BELLS, SPELLS AND MURDERS

Also by Carol J. Perry

It Takes a Coven

Grave Errors

Murder Go Round

Look Both Ways

Tails, You Lose

Caught Dead Handed

BELLS, SPELLS, AND MURDERS

Carol J. Perry

KENSINGTON PUBLISHING CORP.
http://www.kensingtonbooks.com

KENSINGTON BOOKS are published by

Kensington Publishing Corp.
119 West 40th Street
New York, NY 10018

ISBN-13: 978-1-4967-1458-9
ISBN-10: 1-4967-1458-X
First Kensington Mass Market Edition: October 2018

eISBN-13: 978-1-4967-1459-6
eISBN-10: 1-4967-1459-8
First Kensington Electronic Edition: October 2018

10 9 8 7 6 5 4 3 2 1

Printed in the United States of America

For Dan,
my husband and best friend

"All that we see or seem, is but a
Dream within a dream."

Edgar Allan Poe

CHAPTER 1

It was the first day of December in Salem, Massachusetts, my hometown. Wanda the Weather Girl had advised the WICH-TV audience to expect afternoon snow flurries and overnight plunging temperatures and, as the old song says, it was beginning to look a lot like Christmas. I've been associated with the local TV station in one way or another for a couple of years, but this December first was also the beginning of a brand-new broadcasting position for me.

I'm Lee Barrett, née Maralee Kowalski, thirty-two, red-haired, Salem born, orphaned early, married once, and widowed young. I wasn't nervous about the new job. I have a solid background in TV—Emerson College graduate, worked in Miami as a home shopping show host, did a stint on a network weather channel, taught Television Production at a local school, and even spent a short time as a TV call-in psychic. (Not too proud of that one,)

My boss at the station, Bruce Doan, likes all of his employees to wear more than one hat, so in addition to doing occasional investigative reports on the late news, I'd just become WICH-TV's newest field reporter and I was excited about it. It meant that I'd be covering events on location, reporting from the scene where news was happening. It was, I thought, a dream job come true, and just in time for Christmas.

The holiday season is a big deal in Salem. It seems that everything that can hold a lightbulb blazes brightly, and since the year's theme was "Ring in the Holidays in Salem," a whole lot of bell jingling was going on too. My Aunt Ibby had even tied a bell with a red ribbon onto our cat O'Ryan's collar. He was not pleased about it. Aunt Ibby and I share the big old family home on Winter Street, where I have my own apartment on the third floor.

So far on my first morning as a field reporter, I'd stood in front of the bandstand on Salem Common telling the audience about the traditions involved in the decoration of the annual community Christmas tree there. Next, I'd visited with a group of veterans who repaired and repainted donated used bicycles for underprivileged kids as part of a Veterans Helping Santa program.

There was nothing further listed on my schedule until an eleven o'clock appointment with Albert Eldridge. Mr. Eldridge was, among other things, chairman of the Holiday Walk committee, overseeing a popular walking tour through one of Salem's beautifully decorated historic districts. So by nine-thirty Francine, the mobile unit driver/photographer, and I were headed back to the waterfront TV station on Derby Street where a light dusting of snow had begun to fall.

Having the opportunity to work with some of my old friends at WICH-TV on a daily basis made this new job even better. I checked in with Rhonda, the way-smarter-than-she-looks receptionist. "How'd you like your first morning?" she wanted to know. "I watched the Christmas tree segment. You looked good. If you were nervous it didn't show."

"Not nervous," I said. "Excited."

She leaned across the curved purple Formica-topped reception desk, pushing aside an improbable arrangement of glitter-sprinkled lavender poinsettias. "Okay, tell me everything," she said. "You still dating the hot cop?" The "hot cop" in question was detective Pete Mondello and the answer was a resounding "yes." Still dating, still a cop, and definitely, still hot.

I caught her up on recent day-to-day happenings in my sometimes ordinary, sometimes very strange life—carefully omitting the stranger parts. "Aunt Ibby is going to London for the holidays," I told her. "Her friend Nigel invited her when he was here last year."

"Oh? Good for her. But does that mean you'll be alone for Christmas?"

"Not alone," I said. "O'Ryan will be with me and, anyway, Pete's sister and brother-in-law have invited me for Christmas dinner at their house."

"That'll be nice," Rhonda said. "Did you know that the Doans are inviting everybody to a Christmas Eve party here at the station?"

"Got my invitation. I'll probably go." Sometimes Pete volunteers to work on holidays so that officers with kids can be with their families. That meant there was a pretty good chance I'd be spending Christmas Eve with my friends at WICH-TV. New Year's Eve is always reserved for Pete though.

It didn't take long for Rhonda and me to catch up on each other's lives the way good friends can and by ten-fifteen Francine already had the mobile van parked in front of the building, engine running and heater cranked up when she phoned. "Ready to roll, Lee? If this snow doesn't stop you'll have to do your interview with the old guy indoors instead of in front of the fancy-ass mansions."

I glanced at my watch. She was right. We'd be a little early for our appointment, but if Mr. Eldridge wanted to give viewers a peek at some wonderfully decorated old homes we'd better do it right away before blowing snow made filming difficult. I said good-bye to Rhonda, pulled up the fake fur collar of my plaid wool jacket, plunked a knit hat over red hair gone wild, and hurried downstairs. The snow had picked up in intensity. Not the soft, fluffy kind, but the icy, face-stinging variety. I hurried along the sidewalk to the waiting van, pausing only to stuff a few dollars into a camo-painted kettle manned by a bell-ringing Santa with an obviously fake beard and a just-as-obviously genuine smile. I climbed into the passenger seat. "Let's roll."

It's not far from Derby Street to Washington Square, so within minutes we pulled up in front of what one might describe as a stately brick home. A discreet black and gold sign over an exquisite Samuel MacIntire carved doorway identified it as Historical Charities of Salem. The annual Holiday Walk was just one of the numerous fund-raisers Albert Eldridge chaired throughout the year. Some of the proceeds went to maintenance and restoration of Salem's many historical sites and buildings. Other funds supported veterans' causes, aid to needy families, a community Bookmobile (my librarian aunt's favorite) and—especially at holiday time—toys for kids. I felt honored to be able to meet and interview such a prominent and important citizen.

While Francine remained in the van, making camera, sound, and lighting adjustments, I climbed the stairs to the handsome front door and, following instructions posted on the glass inset, entered the reception areas without knocking or ringing. A cushy oriental runner on a polished hardwood floor led to a massive mahogany desk where a diminutive gray-haired woman welcomed me with a smile. A fragrant Scotch pine Christmas tree with Victorian-themed ornaments stood to one side of the desk and a tall wing chair upholstered in green and gold stripes flanked the other. Several comfortable looking club chairs were arranged attractively around the long room.

Only the white plastic topped metal table next to the door seemed out of place. An untidy row of cardboard boxes, canvas bags, and plastic tubs, all filled with a variety of items, were spread across the top. More boxes were piled beneath the folding legs. I saw canned goods, cake mixes, shampoo bottles, candy bars, detergents, packages of diapers. A pile of stamped envelopes in a wire basket marked "outgoing" beside a matching one marked "incoming" was at the end closest to the door. A tall barrel marked "Toys" stood at the opposite end.

"Good morning. May I help you?" The smiling woman greeted me from behind the desk. I handed her a business card, one of my new ones identifying me as Field Reporter. "I'm Lee Barrett," I said. "I'm early for an eleven o'clock appointment with Mr. Eldridge."

"Oh, yes." She peered at the card through granny glasses perched at the end of her nose. "Lee Barrett. Of course. I've seen you on TV. You're Isobel Russell's niece, Maralee. She speaks so highly of you."

"You know my Aunt Ibby?" I wasn't surprised. In her position as head research librarian at Salem's main library, I think my aunt has met just about everybody in Salem at least once.

"Yes indeed. She and I are both members of the Christmas Belles, you know. We're going to start rehearsals this week for our holiday concert." She offered her hand across the broad expanse of desktop. "I'm Lillian Jeffry. Mr. Eldridge's secretary."

"How do you do, Ms. Jeffry. My aunt has told me about the Belles. Sounds like a lively group of musicians."

"We do have a grand time together." She glanced at a grandfather's clock in the corner. "You're quite early for your appointment. Mr. Eldridge likes to keep a timely schedule so I'll announce you at precisely eleven. Meanwhile, just make yourself comfortable." She waved a hand toward the wing chair. "If you'll excuse me, I'll continue with my work while we chat. Mr. Eldridge likes to have all of his holiday cards hand addressed, and as you might imagine, a man of his stature has hundreds of friends." I started toward the chair she'd indicated. "Oh, just a moment, dear. While you're up would you add these cards to the outgoing basket? The letter carrier should be along any minute." I accepted a stack of envelopes, admiring perfect cursive, mentally comparing it to my own back hand scrawl, and added them to the pile.

"You have beautiful handwriting," I said. "No wonder Mr. Eldridge likes to have you address his cards." I paused in front of the table. "Are all of these things for needy people?"

"Yes. Sorry if it looks a little bit messy. People come in and leave donations. Then some of our people pick them up and take them to the right charities. Toys for the kids, new socks and underwear for the vets, diapers go to the battered women's shelter, candy for all of them." She smiled. "I know it looks disorganized, but it really runs quite smoothly. Things come and go from that table all day long. Look, here comes the letter carrier now."

The postman entered, said, "Hi, Lilly. Stayin' out of trouble?" Not waiting for an answer he picked up the outgoing stack of envelopes, dropped a few pieces of mail into the incoming basket, and hurried away.

"'Bye Howie," she said to the already closed door.

The grandfather's clock chimed eleven. "All right, Lee. I think you can go right on into Mr. Eldridge's office now. I know he's expecting you. I checked just a little while ago to see if he wanted me to order some lunch for him, but he's so deep into his work he didn't even answer. A break will do him good. He's been poring over the books since I got here this morning."

"Thanks. We're going to try to do the shoot outside. He'll probably enjoy the fresh air." I walked carefully across the polished floor, hoping the heels of my boots wouldn't mar its perfection, and tapped gently on the door marked "A. Eldridge" before pushing it open.

It was a beautiful room, as one might expect in such a house. Here was more oriental carpeting on gleaming floors and portraits of distinguished men and elegant women lining cream-colored walls. Ashes from a dying fire smoldered in a wonderful huge fireplace with boughs of fragrant evergreen and holly arranged on the mantelpiece. Mr. Eldridge, chin resting on his chest, red Santa hat slightly askew, appeared to be concentrating on a book that lay on his desk. I approached from the right side of his desk. "Mr. Eldridge?" I said. "I'm Lee Barrett from the television station. We have an appointment." No reply. I shook his shoulder gently. "Mr. Eldridge?" The chair rolled back and the man slid forward ever so slowly, feet first, until almost all of him was under the desk. Just his head and shoulders remained propped against the chair seat, the Santa hat at a rakish angle covering one eye. The other eye was open, bloodshot, unseeing.

I backed out of the office. "Ms. Jeffry," I said, trying hard to remain calm. "Please call 911."

CHAPTER 2

Ms. Jeffry's eyes widened. Her jaw dropped, mouth open. But, good secretary that she was, she reached for the phone, dialed 911. "Tell them we need an ambulance." I struggled to maintain a normal tone. "Something is wrong with Mr. Eldridge."

She repeated my words, gave the address, dropped the phone, and ran for the open office door. "The ambulance will be here soon," I said. "Maybe we shouldn't touch him." Ignoring my warning, she knelt beside his chair, pushed the Santa hat aside, and pressed anxious fingers against the side of his neck.

"Cold," she murmured. "So cold."

Sirens sounded outside. Francine appeared in the doorway. "What's going on? There's an ambulance out there. Holy crap!" She moved closer. "Is that him? The guy we're supposed to interview? What happened?"

"I don't know." Steering Francine back toward the reception area, I looked over my shoulder to where the kneeling woman rocked slowly back and forth, shoulders trembling. "He looked as though he was just sitting there, reading," I whispered. "I shook his shoulder and . . ." I shrugged, unable to finish the sentence.

"Oh, wow." Francine covered her mouth with one hand. "You shoved him out of his chair like that? Is he dead? Oh, wow!"

I'd just begun to protest the "shoved him out of his chair" part, when two uniformed EMTs, one man and one woman, wheeled a stretcher past us and into the office. The woman gently helped Ms. Jeffry to her feet and guided her to where Francine and I waited in the doorway. The man moved the chair aside, lowering his silent patient to the floor.

The woman, whose embroidered name tag read T. J. Wells, faced us while her partner focused his attention on Albert Eldridge. "What happened here?" she said. "Did any of you see him fall?" Wordlessly, Francine and Ms. Jeffry each looked at me.

"I . . . I guess I was here when he slipped out of the chair," I said, watching as the male half of the team (name tag: Dom Marafa) placed latex-gloved fingers on the patient's neck, much the way Ms. Jeffry had, shook his head, turned Mr. Eldridge onto his left side, then looked directly at me. "He slipped out?"

"I thought he was asleep. I shook his shoulder to wake him up. Then he just kind of slid out of the chair. I told Ms. Jeffry and she called 911."

"Uh-huh." Marafa touched the back of Mr. Eldridge's head, then carefully removing both gloves and placing them into a red bag, he stood and walked toward us. "T. J., note male patient. Unresponsive. Minimal rigor. Call off SFD. No need. I'll phone in the triple zero." Facing us, he closed the door of the office behind him. "I'm going to call for some police assistance and we'll need to get a little information from you ladies."

I've spent enough time with my detective boyfriend to know what triple zero means. It means that there's no point in performing CPR or attaching cardiac monitor leads, that the patient is beyond their help. Calling off the Salem Fire Department's emergency vehicle offered further proof. Marafa turned his back and spoke into his phone. T. J. Wells spoke softly into her own phone, then, with pen and pad poised, nodded in the secretary's direction. "The patient's name?"

Ms. Jeffry drew herself up to her full height of about five feet, and answered in a firm voice. "He's Albert Eldridge. Executive Director of Historical Charities of Salem. He is a very important man."

"Why are they calling the police?" Francine stage-whispered. "Should I get my camera?"

"No camera," Marafa returned the phone to his utility belt and faced me. "You're Lee Barrett, aren't you? I recognize you from TV. Are you here on some kind of TV business?"

I nodded. "We're here on assignment. An interview." I shrugged and glanced toward the closed office door.

"Okay. I see. Will you ladies give T. J. your full names and addresses, please? The police are on their way."

Ms. Jeffry had resumed her seat behind the desk. She'd placed a box of tissues in front of her. "I'm sorry to say it, but I think Mr. Eldridge may be dead. I touched him, you know. His skin felt cold. Quite cold."

My investigative reporter hat was firmly in place. There was no doubt in my mind that Albert Eldridge was dead. The EMT had told his partner to note "minimum rigor." That meant that rigor mortis had begun and the man had been dead for some hours before I'd touched his shoulder. Besides that, I was quite sure I'd seen a red streak on one of Marafa's gloves after he'd touched the back of Mr. Eldridge's head.

Maybe the very important man didn't die of natural causes.

One at a time, we gave T. J. the requested information. By the time she'd snapped her notebook shut, and Francine and I had each unzipped our warm jackets and chosen one of those comfortable club chairs, the sound of sirens once again split the wintry air. Two uniformed police officers joined us. The room, which at first glance had seemed quite large, had begun to feel crowded. Marafa, once again gloved, opened the office door and the police, one at a time, looked inside but didn't enter.

There was a low-toned conference between the officers and the EMTs. Straining to listen, I picked up enough to figure out that the medical examiner had been called. More than once I heard the words "crime scene."

"As soon as the ME gives the okay," Officer One told the EMTs, "you guys will be able to take your gear and leave. You'd better bring the stretcher out here for now."

T. J. remained with us while Marafa reentered the office. "Be careful," the second officer warned. "Try not to walk in any, um—fluids. Did you move anything when you were in there before? Did you put your bag down on the floor?"

"Moved the chair," Marafa answered. "Left the patient on the floor. Bag was on the stretcher." The wheels made the tiniest squeaking sound as he pushed the gurney out of the room.

The front door suddenly burst open, admitting a blast of cold air. A young man stood on the top step, a Santa hat on his head, his arms laden with gaily wrapped packages, looking just as surprised as I'm sure we all did.

"Hey! What's going on? Somebody sick? What's up

with the ambulance and the TV truck?" He peered around the room. "You okay, Lilly? I got presents here from the church lady. S'posed to pick up diapers for the girls down at the shelter." He pushed his way past T. J. and piled the packages onto the table. "Ooops. Cops." He frowned. "What's going on?" he asked again.

One of the officers moved forward. "Who are you? And what's all this stuff?" He pointed to the table.

"Donations. For Christmas. I'm John Campbell. Santa's helper."

"Don't get smart, kid." The second officer spoke up.

Ms. Jeffry leapt from her chair and hurried to the young man's side. "He's not being smart, officer. John is one of our Veterans Helping Santa crew. There are about a hundred of them around the city. They all wear special Santa hats with a little American flag sewn on. See?" She pointed to the man's hat.

Did Mr. Eldridge's hat have a flag on it? I wasn't sure.

"Okay. Got it. What's all this about diapers then?"

John Campbell answered. "They need 'em down at the women's shelter. Some guys get mean around the holidays. The girls grab the kids and beat it. Don't blame 'em." He picked up the stack of Pampers and Huggies. "I'll just take these and be on my way."

Officer One held up his hand. "Just a minute. You're not supposed to remove anything."

"Oh, for heaven's sake officer, it's diapers." Ms. Jeffry piled one more package of Luvs onto John's outstretched arms. "The babies need them."

Officer One pointed to the table. "Leave them here, son. You can't remove anything from a crime scene. CSI is on the way."

John Campbell put the diapers on the table and held up both hands. "Okay, man. There they are."

"Oh, for heaven's sake." Ms. Jeffry pulled a small metal box from her top drawer, opened it, and removed several bills. "Here's fifty dollars, John. Buy some diapers to tide them over. We'll straighten this out later."

"Thanks, Lilly," he said. He touched the white fur edge of his Santa hat and faced the officers. "Okay if I leave?"

"Okay," Officer One told him. "Don't touch anything on the way out."

"I won't. Anyone going to tell me what's going on here?"

"No," said Officer Two, as John Campbell hurried away. Through the open door I recognized the medical examiner's unmarked black van.

Ms. Jeffry's voice rose just then. "Wait a minute. Did you say 'crime scene'? What crime scene?"

"CSI?" Francine chimed in. "Crime scene investigation? Wow! Just like on TV. Can I get my camera now?"

I was thinking of Francine's camera too, and about how my first day as a field reporter was turning out to be pretty darned interesting. "Mind if I call my office?" I said, already punching in the number. "Rhonda? Tell Mr. Doan to get ready for a breaking news spot."

CHAPTER 3

With a sideways shake of her head, Francine motioned toward the closed front door. I gave an answering nod of mine and together we moved to the exit. I'd just reached for the brass knob when a figure loomed in the glass pane and the door swung open. The medical examiner, traditional black bag in hand, stepped inside the room.

"Well, well, Ms. Barrett," he said, "why am I not surprised to see you here?"

"Hello, Doc." I wasn't surprised that he wasn't surprised. During the past couple of years he and I have met before under similar unfortunate circumstances. Several times, actually. He didn't elaborate and neither did I, so as he disappeared into the dead man's office, and with Francine impatiently poking me in the ribs, I reached again for the doorknob.

This time Officer One noticed the move. "Just a minute, ladies . . ."

He was interrupted by another arrival. The Crime Scene Investigation team had landed and the first person through the door was Detective Pete Mondello. He didn't look surprised to see me either. He frowned. "Hello Lee.

Francine. I saw the TV van outside. Thought it might be you. What's going on?"

"I had an appointment to interview the . . ." I motioned toward the closed office. "To interview Mr. Eldridge."

"Okay. Stick around." When Pete's working, he's one hundred percent all business. No one would guess that he'd just left my bed a few hours ago. "I might have questions," he said.

I waved a hand toward the front door. "Can Francine and I . . . ?"

"Not yet. Your audience will have to wait a while."

I shrugged. Francine pouted. We returned to the club chairs. The ME poked his head out of the office and dismissed the EMTs while Pete introduced himself and his three crew members to a tearful Ms. Jeffry. My phone buzzed.

"Hello Mr. Doan." I grimaced, knowing that the station manager, having been told to brace for breaking news, wouldn't be pleased to hear that we didn't have permission to break it yet.

"What's going on over there, Ms. Barrett?" His voice was even more gruff than usual. "Why aren't I seeing video? I know the CSI is there. The ME too. We stay tuned to the police band here, you know. So does every other TV and radio station. WHERE THE HELL IS MY STORY? Hmmm?"

"I'm on it, Mr. Doan," I said. "I'm inside the building. The other stations aren't. Just need to tie up—um—a few loose ends with the police."

"Okay. Get on with it. Right now." Bam. The connection ended. I knew he'd slammed his phone onto the desk. By then Pete, his three assistants, and Officer One had gone into the office, leaving Ms. Jeffry, Francine, and me with the remaining officer.

Officer Two gave me a sympathetic look. "Your boss?"

"Yep," I said. "He's not happy. I'm supposed to be out front telling our viewers what's going on in here."

"Guess you can't do that, huh? I mean, you can't name names. Notifying next of kin and all that."

"There's no next of kin." Ms. Jeffry spoke up. "No one at all. He was a widower. Had no children. No siblings. His whole life was his charities."

"No kidding. Poor old guy." The officer looked at me. "Say, Ms. Barrett. Want me to speak to the detective? See if you can do your story?"

"Would you? That'd be great."

"I'm a fan." He colored slightly. "I even called you once, back when you used to do the late movie show. When you used to be a psychic."

It was my turn to blush. "I wasn't really a psychic, you know. Just played one on TV."

"Could have fooled me. You found my lost dog for me."

"I did?"

"Well, actually you gave me the number of the Animal Rescue League and they already had him there." He headed for the closed office door. "Anyway, I owe you one. Let's see if I can convince Detective Mondello to let you and your friend go outdoors for a few minutes." He dropped his voice. "Mondello's a good guy."

I already knew that. But did I have to tell the kind officer that Detective Mondello and I were dating? I hadn't been entirely truthful about not having any psychic powers either. Back when I was playing the part of Crystal Moon, psychic, I found out that I'm a scryer. My witch friend River North calls me a "gazer." For some unknown reason, I can see things in reflective surfaces—mostly things I don't want to see.

I decided to keep quiet about both circumstances and

watched Officer Two knock, then enter the closed room. Within the minute, he reappeared. I knew by his grin he'd been successful. "Okay Ms. Barrett. Detective Mondello says go ahead and get your scoop. but keep it brief and come right back inside. No names. He says you know all the rules. Do you?"

"Sure do. C'mon Francine." The two of us zipped up our jackets, pulled open the door, and ran for the van. "If I know Pete we'll have about two minutes to do this. What mic are we using?"

"Handheld in this wind," she said, yanking the van door open. "Here you go."

Without the luxury of taking our time selecting the most advantageous spot for filming, I grabbed the mic and picked a spot on a corner facing the house. A car marked with the logo of a local radio station had pulled up behind the CSI truck but I'd managed to find a location where a large oak tree blocked the view of both vehicles. A bell-ringing Santa near the front door of the place was probably going to be in the shot but that couldn't be avoided. I signaled Francine to start shooting.

"This is Lee Barrett reporting for WICH-TV," I began. "I'm speaking to you from Salem's Washington Square. A 911 call from one of the city's most historic buildings brought emergency vehicles here to the scene of an apparent fatality. An unresponsive man was found alone in his office at eleven o'clock this morning. Police and the medical examiner are presently inside the building." I was just warming up, ready to get to the part about notifying next of kin, even though maybe there weren't any, to intimate without actually naming names, that the apparent fatality involved a person well-known in Salem's historical community. That's when Francine gave the index-finger-across-the-throat signal that meant "Cut." I gave a rapid sign-off. "Stay tuned to WICH-TV for more on this breaking news story," I said, then handed Francine the mic. "What's wrong? What happened?"

Wordlessly, she pointed to where Officer Two stood just out of camera range, frantically waving in our direction. Frowning, I approached him. "What's the matter? I was just getting started."

"Mondello says for you two to come back inside right away."

"What for?" I said. "I don't think I broke any rules, did I?"

"Dunno. He just said for you to come back inside. That's all I know." He shrugged. "Didn't sound too happy about it."

"You did tell me that he said I could get my story as long as I kept it brief and followed the rules, didn't you?"

"Yep."

Puzzled and a little bit peeved, I hoped Pete had some good reason for stepping on my first really important field report.

"I'm sure he doesn't want to talk to me," Francine said. "I'll just stash the equipment and lock up the van. I'll follow you in a couple of minutes."

I hurried up the steps and entered the beautiful, and by-now-familiar front door just in time to see the medical examiner and his associates pushing the gurney with its dark blue covered sad burden toward the exit. "Good-bye, Ms. Barrett," the doctor said. "Perhaps we'll meet sometime under more pleasant circumstances."

"Hope so, Doc," I said, noting the time. It was ten minutes before noon. Ms. Jeffry had started to cry again and I hesitated, not wanting to leave the poor woman alone. "Can I get you a glass of water, Ms. Jeffry, or anything?"

"I told the detective you're here." Officer Two held the

front door open for the departing group. "And I'll get Ms. Jeffry a glass of water."

Officer One appeared then, and beckoned to me to cross the threshold which the county morgue's gurney had just rolled over. "Just step inside here, Ms. Barrett," he said, then held up his hand as I tiptoed carefully over the sill. "No need to come any farther into the room." He reached around me and pulled the door closed. "Here she is, detective."

Everybody says that real crime scene investigation looks nothing like the TV version, but to me, this one did. One of the gloved investigators, holding a camera, stood behind the desk where I'd first seen Mr. Eldridge and appeared to be photographing the book that still lay open. Another man dusted for fingerprints on the mantelpiece and along the hearth, while the third, using tiny scissors, clipped threads from the carpet where the dead man had fallen and placed them carefully into a plastic envelope. Pete, standing in front of a tall bookcase, looked up from his notebook when I entered. He wore the expression I call his "cop face."

"Hello Lee," he said—using his cop voice. "Do I understand correctly that you were the first to discover the deceased?"

"Yes," I said. "I thought he was asleep."

"And you touched him?"

"Yes."

"He slipped from his chair."

"Correct."

I've already made a statement about all this. Did he have to interrupt my stand-up to go over it right this minute?

"Did you touch anything else in the room?"

"No. I don't believe so. I left right away and asked Ms. Jeffrey to call 911."

"Did it occur to you to tell me about this when I asked why you were here?"

"No." I realized that I'd developed a little edge to my voice too. "I told you. I was here to interview Mr. Eldridge. I'd already made a report to the officers. I was here to do my job."

Did I detect a tiny smile trying to break through on the cop-face? "And I'm here to do mine," he said. "If you'll take a seat in the outer office, I'll be out shortly to get statements from you and Ms. Jeffry and Francine."

"Pete?"

"Yes?"

"When can I tell my audience you're investigating a murder?"

Cop-face with negative head shake provided the not-unexpected reply. After all, no one had actually said the word "murder" aloud. My phone buzzed.

"Yes, Mr. Doan?"

"You call that a news break? That piddling little blurb of crap? What's the matter with you?"

"I'm sorry, Mr. Doan. The police . . ."

"Not interested in excuses. How come you're babbling about the historic building while WBZ has a guy in a Santa Claus hat spilling his guts about cops and crime scenes. Do you even know who's dead?"

"I was the one who found the body."

Brief stunned silence. "No shit! You did? Who is it? The old man?"

"That's right. Albert Eldridge."

"I guess it wasn't a heart attack if CSI is there. What else have you got?"

"We'll have to wait for the name release. That shouldn't take long. No wife. No kids." The frowning Pete pointed toward the outer office. "Cops want to question me now, Mr. Doan. I'll call you back ASAP."

I turned to Pete. "WBZ-TV is already interviewing John Campbell. Come on, Pete. Give me something for my station."

"Who the hell is John Campbell?"

"Oh, yeah," Officer One said. "The Santa Claus guy with the diapers. He came in for just a minute to leave some presents. Wanted to pick up some diapers."

"Any other surprises for me?" Pete asked. "Anybody else been wandering in and out of my crime scene in the past eight hours?"

"I saw the letter carrier come in," I said, making a mental note of Pete's eight-hour time frame. "If you're counting the outer office, you should ask Ms. Jeffry. She says there are people going in and out all the time."

"Thank you. I was planning to do just that. But first, tell me in your own words, exactly how you happened to push Mr. Eldridge out of his chair."

I sighed and prepared to explain once again, the difference between a push and a gentle shake. I checked my watch. It was a few minutes past one o'clock. That meant Mr. Eldridge had died sometime between five and six that morning. I needed every useful fact I could pick up. I intended to do my job—even if my favorite man in the world seemed determined to make sure I'd have to work hard for each tiny snippet of information.

CHAPTER 4

The day Albert Eldridge died was the day I got the opportunity to learn firsthand why a real crime scene investigation takes so long. The real thing, at least the way Detective Pete Mondello conducts one, would never fit into a one-hour TV show even if they left out the commercials. There's a lot more to it than taking pictures and snipping carpet samples.

I found out why Pete needed to talk to me so urgently. I was the first one (besides the killer) to see Mr. Eldridge before the positioning of his body had changed. I described to Pete as exactly as I could how he'd looked before he'd slid feetfirst under the desk, where his hands had been positioned on the open book, where his head was in relation to his chest. After that, I recalled, the EMTs had moved him to a laying-down position and Ms. Jeffry had touched him too, even removed his Santa hat. I had a better understanding of why he needed to get the firsthand information before it got mixed up in our minds—but I was still a little bit ticked off about that first report I'd done. Embarrassing.

As the minutes and hours rolled by, Pete relaxed some

of the rules. Francine and I tried to stay out of his way and we managed to hang around most all day. We weren't allowed to walk around in the actual crime scene of course, but we got an occasional peek through the door. We gathered together bits and pieces of information every fifteen or twenty minutes or so, sometimes from the techs working the scene and sometimes from our own observations. Little by little, we were able to keep the viewers of WICH-TV informed about what was going on at the Salem Historical Charities building. Best of all, other than that John Campbell interview thing, we stayed ahead of Boston TV and Salem radio the whole time. Still, no one but me had said the word "murder." We'd heard "upper body trauma" and "head wound," but it seemed pretty obvious that Albert Eldridge's death was neither self-inflicted nor accidental. The man had been murdered. I was sure of it.

Our best break came though, when Conrad Gillette, ignoring yellow-taped warnings and brushing past Officer One, burst through the front door. Gillette, a tall, fit-looking guy I guessed to be around fifty, braced his arms against the front edges of Ms. Jeffry's desk and, fairly shouting, demanded, "Lilly! What's happened here? I just got back. Is it true?"

"Oh, Conrad," she sniffled, "It's true. Albert is . . . gone."

Officer One, moving quickly, had the man's right arm in what had to be an uncomfortable position just as Pete and Officer Two emerged from the dead man's office, the officer with gun drawn. Lillian Jeffrey, moving with surprising agility, raced around the desk and planted her small frame between the gun-wielding officer, the man she'd called Conrad, and Pete. Waving her hands above her head she yelled "Stop! It's all right. It's Mr. Gillette,

Mr. Eldridge's partner! Our executive director! Don't hurt him." With tiny feet firmly planted, she stood her ground until, with gun holstered, Officer Two backed away and Officer One released the man from his hold.

"Ms. Jeffry," Pete said. "It's getting a little crowded here in your office. And I've just learned that many people have been passing in and out of this room today. True?"

Ms. Jeffry resumed her seat and her ladylike demeaner. "Oh my, yes. It's just like Grand Central Station in here. That's what Mr. Eldridge always says." She frowned. "Always said."

"I see." Pete used his most polite cop voice. "Is there another room in the building we could use? One without quite so much public access? I'm afraid I'll have to tape this room off and I'd hate to inconvenience everyone by asking you all to come down to the station for questioning."

"Oh, dear. More of that nasty yellow tape all over our pretty Christmas decorations?" she said, scowling. "Well, I guess it can't be helped." Her expression brightened. "We could use Mr. Eldridge's parlor. It's a lovely room. Wait till you see it. Then of course, there's Mr. Gillette's nice big office at the back of the house. You wouldn't mind if Detective Mondello used it, would you, Conrad?"

By then, the newest arrival to the scene, stood, totally bemused, beside the Victorian-trimmed Christmas tree looking from one of us to the other. "What? No. Of course I don't mind. But could someone—anyone—tell me what's going on here? I got back from a business trip late last night and I woke up to some woman on TV saying that an elderly man had died in this building." He nodded toward the secretary. "Lilly confirmed for me just now that it was Alfred. My partner. My best friend." He looked down, light from tiny twinkling bulbs deepening the lines on his face, and repeated his plea. "Could someone please tell me what's going on here?"

"I'm sorry, Mr. Gillette," Pete said, "that no one thought to notify you." He fixed brown eyes on Ms. Jeffry. "No one so far," his gaze took in Officers One and Two, "had mentioned that the deceased had a partner." He turned toward me. "And I regret that you heard the news about your friend from a television report. Mr. Eldridge suffered a fatal blow to the head sometime this morning. He was at his desk. That's all we know just now. Ms. Jeffry, if you'll direct us to Mr. Gillette's office I'll take your statements as quickly as possible."

The secretary stood. "I guess we can go through the house, but the quickest way would be to duck outside and use the back entrance." She opened a narrow closet door and took a black coat from a hanger. She shrugged into it and pulled a knit hat, much like mine, from a pocket. "Let's go."

Pete opened the door to Eldridge's office a crack and spoke a few muffled words to the crime scene crew. Closing the door, he nodded to Officer Two.

"Stay hcre. Don't let anyone else in. This won't take long."

With Ms. Jeffry in the lead, Pete taking her arm, we ventured into the cold once again. Francine followed them and I maneuvered myself into position next to Conrad Gillette. He was my best shot at getting some inside information about the victim and I was determined to use whatever reporting skills I had to get it. Officer One brought up the rear.

"Mr. Gillette," I began, "It must have been terrible for you to hear about your friend's death from television, and"—I faced him, making eye contact—"I'm afraid I may have been the reporter who gave you the bad news. Lee Barrett. WICH-TV."

He looked at me closely as we rounded the corner of the house and moved down a narrow path toward a broad, open porch. "Yes. I believe it may have been you. Here." He grasped my arm. "This is slippery. Let me help you." I was wearing boots and didn't feel that I was in danger of slipping, but accepted the guiding hand.

"Thank you," I said. "I guess no one has told you, but I was the one who found him."

"Found him?"

"Yes. I had an appointment to interview him about the Holiday Walk. I guess you'll be taking over for him?"

"Yes. I expect I will. But tell me, Ms. Barrett." His grip tightened on my arm.

"Did he . . . do you think poor Albert suffered? Did he . . . was there . . . was it horribly bloody?"

"No. It wasn't," I answered truthfully. *What a strange question.*

I hoped he wouldn't ask me to elaborate. An unexpected interruption was welcome. We'd almost reached the wide porch at the back of the house when Pete suddenly held up one hand. "Stop, everybody," he called. "Don't come any closer."

The reporter in me kicked in. I pulled away from Conrad Gillette's guiding hand and hurried to Pete's side. Distinct footprints in the newly fallen snow led to and from the house. No wonder he'd stopped us. Those prints had to have been made since snow began falling. Not very long ago. Who'd been in the house since the snow started at around ten a.m. that we hadn't seen? Everyone looked at Lillian Jeffry.

"What?" she said, eyes wide. "Oh, the footprints? That would be the Santas."

The expression on Pete's face was one I've seen many times. It's what I call "patient exasperation." He gets it sometimes when my friend River North offers to read the Tarot cards for him when he's puzzled by a case. "The Santas?" he asked. "What Santas? Why is Santa Claus coming to your back door?"

"More than one Santa," she explained. Now Ms. Jeffry sounded exasperated. "There are, oh, I don't know, eight, ten, maybe twelve of them. Not all at once, of course."

"And they are on the porch because . . . ?"

"The money drop. Santas collect cash in those cute kettles. There's a floor safe just inside the porch door. After each shift they come here and drop off their day's collection."

"I'll need photos of the footprints." Pete said. "Officer, would you run back and get one of the techs to come out here with a camera?" Officer One nodded and hurried back around the corner of the house.

I scooted back to where Conrad Gillette waited. No point in wasting time looking at fast-disappearing footprints in the snow. If Gillette was Alfred Eldridge's partner, he'd make a good interview. I motioned for Francine to join me and together we boxed him in, one of us on each side. It was nearly two o'clock. "If Francine grabs her camera, can we shoot a brief interview with you for WICH-TV? Just a few words about whether the Salem holiday events will proceed as usual, even without the guidance of Albert Eldridge? That sort of thing?"

He smoothed graying-at-the-temples hair and stood a little straighter. "Of course. The community should know that all of the planned events will go on, just as dear Albert would have wanted."

I gave Francine a little push. She dashed between the buildings to where the station van was parked and returned with handheld camera and mic just before Officer One and Pete's camera tech returned. I knew there were no next of kin to be notified and if Eldridge's partner announced the death from outside the building I'd have the story Mr. Doan expected. Outdoor shots and interviews are fair game. Witness the John Campbell thing.

While Pete directed his guy to photograph the foot-prints, which were fast filling up with snow, I stood beside Mr. Gillette, careful not to get anyone else in the shot, and asked some of the questions I'd wanted to ask since I'd found the body.

CHAPTER 5

"Ladies and Gentlemen, this is Lee Barrett. We're outside the building that houses the Historical Charities of Salem and is the home of the organization's founder, Albert Eldridge. I have with me Mr. Conrad Gillette, Mr. Eldridge's friend and business associate. When our station reported that a man had been found unresponsive in this building Mr. Gillette, were you shocked to learn the identity of that person?"

"Oh, Ms. Barrett, shocked doesn't begin to describe my feeling on learning of my dear friend Albert Eldridge's passing." He dabbed at one eye with a white handkerchief, whether from tears or the cold wind I couldn't tell. "I've just returned from a business trip, and you can imagine my surprise—my shock, when I heard your broadcast about his death. Horrible. Have the police indicated how . . . who . . . anything?"

"No sir. They haven't released anything further. They've indicated that he didn't die of natural causes. Perhaps you can tell us a little about Mr. Eldridge. You knew him well, I understand. Was he working on anything special, anything out of the ordinary for this year's holiday celebration?"

Anything that could get him killed?

"The usual events. They're pretty well established, you know. People expect things to happen in a certain order at Christmas. The lights on the common, the holiday stroll among the decorated houses, the Christmas music, the carolers, the bells. Yes, Albert was a true traditionalist. For him, every little detail had to be just so." He sighed. "I intend to carry on for him. To be sure that 'Ring in the Holidays in Salem' is every bit the success he envisioned before his most untimely passing. Everyone in this city loved and admired him."

Clearly not everyone.

"Thank you, Mr. Gillette. We appreciate your talking with us at such a difficult time." From the corner of my eye I saw the WBZ-TV reporter racing toward us. He must have spotted Officer One and the tech when they left the building. Hurriedly, I faced Francine's camera as she moved in for a close-up. "Stay tuned to WICH-TV for updates on this breaking story," I said. "This is Lee Barrett reporting from the scene."

Pete motioned for us to approach the porch. The WBZ guy fell in behind me as though he belonged there. "Looks as though we'll have to go over the whole house for evidence," Pete said. "We didn't realize that so many people had access to the place. I can't ask you all to stand around in the cold." He looked straight at Francine's camera and my mic, but didn't comment on either. "Lee, I have the statements you and Francine signed earlier, so you can go along back to work. We'll contact you later if we need more information." I opened my mouth to ask a question, but he held up a hand. "There'll be no official comment on this matter yet, Lee. The chief will probably announce a presser later today. I'm going to ask Ms. Jeffry and Mr. Gillette to come down to the station to answer a few questions, fill out some paperwork. I'll drive them both there in my car. Meanwhile, for the time being, this building"—he gestured toward the house—"is off limits to the press, to charitable donors and assorted Santa Clauses."

The WBZ-TV reporter gave me a little salute. "Hey, Barrett," he said. "What's up with the crack about Santa Clauses?"

"Beats me," I said, keeping a straight face. "Guess we'll all have to wait for the chief's press conference."

"Sure," he said. "See you guys around." He took off at a dead run, back to his waiting much-fancier-than-ours mobile unit. I looked toward the curb where Pete and Officer One shepherded a flustered Ms. Jeffry and a stoic Conrad Gillette into Pete's Crown Vic. Pete caught my eye and gave a little wave. I returned the wave and added a wink.

"Francine," I said. "What do you say we find us a Santa Claus to interview?" My watch said two-thirty-five.

"Shouldn't be too hard to do. They're all over the place."

"My Aunt Ibby always told me the ones in the stores and the others we saw around town were all just Santa's helpers," I said. "That the real one stayed up at the North Pole until Christmas Eve."

"Same story I got." She was right about it being easy to find Santas. We found two of them standing together in front of the Salem Historical Charities building looking with puzzled expressions at the yellow POLICE LINE—DO NOT CROSS tape.

"Hello Santas," I said. "I'm Lee Barrett. WICH-TV. Do you have time to answer a few questions?"

"Questions? Hey, lady. We've got questions." The taller of the two, with what might have been a real white beard, shook a polished brass kettle, which gave a satisfying jingle, indicating the presence of many coins. "The cops have taped all the doors to the Histy."

"The Histy?"

"Yeah." The second Santa, one I recognized both from his friendly smile and his camo painted kettle, answered, being careful to retain his North Pole persona with a ho-ho-ho hearty voice. "The historical place. Anyway, nobody told us where we should drop our money after our shift is over. We always take it to the back door. They got a drop safe in there."

"I see. Hold on. I'll see what I can find out." I pulled out my cell phone and hit Pete's number.

"Hi, Lee. Everything okay?"

"I think so. I guess I still have a job anyway. But listen, I'm about to interview a couple of Santas out here and they don't know what they should do with the money they've collected." I glanced at the kettles, each one displaying a good assortment of bills and coins. "They say they always put it in a drop safe inside the back door."

"Oh-oh. That could be a problem, at least temporarily. Hold on a sec. I'll see what Mr. Gillette wants to do about it." There was a muffled murmur of conversation, then Pete spoke to me again. "Guess they can handle it okay." This time there was a note of surprise in his voice. "Tell your Santas that Mr. Gillette is arranging right now for his bank to be the drop-off point until we're through here." Pete mentioned a well-known Salem bank. "He says to just write HCS, on a slip of paper and include it in your drop-bag."

Wow. That was fast. This Gillette guy doesn't waste any time getting things done.

"You think you'll be through soon, Pete?"

"I think so. Probably one more day should do it."

That statement provided one more bit of information

for my next news break. I said a hurried "thanks" and "'bye" to Pete and turned back to my red-suited new friends. "Looks like the folks at the 'Histy' have you covered." I told them what Pete had said about the bank being ready to accept their collections, then with Francine directing the two to stand where yellow tape was visible, but didn't interfere with the shot, I began my first Santa Claus interview.

"I understand that the money you Santas collect benefits several very worthwhile causes here in the city." Francine moved in close enough to show the overflowing kettles of cash. I held the mic toward the fake-beard Santa with the camo kettle. "Can you tell us a little about that?"

He flashed the great smile I remembered from the brief encounter we'd had outside the TV station earlier. "Sure. Salem can thank Mr. Albert Eldridge for organizing the Christmas programs we have here," he boomed in Santa's voice. "What a great guy." He tapped his companion on the shoulder. "Isn't that right, Harry?" Then, probably remembering that kids might be watching, added. "We're all just Santa's helpers, you know. The real Santa is busy up at the North Pole."

The Santa named Harry agreed in a sincere, but less Santa-like tone. "Yessir. Mr. Eldridge, he figured out how to help just about everybody in Salem who needs help. And how to keep the places the tourists like to see . . . them old houses, you know, how to keep them from falling apart. A great guy. No doubt."

They sound as though they don't know he's dead.

"I understand you and the other Santas volunteer your time. Is that right?" I asked, deciding to tiptoe around the sad fact of the director's demise just in case they hadn't figured it out.

The camo kettle Santa answered, "We do. A bunch of

us are veterans, you know? And the Histy does a lot for us." He turned that brilliant Santa-smile on full blast and faced Francine's camera. "Please, everybody, give as much as you can when you see a Santa with a flag on his hat." He pointed to the furry white band around his hat. "See the flag?"

I remembered Albert Eldridge's hat. I hadn't noticed a flag on it and the furry part had been red. Blood red.

CHAPTER 6

"Glad to share that information with our audience," I said. "I'm sure they'll respond generously. Our sources tell us that the Historical Charities building will probably be closed for one more day, then the city's wonderful Christmas programs will go on as usual."

"That's good news, lady," the Santa-Harry said. "We love that place." He frowned. "Hope they'll be takin' that durn yellow tape down. Folks don't like to think about—you know—what happened in there. 'Specially the little kids."

I get it. They know Mr. Eldridge is dead. They just don't think Santa Claus should mention it.

My respect for the Santa Veterans grew. "Thanks for all you do to help Santa, gentlemen." I pointed to the shiny brass kettle, overflowing with bills and coins. That was a mistake. An image began to form on the shining curved sides. I blinked, willing it to go away. This was a really bad time for one of my "visions" to appear. I'd seen unwanted shapes take form on all kinds of reflective surfaces, but never before when I was live on camera.

I opened my eyes and tried to look away. "Remember

to be generous when you see a Santa with an American flag on his hat," I said, trying to erase from my mind what I'd seen on the kettle. "This is Lee Barrett for WICH-TV. Police Chief Tom Whaley will be on hand for a special press conference this afternoon. Stay tuned."

"You okay?" Francine asked. "That was short."

"I know. The Santas don't want to talk about Mr. Eldridge just now. Don't want to upset the kids. Right, guys?"

"That's right," Fake-beard Santa answered. "That was really bad news. Kids shouldn't have to think about that stuff. Guess I'll go stand in front of Crow Haven for a while." The famous witch shop is the oldest one in Salem and is also within sight of the Eldridge home. "Those witch people are always good for a few bucks. See you later, Harry." He gave a fast jingle of his bell and hurried, jay-walking across the street. Harry gave an answering ca-ching of his own bell, and hurried away in the opposite direction.

Francine began putting equipment back into the mobile unit, giving me a moment alone—a moment to think about what the mirrorlike brass surface of Harry's kettle had revealed.

It was such a quick flash of an image, something I recognized, yet couldn't quite place. Harry and his shiny kettle were gone but the image I'd seen seemed burned into my brain. Where had I seen it before?

My phone buzzed. Bruce Doan's name showed on caller ID. "Hello Mr. Doan."

"I liked the Santa Claus segment. Good job."

I answered with a relieved "thank you." One never knows how the station manager will react at any given moment. "Have you heard yet when Chief Whaley will talk to the press? I know he hates doing those things."

"Right. That's what I'm calling about. He'll be on right in time for the five o'clock news. Scotty Palmer will cover the presser for us."

Darn! I should stick around for it. Now my least-favorite co-worker gets to cover the story.

"You sure? I can do it."

"No need. All he's going to do is make it official that the old guy is dead." Mr. Doan continued. "Now, listen. We're going to lead in with your first promo, then do the interview with the Gillette guy, then the chief. We'll wind it up with the Santa Clauses. Nice package. I'm pretty sure your shift is over by now."

I checked my watch, surprised at the time—it was already three o'clock. "It was over about an hour ago." I said. "I clocked in at seven. Did the Christmas tree segment first while it was still dark enough out for the lights to look pretty, then we interviewed the veterans fixing bikes at around nine-thirty. Arrived at Eldridge's place just before eleven. Guess you know all that's happened since then."

"Yep. Busy news day. We'll let Chief Whaley break the news that Eldridge is officially dead. Why don't you and Francine head for the barn. See you in the morning unless you've got something for the late news."

"No. Not tonight." I was glad that the busy news day was over—for me at least though I would have liked to cover the chief too. Francine and I headed down Hawthorne Boulevard to Derby Street. She dropped me off next to my—beautiful but wildly impractical in the snow—Corvette convertible and I headed—ever so cautiously—for home. (Yes, it's an expensive car for a fledgling reporter, and it blew a bit of a hole in the inheritance from my parents' estate, but I truly love it!)

I pulled into the garage behind our house, glad to see that Aunt Ibby's trusty old Buick was already safely inside. She's supposed to be semiretired from her library duties but she still manages to spend plenty of time at the big brick building on Essex Street, and wouldn't hesitate to drive in a snowstorm for one of her many pet book-related projects.

I scurried through the backyard where snow had begun to accumulate along the garden fence, clinging to the barren branches of forsythia and lilac bushes and making bizarre skinny sculptures from last season's sunflowers and hollyhocks. I'd barely turned my key in the back door when our big yellow cat O'Ryan poked his head out through the cat door. He shook a big paw when he touched the snow, then emerged all the way out, executing a few purring figure-eights around my ankles. I picked him up, hugged him, and together we entered the back hall.

Aunt Ibby's kitchen door is just inside the hall, right beside the narrow staircase leading up two flights to my apartment. I often stop to visit with my aunt on my way upstairs, and this time I particularly wanted to tell her about the hazy, half-remembered picture I'd seen on the kettle. Few people know about my scrying ability. Aunt Ibby has known about it since I was a little girl, even though I'd somehow blocked it out for nearly thirty years. Now that I was aware of, though not pleased about, my so-called "gift," I'd only shared the information with my best friend, River North, who says I am a "gazer" and, reluctantly, with Pete who calls it "seeing things."

I knocked on the kitchen door.

"Is that you, Maralee?" she called, while pulling the door open at the same time. "Come in. Come in out of the snow. I was just watching Wanda the Weather Girl. She says we may get a few inches tonight."

I put the cat down and hugged my aunt. "Glad to be home," I said. "It's been a strange day."

"I gathered that," she said. "They've been showing your reports about the death with each newscast—nine, twelve, two. I guess Tom Whaley is scheduled to announce poor Albert's demise at five."

"Could you tell from my reports that it was Mr. Eldridge who'd died? I tried not to be too specific."

"I think you handled it quite delicately. I guessed who it was right off because I knew you had an appointment with him. Then of course Mr. Gillette tipped it off." She scowled. "Does all the yellow tape mean a crime is involved?"

"We tried not to show it. The tape I mean, not the crime."

"The Boston stations aren't as careful as you and Francine are." She pressed the subject. "Was whatever happened to Albert—was it suspicious?"

"I'll tell you what I know. It's not a pretty story."

She held up her right hand. "Wait. Have you eaten anything today?"

"Not since breakfast," I said, suddenly realizing that I was very hungry. "Pete made waffles."

"Sit." She ordered, pointing to a tall stool beside the kitchen counter. "How does a nice bowl of homemade beef stew and a fresh croissant sound? And maybe a glass of milk?"

"Like heaven." I sat. She ladled. I ate, and between bites, told her exactly what I'd seen in Albert Eldridge's beautiful office. Fortunately, my aunt is not squeamish. I didn't leave anything out.

"Oh, my dear Maralee. How terrible for you. And you actually touched him. How awful." She reached for my hand. "Did Lillian see this?" she asked. "She was so fond of Albert. The poor soul must be beside herself."

"She's holding up well. She tried to find a pulse, but it was too late. She and a Mr. Gillette are at the police station now, making statements."

"That would be Conrad Gillette. I know him. He's been Albert's 'right hand man' for years. Knowledgeable about all of Albert's pet projects." She ticked off items on her fingers. "New England history, architecture, city building codes, music, art, museum collections. . . ."

"I think the charities are in good hands then," I said. "Gillette seems very capable. It only took him minutes to arrange for a bank to accept all the cash the Santa Veterans collect." I dipped the last tender bit of my croissant into the rich thick end of my beef stew. "That was delicious. Thank you."

"You're welcome. Can I get you anything else?"

"Just your opinion. I—um—I saw something."

"Oh, dear. You mean one of those visions?"

I nodded. "Yes. And, as usual, it didn't make the least bit of sense."

"Tell me about it."

"I saw it on a shiny brass kettle. One of the Santas had it. The image was perfectly clear. It's something I've seen before. Just can't place it." I carried my dishes to the sink and began rinsing them. "It's like an illustration I've seen in a book a long time ago."

"I know a bit about books," my librarian aunt said, smiling. "Including the illustrations. Try me."

"Okay. Here goes." I closed my eyes, willing the picture on the kettle to come back. It worked. The picture was in full color. "It's an old man—a really mean looking old man. He's wearing some kind of a stocking hat—oh, it's a nightcap I think. He's sitting up in bed. An old-fashioned kind of bed . . ."

"Got it." She interrupted. "An easy one. Children's Classic Series. I used to read to you from those books all the time. That picture is from a kiddy version of *A Christmas Carol*. I'm pretty sure we still have it."

"Of course. It's Scrooge. Why didn't I recognize it?"

"Maybe because you never liked that particular picture. You used to cover your eyes with your little hands when we reached that page."

"Funny. I don't remember that at all. And why has it come back as a vision?" I put my bowl and glass into the dishwasher. "Not that any of them make much sense at first."

"If you think it might help," Aunt Ibby said, "you could go up to the study and take a look at the book. Try section eight-two-eight."

"Good idea," I said. "I'll stop there on my way up to my apartment. Want to come, O'Ryan?" He followed me through Aunt Ibby's living room and into the front hall, scampering ahead and darting up the wide, curving staircase leading to the upper floors of the house. Our second-floor study is a large room, with floor-to-ceiling bookshelves. (Not too many home libraries are organized according to the Dewey decimal system, but ours is.)

As soon as I pulled the book from the shelf I remembered it. I remembered too hiding my eyes from that one illustration. I'd even pulled the covers over my head when Aunt Ibby read from the facing page. Was it the ghost hovering near the old man that had frightened me? I didn't remember. I flipped through the pages.

"Scrooge was the meanest man in the world. He hated everybody and everything—especially Christmas. Then one cold Christmas Eve, three spirits came toward him and his life forever changed . . ."

A mean old man, some ghosts, Christmas—still none of it computed. The picture no longer brought fright—just curiosity. I closed the book and replaced it on the shelf. "Ready to go back downstairs, O'Ryan? Or shall we go on up to my place?"

The cat didn't seem to care for either choice. He'd curled up on the maroon cushion on the wide window seat, oblivious to the snow swirling outside, pretending to be asleep. I can always tell when he's faking. His whiskers twitch. I went along with the gag, and tiptoed from the room, leaving the door ajar so that he could decide later which way to go.

I climbed the stairs to the third floor, and home. There's something so comforting about being in my own space, surrounded by familiar things. Even though I was raised in this house, it wasn't until I'd returned to Salem from Florida after my NASCAR driver husband Johnny Barrett's death that Aunt Ibby had surprised me with an apartment of my own.

The door from the front hall opens into my kitchen. The other entrance from the back hall, the one Pete most always uses, leads to my living room. (Of course, both entrances have cat doors so that O'Ryan can visit as he pleases.)

I wasn't sure whether Pete would come over after work or just go to his condo. He had plenty to deal with at the Eldridge house, but just in case, I loaded up the Mr. Coffee, and checked the refrigerator for possible evening sustenance. Sending out for pizza during a snowstorm didn't seem like the best option but there was a cheese-and-pepperoni in the freezer, along with one of Aunt Ibby's famous chicken pot pies, a Sara Lee chocolate cake, and a half gallon of vanilla ice cream. With the food question settled—however unimaginatively—even off the clock I still had some work to do for WICH-TV.

Well before landing my current job I'd always been a note taker, with a particular fondness for index cards. Pulling a pen and a stack of the cards from my purse, I sat down at my 1970s Lucite kitchen table and glanced at the vintage Kit-Kat clock on the wall, googly eyes and wagging tail marking the seconds. Chief Whaley's presser would be on the air in about half an hour. Whatever he said would certainly spark community interest in the case and I needed to be ready for what might well turn out to be a series of investigative reports. Meanwhile, I tried to organize my own thoughts about the day's happenings.

By eleven o'clock, Mr. Eldridge had been dead for about eight hours.

Ms. Jeffry touched the body. No one else entered the room until the EMTs arrived.

Marafa wiped blood from the back of Mr. Eldridges's head and the Santa hat was completely red (from blood?).

People came and went from front door often. John Campbell? Santas had access to back door for money drop. Conrad Gillette, Eldridge's "right hand man" arranged with a bank for money drop.

Body removed by ME just before noon. Pete and CSI team arrived.

I was interrupted by a gentle tapping at my door. Aunt Ibby stood in the hall. "It's almost time for the five o'clock news," she said. "Is O'Ryan here with you? He usually watches with me. Happy hour, you know? I have a little taste of wine and he has a nice saucer of milk."

"He's not here," I said. "I left him in the study, snoozing on the window seat. Let's go down and check on him, shall we?" I was concerned. O'Ryan, like the late Mr. Eldridge, did things in a "timely manner," and always seemed to know the time. It wasn't like him to miss happy hour.

We hurried down the one flight to the second floor. The door to the study was still ajar. When we entered the room, O'Ryan looked up at us with an air of absolute innocence, as though he'd had nothing to do with the paperback mystery book on the floor. Then he yawned, lay down with his head on the open book, and once again pretended to be asleep.

The book he'd chosen to use as a pillow was Agatha Christie's classic, *Hickory Dickory Dock*.

"Why, you naughty boy," Aunt Ibby scolded. "I'm surprised at you." O'Ryan looked appropriately apologetic for all of two seconds, then scooted out the open door. I stooped to pick up the book the cat had swiped from its shelf. He has a habit of occasionally knocking things onto the floor. The items he chooses usually have a special significance. (Our cat once belonged to a practicing witch who called herself Ariel Constellation. Some say he was her "familiar." In Salem a witch's familiar is always respected—and sometimes feared.

Placing the books on the desk, I turned to my aunt. "I guess he's trying to tell us something, but what?"

She picked the book up and turned it over, studying the back cover blurb. "If there's a message here I don't get it. Let's go downstairs and watch the news. I want to see what Chief Whaley has to say."

"Me too," I said. "You go ahead. I'll be right down. Mind if I take the book upstairs?"

“Help yourself” She headed downstairs while I went up. Tossing *Hickory Dickory Dock* onto my kitchen table, I picked up index cards and pen, then hurried back to join aunt and cat in her kitchen for happy hour and the five o’clock news.

CHAPTER 7

Chief Tom Whaley walked briskly to his designated spot behind a lectern in front of the Salem Police station, resplendent in full dress uniform, medals and all. He looked extremely uncomfortable, as he always does in these situations. After a couple of throat clearings, paper rustlings, and microphone adjustments, the press conference began.

"As many of you may know, today Albert Eldridge, one of Salem's most admired citizens, was found dead in his office at the Washington Square headquarters of Historical Charities of Salem." The chief read from the prepared statement. "Foul play is indicated in Mr. Eldridge's death. The medical examiner's report cites a blow to the back of the head as the cause of death. The weapon has not been identified. The Salem Police Department requests that citizens who may have observed any unusual activity today in the vicinity of Washington Square during the early morning hours between midnight and six a.m. call the number at the bottom of your TV screen."

He paused, looked to his right, then made a beckoning motion. I was surprised to see Conrad Gillette approach the microphone. Unlike the chief, Mr. Gillette looked totally relaxed. Tom Whaley continued. "I'll turn this over now to Mr. Eldridge's business partner, Conrad Gillette, who will bring you up to date on the many charitable programs that have been impacted by Mr. Eldridge's passing."

"Thank you, Chief Whaley. I just want to assure the citizens of Salem, and the many visitors who come to the city specifically for our outstanding Christmas celebration, that every event scheduled for 'Ring in the Holidays' will take place exactly as scheduled." His tone grew somber. "My dear friend Albert Eldridge would have wanted it that way and the dedicated staff and volunteers of Historical Charities of Salem are working day and night to make this Christmas the best one ever. Any questions?"

"Well, that was brief," Aunt Ibby said. "An unidentified weapon, hmmm?"

"Apparently," I said. "Let's see if anyone asks any good questions."

The usual shouted questions from reporters started. I recognized Scott Palmer's voice immediately. The chief pointed to him. "Yes. You, Palmer."

"Did the ME's report indicate what kind of weapon was used?"

"Blunt instrument."

The WBZ guy piped up. "Like what? Like a baseball bat?"

The chief shook his head. "We don't know yet. It's early in the investigation."

I scribbled "Blunt instrument" on an index card and thought about the blunt objects I'd seen in the room, like the stacked logs in a basket next to the hearth. That would have left splinters in the Santa Claus hat. I'd seen fireplace tools in a brass rack. Too pointy. There was a tall trophy on a side table. It was big and heavy-looking with a marble base supporting a glass globe. Maybe? I hoped Pete would come here instead of going home. He didn't discuss cases with me as a rule, but sometimes he'd let some little tidbit of information slip out.

A woman from the local radio station, WESX, shouted her question. "The police radio said the 911 call came in at around eleven. How come you're looking for activity between midnight and six a.m.?"

Good question. But if anyone had looked into his office this morning, they would have seen what I saw. An old man dozing over his book. If I hadn't shaken his shoulder, he might still be there! It was a chilling thought.

The chief explained that the ME had established the time of death between those hours. After a few more questions—mostly about the existence of enemies, possible motives, and illegal entry into the building—the chief further explained that there were no known enemies or motive, no evidence of forced entry. Chief Whaley, with an appearance of relief, turned the podium over to Gillette for questions about the Holiday Walk, the Christmas Belles concert, the merchant's division coloring contest, the food donations for the needy and homeless citizens of the city. He gave a special plug to the Veteran Santas, encouraging everyone to toss a "little extra something" into the kettles of "the bell-ringing volunteers who've served their country and now serve their city and their fellow veterans."

Scott Palmer tossed the programming back to the studio anchor, Buck Covington, who resumed the regular news report. Buck was the newest of WICH-TVs anchors. Devastatingly handsome with a great voice and the ability to read a teleprompter with amazing accuracy, Buck was dating River North.

"Want to watch the rest of the news?" Aunt Ibby asked. "Seems to be a repeat of the noon edition."

"I'd like to see what Wanda says about this snow. I may take a cab to work tomorrow if it keeps up."

O'Ryan chose that moment to perk up his ears and, abandoning his bowl of milk, raced to the cat door, making a quick exit into the back hall. "That'll be Pete," I said. One of our cat's many surprising talents is his unfailing ability to know when someone is approaching the house and which door that person will use. I followed his lead and pulled the kitchen door open. We were right. Hatless, Pete stepped into the hall, stamping his feet on the braided jute rug, brushing snowflakes from dark hair and leaning forward for a quick kiss. "Sorry I didn't have a chance to call first, babe," he said, bending to pick up a purring O'Ryan. "I just finished up with Ms. Jeffry and Gillette and drove them back to their cars. Practically right around the corner. So I thought I'd come over and see if you'd like a little company."

"Absolutely," I said. "Come on in and say hi to Aunt Ibby. We watched the chief's presser and we're just waiting to see what Wanda has to say about the weather."

"Yeah." He followed me into the kitchen. "I heard the chief on the radio. Nothing new there yet. Hi, Ms. Russell."

"Hello Pete. Come on in. Wine or coffee? Help yourself. Any idea what the weapon was? I guess Chief Whaley isn't buying the baseball bat idea." My aunt is much bolder than I am about asking Pete questions relating to police business.

"Coffee sounds good." He deposited the cat next to the red bowl of milk. I handed him a white ironstone mug, took one for myself, and he filled both from the Mr. Coffee. "Something pretty heavy. Back of the poor guy's skull was pretty much crushed."

My aunt nodded. "You think he died right away?"

"Doc says 'trauma to the brain tissue.' Never knew what hit him." He handed me the cream pitcher. He drinks his black. I wanted to write trauma to brain tissue on an index card, but decided it would be best to wait until later.

"I've been thinking about murder weapons," I said.

Pete smiled, lifting his mug in a sort of toast. "Of course you have, Nancy Drew."

Pete likes to tease me about that famous girl detective, especially since I've been taking an online course in criminology. Pete's the one who encouraged me to take it. I'm in my second year, and doing well. As and Bs. I ignored the Nancy reference. "Really. The only things that popped out at me were the fireplace logs and that trophy with the glass ball on top."

Serious cop face. "Yeah. We've checked them both for prints, blood, damage, you know. The works. Nothing so far."

"What about blood spatter patterns, Pete?" Aunt Ibby asked. My aunt hasn't taken any criminology courses, but she's read about a million mysteries and watched TV a lot too.

"TV detectives depend on them," he said, "and they can be a useful tool. But in real life, they're not very accurate."

"Really?" My aunt's green eyes widened. "I'm so disappointed."

I thought about that blood-soaked Santa hat. "The hat," I said aloud. "Blood didn't spatter much, did it?"

Pete nodded. "Right. Good observation, babe. Did I ever tell you you'd make a good cop?"

"About a million times thanks, but no thanks. I like my new job too much." I raised my mug in his direction. "Even though I have a lot to learn."

"How'd today go?" Pete asked. "I wanted to watch, but . . ." He spread his hands apart. "I got kind of busy."

"I know," I said. "I was there."

"Kind of interrupted you a couple of times, didn't I? Sorry."

"It's okay," I said. "It turned out all right. Got a fairly decent interview with Conrad Gillette. What do you think about him, anyway?"

Cop face back. You know I can't discuss people involved in a case."

"Involved?" My aunt leaned forward. "You mean Conrad is a suspect?"

Pete folded his arms and looked back and forth between my aunt and me. "Ms. Russell, you're as bad as she is." He smiled. "Stop the fishing expedition. Both of you." He pointed to the TV. "There's Wanda. Let's see what's up with the snowstorm."

Wanda the Weather Girl is one of WICH-TVs most popular on-air personalities. That's partly because she's a darn good weather reporter—she has a degree in meteorology—and partly because the males in the audience just plain enjoy watching Wanda. Tonight she wore an all-white mini trimmed with fake bunny fur around the hem and accenting the extremely low—even for Wanda—neckline. According to the weather map, the doppler radar, and the NOAA forecast, the snow would be over by morning and tomorrow would be clear, crisp, and pretty. Wanda gave her trademark low, low bow, blew a kiss to her audience, and turned the five o'clock newscast back to Buck Covington.

Buck, with his usual perfect diction, read the next item from the teleprompter. "Stay tuned, folks," he said. "After a brief commercial break, you'll learn why you should always look into the toilet bowl before you sit down."

Aunt Ibby shrugged, I stared at the TV, and Pete stood up. Our cue to go upstairs. I invited Aunt Ibby to join us for frozen pizza but she declined in favor of her own left-over pea soup and johnny cake. O'Ryan, making a quick decision to join Pete and me, was out the cat door and halfway up the first flight of stairs before we'd even entered the hall.

In New England, five o'clock on a December evening looks like the dead of night. When we entered my apartment I switched on lights in every room, dispelling the gloom, then turned on the oven, while Pete started the preloaded Mr. Coffee. I pulled plates and cups from the cabinet. Pete, who knows his way around the kitchen, put two red place mats on the Lucite table and picked up my stack of index cards. "Where do these go?" he asked.

"Would you just stick them on top of the bureau in the bedroom? I'll put them away later. I'm using them for my notes about the Eldridge case." I waited for the expected smile at my use of the term "case." He thinks it sounds "Nancy Drewish" when I refer to a "case." I wasn't disappointed. Sometimes he even makes up an appropriate book title to go with it. I halfway expected him to say something like *The Case of the Holiday Homicide*. He didn't. Just smiled.

"What about this book?" he asked, holding the Agatha Christie paperback O'Ryan had chosen earlier.

"O'Ryan picked it out," I said. "I guess he thinks I should read it. Maybe it should go on the bedside table."

Puzzled expression. "O'Ryan picked it out?"

"Yep. He was in the study by himself and when we went in there to look for him, he was sound asleep with his head on the open book." I laughed. "Just as though he'd dozed off while he was reading. Cute."

I realized what I'd just said. As though he'd dozed off while he was reading.

"Just like Mr. Eldridge," I said aloud. "That's how Mr. Eldridge looked to me."

Pete turned the book over. "*Hickory Dickory Dock*," he said. "Like the old nursery rhyme about the mouse who ran up the clock?"

"No. Like the mystery," I said. But my mind had gone back in time to a childhood book for the second time that day. This time I recalled an illustration of the little mouse running up the side of a clock. It was a grandfather's clock very much like the one in Lillian Jeffry's office.

CHAPTER 8

By the time the oven buzzer signaled that our pizza was ready, I'd dug half a head of lettuce, a tomato, and a red onion from the crisper. With the addition of some sliced black olives and a bottle of Thousand Island dressing I'd produced a reasonable facsimile of a salad.

"You're quiet," Pete said as he divided the pizza into eight perfect slices. "Are you okay?"

"Sorry," I said. "Yes, I'm okay. I'm was just thinking about some illustrations from books I had when I was a little kid. Like the mouse running up the clock and Scrooge in his big bed."

"You've lost me." He placed two slices on my plate, making sure a round peperoni was centered on each one. "I kind of get the mouse part, because of that book. But Scrooge? Care to explain?"

"I guess I didn't mention that I had a vision today. In one of the Santa Claus collection kettles. A shiny brass one."

"You want to tell me about it?"

Pete's not comfortable with the things I see on shiny surfaces. Why would he be? I'm pretty uncomfortable about them myself. But he encourages me to tell him about them anyway and sometimes he helps me make sense of the damned things.

I told him about the picture from my old Children's Classics book, and about how it had frightened me as a child. "Then when you recited the 'mouse ran up the clock' part of that nursery rhyme, I could see the picture of that little guy running up the side of a tall grandfather's clock. That reminded me of the clock in Ms. Jeffry's office. But what does all that mean?"

"Beats me, Babe," he said. "I think every picture book about that mouse shows a grandfather's clock though. That's the only kind he could run up, isn't it? But the mean old miser in bed doesn't ring any bells."

"Ring any bells," I echoed. "Scrooge is in a Christmas story and there are bells ringing all over Salem. Maybe that means something."

"Not to me," he said, taking a second helping of salad. "But here's a question I've been wondering about ever since we left your aunt's."

"What is it?"

He frowned. "Why should I look into the toilet before I sit down?"

I laughed. "Snake," I said. "Some lady in Australia found a poisonous brown tree snake in her toilet. I saw it on Rhonda's monitor at the station this morning."

That broke the somber mood. There was no more talk of scary picture books or undecipherable visions. I served vanilla ice cream. His with chocolate syrup, mine with Aunt Ibby's strawberry preserves. Alexa shuffled Christmas Carols. Pete poured the coffee and I shut off the overhead lights so that we could watch from the kitchen window as the snowflakes danced past. O'Ryan sprawled his long body along the windowsill and watched with us.

I was the one who broke the companionable silence. "I wonder about the footprints," I said.

"What made you think of footprints? More kiddie books? *Puss in Boots* maybe?"

O'Ryan looked up. "*Puss in Boots* is one of O'Ryan's favorites, isn't it boy?" I reached over and patted his big fuzzy head.

Pete raised an eyebrow. "You're pretty sure the cat can read?"

"Quite sure," I said. "Remember, he's a witch's cat. But anyway, he prefers being read to. Aunt Ibby bought him the audios of all Lillian Jackson Braun's Cat Who series."

"Uh-huh," Pete knows O'Ryan is special. He just doesn't like to talk about it.

"Actually, I was asking about the footprints at the Eldridge house. The ones in the snow. Do you think the Santas made all of them?"

"I think so." He pulled his chair closer to mine. "Hard to tell with all the people going in and out of the place. It's not as though we could make a plaster cast of snow prints. They were almost all filled in when we took the photos"

"It was surprising wasn't it? How fast Conrad Gillette solved the problem of where they should drop the money when you put the whole house off limits."

He agreed. "The guy seems to have connections. He got that bank drop-off fixed with a two-minute phone call."

I pushed my luck with another question. "Do you like him?"

Instant cop voice. "Not my job to like him." He stood and switched the kitchen light on. "Looks like the snow is letting up. Want some more coffee?"

"Okay. And there are some peanut butter cookies in the cookie jar."

Pete and I don't ever have any problem finding things

to talk about. I understand that he can't discuss police business with me, especially now that I'm a reporter. He understands that I'm going to try to get him to talk about it anyway. I know when to stop though, and the cop voice is usually a good signal that it's time to change the subject.

We nibbled on cookies, finished off the coffee, and chatted about this and that, avoiding any mention of the dead Mr. Eldridge, the Holiday Walk, or patriotic Santa Clauses. O'Ryan apparently found us boring and left via the cat door for greener pastures, or maybe a new chapter from Sofie Ryan's Cat Mystery series downstairs at Aunt Ibby's. Together, we cleaned up the kitchen, washed and put away the dishes.

We turned on the ten o'clock news, hoping to get the Celtics' score. The station was rebroadcasting the chief's brief press conference, followed by a replay of my Santa interview. The Celts won, Pete liked the way I wore my knit hat, Wanda had changed into a form-fitting red V-necked angora sweater, and it looked as though tomorrow would be a nice winter day, clear and cold.

"Shall we turn in?" Pete asked. "I'm on early again tomorrow."

"Me too," I said. There's only one bathroom in my apartment, so when Pete stays over, he uses that one and I go downstairs to my second-floor childhood bedroom and use the bathroom there. Grabbing pjs and slipper socks, I headed out the kitchen door to the stairs while Pete started down the hall to the john.

"Pete!"

"What?"

"Don't forget to check for snakes."

I giggled at my own little joke all the way downstairs. I enjoy coming into my old bedroom once in a while. It's like a mini time capsule of the me that used to be. French

Provincial furniture, canopy bed with starched white dust ruffle, dressing table with a round mirror with little lightbulbs all around. One of the best features is the pair of dormer windows overlooking Winter Street with wide, wide window seats and cushy pillows perfect for snuggling up with a book or just day dreaming. There's a rarely ever used fireplace too. I smoothed the rose-sprigged quilted bedspread and headed for the tiny windowless bathroom which I think had once been a closet. It served its purpose nicely with lavender walls, a narrow shower stall, tiny lavender shell-shaped pedestal sink, and a normal-size commode. (Snakeless. Of course I looked.)

I showered, tossed jeans, blouse, socks, and undies down the laundry chute which routes them to a wicker basket between the washer and dryer in the first-floor laundry room, and pulled on flannel pjs. Padding up the stairs to my apartment, a soft "mrrow" behind me let me know that O'Ryan intended to join us for the night.

"Come on, boy," I said. "A nice warm cat is always welcome on a cold, snowy night like this." I held the kitchen door open for him. Sometimes he seems to prefer a human-held door to the conveniently located cat entrance. Alexa had changed tracks from Christmas Carols to country, and Carrie Underwood's "Church Bells" greeted me. I peeked into the bedroom where Pete was already sound asleep. O'Ryan, claws clicking on tile, hurried across the kitchen, hopped up onto the bed, turned around three times (some sort of witch's cat ritual?) cuddled up next to Pete, blinking golden eyes a couple of times, then closing them.

The stack of index cards lay on top of the bureau along with a pen and the Agatha Christie book. I picked them up and carried them back to the table. It was still reasonably early—not quite eleven—and I wanted to make a few more notes about the case. Yes, I said "case." Just call me Nancy. I reread the few notes I'd made earlier, thought for a moment, then began scribbling. I do mean scribbling. I thought about Lillian Jeffry's beautiful handwriting and attempted to slow down.

Trauma to brain tissue. Crushed skull. Died instantly.

Little blood spatter pattern. Santa hat soaked it up.

I paused. Pete hadn't shared much information so far. I decided to include notes about my vision and O'Ryan's book selection. I didn't know what either one signified, but I've become familiar enough with both visions and cat to know that there's a good chance that they're both important. I chose two more blank cards.

Vision in Santa's kettle. An illustration from a childhood book (Children's Classic Series) picture of an old mean-looking man in bed. From child's version of A Christmas Carol. Scrooge.

O'Ryan pulled a paperback mystery book from the study. Agatha Christie's Hickory Dickory Dock. Another possible illustration from the old nursery rhyme? Mouse running up clock? Clock like the one in Lillian Jeffry's office?

I picked up the Agatha Christie book and flipped through the first few pages.

Hercule Poirot's secretary, a Miss Lemon, was described as hideous and efficient. Never ill, never tired, and never inaccurate. Ms. Jeffry was most certainly not hideous, quite the contrary, but it struck me that all the rest of the description fit perfectly. I was quite certain that Ms. Jeffry was to Albert Eldridge what Miss Lemon was to Hercule Poiroit. In the Christie story, at least within the few pages I'd read, Miss Lemon was uncharacteristically screwing things up. I closed the book. Ms. Jeffry, on the other hand, even under the most trying circumstances—and things don't get much more trying than this morning's happenings—had, for the most part, maintained her efficient demeanor. I already had the basic facts on Albert Eldridge. Rhonda had printed out his official biography for me when I got the Holiday Walk assignment. If I was going to get the kind of nitty-gritty inside information Mr. Doan relished, Ms. Jeffry was going to be a perfect source. It was unlikely that I was the only reporter to figure this out. I just needed to be the first one to get her story. I was pretty sure I knew how to get it. Lillian Jeffry and my aunt were friends and I knew that they must have each other's phone numbers.

First thing tomorrow morning I'll call good old Lilly and be on my way to getting my story.

I picked up a fresh index card. *Call Ms. Jeffry,* I wrote, *and dig out every little thing she knows about Mr. Eldridge.* I paused. I'd figured Mr. Gillette might be a good source of information, but so far, he'd turned out to be a bit of a disappointment. Especially when he wanted the gory details of his friend's sad demise.

"Was it very bloody?" he'd asked.

I made out a card for that too.

CHAPTER 9

I woke at seven-fifteen. Pete was already up, dressed. I could smell coffee brewing. I stretched, then sat on the edge of the bed. “Good morning, Sleepy Head,” Pete said. “I’ll grab breakfast on the way to work.” He picked up his regular “to-go” insulated coffee cup. “O’Ryan’s gone downstairs. I’ll call you later. Love you.” He leaned in for a quick kiss and headed for the back door.

“Love you.” I yawned, gave a little wave and, resisting the temptation to fall back into the warm, comfy bed, put both feet on the floor. I didn’t have to be at the station until nine-thirty, when I’d pick up my assignments for the day. I figured Lillian Jeffry for an early riser and hoped she’d have time to talk with me before that. I had time to dress, have some coffee and a toaster Pop Tart before I phoned Aunt Ibby. She’s an early riser too, and I was right about her having the phone number.

“Stop on your way out, Maralee,” she said. “It’s in my office in my Christmas Belles file. I’ll get it for you right now.”

O’Ryan was already waiting for me in the downstairs

back hall when I tapped on her kitchen door, and together we joined my aunt. She'd scribbled the number on a pink Post-it note and handed it to me. I told her about the Agatha Christie character and admitted that I planned to learn all I could about her friend's boss. "I understand, Maralee," she said. "You're doing your job. Please remember to be courteous and professional in your questioning. Lilly is a dear person, and whether she shows it or not, she's suffered a personal loss in Alfred's death. Why, they can't even make plans for his funeral yet, until the police release the body." She made a "tsk-tsk" sound. "Lilly has been his secretary for a long time. And," she added, "you might want to read the rest of that Christie book. An interesting plot."

"Maybe I will," I said, tucking the pink paper square into my jacket pocket. "Thanks for this. I'm going to call her right away." I wished my aunt a nice day, left her warm kitchen, and opened the back door. Wanda had been right about the weather. Clear and cold with only a frosty trace of yesterday's snow on the ground, sparkling in the winter sunshine on bare tree branches, fence posts, and the strings of Christmas lights on decorative hedges bordering our garden.

Our garage faces Oliver Street where the pavement was free of snow. I unlocked the side garage door, hit the Genie, watched the double door rise open, and climbed into the Vette. Then, snug in private, cushy leather comfort, I put the Eldridge bio and my notebook on the seat beside me and dialed Lillian Jeffry's number. If by lucky chance she'd agree to meet with her right away, I'd be ready to roll.

The response was immediate. A chirpy voice answered "Lillian Jeffry." (I've always admired the businesslike impression answering the phone with one's name gives. I've never done it yet myself, but maybe I'll try it someday.)

"Yes. Good morning, Ms. Jeffry," I said. "This is Lee Barrett. Do you have a few minutes?"

"Oh, Lee. Or do you prefer Maralee? Please do call me Lilly. We've shared such a strange and sad experience together, I feel quite close to you, my dear."

That's a good sign.

"Lee is fine, Ms.—I mean, Lilly. I know there'll be quite a bit of coverage about—what happened yesterday, and I'd like to do something special—something about Mr. Eldridge that will help people understand just what an extraordinary man he was." I paused, remembering Aunt Ibby's admonition to bear in mind her personal loss. "It seems to me that you knew him better than most people did. Can you . . . will you . . . help me to do that?"

There was a pause on her end too. Her voice was softer. Not so chirpy now. "I would like to help you, Lee. I'm sure you understand though, that my relationship with Mr. Eldridge over so many years was strictly professional."

The answer surprised me. It hadn't occurred to me for even a minute that the relationship was anything but professional. I consulted my notes. "I know that Mr. Eldridge showed great generosity for the entire community, especially for those in need. I thought perhaps you could tell me something about his unique love for Salem—both for her past and her present."

"And her future," she said, voice sounding wistful. "He had such wonderful plans for creating an amazing historic district showing how regular people lived in long-ago Salem. It involved moving old houses from the neighborhoods, where they're in danger of being torn down, to a new historic district. He was going to call it Heritage Village. I doubt that it will happen now."

"Perhaps Mr. Gillette will be able to move it forward. He seems quite dedicated."

Long sigh. "Perhaps. But Albert had a serving heart. That means everything."

What a great quote! I wrote her words on a fresh card. "A serving heart," I repeated. "I wish I had had a chance to meet him, to talk with him. I know this might be an imposition, but I'd like to get a head start on preparing this piece. Could you possibly meet with me for an hour or so this morning?"

"I have a nine o'clock appointment with Conrad at the Community Center. I could meet you there at say, eight-thirty? That would give us a half hour together. I'm afraid that's the best I can do today."

I checked my watch. It was already eight-fifteen. "That's perfect," I told her. "Thank you so much. I'm on my way." The Community Center was on Orange Street, close to several of Salem's historic homes. If half an hour was all she could spare, I'd make it work. I hoped to have this story ready for one of my occasional "investigative reports" in the late news slot. If my luck held, maybe Conrad Gillette would show up early and I could get some insight from him too. Albert Eldridge had been doing his good works in Salem for years. I was sure the station had plenty of archival film of the man and his various projects. I hadn't heard about the Heritage Village idea before. If Lilly could tell me where one or more of those old houses were, Francine and I could grab some footage of that too. This was starting out to be a good day.

I made a quick call to Aunt Ibby's cell. "I'm still in the garage," I told her. "Talked to Lilly already and I'm on my way to meet her at the Community Center. She's giving me a half hour before she meets with Mr. Gillette."

"Just like her," my aunt said. "The image of efficiency. She won't skip a beat, proceeding with the Salem Historical Charities projects just as though Albert was still in charge."

"Like Miss Lemon?" I asked. "Never tired and never inaccurate?"

"Not exactly," she said. "Read the book."

"I will," I promised. "Ms. Jeffry—Lilly—seemed especially concerned about a project she called 'Heritage Village.' Had you heard about it? She doesn't seem confident that Mr. Gillette will be able to get it done." I started the big engine and rolled out onto Oliver Street. "Gotta go. I'll call you later and tell you how it went."

I was a few minutes early, and wondered if Lillian Jeffry did things "in a timely manner" like her late boss, and would keep me waiting until exactly eight-thirty. There was no grandfather's clock in the reception area of the Community Center but there was a plain large, round, white-faced clock on the wall.

"Hello there, Lee." She beckoned to me from the doorway of a glass-walled room very much like the enclosed study rooms one might find in a library. "You're early. Good. Half an hour is barely enough time to scratch the surface of dear Albert's amazing life. Come right on in here. It's nice and quiet. And private."

Glass walls don't equate with privacy in my world but I hurried to join her in the fish-bowl-like cubicle. "Thank you so much for seeing me on such short notice, Lilly," I said. I draped my jacket on the back of a chair and sat facing Lilly across a square table. I had my pen and notebook ready. The index cards are for my private observations, "my eyes only" as they say on the spy shows, so I'd left them in my car. "I can ask some prepared questions,

Lilly," I said, "but first I'd like you to tell me about some of the things you'd like people to know about Albert Eldridge. I picked up the biographical sketch Rhonda had prepared. "The things that perhaps don't show up in here. For instance, I'm fascinated by the idea of the Heritage Village."

"He was so excited about it." Her smile was so sincere, so genuine, it made me smile in return. For that moment she reminded me of the smiling Santa. "He'd had plans drawn up for it, feasibility studies done, all at his own expense, mind you. Such a generous soul." She sighed, the smile replaced with a slight frown. "He'd planned to submit the idea to the city council right after the holidays. Now,"—she spread her hands apart in a helpless gesture—"now, I just don't know."

"It would be a wonderful addition to Salem's many historic buildings," I said. "People love the mansions and great homes, but a neighborhood of houses that ordinary men and women lived in would be so interesting. They'd be for sale or for rent, I imagine?"

"Yes indeed. But it will be an expensive project. Most of the houses Alfred selected are well built, but in sad disrepair. There are a couple of them not far from here." She mentioned a street where workers had been housed back when some world-famous mills had been located in Salem. "But, dear Lee, if you can tell people about Albert's dream, make them see how grand it could be, who knows? Maybe it could happen after all!" She clapped her hands together like a little girl. She looked away from me for a moment. "And look who's here." She pointed to the glass wall behind me. "It's Conrad." She made a beckoning motion and the door opened, admitting Conrad Gillette.

"I'm a tad early for our meeting," he said, "but when I saw our charming new friend Lee Barrett here with you, Lillian, I decided to take the liberty of interrupting. Hello there, Lee." He pulled up a chair and sat between Lilly and me, looking from one of us to the other.

Charming new friend?

"I was telling Lee about Albert's dream for the village," Lilly told him. "I think she may be able to help us by publicizing it. But for now, she's gathering impressions of the dear man. I'm sure you have special memories of him to share. She wants to make an investigative report about him."

"Investigative?" Gillette looked confused. "About his death?"

"Certainly not." Lillian Jeffry frowned. "About his devotion to Salem's history."

Gillette nodded, and spoke in an officious tone. "So conversant with history. Albert had an amazing knowledge of the city, as well as an encyclopedic memory. He could spout names and dates and places covering centuries." He leaned forward, putting both elbows on the table. "He will be sorely missed. No doubt about that." He moved his left wrist slightly, glancing at his watch, which if it wasn't a Rolex, was a remarkably good fake.

I took the hint. "I must be keeping you two from your meeting. Lilly, I appreciate your seeing me on such short notice. Perhaps we can meet again when you have more time." I picked up my notebook and papers and stood. "Good to see you again, Mr. Gillette. I'm sure you both have a lot of Historical Charities business to discuss."

Surprise showed on both faces. Oops. Maybe they're here to make funeral plans.

Lilly spoke first. "Oh dear, this meeting is about music for 'Ring in the Holidays in Salem.' Conrad is our musical director. He knows your Aunt Ibby too. He'll be directing the Christmas Belles performances. We only have a couple of weeks before our first concert."

CHAPTER 10

I had a lot to think about while I drove from Turner Street to the WICH-TV building on Derby Street. I hadn't learned as much as I'd hoped for about Albert Eldridge, but I still wanted to do an investigative piece about him on the eleven o'clock news.

And I want to do it tonight. Before somebody else does it.

Who else could I talk to who'd have some personal insight into what made the man tick?

Whoops. There goes another clock analogy!

I pulled into the station's parking lot and eased into my designated spot. It was the same one I'd had back when I was Crystal Moon, phony psychic, and it was as far away as I could get from the sea wall where I'd found Ariel Constellation's drowned body. Gathering up notebook, papers, and purse, I looked at the digital dashboard clock. Nine-ten. That left me twenty minutes before I had to check in with Rhonda for today's schedule. I stepped out of the car, locked it, and started across the lot, concentrating on how I could cobble together the kind of program I wanted to produce, and at the same time trying to avoid the patches of slush on the ground. Maybe I shouldn't have worn my

Dolce and Gabbana boots with heels before the ground was clear of snow, but they were so cute and I knew they'd look good on camera. Okay. The convertible isn't my only extravagance. I really like designer shoes and handbags too.) I'd just about reached the sidewalk in front of the station when my right foot hit a patch of ice under the slush. I braced myself for an inevitable embarrassing and perhaps painful crash.

"Whoa, little lady. What's your hurry?" Strong arms grasped my waist, lifted me, and set me upright, steadying me. I turned to face my rescuer. It was Santa Claus. The same smiling Santa I'd seen in front of the building the previous day.

"Thank you," I breathed. "You were here in the nick of time."

The smile broadened. "In the Saint Nick of time, you might say. You all right?"

"Fine," I said. "Thank you so much." I bent to pick up notebook and purse while my benefactor retrieved the stapled pages of the Eldridge biography.

"I see you're reading up on Mr. Eldridge." He handed the papers to me. "Great guy. You going to do a TV show about him or something like that?"

"Something like that," I agreed. "You said that before, when I interviewed you. That Mr. Eldridge was a 'great guy.' Did you know him personally at all?"

"You picked that up, huh? Yes. I did." He turned in the direction of the camo kettle which was on the curb near the front door of WICH-TV. "Sure did."

I waited for him, to continue. He didn't. I pushed. "Tell me about him," I said. "Did you and he have one-on-one conversations? Did he have interests besides his organizations?" I waited, realizing that, for such a public figure, Albert Eldridge was turning out to be a surprisingly private person.

The Santa looked down, not smiling now. He towered over me, even though I was wearing boots with three-inch heels. "We understood each other. We were both combat vets. Neither of us liked to talk about that. We talked about normal stuff. Sports. Politics. Besides that, he liked his organizations. That's what he liked to talk about." He frowned. "You got a problem with that?"

I took a half-step back. "No. Of course not. I'm just interested in learning all I can about him. His secretary said he had a 'serving heart.' I guess you agree with her."

The smile returned. "Lilly said that? That's nice. She's right. He liked serving other people. All the time. That was him."

I felt as though I'd been dismissed. I clearly wasn't going to get any more information here. "Well, thanks again, Santa, for keeping me from falling. Say, I can't keep calling you Santa. What's your name?"

He walked toward his kettle, reaching it in two long strides. He gave me a red-gloved thumbs up. "You can call me Nick."

"Okay then, Nick," I said, hurrying past him and up the two granite steps leading to the station's front door. "Thanks again."

I took the clanking elevator up to the second-floor suite of offices. Rhonda was at the reception desk and the gold sunburst clock on the wall read nine-twenty-five. On time for work with minutes to spare. "Hi, Rhonda," I said. "Anything interesting on the docket for me today?"

"Yep. We just got word Chief Whaley's going to do another presser at ten. Scottie's not here so you get to cover it. Guess it's about the dead guy you found yesterday." She handed me an assignment sheet. "After that you've got some ladies at the senior center who've been knitting little Christmas hats for newborns at Salem Hospital and there's a big push for people to adopt shelter pets down at the Northeast Animal Shelter on Highland Avenue. Francine is already in the van. She says she'll be out front in two minutes." Rhonda leaned over the counter around her desk. "Cute boots."

"Thanks. Not good on slippery pavement though. See you later." I hurried down the elevator and out the front door. Francine was there. Nick wasn't.

I climbed into the passenger seat. "Might as well head right over to the police station," I said. "Let's get a front row position."

"Yep. That's what Scotty always does when he gets this assignment. Even if we're not the first ones there, he elbows his way up to the front." Francine glanced over at me. "'Course he's a lot bigger than you."

"True," I said, sneaking a look at my own elbows. "I'll try saying 'excuse me, please.' Think that'll work?" No reply.

We pulled up into the parking area of the police station. Francine handed me a mic, pushed a few buttons on her control panel, grabbed a shoulder mount camera, and the two of us ran toward where the chief's lectern had been set up. No sign of the chief yet, and I didn't see any of the Boston mobile units.

"Hurry up, Lee." Francine was ahead of me. (Of course she was wearing sensible boots.) We got a good position anyway without using either elbows or polite requests. I stood between a rep from the radio station and a new guy from the *Salem News*.

"You got any idea what's going on?" the WESX rep asked. "Maybe some new info about the Eldridge murder, don't you think?"

"Could be," I said. "You heard anything?"

"One of the guys at the station lives next door to the old man's secretary and he says there was a cop car over there last night." She shrugged. "That's all I know."

Hoping there was nothing wrong with Lilly, I focused my attention on the big window behind the lectern where a few uniforms had begun to gather. The chief walked into view with Pete right behind him. The door opened and Chief Whaley took his customary spot behind the mic, wearing his customary "I'd rather be any place but here" expression, along with his medals and gold braid. Pete stood beside him, cop-face in place. I looked behind me, where some of the Boston reporters had begun to show up. I resisted a couple of elbows and maintained my front-row status.

"Good morning," the chief said. "I'll have a brief statement and then I'll turn the microphone over to Detective Mondello for any questions." He nodded in Pete's direction, then, reading from a single sheet of paper, began. "As you know, yesterday morning it was learned that Mr. Albert Eldridge was found dead in his home office. The medical examiner has determined that death occurred due to a blow to the head from a blunt instrument. In short, this was a murder committed by a person or persons unknown. We are asking once again for the community's help in apprehending the perpetrator. If you recall seeing anyone in the vicinity of the Historical Charities of Salem building on Washington Square—between midnight and seven yesterday morning, call the number on your screen. Anyone at all. If you can identify that person, do not attempt to apprehend him or her. Call the number at the bottom of your screen. All calls will remain confidential. I speak with some urgency because last night at eleven-ten p.m., a person closely associated with Mr. Eldridge reported an attempted break-in at her home. We have reason to believe the attempt was associated with Mr. Eldridge's death. We have taken necessary steps to protect this person. I'll turn this program over now to Detective Mondello who is the lead detective in this matter. Thank you." He picked up his paper and hurried back into the police station.

Someone tried to break into Lilly's house. She must have been terrified.

Pete moved into the position behind the mic which the chief had just vacated. He held up one hand. "Questions?"

I raised my hand.

CHAPTER 11

"Yes?" Pete pointed at me.

"Lee Barrett, WICH-TV," I said. "How do you know the attempted break-in had to do with Mr. Eldridge's death? That it wasn't just some random thing?"

"We don't know for sure," Pete admitted, "but the householder has reason to believe that it does. I can't give out any more information at this time."

Maybe he'll be able to give it out later. To me.

Questions after that came quickly. Answers were pretty much as vague as the one he'd given me. "Why do they even bother?" Francine mumbled. "They could just put the information online. They must just like the face time on TV."

"Not the chief," I whispered back. "Not Pete either."

The *Salem News* reporter asked Pete if the person whose house it was knew what the perp was after. It was a good question. I should have asked it.

"She believes she knows and has turned over relevant material to us."

That was new information. The print reporters were on their tablets and phones. A few cameras clicked and flashed. Follow-up questions didn't result in much. Pete repeated the chief's request for help from the community, then ignoring a few shouted requests, ducked inside the big glass doors and disappeared from sight.

I thought about how Pete had left extra-early for work. I figured that he probably knew all about Lilly's call to the police. Son of a gun. You'd think he would have told me that much!

Francine and I headed back to WICH-TV and picked up the information sheets on the knitting ladies. "That's nice," Francine said, looking over her copy as we rode down in the elevator together.

"What's nice?" I asked. "Red and green bonnets for the Christmas babies?"

"That too," she said. "But I meant that the ladies get together and do something like that. They don't just sit around and get old."

"You should meet my Aunt Ibby," I told her. "She's a pistol! She's well over sixty, still works part time, is a computer whiz, she's writing a cookbook, still dating, does church work—she'll never grow old!"

"I hope I'll be like that," Francine said as we approached the Senior Center on Essex Street.

"Me too," I agreed. "My aunt's even in that Christmas Belles group that Lilly Jeffry mentioned when we were there yesterday."

"Yeah. I remember. I went to their concert last year. The one where they all sang Christmas Carols from other lands. And I loved the one a couple of years ago when they wore costumes and each one played Christmas music on a different instrument."

"I missed a lot of the concerts when I was living in Florida," I said, "but I saw last year's. I loved the part when they sang the Gaelic carol and tried to do an Irish step dance. They all got laughing so hard they couldn't sing. I think what people love most about the Belles is that they don't take themselves too seriously. But I know they each play one or more instruments. Aunt Ibby plays both piano and flute."

"They don't always do music, I guess. I remember once when they did a funny version of *A Christmas Carol*. What a hoot. All those ladies playing the guys' parts. What are they going to do this year?"

"I haven't asked. I'll find out tonight and let you know. Whatever it is, everyone says the Belles always put on a good show."

We met with the "KnitWits" as they called themselves. Their ages varied from young moms to some great grandmas. They were an interesting and funny group, and the interviews and displays of the tiny hats and bonnets filled a good ten-minute segment. We moved on to the pet shelter where it was all I could do to resist taking a new furry friend home with me. (Would O'Ryan like a new sibling?) The shelter had dressed up some of the kitties and puppies with Christmas-themed collars and even skirts and bonnets. Another fast-moving ten minutes, and Francine and I were on our way back to the station.

I hoped to have time to call Lilly Jeffry. I hoped she was okay although naturally having someone try to break into your house would be terrifying. I knew it from experience. I also hoped that she'd be willing to share some new information about her late boss. He must have had some interests besides his charities. He must have had some acquaintances besides his associates in the Historical Charities of Salem. And frankly, even though I didn't like to admit it even to myself, I found it hard to believe that the man had no flaws. Was he some kind of saint who thought of nothing but good deeds? Maybe.

There was nothing new on my schedule. Rhonda was going to lunch at the Scratch Kitchen, down Derby Street a little way from the station. I asked her to bring me back a chicken salad sandwich—toasted, and a diet Pepsi. That gave me time to call Lilly. She answered on the first ring.

"How very kind of you to call, Lee. Yes, it was frightening. Especially right after . . . you know."

"If you don't feel safe there, Lilly," I said, "we have a guest room. "I'm sure Aunt Ibby would love to have you stay with us—as long as you like."

"You're very kind," she said again. "The police have arranged for me to stay at the Hawthorne for a while. Isn't that something? I'm sure my home is safe though. It was my alarm system that chased the burglar away."

"We have a good alarm system too," I said. "Do you have any idea what they were looking for?"

"Whoever it was tried to get in through my home office window. I suppose they were after my computer. It's nothing special as computers go. It's not new, but it does contain everything the computers at the Historical Charities do. Mostly dates and times for events and, of course, all the financial records. Did you know Mr. Eldridge kept a ledger—an old-fashioned ledger? He didn't believe in computers." She paused and her voice quavered just a little. "That's what he was studying when you—you know, shook his shoulder."

Interesting. An old-fashioned ledger. I can use that.

"I guess the police took the computers and the ledgers from the office?" I asked.

"Right."

"So you think maybe someone else is interested in what was on them. Did the police know you had duplicate records?"

"They didn't ask. They know now."

"This'll give you a few days off, I suppose," I said. "What'll you do with all that time?"

"Oh, this and that. Housework, long neglected. And," her voice brightened, "I'll have time for the Belles' concert rehearsals."

"Francine and I were just talking about that. What's the theme this year?"

"Well dear, it's in perfect harmony with the theme for the holidays. We'll be bell ringing!"

"Bell ringing?" A mental picture of the Santas flitted through my head.

"Yes. We're really excited about it. The handheld bells are beautiful, of course. Bright brass. And the sounds! Amazing. We each hold two or sometimes three bells and the sheet music tells us when to ring them. Conrad has had experience with them before so he's the perfect director."

"He has a musical background I understand. How did he wind up with a historical society?"

"He and Albert met some years ago at a Boston Pops concert. Conrad's family owned a construction company Albert had hired to do some work on one of our historical homes. Conrad was involved in giving estimates on reconstructing older buildings. Conrad and Albert were both Boston University alums and Conrad's major at BU was business administration with a minor in music. It was a perfect match!"

"Fascinating," I said. "I'm trying to gather enough information to do a piece on 'Albert Eldridge, the man.' He's so well-known for his charities, his good works for the poor, and the vets and the homeless. I'm looking for more. His interest in music gives another facet. I'd like to know more about that part of the man."

"He was a very private person, mostly staying in his

office, letting me face the public, letting Conrad take care of the business of keeping all the properties in good repair. But the music was something he loved. For instance, he bought the set of hand bells for us."

"He did? I remember that we had bells like that when I was in second grade. They were different colors and the music had colored dots."

The silvery laugh. "Oh no. The principle was the same. But these are professional choir bells. The set cost several thousand dollars."

"Wow. I guess those are kept locked up tight."

"Of course," she said. "Well, Lee, thank you for calling me. Tell dear Ibby I'll see her at Belles' rehearsal. Must go now. 'Bye."

That was apparently all I was going to learn from Lilly Jeffry for now. I'd picked up a couple of bits of information though. He was a music lover and kept his records the old-fashioned way. Didn't trust computers. That would fit in with his desire to rehab those old houses, to make things the way they used to be.

Rhonda returned with my lunch, checked the schedule for more appointments. Nothing yet, so she gave me the key to one of the little cubicles the station reserved for reporters to use (but made sure they were readily available if needed). Mr. Doan called them "Dataports." I carried my lunch, purse, Eldridge bio, and notebook into the small room. There was a desk, a computer and printer along with copy paper, one pen, one pencil, and a gooseneck lamp. Sparse, but adequate.

I checked online for more information. Disappointed. Nothing new there. What I needed, I realized, was someone who was an expert at digging out facts. I needed my tech-savvy, research librarian, information guru, Aunt Ibby. Fishing my phone from a cluttered purse, I called her.

"Help," I said when she answered. "I need some inside information on Albert Eldridge. Human interest, you know." I explained what I wanted to do for the news segment. "Fifteen minutes worth will do it I think. Therese and Francine are looking up film clips for me."

The calm voice was full of reassurance. "Of course I can. I take it this isn't to be about his death, but about his life."

"Exactly." My feeling of relief was immeasurable. After we hung up, I whipped together a bit of introductory script which sounded all right when I read it aloud to myself. I leaned back in the not-too-steady chair, finished off my sandwich and Pepsi, printed out the couple of pages I'd produced, and trusted in my aunt's able assistance for the rest. I'd just reached to click off the gooseneck lamp when Rhonda buzzed me on the intercom.

"Got another stand-up for you and Francine, Lee," she announced. "You need to go over to the yacht club and check out the lighted boat parade they're planning for next week. After that, Mr. Doan says you can go on home if you want to. Scott Palmer will be doing the High School basketball game live. Doan really likes the puppies and kittens thing you did this morning. Plans to run it after the five o'clock news. I told him about your investigative thing on old man Eldridge. Loves it. He's blocking out fifteen minutes on Covington's eleven o'clock. Hope that was okay."

I hoped it was okay too. My newfound confidence lagging just a bit already, I grabbed coat and hat and met Francine in front of the station. It had become a habit to look for the Santa named Nick. He wasn't there but I was happy to see that another Santa had taken his place.

This one didn't have a camo or brass kettle, but a rainbow painted one. I guessed that before long, I'd learn to identify them all by their individual kettles.

Another idea for a story! Maybe I'm getting good at this!

Maybe.

CHAPTER 12

I'd covered a few lighted boat parades at Christmas time back in Florida, but wondered how they planned to pull it off in December in Massachusetts. What if the harbor was full of ice? What if we had a blizzard?

Turns out, they had a pretty good plan. The lighted boats would tie up at Pickering Wharf. If weather permitted, they'd parade around that section of harbor. There were plenty of viewing places, restaurants, and hotels on the wharf, and along Derby Street, benches here and there, bordering the harbor. If they couldn't leave the wharf, the many lighted yachts around it would be pretty anyway. Even the upper floors of WICH-TV would have a clear view. Either way, it would make for good television.

I interviewed the Commodore and a couple of yacht owners who were already installing elaborate lighted decorations on their boats from stem to stern. If the weather cooperated, this would be a great show. Francine was excited about the videography possibilities and we both wished them all well on the idea.

When we returned to the station, Francine dropped me off in the parking lot. I started the big engine and waited a few minutes for the heater to kick in. (Okay. I know a convertible isn't practical in Salem in the winter, but she's so pretty!) I called Aunt Ibby and told her I was on my way.

As Dorothy famously said, "There's no place like home." I parked my car, locked everything up, and started up the path to the back door. I was about halfway past the garden when O'Ryan poked his fuzzy head out of his cat door, looked back and forth, then hurried down the path to meet me with joyful "Mmrows" and ankle rubbings. Things got even better when I entered the back hall and smelled something wonderful cooking in my aunt's kitchen. O'Ryan ducked through that cat door. I knocked and waited for Aunt Ibby's "Come in Maralee. It isn't locked" and followed.

I draped my jacket over the back of a captain's chair and tossed hat, gloves, and purse on the seat and gave my aunt a hug. "Smells great in here. What's cooking?"

She waved a wooden spoon. "Beef Burgundy. It's not quite ready yet but you can have a tiny taste before we get to work on your project." She lifted a steaming ladleful of the rich brown stew from the black iron pot into a small Franciscan ware bowl and put it on the round table. "Tell me what you think," she commanded. "It's one of Tabitha's recipes. I altered it a tad. I don't think she'd mind." I pushed hat, gloves, and purse aside, sat and tasted. She sat opposite me, watching as I lifted the spoon to my mouth. The Tabitha my aunt referred to was Tabitha Trumbull, the namesake of the Tabitha Trumbull Academy of the Arts where I'd recently taught Television Production. Aunt Ibby had discovered a cache of Tabitha's recipes and was busy preparing a Tabitha Trumbull cookbook for a library fund-raiser.

"It's wonderful," I said, absolutely truthfully. "Just right. It's familiar, but has a little something extra."

"Ha!" she said. "Good. That's what I thought too. Okay.

Finish up. I'll turn the heat down to low and we can get to work. The eleven o'clock news, you say?"

"Right. Do you think we can do it?"

That brought a haughty look as only she can do it. It's sort of a "Do you know who you're talking to?" look. "Sorry," I said. "Silly question." I finished every last delicious bite, poured the last few drops of rich broth into the cat's red bowl, and followed her to her office.

"Come and sit by me and I'll show you what I've found so far," she said. "I started searching the minute you called." She tapped the big monitor screen. "There's a picture of Albert when he was young."

It was hard to reconcile the image of the dark-haired, handsome young man on the screen with the distorted features of the man I'd seen with his head propped against a chair, a blood-soaked Santa hat covering one eye. "Where did this picture come from?"

"The *Salem News* microfilm" she said. "I used my library access. The Eldridges are an old Salem family. They've been photographed and written about many times. This one was from his graduation from Boston University. Suma Cum Laude of course. There are several photos taken through the years, but remarkably little information other than just the facts surrounding each picture. He served during the Korean conflict. Look, there he is in his uniform. He was a marine. Received the bronze star and a purple heart. Joined his father's real estate business. Never married. He began buying the old mansions as they came on the market, one by one. Founded the Historical Charities back in the sixties. The foundation itself raises money to maintain and repair the buildings. They've bought several new properties lately. Not mansions this time. Mostly older houses built in the 1930s and 1940s."

"I know a little about that," I said. "Lilly told me." I

explained about Heritage Village and how Mr. Eldridge was looking forward to completing it. "Too bad, isn't it, that he never got to see it done."

"It is," she said. "If you were looking for any deep, dark secrets about Albert, I'm afraid you're going to be disappointed. His life was, as they say, an open book."

O'Ryan had joined us by then and sat on top of a nearby bookcase, grooming his whiskers and listening to our conversation. (We can tell when he's listening because he cocks both ears forward in a rather peculiar way.)

Aunt Ibby returned to manipulating screen images, putting together a nice montage of the dozen or so photos of Albert Eldridge she'd discovered, covering several decades of his life. "I talked to Marty at the station and she said if I sent them to her, she'd arrange them to work with your script as you see fit. She said to tell you the station has footage of the holiday houses from previous years along with a nice film of the old gentleman receiving an award from the Chamber of Commerce last year. I'll print out what I've found. Hope it's useful to you."

"Thanks," I said. "It certainly is. With this, and what I've learned from Lilly, I think I can easily fill fifteen minutes. The pictures will help a lot. And the part about his being a decorated marine and a B. U. grad, and the family being in real estate, it all gives a little clearer picture of the man, don't you think?"

"I think it does. I wish I could have learned more to help you. I'll keep at it. Meanwhile, you'd better get to work on that script. You only have a few hours."

"I know. I'm getting kind of used to it. That's how the reporting business works. News has to be fresh, you know?"

"Scoot along upstairs then," she said. "I'll finish up the beef stew and maybe make some biscuits. You'll have a proper sized bowlful before you go out again. Wanda says it's going to get colder tonight. And please, take my car. It's warmer."

"I will." I leaned and gave her a kiss on top of her head. "What would I do without you?"

"I have no idea," she said. "Now get busy."

I laughed "You sound just like you did when I was in high school and had homework to do."

"Same thing."

I took her advice, just as I had in high school, and with O'Ryan tagging along, I gathered up my belongings and climbed the narrow back stairs to my apartment. We entered my living room door together. He didn't use the cat door. Sometimes he likes having the big door held open for him. "You can watch TV while I work," I told him. "You're just in time for *Wicked Tuna*." He loves programs about fish. Climbing into his favorite wing chair, the one with zebra print upholstery, he turned around three times, then in curled-up cat position, settled down to watch Captain Dave Marciano. I selected the proper channel, then walked down the short hall to the kitchen.

My laptop was still on the table. I kicked off my boots, wiggled my toes, and went straight to work. Back when I was doing the shopping channel show in Florida, my words-per-minute speech pattern was figured at about a hundred words a minute. I guessed that the short films and still photos would account for pauses in the voiceover section. If I could write a script for about eight minutes worth of comment, memorize the important parts, and work with Marty on the order of the piece, I should be able to deliver a short, but informative bio of the dead man.

Working alone in my kitchen, with only the sound of a ticking clock and a wintry wind blowing outside, with no interruption, no cat-comments, I had a usable script in less than an hour. I watched Kit-Kat's wagging tail for timing, read the piece aloud, printed it out, and still had time to shower, change clothes, and to call Pete and tell him I'd be on the late news. He promised to watch. I wanted to ask him a few questions—quite a few actually, but that would have to wait. By nine-thirty, with a tummy full of beef stew and a hot baking powder biscuit, and with a polished script in my purse, I phoned Marty to tell her I was on my way, backed the Buick out of the garage, and headed for WICH-TV.

There were still a few Santas standing beside their kettles, ringing bells, along my short route to the station. I admired their dedication and hoped those red suits were as warm as they looked. I started to pull into the parking lot and noticed a kind of thin-looking Santa at the edge of the sidewalk. I reached for my purse, intending to donate a few more dollars. But something about this guy didn't look quite right. He didn't have a colorful kettle like the others. He had what appeared to be a sand pail in his hand. His beard looked like a bunch of glued on cotton balls. No bell, either and I didn't see a flag on his red hat.

I think I'll pass on that one. I'll bet he's not even a Santa's helper.

I parked the Buick in the space my Vette usually occupied at the far side of the lot, avoiding the Santa, and thinking that my old spot near the seawall which, although it held bad memories, would be much more convenient on a cold winter night. I picked my way carefully and slowly across the pavement which was beginning to feel slippery. Although there was no snow, the spray over the seawall had begun to form a thin glaze of ice. Using the side door that led directly to the downstairs studio, I punched in my employee code and stepped gratefully into the long, dimly lit but comfortably warm room.

"Hey, Moon! Good to see you." (Marty McCarthy will

probably always use my make-believe psychic name Crystal Moon.) She motioned me over to the Tarot Time with River North set (the same stage where I'd done my show—*Nightshades*). "River won't be here for another hour so I've set things up here so you can see if it all works. Try your lead in, then we'll figure out the sequence of pictures and video. Okay?" She ducked behind the large, wheeled camera. "Jeez, Moon, it takes as much work to set up a fifteen-minute shoot for the news department as we used to spend on a whole hour call in show."

I shed my coat, smoothed my green velvet pantsuit, and straightened the collar of a beige silk blouse. "Seems so," I agreed. "Shall I stand here?"

"That's fine. Go."

"Albert Eldridge was a well-recognized figure in Salem," I began, "but such a modest person that we didn't know a lot about him. Let's take a tiny peek into the life of this beloved and very private man."

With the ease that came from working so closely together on *Nightshades*, Marty and I coordinated photos, scripted explanations, archived video clips, commentary, and closing remarks. It took some adjusting (apparently I no longer speak one hundred words a minute, more like eighty), but after fiddling around with pacing, selecting the best photos, and some judicious editing of old films and videos, we felt that we'd nailed it at exactly fifteen minutes. It was twenty minutes before eleven when we climbed the stairs to the second-floor newsroom.

Buck Covington was already behind the news desk and welcomed me with his best smile. "Hello Lee. Mr. Doan says you're doing an investigative piece about that poor guy that got killed. Have you figured out who did it already?"

"Not that kind of investigation I'm afraid, Buck," I

said. "I was hoping you'd have something about that in your newscast."

"Don't know. Haven't read it yet. You'll go on right after the hard break at eleven-thirty. Okay?"

"Okay." Buck had the amazing talent of being able to read cold from the teleprompter with absolute accuracy, never missing a word, never mispronouncing one, always using the correct expression on his handsome face. Mr. Doan characterized the man as "dumb as a brick but with great pipes." My friend River North and Buck were dating and River didn't find him dumb at all. Quite the contrary.

Scott Palmer was seated off to the side in the director's chair and motioned for me to join him. I took the offered seat. "I've read the newscast," he said, "even if Buck hasn't. The cops have made some progress. They've already identified the punk who tried to break into Ms. Jeffry's place."

"No kidding? Got a name?"

CHAPTER 13

"Yep. You'll see." I wasn't going to get any more from Scott. Our relationship hasn't been what you'd call friendly for quite a while, and my becoming the station's second field reporter wasn't sitting well with him. He'd been the first and only for a couple of years.

I busied myself with the script. I'd memorized the lead, and I'd be sitting next to Buck at the news desk for my segment with my notes out of sight in my lap. I had the usual jitters that come just before the camera lights go on, but nothing really worrisome.

At eleven, Buck led off with some national headlines, then read (with perfect diction and appropriate facial expression) a breaking news segment. "Salem police have made an arrest in an attempted break-in at the home of Albert Eldridge's secretary. Mr. Eldridge, you have undoubtedly heard, was found dead yesterday under suspicious circumstances in his home office on Washington Square. It is unclear at this time whether the attempted break-in and Mr. Eldridge's death are in any way connected. The suspect was identified by fingerprints at the scene and was taken into custody without incident. He is

Vincent Drake, called Vinnie, and has a long arrest record for similar crimes." A mug shot photo covered the screen. He was a fairly young man and his face looked vaguely familiar to me, although the name didn't ring any bells.

Ha! Ring any bells. Very funny.

There was a brief sports report, a weather update from Wanda, wearing white shorts and a navy crop top with the trademark deep V neckline, and some back to back commercials, coverage of the city council meeting where City Councilor Lois Mercer announced passage of a new ordinance regarding off-street parking. Hard break for network ID. I took my seat beside Buck, prepared to present my fifteen-minute report, while still puzzling over where I'd seen Vincent Drake before.

The segment went off just as rehearsed. A thumbs up from Marty, a fist bump from Buck Covington, and an approving nod from Scott signaled the end of a hastily put together and not entirely complete investigative report. It was, I thought, a good job.

I went back downstairs to the first-floor studio where I'd left coat, hat, and boots. River's Tarot Time set was lighted, and River, glamorous in bright red velvet, silver stars woven into her long black braid, ran to greet me. She embraced me in a patchouli scented hug. "I watched from here." She pointed to the monitor on the wall. "You were great. And isn't Buck a wonderful news anchor?"

"He is. You thought it went well?"

"It was really nice, Lee. I liked the pictures of the poor man when he was young. What a lot of good he did for Salem. Who would kill a good guy like that?"

"I know the police are working 24/7 on finding out," I said. "It was a terrible thing." Once again, the sight I'd seen in that office flashed across my mind. "A terrible thing."

"I'll be reading the tarot for him tonight on my show,"

she said, indicating the stack of cards spread out on the table in front of her high-backed wicker chair. I've selected the Hermit card to represent Mr. Eldridge." She picked up a card with a picture of a man holding a lantern, standing on a snowy mountain peak. "Will you watch? The tarot may help to solve the puzzle. It often does."

"I know it does," I said, and it was true. More than once River's talent with her beautiful and mysterious cards had helped to unravel difficult problems. "Doing that reading tonight is a really good idea. I'll be watching. What's the movie?" River's show follows approximately the same formula mine did. River does tarot readings before and after a scary movie. *Nightshades* was similar, but I did my phony psychic readings before and after scary movies.

"I'm showing *Nightmare Before Christmas* she said. "Not quite as scary as most of my movies, I know, but it's a good Christmas story."

"I remember. I always thought Jack Skellington seemed so lost in *Christmastown*."

We laughed together, I put on my outdoor gear, gave my friend a hug, promised I'd watch the Eldridge tarot reading, and maybe the movie too, if I could stay awake. I used the downstairs studio exit and stepped into a brisk wind, a dark night, and a slippery, near-empty parking lot. Across the harbor at Pickering Wharf I could see a few yachts, already showing their holiday lights. I walked gingerly, slowly and extremely carefully to the Buick, unlocked it, and climbed inside. The clock read eleven-forty-five. I'd be home in time to catch most of River's show and I knew Mr. Doan would run my report again on the morning news, so I'd have a chance to critique my own performance.

Aunt Ibby's windows were dark when I made my way along the garden path to the house but O'Ryan was wide awake and waiting to greet me just inside the back door. "Want to watch a little more television, boy?" I asked, as together, we climbed the two flights up the twisty stairway to my cozy home. The television was still on in my living room. Our clever cat knew how to shut it off, but hadn't chosen to do so. I changed the channel to WICH-TV, then hurried to my bedroom to change into pjs. I hung the green velvet outfit in the closet, stopped at the bathroom to toss undies into the laundry chute, wiped off makeup, then joined O'Ryan on the couch. We were just in time for River's first reading—the one she'd dedicated to Albert Eldridge. Buck Covington was on hand to shuffle the deck, as he'd often been ever since he and River had started dating. She thanked him prettily, bid him good night, and began the placement of the cards on the table. "The Hermit is the card I've selected to represent Albert Eldridge," she explained, holding the card toward the camera. "The man stands alone on a snowy mountain. He carries the staff of a patriarch. An elder. A leader. In his other hand he carries a lantern. We call it the lantern of truth." Placing the Hermit card, face up, in the center of the table, River bowed her head. "May only the higher forces surround this seeker while this reading takes place and may the truth of the matter concerning him be revealed." Then, in what she called the ancient Keltic method, River arranged ten more cards, faceup.

The second card lay across the Hermit card. The Two of Pentacles showed a dancing man balancing two five-pointed pentacles. There were ships in the distance on high seas. River tossed her braid, silver stars sparkling in the studio lights. "Mr. Eldridge was balancing two situations at the same time, striving for harmony while things around him changed. A new project was proving difficult to launch." She tapped the card against her cheek. "It's possible that a message brought him disturbing news." A pretty shrug. "Maybe." She returned the card to the table and picked up another. This one was upside down.

"The Five of Swords reversed," she said. "A knave has captured the swords of his opponents. Not good." She tilted her head to one side. "Loss and defeat. A funeral. Not a surprising card, under the circumstances." She lifted the next card. "The Four of Pentacles shows a miser hanging onto his gold. There's a city in the background. Someone in Mr. Eldridge's city—that would be Salem, friends—someone is seeking power and money, but the person is not generous."

The camera closed in on the fifth card. The Five of Cups. "Here we see a man in a long black cloak. Looks sad, doesn't he? See the three spilled cups of wine? Unhappiness. Loss of friendship. But there are still two full cups. He ignored them though." River replaced the card, a look of sadness on her pretty face. "Poor guy," she said.

The Ten of Wands came next. It showed a man struggling to carry ten long poles toward the city. "Looks bad, doesn't it," River asked. "But maybe not. It could be a painful, difficult test, but there's a good chance a problem will soon be solved." She looked into the camera. "Let's all hope so."

The next two cards were the Wheel of Fortune and the Ten of Pentacles. Both apparently good ones. River told her audience that the Wheel of Fortune card promised an unexpected turn of luck, a change of fortune. The Ten of Pentacles showed a man River called "a patriarch," resting before his coat of arms with his family and his dogs. "This may indicate the solidarity of the historical society Mr. Eldridge founded carrying on in prosperity," she said. "It often refers to the acquiring of real estate."

Next came a pretty card. A young man (Or is it a woman?

Hard to tell.) holds a sword with both hands. A flock of birds fly overhead. The card is reversed. "Oh dear," River said. "An imposter may soon be exposed, maybe through a message. Everybody, be prepared for the unexpected! Here's our last card for this special reading." She held the card in front of her face. "It's the Seven of Swords. Not surprising under the sad circumstances of this reading. Someone, like the man on the card who is apparently in the act of stealing five swords, is attempting to get away with something dishonest. There are still two swords stuck in the ground, so the thief has been partly successful."

River swept up the cards with one graceful hand and returned them to the deck. "After these commercial messages, stay tuned for tonight's special holiday movie. It's one of my favorites, and I hope it'll be one of yours. After the movie I'll be back to read the tarot, maybe for you! Phone lines will be open after *The Nightmare Before Christmas*. Don't go away!"

River leaned back in her chair and I leaned back on my couch. A commercial for Crow Haven filled the screen. "Well, cat," I said to O'Ryan who'd been paying close attention to River's reading which may be because he understood it all, or just because he loves River. "What do you think? Did the reading reveal 'the truth of the matter'?"

He moved over closer to me and gave my chin a lick, then jumped down from the couch and started down the hall to the kitchen. Naturally I hadn't expected an answer from the cat, and I had no idea myself whether the cards had revealed anything at all. I wondered if Pete had stayed awake throughout the whole reading.

My cell phone buzzed. I had my answer. He'd stayed awake. "What did you think?" I asked.

"I thought your part of the news was excellent and you are gorgeous, Pete said. "River's hocus-pocus was as confusing as ever. Just wanted to say good night and tell you I love you."

"Good night," I said. "Love you too."

I truly had meant to watch at least the beginning of the movie from my bed where O'Ryan already waited. I sat on the edge of the bed, waiting for the cat to decide where to lie down. The tall antique oval mirror in its cherry wood frame was tilted toward the kitchen window so that I couldn't see my own reflection from my bed. This was on instruction from River who, in addition to her tarot talent, was also an expert on feng shui, and advised me regularly on such matters. O'Ryan did his usual three-times-turn-around, but didn't lie down right away. Instead, he reached across the edge of the bed and tapped the frame of the mirror. I found myself looking directly into the beveled glass. Immediately the flashing lights and swirling colors that usually precede a vision spread across the surface. The glass turned misty for a moment, then a picture formed covering the oval plane. It was almost identical to the card River had chosen to represent Albert Eldridge, except that the Hermit's face was the face of the young marine we'd shown on the news. And in place of a lantern he held a brass kettle.

"What in blazes is that supposed to mean," I complained out loud. O'Ryan turned his head and stared at me. "I know," I grumbled. "They never make any sense at first anyway. I'm just not going to worry about it." I gave the mirror a little tap with my foot, sending it back to its correct feng shui position, reflecting the kitchen window.

Not just the kitchen window. Outside on the sill sat a large but skinny white cat. "Look, O'Ryan," I said. "Frankie's back."

Frankie was sort of a mystery to us. She shows up in our backyard once in a while. Comes over the tall back fence. At first we thought she belonged to the next door neighbors, but they claim they don't have a cat, and furthermore, they've never seen her in their yard at all. Strange. (I gave her the name Frankie because of an old Ben Franklin quotation, but that's another story.) One more thing. She only shows up when strange things are happening in our lives. This was such a time.

O'Ryan made a dash for the window and sat on the wide sill on our side of the glass and gave an insistent yowl. The white cat responded with a similar cry. "She must be freezing," I said. "Shall we invite her in?" I pulled the lock at the top of the frame aside and lifted the sash. Aunt Ibby thinks that Frankie is a feral cat who became friends with O'Ryan and comes to us when she's cold or hungry. This time she looked as though she was both. With a combination of purr and meow, and with dainty girl-cat feet she alighted on the chair closest to the window, then to the floor, then to O'Ryan's red bowl where he'd left a bit of kibble (in case he wanted a midnight snack, I assumed), and with an inquiring glance in O'Ryan's direction, she hunched down over the bowl and ate every bite.

Frankie's not the sort of cat who gets close to people easily, so I put a folded soft blanket in a warm corner of the kitchen, put some more kibble into O'Ryan's bowl, and fixed a blue bowl full along with a saucer full of milk for her. I went back to bed. O'Ryan stayed in the kitchen with his friend.

I didn't fall asleep easily. When I did it was with a troubling dream of the tarot card man with the young marine's face ringing a pair of those second-grade brightly colored hand bells. Didn't make the least bit of sense.

CHAPTER 14

I woke to the ringing of the house phone. I reached for it, thinking it was probably Pete, since very few people have the number. (Aunt Ibby and I each use our smart phones most of the time, but as she explained, the old-fashioned phones still work even when the power is out.)

I was right. It was Pete.

"Morning, babe. Ready for an early breakfast?"

"Love to. What time is it?"

"Six. That okay?"

"Sure. You on your way over here?"

"Almost there. I'll let myself in."

"Good." I sat on the edge of the bed. "I'm getting up right now. Oh, Pete. Remember that white cat, Frankie? She's back."

"In the house?"

"Yep. She was cold."

"She shows up at weird times. You did great on the news last night. I'm so proud of you."

"Thanks. Love you." I hung up the phone (a great 1920s black candlestick telephone reproduction) and headed for the bathroom. Early breakfast means one of our favorite places. It's on a side street in an ordinary looking two-story house. The only sign is a neon OPEN sign in one of the windows. It's a perfect place for morning people. Fishermen, nurses, kids going to early morning hockey practice, third-shift people going home, first-shift people going to work, taxi drivers, cops.

I was showered, dressed in warm cozy gray sweats, with hair reasonably tamed when I heard Pete come in through the living room door. O'Ryan ran to meet him. Frankie was still asleep on her blanket, so I was extra quiet as I rinsed out the red and blue bowls and tiptoed out into the hall to greet Pete. We shared a long, really sweet kiss. "It seems as though I haven't seen you for a long time," he said, his voice husky.

"I know. I missed you."

"We saw each other yesterday."

"I know. It was all business though."

"I'm ready for pleasure," he said, holding me close. "But I guess I invited you for breakfast, huh?"

"You did."

"Did the white cat sleep over?"

"She's still asleep."

"Think I can sleep over tonight?"

"Absolutely." Another long kiss. I pulled on the plaid jacket, knit hat, and boots and followed Pete down the narrow staircase and out into the cold.

When we were seated in our favorite corner booth in the restaurant, where two steaming white ironstone mugs full of coffee had been placed on the table as soon as we came through the door, I told Pete about the two visions, the one in the brass kettle and the one in the mirror. "As usual," I said, "they don't make sense to me. How about you? Anything?"

He leaned closer to me, looking into my eyes. "I don't understand anything about how they work, Lee. The kettle one, of the picture book Scrooge—an old man wearing a stocking cap could relate to Eldridge with his Santa hat I guess, although he was no Scrooge. The guy on River's tarot was meant to be Eldridge. So they both have to do with his murder. What, I don't know."

"Does the man who tried to break in to Lilly's house have to do with it too?"

"Vinnie Drake?" I kind of doubt it. We've pulled him in for other attempts. A couple of times he got inside some unoccupied houses." Pete's smile was wry. "Actually, he's not very good at his work."

"Lilly thinks he was after her computer."

Pete shrugged. The waitress arrived and took our orders. Veggie omelet and fresh fruit for me. Ham and eggs and pancakes for Pete. More coffee for both.

"Do you think he was after her computer because of the Historical Charities' records?" I persisted in my question.

"I know she thinks so. But we checked it. Just as she said, other than her personal e-mail and some miscellaneous household figures of her own, it's just as she told us. Duplicate records of the Historical Charities' finances. Boring stuff. If he was after the computer, it was because it's a fairly new one and he could sell it. We'll return it to her today."

I pushed the grapes and melon around on my plate. "I keep thinking I've seen that Drake kid before. The mug shot on the news looked familiar."

"You might have seen him around. Local talent."

"Hmmm. Maybe. Speaking of talent, did you know that

Conrad Gillette is the director of the Christmas Belles? The musical group of gals my aunt is part of?"

"Yes. He told me about it. Mr. Gillette is quite proud of his good works. I guess he plans to step directly into Eldridge's shoes."

"He seems very efficient. Gets things done fast."

Pete signaled the waitress for more coffee. "Like the bank drop off point for the Santa Claus money?"

"Right," I said. "Oh, wow Pete! That's it. He was a Santa Claus! Vinnie Drake was a Santa Claus. But he didn't have a flag on his hat and his beard was all wrong. That's where I saw him. He had a sand pail instead of a kettle. A fake Santa Claus!"

"Sounds like something he'd do. Picking up cash anyway he can."

"That's just wrong. Taking money from people at Christmas like that. Do you think he could be the thief in River's reading? The sword stealer?"

Pete laughed. "No, Nancy Drew, I don't think so. Vinnie's a small-time punk. Not important enough to show up in a tarot reading. He'll probably be in jail until after Christmas so he won't be playing Bad Santa for quite a while."

"Well, that's good. But we were talking about Mr. Gillette," I said. "Did I tell you the Belles are playing hand bells this year for the concert he's directing? And that these particular hand bells cost more than five thousand dollars for the set?"

That brought a low whistle. "No kidding? You could buy a good used car for that much money. Who told you that?"

"Lilly Jeffry. She ought to know."

"The woman's a whiz with numbers," he said. "She

could recite most everything that was on her computer at the Historical Charities from memory."

"Just like Miss Lemon," I said.

"Who?"

"Miss Lemon. She's in the *Hickory Dickory Dock* book."

"Mouse ran up the clock?"

"No. The Agatha Christie one. It's a mystery."

Pete signaled for the check. "So are you sometimes, babe. In a good way."

Pete dropped me off at home and he went along to work. I still had a few hours to kill before I had to check in at the station. O'Ryan waited for me inside, his pink nose pressed against a frosty pane in the narrow row of windows beside the front door. It was only seven-fifteen so I knew Aunt Ibby would be up, dressed, and busy working on the *Boston Globe* crossword puzzle in ink).

I poked my head into her living room which opens through an arched opening from the foyer. "Aunt Ibby, it's me," I called.

"I'm in the kitchen, Maralee. Coffee's on."

The cat and I followed the sound of her voice and the aroma of fresh cinnamon rolls. I took off jacket, hat, and boots, and helped myself to a cup of coffee. "Are the cinnamon rolls for us or are you taking them somewhere?"

"They're for us. One of Tabitha's holiday recipes. Pretty aren't they?" They certainly were. Each perfect swirl was topped with frosting. "A little labor intensive for today's add-an-egg-to-a-packaged-mix cooks, but worth it. Have one."

"Maybe later," I said, patting my tummy. "Just had breakfast with Pete."

Wise old owl look. "Learn anything new?"

"Why Aunt Ibby! Do you think we discussed police

business?" I pretended shock. "Of course." Her eyes sparkled and she put the newspaper down. I told her about Vincent Drake and how I'd remembered where I'd seen him before. "Lilly's staying at the hotel until they get through investigating. Guess they need to figure out if there's a connection between the attempted break in and—you know—what happened to Mr. Eldridge."

"Why, she could have stayed here with us."

"I know. I told her she'd be welcome. But Pete says she can have her computer back today so I guess she'll go home. By the way, I found out something else interesting. Did you know the hand bells you girls will be using are worth thousands of dollars?"

"My goodness! I knew they were valuable, but that's a great deal of money. They say we'll be rehearsing with a less pricey set, and we even have to wear gloves to use those. The real ones will be revealed at the concert. No wonder Mr. Eldridge always kept them under lock and key."

"I suppose that's where they still are," I reasoned. "But I'm sure Mr. Gillette will be able to get them released. He seems very competent."

"I'm sure he will," she said. "Conrad truly was Albert's good right hand."

"Between Mr. Gillette and Lilly Jeffry, he had a super efficient staff to keep things running smoothly, didn't he?"

She nodded, and poured herself another cup of coffee. "So he always said. Sure you don't want one of these cinnamon rolls while they're still warm?"

"Stop twisting my arm. Maybe I'll take one upstairs and eat it later."

"Suit yourself. They're better warm though." She lifted one of the rolls from the cooking rack and took a bite. "Yum. Say, we have our first rehearsal on the hand bells tomorrow evening. If you're free, would you like to come along and see your old aunt make a fool of herself on an instrument she's never played before?"

"It's easy. I did it in second grade, remember? Sure. If nothing urgent turns up at the station, I'd love to." I picked up the promised cinnamon roll, wrapped it in a paper napkin, and headed for the front hall, then peeked back around the corner. "Will there be Irish step dancing?"

CHAPTER 15

Laughing at my own little joke, I followed O'Ryan through the living room and out into the foyer. I heard Aunt Ibby laughing too. Good thing we both have the same silly sense of humor. I hurried up the wide, curving front staircase. Seven-forty-five. Maybe I could still catch the early news and see how the shortened version of my investigative report looked.

O'Ryan had already pushed his way through the cat door by the time I let myself into the kitchen. He and Frankie sat expectantly together in front of the cabinet where I keep the assorted varieties of cat food and treats. "Breakfast time for you guys too I guess." I filled their dishes with one of Rachel Ray's latest delicacies for kitties and added a big bowl of fresh water. I clicked on the kitchen TV, then went into the bedroom and turned that one on too. That way I could make my bed, reheat last night's coffee, get dressed for work, move back and forth between the rooms, and not miss anything on Phil Archer's morning news show.

Is that multitasking?

I poured a cup of coffee and pulled out a stool at the

kitchen counter. I'd missed a little of the intro, but that was usually traffic reports and weather. I'd already been out so I knew the weather was clear and cold and the traffic was the same as it is every weekday when the tourists aren't here. Albert Eldridge's death—Phil Archer wasn't exactly calling it murder—was still leading the news cycle in Salem. "Funeral plans for Mr. Eldridge, who died under suspicious circumstances, will be announced later today, according to Conrad Gillette," Archer announced, as a photo of Albert Eldridge at his desk appeared on the screen. "Mr. Gillette has taken over the operation of Historical Charities of Salem by unanimous vote of the organization's Board of Directors."

That was the first I'd heard about a board of directors. Made sense that there'd be one of course. I wondered if Lilly Jeffry was a member. That would make sense too.

I'd better get a list of the members, set up some interviews, pronto. Should have thought of it sooner.

"I have a lot to learn in this business," I told the cats. O'Ryan gave me a one ear up, one ear down look that said something like "Well, duh," while Frankie concentrated on washing her white coat.

Phil gave a brief lead into the Eldridge bio portion of my previous night's report. I peered closely at the screen, deciding that the green velvet photographed well and looked good with my red hair. Marty had done an excellent job of editing my fifteen minutes down to five, and Phil threw in a few complimentary words about the piece at the end of the segment. I was pleased about that. Phil was a newsman from way back and his opinion meant a lot to me.

I retreated to the bedroom then and opened my closet. I debated mentally for a minute about what to wear to work and decided on skinny jeans and a warm blue parka.

I pulled on tall Marc Jacob boots, picked another knit hat just like the one I'd worn to breakfast, but a different color. Red this time.

I remembered to retrieve my roll, no longer warm but still beautiful, pop it into a plastic bag, and put it, along with notebook, index cards, and pens into a big leather Jacki Easlick hobo handbag. Said good-bye to the cats and headed downstairs. Once outside, I turned up my collar against the biting cold, and sprinted toward the garage.

Within a few more minutes I was on my way to the WICH-TV studio. As I rounded the corner onto the north side of Washington Square, I looked across the Salem Common toward the Eldridge house on the south side. Was the yellow tape gone? Looked that way from where I sat. I wondered if that meant Lilly would be back to work, that the Santas could drop their cash in the back-porch safe, and that the flow of groceries, diapers, toys, candy, and socks could again be on their way to those in need. I hoped so.

It had become a habit to look for Santas as I drove along Hawthorne Boulevard toward Derby Street. There were several already ringing their bells. They all looked appropriately jolly and each one had the stars and stripes on his red hat. No skinny Santa with a cotton ball beard, and if Pete was right Drake wouldn't be seen on Salem's streets for quite a while. . . .

The camo kettle Santa was once again stationed in front of the WICH-TV building. I parked in my usual spot and walked (carefully) across the lot, pausing to say, "Good morning, Nick," and to put a few dollars into the kettle. I was rewarded with a big smile and a hearty "Ho-ho-ho Merry Christmas, Ms. Barrett!"

"Ho-ho yourself, Nick," I said and dashed inside.

Rhonda handed me a really short list of assignments.

I had mixed feelings about that. I wanted to get as much experience in this new job as I could to prove to Mr. Doan—and to myself—that I could handle on-the-spot, unrehearsed reporting. On the other hand, I relished having more investigative time to delve into the growing mystery surrounding Albert Eldridge's murder. "Short list," Rhonda said with a smile, "but I think you're going to like the first one on it."

She was right. First location on the list was the Tabitha Trumbull Academy of the Arts. The Tabby. I was to meet with Rupert Pennington, the director of the school and until very recently, my boss. The topic line read, rather cryptically, "problem with the acting division's holiday production."

"Problem?" I was puzzled. "What does that mean?"

Rhonda, as everyone at the station knows, is a never-ending font of knowledge on darn near anything. I had confidence that she'd have the skinny on Mr. Pennington's dilemma. She dropped her voice and looked around as though there might be spies lurking behind the lavender aluminum Christmas tree (Mrs. Doan's latest addition to the office decor). "The problem is the subject matter. They've been in rehearsal for months. Who knew there'd be a murder in Salem right before Christmas?"

"Subject matter?"

"Oh, yeah." Rhonda patted her hair. "The play is *Hercule Poirot's Christmas*."

"Poirot," I echoed. "Agatha Christie?"

"Right. Here's a hint. The original title was *A Holiday for Murder*."

"Oh, boy."

"Yeah. They can't scrap the play. Too much work has gone into it. But how can they produce it now, after the Eldridge thing?"

"So my job is to make a staged holiday murder acceptable to the public right after a real holiday murder?"

"You got it."

"Great." I looked back at the assignment sheet. "I hope the second one is easier."

"Should be," Rhonda said. "The women's shelter. They're trying to make Christmas special for the moms and the kids. Tear jerker."

"I think that's one of the projects the Historical Charities helps with." I thought of John Campbell and of Lilly giving him money to buy diapers when he wasn't allowed to take the donated ones.

"They did a lot of good stuff." She looked at the sunburst clock. "You'd better get going. Francine said she'd be out front at nine-thirty. It's nine-fifteen now. Lots of luck with the Tabby thing."

"Thanks. I'll need it."

I did as she suggested and with the assignment sheet stuffed into my purse, took the elevator back down to the street level, crossed the black and white tile floor, pushed the glass door open, and stepped back into the wintry day. Francine gave a friendly toot of the horn and I climbed into the passenger seat. As we pulled out onto Derby Street I noticed that the camo kettle Santa had been replaced by a kelly-green-kettle-with-a-shamrock-on-it Santa.

"Rhonda says we're going to the school where you used to teach," Francine said. "That'll be fun for you."

"Yes and no," I said. "It'll be good to see the friends I used to work with. Students too. I'm supposed to interview the director of the school. Rupert Pennington, my old boss. That may be a problem."

"Why? Don't you like him?"

"Oh it's nothing like that. I like him a lot. My aunt even dates him sometimes."

"Your aunt and your boss? Aren't they old?"

I turned to look at her. "Older people still date. Actually, my aunt is flying to London later this month to spend the holidays with another gentleman friend." That didn't sound quite right. I hurried to correct the impression. "She's traveling with another lady, Mrs. Abney Babcock, so of course it's all quite proper."

"No kidding!" An understanding nod from Francine. "I get it. It's proper and all, but the school director is still jealous of the London guy. That's the problem."

I hadn't given that triangle even a passing thought. "Hmmm. Maybe he is but that's not it. It's all about a play the acting division at the school is planning. A Christmas play."

"And . . ."

"The play is about a murder during the Christmas holidays."

Francine gave a quick intake of breath. "Uh-oh. Awkward."

"Awkward is right. I haven't ever read the play or the book. I wish I'd had a chance to talk to my aunt about it. She's read everything".

"So you're supposed to make it sound like it's just a play. No big deal."

"Well, yeah. It is just a play, after all. Fortunately, they've advertised it as *Hercule Poirot's Christmas*, not by the original title."

"Which was?"

"*A Holiday for Murder*. Agatha Christie wrote it."

"The mystery lady."

"Right."

Agatha Christie again.

CHAPTER 16

The parking lot beside the Tabby was almost full. Of course, it was a school day and the excellent reputation of The Tabitha Trumbull Academy of the Arts had by then spread well past the boundaries of Salem. Students from all over the country had been attracted to the place, which was housed in an old department store. The various arts courses offered held appeal for people of all ages who'd always wanted to act or paint or dance or sing or write—or as in the case of my classes—to be involved in the world of television, either behind or in front of the cameras. The tuition was pricey and no degrees were offered, but the success rate of "graduates" was impressive.

Francine pulled in as close to the building as she could get. We gathered up microphones and lights and camera and walked to the front door. I gave the student-receptionist my card, mentioning that Mr. Pennington was expecting us.

"Oh, yes, Ms. Barrett," she said. "I really wanted to take your course, but I switched to acting. I'm Nancy, playing Pilar in our Christmas production!"

"Congratulations," I said. "Is Mr. Pennington in his office?"

"Yes." She pointed to the broad stairway. "Top of the stairs. Second door. Oh, I guess you know that."

"Thanks, Nancy," I said. "Break a leg!" Francine and I started up the broad, polished staircase, passing the mezzanine landing where my TV Production classes had taken place in the old Trumbull Department Store's shoe department. I peeked into the darkened space where apparently nothing was happening.

Maybe they think I'll be back.

"This is a beautiful staircase," Francine said, running her free hand over the broad bannister. "Ever slide down this?"

"Actually, yes, I did once," I told her. "Someday I'll tell you about it." We'd reached the door marked Director. It was open. Mr. Pennington prided himself on his open door policy.

He stood as soon as we entered. "Oh, my dear Ms. Barrett. I am so very glad to see you." He nodded in Francine's direction, "and your most efficient associate."

"Mr. Pennington, this is Francine. She'll be filming our interview. Do you want to do it here, in your office?"

"How do you do, dear lady." He gave a little bow in Francine's direction. "I thought we might do it in the rehearsal hall. They're onstage right now and it will give you a bit of flavor of the production. I do hope you can help us clarify the fact that *Hercule Poirot's Christmas* is just a rollicking good whodunit and the um—recent unfortunate happenings should not dim the public's enjoyment of our efforts." He ran a hand across his brow. "I hope no one will be offended by the content—or even worse, stay away from the play because of it." He lowered his voice. "This is, after all, the acting department's major fund-raiser of the year."

"We'll do our very best, sir," I promised. "Shall we take the elevator up to the hall? Francine's camera is heavy."

"Yes, let's." He led the way to the elevator and pushed the Up button. I was glad to see that the old department designations remained on the hammered tin walls. Lingerie, notions, luggage, millinery . . . we stepped out on the third floor, and followed the man to what had once been the store's Green Stamp Redemption Center—and now held a rehearsal stage, a costume area, and several makeup stations.

On stage, several actors rehearsed their lines. One was a sturdy looking gentleman with a quite luxuriant handlebar mustache. I pointed. "Hercule Poirot?" I whispered. "What a fine mustache. Is it real?"

Mr. Pennington smiled. "It is," he whispered back. "The student grew it for the part, but has become quite attached to it. Literally."

Looks a lot better than the fake facial hair I've seen on some Santas lately.

"The fellow Poirot is addressing," he continued, still whispering, "is the Police Superintendent."

I was pleased that I'd have the opportunity to see at least at bit of the production so that I wouldn't be flying entirely blind on this assignment. Francine busied herself with her lighting setup and camera tripod, while I focused on what was happening onstage.

The superintendent spoke first. Poirot twirled his elegant mustache. "Mr. Lee telephoned me yesterday afternoon," superintendent-actor said. "He wanted me to come and see him. What's more, he told me to tell the butler I was collecting for some Police Charity."

"Indeed. A Police Charity?" Poirot spoke with a pretty good representation of a Belgian accent.

"I did as he said." The superintendent had a sort-of-British sound. "He told me that several thousand pounds worth of diamonds had been stolen from his safe. So he thought."

Another mustache twirl. "He thought?"

Mr. Pennington suddenly clapped his hands. "Take a break, people," he said. "Good job." He waved in my direction. "The media is here to give us some free publicity."

The actors disappeared into the wings. I wished I could have seen a little more of the action. "Before we begin, Mr. Pennington," I said, "want to give me a little background on what the audience might find—upsetting in the play?"

"Just the unfortunate timing of it, Ms. Barrett. It's a charming piece, really. Holds up well. The book's from 1939. We're using a TV adaptation from 1994. But," he sighed heavily, "but, it concerns a murder of a wealthy, prominent man during the Christmas season." He held up both hands in a gesture of helplessness. (Mr. Pennington isn't without considerable acting ability himself.) Another sigh. "Alas." Downcast eyes.

I decided that since my knowledge of the play was zilch, I'd keep my questions simple and brief and let him do the talking. If anything messed up, we had time to edit.

"You about ready?" Francine tapped her watch. "We still have a date at the women's shelter."

"Ready, Mr. Pennington?" I asked. "Shall we use the stage set for background? Those chairs look comfortable and the Christmas tree in the background is a nice touch."

"Fine," he said. So that's what we did.

It was the right choice. I asked some basic questions, such as "Tell us a little bit about the background of the story," and "Can you tell us about the cast? I met the charming young woman who plays Pilar, and your Poirot is simply perfect in the part!" I played it straight on the touchy part about the similarity between the murder in the play and the local real-life version. I phrased the question carefully, speaking softly, leaning toward him. (I'm not without some acting chops myself.) "I understand that you have some concern about the timing of this production, following so closely the sad circumstances of Albert Eldridge's passing." I paused, giving Mr. Pennington the opportunity to bow his head in sadness. "I've had the privilege of seeing some of your amazing actors in rehearsal. And it's an Agatha Christie play! I'm sure the sophisticated Salem theatergoers will enjoy the performance for exactly what it is—a rollicking good mystery!"

Pennington's expression brightened "You're exactly right, Ms. Barrett. Why, Agatha Christie's play *The Mousetrap* opened in London's West End in 1952. It's still running! That's the longest initial run of any play in history! True theater lovers will relish the opportunity to see a genuine Agatha Christie play right here in Salem. Orchestra seats will sell out fast. Tickets are available at the box office at the Tabitha Trumbull Academy or online or by phone." He smilingly gave the correct numbers. I made a mental note to be sure to have the station scroll them at the bottom of the screen when the piece ran. I thanked him for being our guest on WICH-TV. He beamed and thanked me.

Cut.

Francine began to pack up her gear and I shook hands once again with my old boss. I could tell that he was relieved. "Give my regards to dear Ibby, won't you, Ms. Barrett? And thank you so very much. I think this will help sales immensely, don't you?"

"I do, sir. You made an excellent case for everyone to rush right out for tickets. Thank you again."

We took the elevator down to the ground level and hurried out to the van. "That was good," Francine said as we approached the mobile van. "I might even go to see it. The tickets are pretty cheap too."

"They keep it reasonable. That's why they need to fill the house. They want people to see the talent they're producing. At least one alum is in Hollywood now."

"I know. Daphne Trent. So cute." We loaded our gear into the van and started toward South Salem and the women's shelter. "I hope they can give those poor souls a nice Christmas. At least the little kids."

"I'm sure they will. From what we've seen at the Historical Charities, they not only get plenty of merchandise donations, but I get the impression that they're really well funded. From what I've seen of the wall-to-wall Santa Clauses with kettles full of money, I'm betting the kids will have a merry one for sure."

We parked on a narrow strip of pavement behind the four-story brick building. The place looked plain, simple, unadorned with shutters or window boxes like some of its neighbors. The gray steel back door bore a small hand-lettered command.

RING BELL

CHAPTER 17

"You sure this is the right place?" I asked Francine. "I don't see any signs of life."

"This is it," she replied, pushing the bell. "Directions were clear. I guess they don't want to attract any attention. These women are hiding from bad situations."

"Makes sense," I agreed.

A small panel in the door slid open. "Donations?" asked a husky voice.

I held my card up to the oblong space. "WICH-TV," I said. "We have an appointment."

"Oh, sure. Wait a sec." The door swung open. "Come on in." The middle-aged woman wore blue scrubs with pictures of Hello Kitty on it. A name tag identified her as Doris. "Darn. I was hoping you were one of the volunteers bringing diapers and formula. We're running low." Her expression brightened. "But, hey! We're glad you're here. TV publicity is a good thing. Come on upstairs. You can meet some of the kids and moms." She looked at the camera on Francine's shoulder. "But you can't take pictures that show their faces."

I introduced myself and Francine. We followed the woman to an elevator that appeared to be of about the same vintage as the one at the station and clanked and growled our way up to the floor marked three. We heard the kid's voices before the doors parted.

"Christmas nerves." Doris smiled. "They're not usually quite this noisy." About twenty big-eyed children stared at us. I stared back. All I could think of was one of those UNICEF Christmas card illustrations showing happy kids of every color playing together. That's how those beautiful little ones looked to me.

Several women I guessed to be moms were seated together toward the back of the colorfully decorated room. A couple of them smiled in our direction. One waved. "If we blur their faces and disguise the voices, can we talk to the moms?" I asked.

Doris agreed that we could. I'd taught the pixilating and blue spot techniques in my TV Production 101 course at the Tabby, but this would be the first time I'd actually put it into practice. "And if the kids have their backs to us while they play with some toys, can we film them that way?" I said, trying to push my luck.

"Yes," Doris said. "We've done that before."

"Good. Thanks. Could we talk with you first?" I peered at the plastic covered ID tag she wore on a pink lanyard. It identified her as General Manager. She agreed, spoke briefly to one of the moms, and motioned me to a far corner where two yellow vinyl-covered club chairs were arranged beside a round maple table bearing a small artificial Christmas tree and a silver menorah.

Francine steadied her camera against a battered but sturdy indoor slide while I held the hand mic.

"Hello, viewers," I said. "Lee Barrett here and this morning we're visiting a local women's shelter where holiday preparations are in full swing." I held the mic in the direction of the chattering children across the room. "Perhaps you can hear the voices of some of the kids who, with their moms, will spend the holidays here in a safe and caring environment. I'd like to introduce Doris Ahern, the GM of the shelter. Doris, would you tell our audience a little about the services you provide here?"

The woman obliged with a succinct but heartfelt description of the purpose of the place and the 24/7 care the largely volunteer staff provides. "Of course we have paid staff too, professional people, especially trained for this type of work. Counselors, a psychiatrist, a registered nurse. That uses up a lot of our funding."

"When we arrived here today, you mentioned that you were running low on diapers and baby formula. I understand that donations are needed and welcome?"

"Oh, yes." She looked directly into the camera. "The money available for our supplies has been cut back in recent years, so we depend on outside donations a lot more than we used to. If you can donate packages of diapers or cans of formula, you can drop them off at the Historical Charities office on Washington Square and they'll be delivered to us. We need clothes and shoes too." Her smile faded. "I mean, I'm sorry. You can donate as soon as they open up again after—after what happened over there."

"Yes, thank you Doris." I said, racing to change the subject. "I believe the normal operation of the society will resume very shortly," I said, remembering that the yellow tape was gone this morning. "We were greeted by a group of excited kids this morning, I guess they're expecting a visit from Santa soon."

Doris's smile returned. "Aren't they adorable? We've already given them some of the toys that arrived unwrapped."

That'll make a good shot. Kids, backs to the camera, playing with some new toys.

I asked a few more of my prepared questions, like how many women and children do you house here on an average week? How long are they allowed to stay?

Her statement about lack of funding bothered me. This project is an important one, so I pressed the issue. "How, exactly is the shelter funded? By the state?"

"Many different ways," she said, beginning to tick them off on her fingers. "The state gives us a generous grant. The county too. Then the rest comes from various charities. A lot of it is from the Historical Charities of Salem. You can get a list from the office downstairs."

I faced the camera and Francine zoomed in on me. "After the following brief commercial message, we'll talk to a few of the women who are staying here, most with children, a few by themselves." If there's ever a pause when we're recording a shoot, Mr. Doan likes to make it pay for itself with a "brief commercial message."

Francine and I walked across to where a row of four moms sat in folding chairs. They chatted among themselves as we approached, but I noticed that they all were keeping watchful eyes on the children playing nearby. Doris introduced us to the women, using their first names only. "This will be on television. WICH-TV," she said. "But they're going to blur out your faces with those little squares or a big blue dot or something and change your voices somehow. Okay?"

To a woman, they agreed and willingly told their individual stories. Powerful stuff. I realized that even though I'd withstood some painful times in my life, I was truly fortunate. Their words made me both sad to the point of tears and angry to the point of ferocity. These brave and, at the same time, frightened women and their children deserved all the help, physically, financially, and spiritually a community could give.

Here's a cause I can get behind! After this field report, I'm going to put my Investigative Reporter hat on and do something.

We spent longer at the shelter than we'd meant to, but neither of us minded. Trying to get a bunch of hyper-holiday-excited little boys and girls to all sit facing away from the camera at the same time is like trying to herd cats. But kind of fun.

Once finished, and satisfied that we had a good piece of video to share with the WICH-TV audience, we said good-bye to our new friends, got some hugs and candy-sticky kisses from the beautiful children, stopped at the office, picked up the promised charity list so we could give credit to those generous folks, and headed back to the station.

We'd worked right through our lunch hour. "I'm hungry," I said. "Want to split a cinnamon roll?" I pulled the cold but still wonderful-smelling bun from my purse and broke it in half. "Let's get some drive-through coffee to go with it."

Francine pulled the van into a nearby Dunkin Donuts, and the two of us happily munched and sipped our way back to WICH-TV, then sat in the parking lot with the heater going and the radio playing Christmas carols until we'd finished every last crumb. "That was good," Francine said. "Better get this material over to the production guys so they can do their magic."

Rhonda didn't have anything new scheduled for me, so I went downstairs to watch the two men who handled editing/bleeping and special effects on footage to be aired later. I was especially interested in watching the morning's work materialize, particularly the shelter segment. I was pretty sure the Pennington interview would run just the way we'd shot it.

Francine had deliberately avoided showing the front of the shelter building. We didn't want any abusive husbands or boyfriends to recognize it and show up and cause trouble. All she'd shot of the back was the sliding panel with a shadowy figure behind it, but that was enough to convey the message that the place was secure and safe.

I watched the rough cut of the shelter piece on a small camera-mounted monitor and marveled again at the beauty of those multihued children. And again, I was troubled by the plight of their mothers.

When I do my investigative story, I'm going to take my time. Do it right. No rush job like the recent Albert Eldridge effort.

Maybe I'd get in touch with the organizations Doris had mentioned, the ones that already donate money regularly, even though they may have had to cut back on the amounts. Their stories might encourage other groups to take up the slack. I fished in my big purse and pulled out the sheet of paper with the charities listed on it. Not as long a list as I'd thought it might be.

Although most of the happenings I'd be reporting on at WICH-TV would appear on the printed schedule Rhonda handed to me each morning, it was pleasant to think about a topic I'd chosen myself. The brief visit to the shelter had provided the inspiration. Now it was up to me to put in the research, the footwork, the dedication that a good investigative report requires.

Having made that decision, I put that project out of

my mind and focused on what I was supposed to do for the rest *of this* day.

As sometimes happens, fate wandered in and decided that for me.

I was still checking the Pennington footage which, as I'd thought, could run just about the way we shot it. Mr. Pennington's acting background, which included quite a bit of onstage Shakespeare, a few movies, and even some early TV productions, made him an easy interview. He knew the rules. He knew how to play to the camera. As Marty McCarthy was fond of saying, "a piece of cake."

Cake reminded me that I was still hungry. A nice cinnamon roll can provide a good sugar rush, but it doesn't last long. I thought that probably Francine was experiencing the same nutritional let down I was. I called her. "Want to meet me at the Scratch Kitchen for some lunch?"

"On my way," was the brief answer. I decided to walk the couple of blocks to the restaurant. It was still cold outside but it was, for winter, quite a pretty day. I zipped up my parka all the way to the top, pulled the red hat down to cover my ears. Gloves and boots were both warmly lined.

I was within a few feet of the Scratch Kitchen's front door when I heard a blare of sound from behind me. Police cars. Several of them, all with red, white, and blue lights blazing and sirens screaming. Pulling my phone from my pocket I called Rhonda. "What's up? A bunch of cop cars just went flying by me. You monitoring the police channel?"

"Doan is. It's a guy threatening to jump off the top of a building down near the Willows road."

"Francine will be with me in a minute. Does he want us to go over there?"

"Do you have to ask? He says to get good close-up footage." Short pause. "Especially if the guy really jumps."

"What a sick puppy," I said. "Here comes Francine. We're on it." I waved at the oncoming van which barely slowed down long enough for me to climb into the passenger seat.

"Jumper?" Francine asked.

"Looks that way. On the Willows road, Rhonda says."

"Yeah. I got the call from Mr. Doan. Told him we're already on the way."

The sound of sirens had trailed off and stopped, but the flashing lights were just ahead of us. I didn't see any other mobile units around. "Looks like we're first, huh?"

"Yep." Francine pulled the van into a vacant lot full of frost killed grass and straggly brown weeds, next door to one of Salem's nondescript aged wooden buildings. It was four stories high with boarded-up windows here and there on the upper floors. Not a pretty place, but not the worst I've ever seen either. I clipped my laminated press pass to my collar. Francine still wore hers from the morning assignments. She handed me my mic and lifted her shoulder mounted Panasonic from its case.

Together we ran toward the building. I searched the roofline as I ran and spotted the man standing at the front edge. He looked very, very small up there. And terribly alone.

CHAPTER 18

More sirens. The fire department had arrived. I knew that meant there was an aerial ladder that would easily reach to the roof. Good.

"Let's move a little closer," Francine said. "You seem to know a lot of cops. Know any of those over there? Anybody who can help us out?"

I squinted at the cluster of blue uniforms gathered near the door of the building, spotting a couple of men and one woman I knew by name. Dating a detective means I get to recognize—and be recognized by—more police (and maybe more lawbreakers) than the average citizen might.

"Yes. I know some of them. I'll see what I can find out. You just start getting some footage of the man up on the roof. Okay?"

"Gotcha."

I approached Police Sergeant Joyce Rouse. I'd gone to high school with her. "Joyce, do we have the man's name yet?"

"What? Oh, hi Lee. Yes. He's Joseph Marshall. He works here. Does electrical work."

"Do you know what his problem is?"

"Nope. But we've got our best crisis negotiator on the way up there. Hopefully, he can talk the guy out of jumping."

"I sure hope so." I looked up at the building again. "It's a long way down. Is it okay if my photographer and I set up over there near that work truck?" I pointed to a white Ford cargo van with magnetic signs on the doors that read PRESTIGIOUS ELECTRICIANS. SALEM, MASSACHUSETTS. It was parked on a flat area of ground about halfway between the building and the area where our mobile unit was parked.

Joyce looked at the spot I'd indicated and nodded agreement. "Looks about right. Just stay out of the way, okay? And if he jumps . . . " She didn't finish the sentence.

"We'll be careful. Thanks, Joyce. Anything happen so far with the negotiator? How's he doing?"

"I don't know yet. But we've got Marshall's mother on the phone with him now. That works sometimes." She shrugged.

"Hope it does here," I said, meaning it with all my heart. I sure wasn't looking forward to seeing the result of a body falling four stories to the street below. The red stain on Albert Eldridge's Santa hat was more than enough blood for me.

I ran back to where Francine had already begun filming. With my mic live, I began describing the scene. I didn't give the man's name, of course, but told my audience about the crisis negotiator who'd been sent up there to talk to him. The two figures were now both in view, one dressed in tan, the other in a business suit. There was a considerable distance between them. (I was able to describe for my audience what a negotiator does because I'd studied the subject fairly recently in my online criminology course.) "Police have contacted the man's mother," I added, "hoping that she can dissuade him. She's on the telephone with him now." Francine panned across the row of fire trucks. An ambulance had arrived too. "Emergency personnel are on hand," I reported. One of the police officers had taken a position on the street, directing traffic which had begun to build, as the curious "looky-lous" began to arrive. I cautioned drivers to avoid the area if possible.

The two figures suddenly backed away from the roof's edge and out of range of the camera. Motioning for Francine to follow me toward the building, I approached Sergeant Rouse once again. I held the mic in her direction. "Can you tell us what's happening, Sergeant?" I asked.

"They're coming down," she said. "Excitement's over. Excuse me." She turned away from the camera and hurried into the building. I looked around for someone else who might have information to share. No luck.

Francine focused on fire trucks pulling away from the curb, leaving the ambulance and the police cars, lights still flashing, along with a few civilian cars which had apparently stopped to get a better look at the action. I continued talking—Mr. Doan doesn't tolerate dead air graciously—speculating on how maybe the mother's phone call had saved the man—all the while hoping the would-be jumper would appear in the doorway so that maybe we'd get some answers as to the how and why of his obvious distress. I talked a little bit about the fire department's modern rescue equipment for such cases, and how years ago they'd used nets and tarpaulins for people to jump into, sometimes with disastrous results.

The driver's side door of one of the parked cars, a recent model Lexus, opened and a man stepped out. He passed

Francine and me, glancing at the camera and favoring us with a warm smile. Walking with long strides to the doorway, he handed a piece of paper to one of the officers, and was quickly waved inside the building.

Who's he?

I didn't have much time to wonder. A man wearing a khaki work uniform appeared in the doorway with another man I recognized as one of Pete's fellow detectives. Although I didn't see any handcuffs, the detective had what looked like a tight grip on Joseph Marshall's arm.

Francine and I moved in close enough so that we could get a clear view of the detective and his prisoner. Close enough to call out a question. "Mr. Marshall! Was it your mom who talked you out of it?"

I didn't really expect an answer. But I got one. "Yes, she did." His eyes were downcast, expression doleful. "Sorry about this, Mom."

"Is he charged with anything?" I shouted in the detective's direction. Didn't expect an answer to that one either and I didn't get one. The khaki suited man was assisted into the backseat of a cruiser with the usual hand-on-the-head method. His shirt was embroidered with "Prestigious Electric" in bright red. The detective sat in the backseat beside him. Francine got a good shot of the sad-faced electrician looking out the window before the cruiser pulled away, lights flashing, sirens screaming.

I looked back toward the building where things had grown quiet. The remaining vehicles, both official and civilian, began to leave. All of the police vehicles and most of the curious lookers drove away until only one police car and the Lexus remained.

The excitement over, it was a good place to end the live broadcast. "This is Lee Barrett," I said, "at the scene of a human tragedy averted. The intervention of a trained crisis negotiator and a telephone call from a man's mother may have saved someone here in Salem today. Stay tuned to WICH-TV for updates on this unfolding story."

"Okay, let's head down to the police station," I said to Francine as we stashed our equipment in the van. "And see if we can find out how all this happened."

"On camera?" she wanted to know.

"Nope. Not yet. Just snooping around. That works better when there aren't any cameras."

"Okay. How about if I drop you off at the station while I go find us some cheeseburgers or something." Her expression brightened. "Great idea, huh?"

"Excellent," I said. "I'll see you back later. With food."

I checked to be sure phone, notebook, pens, and pencils were in the purse, and stepped down from the van right in front of the big glass doors of Salem PD. I saw the lectern the chief uses for press conferences pushed over to the side of the covered area.

Must be planning another presser. Maybe it'll be about Joseph Marshall.

My phone buzzed before I could push the doors open. "That you out front, babe?" It was Pete.

"It's me. Where are you? In your office?"

"Yep. I saw the van pull in from my window. I'll be right out."

He appeared before I'd reached the front desk. I had my press credentials and ID ready for inspection and handed them to the officer behind the tall desk. He already knew who I was, but procedure is procedure.

"Are you here to see me," Pete asked. "Or are you snooping around about the guy on top of the Octagon building?"

"The Octagon building?"

"Oh, that's just the name of the corporation who owns the place. Real estate outfit. They buy and sell older buildings in the area. No big secret about it. Nothing high end, but they're legit." We walked together down a glass-walled corridor toward his office. "So, snooping?"

"Right," I agreed happily. "Can you answer some questions?"

Cop face. "Maybe. What about?"

"Can you tell me where they took Joseph Marshall? Is he under arrest?"

"No. It's not against the law to threaten to kill yourself. I guess he'll be checking into a mental health facility for a little while. But he's here. We have some questions to ask him. There's a little problem with his license."

I wrote "license problem" in the notebook, bringing a semiamused look from Pete.

"What's the problem with the license—if you can say?"

"It seems to be—um—inadequate for the work he was doing. We have a few questions we'd like answered."

I wrote "inadequate" with a question mark after it, then looked out the window while I thought about what to ask next. "Pete," I began, "what happened with the person who tried to break into Lilly's house? Is he still locked up?"

"Yes," was the cop-voice answer. That question obviously was going nowhere. I stared out the window some more. That's when I noticed the black Lexus pulling into the guest parking area. The same tall man who'd smiled at Francine and me when he was going into the Octagon building climbed out. I pointed. "Who's that, Pete? I saw him today just before they took Marshall away."

Pete swiveled his chair around so that he could see where I pointed. "That's Richard McNally. He heads up the real estate firm I told you about. He's probably coming here to check up on his tenant. Not my case, but that'd be my guess."

I saw the WICH-TV mobile van pull in. "Makes sense,"

I agreed. "If you're not going to tell me anything about Marshall though, I guess I'll go by City Hall and see if I can dig up anything about licenses. See you tonight?"

"You bet. Want me to bring anything?"

"Chinese?"

"Sure thing."

Pete walked me to the door. "Chief going to talk again today?"

"Don't know." Cop voice.

I gave up, smiled, waved good-bye, and hurried across the lot to where Francine waited, hopefully with bags of fast food to share.

CHAPTER 19

Nothing like cheeseburger, fries, and a chocolate milkshake to generate a new burst of energy. Just as I'd suggested to Pete, a visit to City Hall was next on my to-do list. Once again, Francine left cameras and mics in the van while we visited that historic building, following signs to the upstairs office. My questions were answered politely. "Yes, there's an electrician by that name registered at that address. Yes, the board is investigating a complaint regarding his license. No, I'm not at liberty to give you any more information at this time. Have a nice day."

So much for that. We decided to go back to the station, Francine to vacuum some burger bun crumbs and a few scattered fries from the front seats, me to compile my scattered notes into some kind of order. I was greeted by both Rhonda and Mr. Doan with enthusiastic congratulations on our live report on the almost-jumper. Even Scott Palmer offered a fist-bump and a "Good job, Lee." I promised Mr. Doan that there'd be some interesting updates on the story to look forward to, but that I needed a little more time on that. "I stopped by the police station,"

I added, "and it looks like the chief's lectern is about to get dragged out front again. Anybody here heard anything?"

Nobody had, or if they had they weren't sharing the information. I asked for a key to the dataport again, planning to pull together what little information I had on Joseph Marshall and the Octagon building.

Spreading notebook pages and index cards on the desktop, I stared at them. No inspiration. After a moment I selected a new index card. "Richard McNally," I wrote. Real estate person. Owns the building Joseph Marshall tried to jump from. Owns other buildings in Salem also (Not "high end."). I added that card to the pile.

I thought about the name I'd seen on the truck, PRESTIGIOUS ELECTRICAL, and entered it on my tablet. Maybe his company webpage would tell me something.

No result.

"That's strange," I muttered aloud. "Is business so good that he doesn't need to advertise?" I tried Facebook and LinkedIn. Nothing there either.

There can be times when finding nothing is more interesting than finding something. This was one of those times. I scribbled very fast on the card, hurrying before any thoughts got away. Then I called my Aunt Ibby.

"My goodness, Maralee," she said. "I saw that newscast you did. How frightening. And how fortunate that the poor man was rescued. What will become of him now?"

"Pete says he'll probably spend some time in a mental health facility. But listen, I need your help on something. Something about Joseph Marshall." I explained how I'd been unable to find information on him, or even more strangely, on his business. "I tried the usual social media sites, but he doesn't turn up anywhere. That's just not normal these days. I know the library must have more resources than I do. Can you check?"

"I'll be happy to, dear. You know how much I love helping you on your cases."

"Shhh. Don't let Pete hear you call it a 'case.' But, I have to admit, I think it might be one!"

"I'll get on it as soon as I can" she promised. "I'll be working at the library tomorrow and I'll see what I can turn up. You'll be going with me to the Belles' rehearsal tomorrow evening, don't forget. We can talk about it then. And by the way, didn't Rupert do a fine job of explaining the Agatha Christie mystery? I think the play will be a big success. And it'll be partly because of WICH-TV."

"He's an easy interview," I said. "I don't think there'll be any problem with the play at all. Wait until you see the fellow playing Poirot. That mustache is real!"

"I can hardly wait. Agatha seems to be following you around these days, doesn't she? The *Hickory Dickory Dock* book and now the Christmas play."

"Don't think I hadn't thought about that. Has O'Ryan selected any more books lately?"

"Not that I've noticed," she said. "He and his lady friend came through here a while back and she exited through the cat doors to outside. O'Ryan is in here with me, keeping warm."

"Smart cat," I said, "and thanks for any help with the mysterious electrician. See you this evening. Pete's coming over."

"Does he know we're working on the case?" Sly laugh.

"No! Good-bye Aunt Ibby. Love you."

I wrote one more card. "Reminder: Ask Lilly for names of the Board of Directors."

Then I gathered my papers, stuffed them into the purse, and using stairs instead of the elevator returned the dataport key to Rhonda. "Anything on the docket for this afternoon?"

"Nope. Four o'clock already. Looks like Salem is pretty quiet. Maybe everybody is out Christmas shopping."

That was a smack-yourself-on-the-forehead moment. "Shopping!" I said. "I haven't even started."

"Why don't you head for the mall then?" she asked. "You and Francine have had a pretty full day and you'll be off at five anyway. Mr. Doan has already left and Scott Palmer has clocked in. If anything turns up I'll toss it to him."

"What if the police department calls a presser? They've got the TV setup ready down there."

"Scotty can handle it."

I knew she was right. "Okay then. I think I will." With hardly any qualms about taking off early, within minutes I was on my way to the North Shore Mall. If I hadn't been infused with holiday spirit already, I would have been as soon as I landed at the sprawling complex of stores. Giant nutcrackers, enormous wreathes, gorgeously decorated trees, greetings in several languages flashing in neon—all against a background of instrumental Christmas music. Who could resist? I dove right in.

By five-thirty, with a shopping bag from Macy's in one hand and one from Barnes & Noble in the other, each one holding professionally store-wrapped gifts, I started back toward the parking lot. Fluffy towel sets for all my married cousins, books for all their kids. Proud of myself for achieving a lot in a short space of time and humming "Jingle Bell Rock," I passed Best Buy then took a step backward for a second look at the window display TV. The sound was off, but the closed captioning was on, and the picture showed a close-up of my fellow field reporter, Scott Palmer, standing in front of an empty lectern in front of the police department. "We're expecting a spokesperson momentarily," the caption read, "with breaking news relating to the recent suspicious death of Albert Eldridge." I moved closer to the window and put both shopping bags down. The camera focused on the lectern as a figure emerged from inside the station. I recognized Joyce Rouse as she adjusted the microphone and began to speak. The close captioned words read, "I'm Joyce Rouse, detective sergeant with the Salem Police Department. Today a video was brought to our attention and we are requesting the help of the community in identifying the person shown on it. The video was taken from a security camera mounted above a hotel overflow parking lot adjacent to the Eldridge property at approximately 5:50 on December first. The figure is indistinct. If you recognize the person highlighted, please call the number at the bottom of your screen. The person is not a suspect, but a person of interest in this matter. If you were in the vicinity of Hawthorne Boulevard and Washington Square and happened to see this person during the early morning hours of December first, we'd like to speak with you. Please call the number at the bottom of your screen."

The black and white film was dark and grainy. A bright circle highlighted the figure of a person. (Man? Or woman? Hard to tell.) Whoever it was carried a large suitcase and moved quickly from the left side of the screen to the right, passed a row of automobiles, then disappeared. His (or her) clothing was dark colored and he (or she) wore a baseball cap pulled low. The film ran several times in succession as the close captions advised viewers that although the face of the person was not clear, they should look for body language, distinctive clothing, or mannerisms that might be familiar. Then back to Scott who repeated the call-in number. I picked up my shopping bags and started for the exit, holiday spirit fading fast.

CHAPTER 20

The dashboard clock read five forty-five when I pulled out onto Route 128 and headed home. Pete wouldn't finish work until around six-thirty, and thanks to him I didn't need to cook. He'd still have to pick up the Chinese food and that should leave me plenty of time to shower, dress, and maybe find a few minutes to empty my purse and organize the day's notes. Or at least enough time to smooth out the wrinkled papers and brush the cinnamon roll crumbs from the index cards.

O'Ryan was on the back steps when I arrived home. I looked around to see if Frankie was anywhere in sight, but she wasn't. "Coming inside with me, big boy?" I unlocked the door and O'Ryan trotted into the hall beside me, then dashed ahead of me up the two flights. The shopping bags slowed me down a little. Once inside, I followed my plan. I put the bags of gifts on top of my bureau, hung my plaid jacket in the closet, then dumped the contents of the purse onto the kitchen table. I grabbed clean undies, jeans, and a pink cashmere sweater and headed for the bathroom. In near record time I showered, washed my hair, then dressed, and barefoot with towel-wrapped head, approached the disorganized mess on the Lucite table.

Of course that's when O'Ryan ran for the living room door and Pete showed up early, carrying a bouquet of supermarket flowers and a big brown paper shopping bag with red pagodas on it. Putting the bag on the counter and the flowers in the sink, he pulled me close for a long, satisfying kiss. "Missed you," he said.

I snuggled a little closer into his arms. "You saw me this afternoon."

"That was business. This is pleasure." His voice was sort of muffled by the towel but I got the message. A little more kissing, a little more snuggling happened. After a while though, we remembered the dinner. "I suppose our Crab Rangoon is getting cold," he whispered.

I straightened my terrycloth turban. "I'll pick up the stuff on the table if you get the plates and silverware."

"Do you have a vase for these?" He held up the flowers.

"I'll get it," I said. "It's in the hall closet."

"Where do you want me to put all this stuff then?" Pete asked, pointing to the dumped contents of my purse.

"I don't know." I pulled the blue satin glass vase from the closet. "I was going to sort it out. Change handbags. Just put it on a chair I guess. I'll fix it later."

"Okay. How come it all smells like cinnamon?"

"Long story."

I toweled my hair damp-dry, resulting in the usual red-haired-Shirley Temple tangled curl look I outgrew about twenty-five years ago. "Sorry about this." I pointed at my head. "Didn't have time to fix it."

He shrugged, smiling. "I like it." He pulled my scattered papers into a pile, then began to stack the index cards into another. He lifted one and sniffed it. "Cinnamon," he said, then looked down at it. "You're checking up on Prestigious Electrical? How come?" He turned over the next card. "Octagon Real Estate too?"

I arranged the flowers in the vase and put it in the center of the table. "You look like River arranging the Tarot cards," I said. "I was looking for a website for the electrical business. There isn't one. Don't you think that's odd?"

"Yes. It is."

Oh-oh. Cop voice.

I spooned Veggie Delight into an orange Fiesta ware bowl. "The owner Richard McNally, seems to be who he says he is, right?"

"Sure does." He pulled the rest of the cards together and put papers and cards in a neat pile on a chair. "I don't know what to do with all the girly stuff." He held lipstick, comb, Chapstick, tissues, and the rest of my necessities in both hands. "On the chair too?"

"That'll be fine. I'll sort it out later. I saw Joyce Rouse on TV. The video was a surprise. Oh, good. You remembered to get the duck sauce. Do you think anybody will recognize the guy? Pretty grainy film."

He joined me at the counter and arranged half a dozen egg rolls in a neat pyramid on a green plate. "Okay, Miss Nosey reporter. Here's an early scoop for you. We have a witness who saw the person of interest leaving the Historical Charities building at around six-thirty that morning."

"No kidding? You know who it is?"

"Nope. We just have an eyewitness. Still no ID."

"Reliable witness?"

"Maybe not. It's Vinnie Drake."

I filled a blue bowl with fluffy white rice. "The bad Santa?"

"Yep. Our little cat burglar. Oops. Sorry O'Ryan."

The cat on the windowsill gave an angry swish of his tail. "No offense intended."

"What did he say he saw?" I resisted a strong temptation to reach for the notebook and start taking notes.

"Said he was just on his way home from 'hanging around.' He was over near the statue of Hawthorne and he saw a man carrying a big suitcase near the overflow parking lot. He admits he thought about robbing the guy, but it was starting to get light and there were too many people around."

"There are probably some better witnesses then."

"Probably. But a man carrying a suitcase next to a hotel isn't unusual at any time of day. Not something you'd notice particularly."

He was right. "Maybe somebody got a closer look at him though," I said. "Enough for some kind of ID."

"We hope so. We'll keep running that video. What do you want to drink with this?"

We decided on iced tea with dinner and coffee after. And ice cream. Pete poured iced tea into my glass. "Pete," I said. "Do you think that whatever is in the suitcase is important? I mean, if that man is important at all."

"Could be. Or not."

"Five swords," I said, almost to myself.

"Huh?"

"I was thinking about River's reading. The man who's stealing five swords. He left two in the ground."

"Don't go all witchy on me, babe," he said. "You know I don't get River most of the time. Like her fine. Just don't understand her."

"I don't always either," I admitted. "But that card shows a thief. We know Vinnie Drake is a thief, but he was down the street."

"So he says."

"Well, if he's telling the truth, maybe the man in the video is stealing something. Something in that suitcase. Maybe though he left something important behind." I was beginning to warm up to the subject. "What do you think?"

"Two swords?"

"Two figurative swords. The Tarot isn't supposed to be literal."

"Okay. Let me try to follow this." He picked up two egg rolls, putting one on my plate, one on his. "Two swords. Two egg rolls. Same thing. You think the video guy killed Eldridge, then stole something from his office, something in the suitcase, but left something behind."

"Well, it's possible, isn't it? I mean, swords could represent weapons." I took a bite of my eggroll/sword. "Maybe he carried away the weapon. That's why you haven't found it."

He ate his eggroll in two bites. Big smile. "Look. We're destroying Tarot card evidence here."

"I'm serious," I insisted. "The cards have been right before."

"My love, I'm a cop. You know I can't take River's card tricks or even your mirror pictures as evidence of anything. I deal in facts."

"Okay," I agreed. "But I can't help thinking about what River said. You wait. I'll bet even if you can't find the weapon that killed him, you'll find two clues he left behind right in the Histy."

"The Histy?"

"Santa Claus name for the historical society."

"I'll take the two clues bet. Dinner at Gulu-Gulu?"

"You got it." I reached across the table and shook his hand. Then together, we cleared up the dishes and ate ice cream and drank coffee, talk of murder and swords and Santas put aside.

At least for the moment. But I'm not forgetting any of it.

CHAPTER 21

I was awake and out of bed before Pete. Switching the big Jacki Easlick bag for a cross body Kate Spade, I arranged the cosmetics, pens, phone, and notebook into neat, zippered compartments. Organizing the index cards with a rubber band, and stapling loose papers together, I tucked them all into a desk drawer. I turned on the morning coffee and then with the aid of blow dryer, hair spray, and electric straightening brush I tamed my unruly hair. By the time Pete got ready for work, I'd already had a cup of coffee and a strawberry Pop-Tart. I was ready to face the new day.

It turned out to be a comparatively uneventful one. One field report—interview with a couple who do Christmas puppet shows for kids. Something about Rudolph and the Gingerbread boy. Cute, but not exciting. There was no more breaking news about Eldridge's murder except that they were now actually calling it "murder" instead of "unexplained death," or "under suspicious circumstances," or the other dozen or so euphemisms broadcasters use when they mean murder. As Phil Archer had promised on the previous day's show, funeral plans for Mr. E. were announced. He was to be cremated, according to his expressed wishes. No formal ceremonies were planned at this time. A celebration of his life would be scheduled after the Christmas holidays. They did, as Pete had promised they would, run the video of the man with a suitcase at intervals during the entire day.

I even had time to do a little local Christmas shopping. The people I used to work with in Florida remain fascinated with Salem's witchy past. I ran over to Crow Haven and bought a few candles presumed useful in casting various spells. I bought some for love (pink) and some for money (green), figuring I couldn't go wrong with those. I threw in one for justice (orange) for Pete.

I hadn't forgotten Aunt Ibby's invitation to go with her to the Belles' first rehearsal with the hand bells. Compared to the rest of my day, that seemed downright fascinating. Besides, it might give me a chance to ask Lilly Jeffry for the names of those board members. At least I'd have one thing to write in the notebook. I hoped Aunt Ibby would have something for me to write down too, about Joseph Marshall.

Pete had hockey practice with his Police Athletic League Pee-Wee team, so my evening was completely free. I took time for a leisurely hot bath with a gardenia bath fizz, dressed carefully in the green velour with a fake mink jacket and knee-high boots. Took my time with makeup, trying to implement the tricks I'd learned from Carmine, Wanda the Weather Girl's makeup man. (Even at my age, I want my aunt to be proud of me when we meet with her friends.)

We left in the Buick for the Community Center at seven for the seven-thirty rehearsal. She seemed excited about playing the hand bells. She didn't mention Joseph Marshall so neither did I. That information, if she'd found any, would keep until later. The ten Belles took the stage, all of them wearing black choir robes and white gloves. They seemed to be arranged according to their height. At least it seemed so to me. Lilly Jeffry, of small stature, was at one end of the row, with my tall, slim aunt at the other. The bright brass hand bells were arranged in front of them in two rows of graduated sizes. One row with black handles, the other with white ones. My aunt had explained that the bells worked in a similar way to piano keys—the white keys and the black keys. The fact that all of the women played other instruments and could read music made the task much easier than it would have been for those of us, like me, whose musical background consisted of childhood piano lessons and second grade numbered hand bells and a middle school orchestra triangle.

Conrad Gillette, in conservative blue suit with striped tie, took the stage, gave a brief history of the hand bells, then, with his back to the small audience, picked up his baton. "We'll begin with a simple one-octave piece. 'Good King Wenceslas.' You each have your sheet music before you? Begin."

Considering that this was their first effort with the bells, it wasn't bad at all. The old song was fairly recognizable. Gillette had them repeat it several times. By then it sounded really good. "Very well then, ladies," he said. "Turn to another one-octave number. 'Oh, Holy Night.'" This one sounded even better. The girls were clearly getting the hang of this bell thing, even though the one-octave songs didn't call for Aunt Ibby's third bell, the tall C-3, to ring at all. The rehearsal took about an hour, then they adjourned for cake and coffee. I and the rest of the audience were invited to join them. Mr. Gillette stayed for a few minutes, then beat a hasty retreat. Couldn't blame him. That was quite a bunch of chattering girlfriends, even for me. I maneuvered myself into position beside Lilly Jeffry. "Nice to see you, Lilly," I said. "The Belles sound as good as ever."

"Thank you, Lee." Big smile. "It's such fun to get together with old friends. It seems that we're only all in the same place at the same time, once a year. This is it."

"Aunt Ibby loves it too," I said. "By the way, I believe you mentioned that the board of the Historical Charities also meets only once a year. Who are the board members?"

"Are you working on a piece?"

"I am," I said truthfully. "The society is very interesting." *True also.*

"Let's see," she said with one finger under her chin in a thoughtful position. "I'm not sure I can name them all. It's like trying to name the seven dwarfs." The silvery giggle, then she began to count on her fingers. She named the president of a bank (the one Gillette had chosen for the Santas' money drop), a member of the city council, a history professor from Salem State. "Myself, of course," she said, and—oh yes, Richard McNally. He's in real estate."

It seemed like a perfectly logical mix, on the surface of it. The banker, the historian, the city representative, the secretary, and the real estate man. Why not?

Again, River's reading flitted across my mind. Was it the Ten of pentacles that referred to real estate? And the miser was all about money. She'd mentioned the city when another ten turned up. Ten of wands?

Maybe I'll watch it again. River's shows are all archived I'm sure.

When my aunt and I once again got into the Buick and started for home, I couldn't contain my curiosity any longer. "So? What did you learn about Joseph Marshall? I'm dying to know."

"You know, Maralee, I hate to admit defeat. I've always

believed that a good researcher, digging deeply enough, can find almost anything." She shook her head. "This one has me stumped. So far, that is. I'm not giving up."

I was incredulous. "Really? You mean you couldn't find anything about him either?"

"I found out that someone by that name was born in Revere, Massachusetts, forty-two years ago."

"And?"

"And that person died sixteen years later. Automobile accident."

"So you think our Joseph Marshall somehow assumed the identity of the dead Joseph Marshall?"

"It could be. It's not hard to order a birth certificate by mail, you know, and once you get that you can get a driver's license—just about whatever document you need. Anyway, I'll keep digging."

"Me too," I said. "And I think Pete ought to know about it, don't you?"

"Yes, indeed he should. Between the three of us, we'll crack this case."

I had to laugh at that. "Aunt Ibby, you're watching too much TV. Or reading too much Agatha Christie. Pete isn't Hercule Poirot, and we're not Charlie's Angels."

She pulled the Buick into the garage carefully as always, stopping when the suspended tennis ball hit the windshield, and we hurried past the frosty garden to the back door where, as always, O'Ryan waited for us.

"Coming upstairs with me?" I asked the cat, "or staying down here." He looked from Aunt Ibby's open kitchen door to where I stood on the back staircase as though making a thoughtful decision, then chose to follow me.

"Good night Aunt Ibby," I said. "See you tomorrow. Thanks for inviting me. It was fun."

"Good night, Maralee. Sweet dreams."

Sweet dreams seemed like a really great idea. Dreams with no fictional characters, no dead bodies, nobody jumping from buildings, no Tarot cards, no Santa Clauses. Visions of sugar plums might be okay, if I knew exactly what a sugar plum was. Must ask Aunt Ibby.

I put on a long flannel Lanz nightgown with red and blue hearts and flowers on it, a gift from Aunt Ibby last Christmas, fixed myself a cup of hot cocoa, put a few vanilla wafers on a plate, and turned on the living room TV. House and Garden TV was showing a film on Christmas tree decorations. I hadn't even bought a tree yet, or brought decorations down from the attic. There's a big bay window in my living room, overlooking the backyard and Oliver Street. Most of the year my antique carousel horse has the place of honor there, but it's a perfect spot for the tree.

"What do you say O'Ryan?" I asked the cat, who'd curled up beside me. "We'll get our tree this week and get the lights and decorations down from the attic."

"Mmrrow" he said in an agreeable purry sort of way, not opening the golden eyes.

"Good. Want to come up in the attic with me?" That attic holds some bad memories for me. O'Ryan doesn't like it up there either. If I make him come with me on the rare times I venture up to the fourth floor, he walks in a kind of crouch, ears flattened, tail switching.

"Meh," he said.

"Right. We don't have to do it tonight." It wasn't time for the late news yet, so we watched the last half of *Prancer*, one of my all-time favorite Christmas movies. By eleven o'clock, feeling a little drowsy from the warm room, the flannel nightie, and the hot chocolate, I was tempted to skip watching Buck Covington deliver the nightly headlines. But I snapped to wide-awake attention when I heard my own voice issue from the screen.

"Was it your mom who talked you out of it?" Buck was showing the portion of my report when Joseph Marshall was being escorted out of the building. I heard the man's soft message to his mother. "Sorry, Mom."

"We have Mr. Marshall's mother here in the studio with us tonight to update us on how she may have saved her son's life," Covington said. "Good evening, Mrs. Marshall."

Uh-oh. Buck's going to have to do this live—without the teleprompter. I crossed my fingers and hoped he'd get through it without messing up. I moved closer to the screen.

Plump, with permed gray hair, wearing a polka-dotted navy dress, the woman was so motherly looking she could have come from Central Casting. "Oh, thank you, Buck. But my name is Mrs. Prescott. My son went by his cousin Joey Marshall's name. For business reasons. That's what he told me. Business reasons." She gave a fluttery little gesture with her hands. "They were great friends, him and Joey. Same age. Poor Joey died young. Too bad."

Aunt Ibby had nailed it! The suicidal electrician had assumed the identity of someone else. His cousin. And I hadn't had a chance yet to tell Pete about what my aunt had discovered. I turned my attention back to Buck Covington. How was he going to handle this turn of events?

He didn't skip a beat. Completely ignoring the name-change information, he stuck to the original script. He was supposed to find out how the mother had saved the son with a phone call. That's what he did. "Would you share with us what you said to Joseph? The words that made him change his mind? To leave the edge of that tall building?"

"Why sure, hon. I said what any mother who loves her child would say. "I said, darlin' get your fanny down off the edge of that roof and come on home. There can't be anything so bad that you and me and Jesus can't fix it and make it right. And he did what I said. Just like always." Shy smile. "Well, most always."

Covington nodded and favored her with one of his heart-melting looks that women of every age respond to. "Thank you so very much for sharing your story with us. I hope you and your son will be reunited soon. Now here's Wanda with tomorrow's weather."

And that was that. No searching questions about Marshall's reason for the threatened jump. No curiosity about the name change. No pressing her on the "almost always." I guessed I didn't ever have to worry about Buck wanting my investigative reporter gig. I uncrossed my fingers. At least he hadn't actually messed up. I wondered if Scott Palmer was sitting in the director's chair tonight. If he was, he must be tearing his hair out.

I was sure Pete would be at his apartment by then, or maybe at his sister Marie's house. Sometimes he stays and visits for a while after he brings her two boys home from hockey practice. I hoped he wasn't home asleep. I wanted to tell him what Aunt Ibby had learned about the Joseph Marshall from Revere, who'd died in a car accident when he was sixteen—our Joseph Marshall's cousin Joey.

He was at Marie's and wide awake. "What's up, Lee? Everything okay?"

"Yes. I'm fine. Are you watching the news?"

"No. We're watching *Blue Bloods* on Netflix. Why?"

I explained what Marshall's mother had revealed and what Aunt Ibby had learned earlier about the two Joseph Marshalls. "Just thought you might want to know right away," I said.

"Thanks, Lee. And thank your aunt too. I'll pass this on to Rouse. She's the detective working this one. Good job, you two. Call you tomorrow. Love you."

"Love you too. 'Bye."

Wanda promised that tomorrow would be another cold but pleasant day and warned that colder weather was on the way to New England via the "Montreal Express." O'Ryan watched the screen until the end of her report, then jumped down to the floor. He likes Wanda. Most males do. He looked back at me, opened his mouth wide in a yawn, then trotted down the hall toward the bedroom. It was almost time for River's show, but I knew I couldn't stay awake for it, so I turned off the TV and followed the cat.

Ever since Frankie had reappeared in our lives, I found myself often looking at the windowsill, halfway expecting to see her outside. I thought I saw a little flash of white when I passed the window and moved closer. "That you, Frankie?" I said aloud.

There was no cat on the windowsill. Instead, on the frosted pane was a display of swirling colors followed by flashing lights. I sighed and closed my eyes, even though I knew that when I opened them I'd see something more.

CHAPTER 22

I've seen some frightening things on a weird variety of reflective surfaces. Too many of them involved death. When I opened my eyes this time I saw something that wouldn't bother most people one bit. It was a door. Not an unattractive door, but one nicely painted white with vintage carved wood bull's-eye corner trim on the door frame. The problem with it for me was this particular door led from the hall outside my kitchen to the attic—the attic where the Christmas decorations were stored—the attic where I'd once, not so very long ago, barely escaped death myself.

I turned away from the window. When I looked back I saw nothing there but a lacy tracing of white frost. No white cat. No white attic door. Glad the vision was gone, but mostly confused about why it was there in the first place, I turned off the kitchen light and joined the cat on my bed. "I don't know what that was all about, O'Ryan," I told him, "but we're not going up there alone any time soon." He gave me a little lick on my chin, then turned around three times, snuggled up close to my side, and went to sleep.

Sleep didn't come quite so easily to me that night. It's long been a habit of mine, when the body is tired but the mind refuses to shut down, to make a to-do list in my head. Tops on the list this time was to contact Joseph Marshall's mother and ask her the questions Buck Covington had missed—and preferably to do it before Scott Palmer did.

Next on my list was another list. Christmas shopping. At least I'd made a start on that one. I needed to buy a tree. (I needed to decorate it too, but I pushed that need to the end of the line.) Holiday cards for friends and family. I thought of Lilly Jeffry's neat stack of beautifully hand-addressed cards. Addressing mine would be a chore. I think that was the point at where I finally dozed off.

I put my list into my purse in the morning and arrived at the station before eight. I knew that Rhonda would have the contact information for the electrician's mom, Mrs. Prescott, and I hoped the woman was an early riser because I had every intention of calling her immediately.

Bingo. She answered on the first ring and remembered seeing me when I called out my questions to her son. "Oh, Ms. Barrett," she said. "Because of you, my friends think I'm a big TV star. Did you see me with that cute guy, Mr. Covington, on your station?"

"I did. You did a good job with the interview. How is your son? Have you been able to see him?"

"Thanks for asking, hon. Yes, he's in a kind of rehab place. Lots of doctors. All kinds of doctors."

"I'm sure he'll get whatever help he needs. If you have a few minutes, I'd like to ask you a few questions—off the air. Ever since I saw you with Buck last night, I've been curious about a couple of things you mentioned."

"Oh, sure dear. What can I tell you?"

"I wonder, as I'm sure others do, if you know what

made your son want to do such a thing. He's a young man, with what seems like a good job and an obviously loving mother."

"You know, that's the first thing I asked him. Why? Why would you do such a dumb thing?"

"What did he say?"

"What a silly kid. He said he might be in trouble because he made some mistakes when he got his business cards printed."

That was a surprise. "Business cards?" I echoed.

"Yeah. Did you see his cards? They're nice. Made out of that shiny white cardboard, with a little cartoon of a yellow lightbulb with those little lines coming out so you can tell it's turned on, you know?"

"Uh-huh. Go on."

What in the world do business cards have to do with anything?

"It wasn't about the picture. It was about the words."

"The words?" Again, I echoed her, sounding astonishingly unprofessional in the process.

God, I'm glad no one is recording this.

"It was the part about him being 'licensed and bonded.'"

"That's on most cards people in that business use, isn't it?" I asked, finally managing a full sentence.

"I guess. Only he isn't."

Wow! "You mean he's not really an electrician?"

"Well, I think he is. I mean, he's real handy about that stuff. Always has been. But I guess he didn't get around to getting the license and all." A sigh. "The boy never was much for doing paperwork."

"I see. Well, I hope he can get that problem straightened out," I said, thinking that Joseph was probably in a world of trouble with whatever agency keeps track of such things. Moving right along, I asked my next question.

"Another thing I wondered about was why he wanted to use his cousin's name and how he managed to do that."

There was the tiniest giggle from her end of the line. "He was naughty. Just drove up to Portland to his Auntie Mae's house and swiped Joey's birth certificate out of her desk. We all know where she keeps it. He put it right back after he was through with it. No harm done. She never even missed it."

"I think you said he did it for 'business reasons'?"

"That's right. That's what he said. Business reasons. That's all I know about that."

All right. On to the next one.

"I can tell that you two are really close." I led into my final question.

"Oh, yes. He loves his mom."

"You told Mr. Covington that he almost always takes your advice. Can you think of any times that he didn't?" I asked.

"Sure. More than once or twice, like any kid. For instance, I've tried to get him to give up bad habits. Just like every mother does. Smoking, drinking, gambling, that stuff. You know?" Another sigh. "Dying his hair, growing a mustache. Well, at least he cut down on the smoking, and I'm pretty sure he's not gambling any more. I make him go outside to smoke so he don't stink up the house."

"Does he live at home?" That was a surprise.

"Oh yeah. He's tried to go out on his own a few times, but he always comes back to his old room."

"I see." I did see too. After all, I'd done the same thing just a few years ago when I moved back into the house on Winter Street—my childhood home. Another question popped into my head, so I asked it.

"Do you call your son Joseph at home? Or do you use his given name?"

"Oh, I call him by his real name."

"What's his name?"

"Anthony. Anthony Prescott. Named for a saint, he was." Another pause. "He's no saint I guess. But I love him to pieces."

"I understand completely. Thank you, Ms. Prescott. I appreciate your talking with me."

"Any time, hon. You call me anytime. Enjoyed chatting with you. 'Bye now."

I reached for my ever-present stack of index cards, happy to have something new to record, not at all sure of where this recent information might lead. So, as usual, I called my aunt.

"Aunt Ibby? I've found Joseph Marshall's real name. He's Anthony Prescott. Want to see what you can dig up on him?"

"I can hardly wait to get started!" I could tell by her tone of voice that she meant it sincerely.

"I found out about his license problem too. The problem is, he doesn't actually have a license at all. I'm betting he got a phony one somehow with Joseph Marshall's name on it."

"Could be. I'm on it." She sounded gleeful. She loves this stuff.

Time to start my day job. Rhonda handed me the neatly typed list with times and places highlighted in yellow. First one looked promising. I was going to Leavitt Street to treat the viewers to a tour of the production area of a chocolate candy workshop.

I'll do some Christmas shopping there. Who doesn't like a big box of chocolates?

Francine loved the idea too. "I've gone past that place a hundred times," she said. "You can smell the chocolate just driving by." Later in the day we had appointments at three of the decorated mansions we'd planned to see the day Albert Eldridge died.

"We'll film the chocolate shop tour, then send it back to Marty to edit," Francine said. "I wonder if they have free samples for the media."

"If we don't come back with candy they might not let us in," I said. We moved slowly along Leavitt Street, then parked across the street from the neat brick building with its identifying oval sign. We didn't need a sign to find it though. Francine was right about the yummy chocolate aroma. We just followed our noses through the front door to the candy kitchen.

A knowledgeable guide made my job easy. From a brief explanation of the care with which the cocoa beans are harvested, through the hand dipping of the lovely stuff, she gave the viewers an entertaining ten minutes. I knew the audience would love it, and yes, they gave us a generous sample pack of the chocolates.

After we (reluctantly) left, and headed for the first decorated house on our list, we passed the narrow road Lilly Jeffry had once mentioned as a possible site for Mr. Eldridge's hoped-for Heritage Park.

"Francine, can you drive around the block one more time, and stop on the corner of that little alley back there." I said.

"Sure. See something interesting?"

"Not sure." I rolled down my window, focusing on a white van parked in front of a modest clapboard house. "Looks the same. But it can't be."

"What can't be?" Francine coasted the vehicle to a stop and peered over my shoulder. "What do you see?"

I pointed. "That white cargo van. The 2007 Ford E150. Right over there. Recognize it?"

"Yeah. It's big and white. How do you do that anyway?"

"Do what?" I pulled an index card from my purse and jotted down the license number of the van.

Francine leaned closer to my window. "How do you always know the year, make, and model of every darned thing on wheels?"

"Oh that. I was married to a professional driver, remember? I hung around cars a lot. Like 'em," I said. "Look, can you pull into the alley? I want to read the sign on the side door of that van."

She did as I'd asked. "That's funny," I said, puzzled. "I was sure it was the same one."

"Same one as what?"

"The Prestigious Electrical van. The one we saw in the yard where the man was going to jump off the roof."

"Yeah. It does kinda look like it." She leaned back in her seat. "Ready to go?"

"Not just 'looks like it.'" I said, writing down the name I saw on a magnetic sign on the van's driver side door. "It is it."

"Can't be," she said. "Sign says Acme Plumbing."

"Right, I said. "Wait a sec. I need to take a picture." I pulled my phone from my purse and climbed out of our van. I walked up to the white Ford and took pictures of the sign and the number plate. I was just about to photograph the passenger side where a long scratch marred the white paint when the door of the house opened and an angry male voice bellowed, "Hey! What the hell do you think you're doing?"

"Come on, Lee!" Francine yelled. "Let's beat it."

She didn't have to say it twice. I jumped back into my seat. Gravel from the rough road scattered in all directions as we sped away. Francine was quiet for a minute, concentrating on her driving. We were a couple of blocks away when she spoke again. "Okay, Lee. Like the mean man said, 'what the hell do you think you're doing?'"

"It's the same cargo van," I said. "As soon as I saw that scratch down the side I knew it was. But the sign threw me for a minute. It's an electrical work truck one day and a plumbing truck another day? How can that be?"

"Don't know," she said as we turned onto Chestnut Street heading for our first mansion. "But I'm pretty sure you're going to find out. Right, Miss Investigative Reporter?"

"Darn right," I agreed. "Or die trying."

CHAPTER 23

We were back to being all business when we set up Francine's camera and my mic in front of a beautiful Chestnut Street home where baskets of fresh pink and red poinsettias flanked granite steps leading to one of the magnificent, often photographed front doors this street is famous for. The flowers were a far cry from the glitter-sprinkled lavender plastic ones on the reception desk back at the station. Rhonda had provided us with an information sheet on Historical Charities of Salem stationary providing details on the age of the house, a bit of its history, and a nicely worded description of the decorations. I detected the efficient hand of Lilly Jeffry in the printed copy.

Our next two mansion stops went just as smoothly as the first one. Between the bright and articulate guide who'd conducted our chocolate kitchen experience, and the neatly prepared scripts and gorgeous buildings on our decorated mansion assignment, our day's work had been the proverbial "piece of cake," or in this case, "pound of candy."

We, along with our sweet chocolate offering, were welcomed back to the station with open arms or more accurately, extended fingers, reaching into the gold foil covered box for truffles and nougats, fudge and clusters.

I asked Rhonda if she had anything else on the docket for us. She had nothing further on her schedule, and it wasn't even two o'clock yet. "Want to go to lunch with me?" Francine asked.

"I'm not hungry yet," I said. "Too many candy samples I guess. You go along. I have a couple of phone calls to make." Once again, I headed for the privacy of my cozy little dataport.

Who should I call first? Pete or Aunt Ibby?

No contest. Pete needed to know about the cargo van and its two identities. I had no idea what it meant, and as far as I knew there was no law against using one vehicle for two different businesses. But it seemed unusual enough to warrant some official attention. Besides that, if the guy who chased me away from it reported me for trespassing, it was best that I notify the police department myself.

I told Pete what I'd seen and sent him the two photos. "I thought you might be interested," I told him. "It just seems . . . odd. And it was on a road that Mr. Eldridge was interested in." I told him about the man who'd yelled at me too. "Maybe I was trespassing," I said, "or maybe I shouldn't have taken pictures."

"Yeah, well, it's possible that he might have taken a pretty dim view of some random redhead wandering around on his property. Especially if she's taking pictures."

I could see his point. "I guess so," I said, "but don't you think . . ."

He interrupted. "Yes, I do think. And I'll look into it. But Lee, for God's sake be careful. This reporter thing could put you in danger. I mean, there's been a murder, remember?"

"I know. I *am* careful," I insisted. "It was broad daylight with cars and people all over the place. What could go wrong?"

"Things can go wrong anywhere. Any time." Exasperated cop voice. "Just be careful. I'll call you later. Okay?"

"Okay." I know Pete's just being protective when he delivers his occasional "for God's sake be careful Lee" lectures, but sometimes I wish he had more confidence in me. I called Aunt Ibby immediately. She wouldn't lecture.

"Oh, Maralee, that's interesting, isn't it? I wish I'd been there. You say it's the very same big truck you saw when Joseph Marshall was thinking of jumping?"

"Yes. A white Ford cargo van." I told her about the scrape on the side. "I know there are a lot of those Fords around, but they don't all have identical scrapes, and magnetic signs instead of painted graphics."

"I'm sure you're right about that. You know about such things. What did you say the name of the plumbing company is?

"Acme Plumbing. Not very original, is it?"

"Not very. I'll see what I can find out about it. And you think it was parked near the spot where poor Albert had planned his little village of old houses?"

"From what Lilly described, I'm quite sure it's the same place," I said. "Do you think maybe somebody has started work on the project? The house the man ran out of looked like it was maybe from the 1920s or 1930s."

"Just about right for preserving how things looked for the regular folks back then. I hope somebody is going ahead with it."

"I told Pete about it," I said. "He seemed to think I

might have put myself in some kind of danger by getting out and taking those pictures."

"He did? I wonder why." Long pause. "For goodness' sake, Maralee. Be careful."

"Thanks, Aunt Ibby. See you when I get home."

Okay, she's protective too.

I made notes on fresh index cards, trying to recall every detail from the time I'd asked Francine to back up the mobile van until we'd sped away toward the TV station. I tried to remember exactly what the yelling man had looked like. Closing my eyes, I tried to visualize his face. No luck. His expression had been angry, I was sure of that. But his features wouldn't materialize for me. Maybe later I'd have more luck. I put the rubber band back around the growing stack of index cards and stared at them. Blankly. No inspiration there either.

But the cards made me think of River and her reading of the Tarot. One had come up during her Eldridge reading that meant the acquiring of real estate. The ten of something? Pentacles? I'd check it out later. I hoped it might mean that Heritage Village might become a reality, a tribute to a man who'd done so much for Salem. That at least was a positive thought in the midst of my tangled mess of thoughts leading nowhere in particular.

I packed up my papers and cards once again, locked up the small room, and dropped the key off with Rhonda. "Anything happening anywhere yet?" I asked her. "Salem can't be that dull. No traffic jams? Brush fires? Cats in trees needing rescuing? Anything?"

"That's the way it goes sometimes," she said. "You'll get used to it. Scott always complains about it too. That's how come he took on so many extra jobs around here. They're not all going to be crazy busy days with murders and suicide jumpers you know. Sometimes it's just candy and Christmas lights. Then you just have to sit around and be ready in case something breaks." She gave me an encouraging smile. "You'll get used to it. Here. Have a chocolate raisin cluster."

I held up my hand. "No thanks. I think I'll run across the street and grab a sandwich or something. Just buzz me if anything breaks."

Something broke.

I was nearly finished with my BLT and had already signaled the waitress for a second cup of hazelnut coffee when my phone jingled. Caller ID read "Isobel Russell."

"Hi, Aunt Ibby."

"Hello Maralee. I believe I've found something quite interesting."

"Good," I said. "In reference to what?"

"To the case silly child! What else?" I could almost see her raised eyebrow. "In reference to Anthony Prescott in particular—the overall case in general."

I wasn't sure what the "overall case" consisted of, so I didn't comment on that part. But anything she'd been able to learn about Anthony Prescott was definitely welcome. "I talked with Anthony—Joseph's—mother this morning," I told her. "Picked up a few things. I can hardly wait to hear what you've been able to come up with."

"All right. Here goes. You were right when you guessed that he isn't properly licensed to do the work he's doing."

"Not a surprise," I said.

"Just about the only electrical training he's had—at least the only thing I've found so far—is the fact that he took lots of shop classes when he was in high school."

"Oh, boy. He's in a heap of trouble, I'd say."

"I agree. Although I must say he had As in all of his classes, so he could undoubtedly do a lot of the things he has to do in that job."

"His mother says he's always been handy at that stuff."

"I'm sure he is. Now, about the other name. He has a Massachusetts driver's license in the name of Joseph Marshall and the address on it matches his mother's address." She paused, maybe for effect. She had my full attention. "He also has one in his own name. Same address. I guess that's not uncommon these days, what with people living together and all. Anyway, the pictures on the licenses looked very different from one another. Joseph Marshall looks like the picture they showed on the news. Anthony Prescott is a platinum blond with a mustache and sideburns. Looks like he even has different color eyes."

"He had access to original birth certificates for both identities. Peroxide, facial hair, and contact lenses would account for the rest," I reasoned aloud. "But why would he go to all that trouble? Does Anthony have an arrest record he's trying to dodge? Anything along those lines?"

"Not that I could find. Nothing serious. Couple of speeding tickets and a DUI about ten years ago."

"I suppose Pete already has all this. No reason he'd share it with me,' I said, more to myself than to my aunt. "But I guess I should tell him about the two licenses anyway."

"He'll know we've been snooping."

"That's my job now, remember? I'm an occasional investigative reporter."

"True enough. Oh, there's one more interesting thing. It's about that van you took a picture of."

"What about it?"

"It's registered to an R. M. Real Estate Company. I think you mentioned that name once in connection with the Board of Directors at the Salem Historical Charities."

"Very interesting," I said. "And I'll bet Pete has that information too."

"Maybe," she said, "and maybe not."

"He has a whole police department to dig up facts," I said. "That's hard to beat."

"He doesn't have a professional, multidegreed, research librarian and certified snoop like me," she announced. "Better tell him about the real estate company."

"I will," I promised. "And thanks, Aunt Ibby."

"My pleasure," she said. "My absolute pleasure. Well, back to my snooping. See you for dinner this evening? Around seven? I'm making a lovely roast beef dinner. Perfect for a cold night. Wanda says snow flurries likely."

CHAPTER 24

Pete's call came right after Aunt Ibby's. Turns out I was right about the Joseph Marshall/Anthony Prescott driver's licenses. The police had all of the information we had. Pete knew all about the real estate company owning the electrical company/plumbing company work van too.

"One more thing about that real estate company, Pete," I told him. "I'm pretty sure the owner of that company is on the Board of Directors for the Salem Historical Charities Society."

"He is?" There was surprise in his voice. "Where did you get that? Not from a vision or something River saw in those cards was it?"

"No. Of course not! Lilly Jeffry told me. And Pete, he's the same man we saw outside the window in your office. Richard McNally."

"Hmm. It's not my case, you know. But maybe I'll look into it."

"Will you tell me what you find out? Maybe it's just a coincidence, but all of a sudden that name is turning up all over the place."

Another "hmm" on his end of the phone. Then in

matter-of-fact cop voice, "You know I don't believe in coincidences."

I pressed my luck. "But you'll tell me what you find out?"

"I'll tell you as much as I can if you and your aunt will stop playing detective and knocking on doors you have no business opening."

Doors? What's up with doors lately? Like the attic door in my vision.

I must have said the word aloud.

"It's a figure of speech, Lee. I didn't mean real doors. Hell, it's bad enough that you trespassed in some guy's yard taking pictures."

"That man didn't make a complaint about me, did he?"

His tone softened. "No babe, don't worry. He didn't. Not to us anyway, but if you and Francine were riding around in that big van with WICH-TV written all over both sides, and he was as mad as you think he was, I wouldn't be surprised if your station manager hears about it."

I'd never thought about that. If the yelling man did complain to Bruce Doan though, I'd just explain that I was working on an investigative report idea. Which was the truth. And the more I thought about it, the better I liked the idea.

Pete gave me a few more warnings about being careful, not sticking my nose into other people's business, and that he worries about me so much because he loves me. It was all kind of nice, really. I promised to be careful, which I thought I already was, to avoid the nose thing as much as possible considering my job requirements and told him I loved him and worried about him too. Which was also the truth.

I paid my tab, finished my rapidly cooling coffee, and walked back to the station. Cold, but no snow flurries yet.

The camo kettle Santa was once again at his post near the front of the building. His white beard and mustache, though much too perfectly waved and clearly made from Dynel or some other synthetic fiber, somehow looked just right on him. His ruddy complexion, what I could see of it behind the bushy beard, was probably from brushed-on blush, but it looked good too. I paused and tucked a five into the kettle. "Looking good, Nick," I said. "I guess the beard keeps you warm in this weather."

"Ho ho ho," he said, in that hearty Santa voice of his. "Thanks Ms. Barrett." He tapped the top of the round belly. "Padding helps too. Merry Christmas."

I found myself humming an off-key version of "Good King Wenceslaus" while I waited for the elevator. Must have been all those Christmas lights on the mansions and maybe a little sugar rush from the chocolate, but the proverbial Christmas Spirit had quite suddenly hit me full force along with a happy urge to buy gifts, address cards, decorate a tree, even to bake cookies. I stepped off the elevator on the second floor, still humming, and pushed open the door to the reception area in all its purple splendor. Rhonda looked up from her *People* magazine. "Well, you're all smiles and happy-faced," she said.

"Feeling good," I said. "I think I'll do some more Christmas shopping tonight after dinner."

"You still shopping?" Astonished look. "I have mine all done and wrapped and under my tree."

"Your tree is up and decorated already? Shopping done?" It was my turn to do the astonished face. "How did you find time?"

Francine appeared just then and joined in the conversation. "I put my tree up last weekend. My roommate decorated it and I still have a little shopping to do. I don't send cards anymore. Just the cute e-mail ones."

Am I surrounded with Miss Lemons? Is everybody efficient but me? Happy face fading fast.

Pete to the rescue. I could hardly believe the timing of his phone call. "Hi babe," he said. "Want to go Christmas tree shopping with me tonight? I promised Marie I'd get a little one for the kids' room. And I know you don't have one yet."

"That is an absolutely great idea! Want to come over for dinner? Aunt Ibby is cooking roast beef. Around seven?"

He said yes. Happy face back.

"Here comes Scotty." Rhonda pointed to the glass door. "Guess you two can leave. Old Eddie will drive and Scott'll do the reporting. If anything happens, that is."

Scott Palmer came through the door, tossing a wool hat and a long maroon scarf onto the counter and peeling off a leather bomber jacket. "Want to stick these in the coat closet, Rhonda? Looks like a quiet night around town. Dead as a doornail out there." He pulled his wallet from a back pocket and looked inside. "Except for the darned Santa Clauses every two feet. I must have stuffed twenty bucks into those kettles today."

"All for a good cause," Rhonda said, "and hang your own clothes up. You're a big boy."

"Okay," he said pleasantly. "It was worth a try. "Hey, Moon." He put the offending garments into the coat closet, then faced me. "Heard you and Francine were wandering around some guy's yard and he got really pissed."

"How'd you hear that?" This was not good news.

"Don't worry. I took the phone call. Doan doesn't know about it. I figured you had some good reason." He looked into my eyes the creepy way he does to everybody. "What were you girls doing over there anyway? You onto something I should know about?"

"What did you tell him we were doing?"

"I told him you were looking for Monarch butterflies."

I laughed. "In December? Did he believe you?"

"I told him a bunch of them got blown off course on their way to Mexico." He shrugged. "He seemed to buy it." He stared off into space. "It would make a great story if it was true though, wouldn't it? Clusters of shivering butterflies clinging to the Christmas tree on the common, warming themselves by the lights?"

One thing I'll say for Scott, he has a great imagination.

I decided to share the reason Francine and I had stopped next to that particular yard though. After that butterfly story I felt that I owed him one. "We don't know exactly what we're onto. Maybe you can make some sense of it." I gave him a quick rundown on why we'd stopped, how I'd recognized the white van because I'd seen it when we covered the man on the roof story. "I know there's no reason why somebody couldn't use the same truck for two companies, but does it mean anything that both companies belong to a Historic Salem Charities board member?"

He did that eye contact thing again. "Are you thinking that has something to do with Eldridge's death? Murder?"

"I'm not sure what I think about it," I admitted. "But I can't stop thinking about it."

"Hmmm. I'll think about it too. Maybe do a little digging. I'll let you know if I turn up anything interesting. Have a good evening. See all you gorgeous ladies later." He left through the metal door leading to the news department and the downstairs studios.

I said good night to Rhonda, zipped up my jacket, and headed for the elevator. According to the gold sunburst clock it wasn't yet five o'clock. I wouldn't have time for a trip to the mall, but I could check out a few of the local shops for gifts before dinner time. Much of Salem's downtown Essex Street is arranged in the form of a pedestrian mall, which lends itself to easy shopping, strolling at one's own pace from store to store. Holiday season makes it extra festive with lights twinkling everywhere—strung across the street and from building to building. I parked in the municipal lot near the museum, locked the car and joined the crowd. A rocking version of "Rudolph the Red-Nosed Reindeer" was being piped in from some invisible source, and it seemed that everyone on the street—including me—walked in rhythm to the beat. Even the officer directing traffic on Hawthorne Boulevard had adapted his white gloved hand signals to the upbeat tempo of the old song.

The museum gift shop is always a great source of inspiration for people like me. I found a soft chiffon scarf for Aunt Ibby with detail from Childe Hassam's painting of Poppies, Isle of Shoals. I knew she would love it. I bought a box of Christmas cards with a color photo of a snow-covered House of Seven Gables. For Pete's oldest nephew, Colin, I decided on an optical illusion gadget called an infinity light. The one on display fascinated me. A series of lights within a picture frame appeared to lead off into, well—infinity. Unfortunately they also closely replicated the flashing lights that precede a vision. Before I could look away, the swirling colors materialized on the oblong surface too. Then the vision.

It's bad enough when these things pop up when I'm alone in my room, but this is a public place, with people all around.

Fortunately, it was a fast one. Blink. It was gone. But it had made its impression on my mind. This one seemed straightforward enough. It was my own front door, the door of the house on Winter Street. Not so elegant perhaps as the doorways of the mansions Francine and I had filmed, but quite beautiful in its own way. There was a

Christmas wreath surrounding the brass door knocker in the center of the white paneled entrance. The narrow windows on either side had traces of lacy frost accenting each pane. I'd automatically looked for O'Ryan's fuzzy face in his accustomed place behind the glass, waiting to greet me. He wasn't there. Instead I saw Frankie. Her mouth was open wide in, had I been able to hear it, what would have been an agonized yowl.

Trying hard to control shaking hands, I carried the scarf, the cards, and one of the prepackaged infinity lights to the cashier. Within minutes, my purchases wrapped and tucked into a holiday-themed museum shopping bag, headed for home. I was tempted to use the Winter Street entrance, just to see if O'Ryan would be in his usual place behind the glass.

That's just plain silly.

I drove down Oliver Street instead, hit the garage door opener, and put my car safely away beside my aunt's Buick. Balancing my purchases I made my way carefully along the darkened path, past the garden where leafless frozen branches had already taken on their fearsome nighttime shapes even though it was not yet even six o'clock. Would O'Ryan be waiting behind the back door as he always is when I use that entrance?

Of course he was. Why wouldn't he be? The cat unerringly knows which door he should choose for his welcoming greeting. Not just for me. He does the same for Aunt Ibby and Pete and River and sometimes for the pizza delivery man.

So where was he in the vision? I felt a chill that had nothing to do with the weather.

CHAPTER 25

I was so happy to see O'Ryan that I picked him up and gave him a kiss on top of his head. He accepted the unusual display of affection with typical catlike aplomb, giving me a lick on the cheek in return. Wonderful aromas wafted from Aunt Ibby's kitchen. I tapped on her door which she opened immediately. "Come in, Maralee. You too O'Ryan." She eyed the colorful shopping bag on my arm. "Christmas shopping?"

O'Ryan hopped down and ran to his favorite captain's chair. "I'll just drop these off upstairs," I told her, "and I'll be right back. Oh, I invited Pete for dinner. That's okay, isn't it?'

"Of course. I thought you might. Roast beef is one of his favorites. I baked a pie too."

I hurried up the stairs to my apartment, passing through my living room, picturing how a lighted tree would look in the big bay window, and clicked on the kitchen overhead light. I draped my jacket over the back of a Lucite chair, knowing I'd be wearing it later in the evening, and put my new purchases on top of the bureau with the others. The pile was growing. Well begun is half done.

That's one of Aunt Ibby's favorite sayings. I know it applies to more than Christmas shopping.

But a pile of scribbled index cards that added up to total confusion, a string of visions that made no sense at all, and unanswered questions about murder—these were not well begun and certainly nowhere near done. I exited through my kitchen door and stepped out into the maroon-carpeted hall. I avoided looking at the attic door and started down the curving stairway to the first floor.

Aunt Ibby's living room opens directly into the front hall. Her Christmas tree was so beautiful, I had to stop in the arched doorway and just stare at it. All of the decorations and lights I remembered so fondly from my childhood in this house were there—the bubble lights and the blond angel at the top. Good memories. I heard Pete's voice and hurried through the dining room and back to the kitchen.

"Hi, Ms. Russell. Smells great in here." He'd apparently picked O'Ryan up in the back hall and carried him inside, much as I had. If the cat was surprised by such unusual attention, he was much too cool to show it. Pete deposited him gently on the floor and greeted me with a discreet hug. "Hi Babe. Thanks for inviting me. Ready for some Christmas tree shopping? That big tree lot over on the Boulevard got a new shipment of nice blue spruce from North Carolina this afternoon."

"I can hardly wait," I said. "The proverbial spirit of Christmas hit me just today. It's everywhere. Christmas music on Essex Street, a dancing traffic cop, it's all good."

"Can we help you with anything, Ms. Russell?" Pete glanced around the kitchen.

"I seem to recall that you're good with a carving knife, Pete." She gestured to the beautiful roast on the cutting board. "And Maralee, want to mash the potatoes?"

"I guess I can handle that." My aunt instructed Alexa to play Christmas music and together the three of us carved and mashed and ladled and arranged the lovingly prepared food in beautiful vintage bowls and plates and carried our bounty into the dining room where the table was set with Aunt Ibby's best Christmas dinnerware with its bright borders of holly. The centerpiece was a silver prancing reindeer surrounded by red carnations among evergreen boughs and flanked with red candles in tall silver holders.

"Wow. I feel as though I should have dressed up for dinner," Pete said.

"Me too. This looks extra festive."

My aunt looked around the room with satisfaction. "You know, I won't be here to share Christmas with you, so I'm planning to celebrate the season as much as possible before I leave. I love decorating. I love grandmother Forbes's silver reindeer and all the old lights and tree decorations."

We took our seats, snowy white napkins in our laps. "When are you flying off to London, Ms. Russell?" Pete asked.

"Louisa and I have reservations for the week before Christmas, the day after the Belles concert," she said.

"I'll bet Nigel has some exciting adventures planned for you over there," I said. "London must be beautiful at holiday time."

"He knows the city very well. I don't know exactly what he has planned for us." Did I detect a hint of a blush? (She's so darned cute I just wanted to jump up and hug her.) Nigel is with New Scotland Yard, so I was sure he knew London the way Pete knows Salem. It goes with the policeman's job. That made me think of the house I'd been chased away from by the yelling man.

"Pete, do you know if that house where I got yelled at belongs to the Historical Charities?"

He looked quickly in my aunt's direction. "It's okay. She knows about my little adventure."

Aunt Ibby made a small "tsk-tsk" sound and shook her head.

"Not yet," he said, putting a second helping of spinach soufflé onto his plate. "Although according to Gillette they have an option to buy that one and a few others on the same street."

"I guess then that it's the proposed site for Mr. Eldridge's Heritage Village."

"I hope they'll be able to complete his plans," Aunt Ibby said. "What a shame Albert can't be here to see it. That dear man will be missed by so many. Pete, have you learned any more about the man on the video? The man with the suitcase?"

"We've got some tech people trying to enhance the thing. Hoping we can get a look at his face, but so far nothing new there."

"What about the witness? Vincent Drake? Has he remembered anything else?"

"He's added a little something to his story. He's not the most reliable person in the world you know, but he says he thinks the guy might have had somebody else with him."

Aunt Ibby's eyes sparkled with interest. "Really? What makes him think so?" I had to smile at her enthusiasm. *Charlie's angel?*

"This doesn't show on the video at all, but he says that he saw the man making a signal with his free hand, like this." Pete extended his right hand with the palm cupped and moved it back and forth as though he was beckoning someone to come to him. "He says he kept doing it until he was out of sight. As though he was telling someone with him to hurry up."

"Of course," I reasoned. "It happened near the hotel and maybe it was just a couple of people checking out and one was lagging behind." That made sense to me.

"Uh-uh. We checked with the hotel. No early checkouts at all that day," Pete said. "I think the guy might know something about this case. So does the chief."

"Your work is so interesting, Pete. Here, have some more mashed potatoes." She piled some onto his plate. "More gravy? What does Chief Whaley think about the poor boy who tried to jump off that rooftop? Do they know why he did it?"

"I haven't discussed it with him," Pete said, accepting the gravy boat. "Sergeant Rouse is working that one."

"I went to school with Joyce Rouse, Aunt Ibby. I could call her."

"That would be nice," my aunt said. "His mother seems like a good person. Did you watch Buck Covington's interview with her, Pete?"

"Nope. Lee told me about it though."

"I talked to her after the interview." I took one last bite of the perfectly pink-centered roast beef. "I asked her a few of the questions Buck missed. Off the record, of course."

"Anything I should know about?" Pete asked.

"You already had all the important stuff. It was about the driver's licenses and birth certificates."

"Yeah. Guess Joseph Marshall will have all that to deal with when he gets out of the hospital. Doesn't look good for him."

"Bad enough to make him want to die?" I wondered aloud.

"I don't know the answer to that one, Babe." Pete

looked down at his plate. "People do strange things sometimes. Things that make no sense."

"You've got that right," I said. "There seem to be a lot of things that don't make sense going on around here lately.'"

"More than usual?" Aunt Ibby stood up. "Maralee, if you and Pete will clear the table, I'll bring in dessert."

"I think so, even for Salem." I gathered the plates and glassware while Pete piled the serving dishes and glassware onto the wheeled serving cart which has been in the dining room for as long as I can remember. It is, I suppose, a remnant of the days when people had household help. The two-tiered cart has a glass top covering assorted butterflies arranged on white cottony stuff Aunt Ibby says is milkweed.

"This thing is so cool," Pete said, wheeling it carefully into the kitchen. "Except for the dead butterflies."

"Shhh. It's a family heirloom. Belonged to my great grandmother," I whispered, then giggled, remembering Scott's preposterous butterfly story. "You were right about the man calling the station about my trespassing."

"Uh-oh. Did you get in trouble?" Pete asked.

"Oh dear, Maralee. You didn't tell me that." My aunt lifted the mile-high lemon meringue pie carefully from the refrigerator. "Pete will you pour the coffee?"

"I'd kind of forgotten. Nothing happened. Scott Palmer took the call and gave the guy the most amazing excuse."

As we returned to the dining room, following Aunt Ibby with the pie on the cart, Pete carrying our coffees on a tray, I repeated Scott's tale of the shivering butterflies on the Christmas tree.

"That is a wonderful Christmas story!" My aunt put the pie on the table. "Scott should put it into a children's book. Think of the illustrations. Marvelous!"

"And Santa Claus can take the butterflies to Mexico on his sleigh," Pete added.

"Yes," Aunt Ibby agreed.

"It's not my story," I said. "But I'll suggest it to Scott."

"See, babe? Some things make sense after all," Pete said. "And the most sensible thing I can think of is let's cut this beautiful pie and eat it."

Aunt Ibby cut the pie into generous slices. "Maralee, exactly what things don't make sense to you? You sounded quite serious about that."

Wishing I hadn't even mentioned it, I tried to dodge the subject. I realized that most of what didn't make sense to me—as usual—was the damned visions and I didn't want to talk about them. "I guess I'm overreacting. Too many things on my mind."

"You did sound serious, Lee." Pete frowned. "Anything I can help with?"

I had to say something. "I don't think so. First, of course is Mr. Eldridge's murder. Why would anyone want to harm him? And other than a shadowy figure on a grainy tape, you have no real suspects, do you?"

"Not yet. I mean it's one of those times when no one is a suspect because everyone is a suspect. You could be right that the guy on the tape has nothing to do with the murder." He put his fork down. "But I sure would like to talk to him. Maybe he saw something."

I was getting warmed up to the subject. "Do you even know how the killer got into his office? There are doors all over that house. Inside and outside. Front and back and side. Yet the officer said there was no sign of a break in."

Doors again. Why?

"True."

Aunt Ibby pointed in my direction with the pie server. "I've been thinking about the case too, Maralee. Why did

Albert have a Santa Claus hat on so early in the morning? Do you know, Pete?"

"That's an easy one. I asked Ms. Jeffry that almost as soon as we started the investigation. He'd decided to surprise some of the people who helped the society by delivering their Christmas gifts in person. He'd had her select a Santa hat for him the day before. She said he was already wearing it when she saw him working on his ledger when she arrived at work."

"Delivering gifts wearing a Santa hat. That's the kind of thing Alfred would do," Aunt Ibby agreed.

"But he wasn't working on his ledger, was he?" I asked. "He was already dead."

"That's right. But she couldn't know that. You didn't know it until you pushed him."

"Tapped lightly," I insisted. "Didn't push. But you're right. He didn't look dead. He looked like he'd dozed off."

"I know. Shocked poor Ms. Jeffry big time."

"Me too. But had he delivered any of the gifts?" I wondered. "You said she'd given him the hat the day before."

Pete looked surprised. "I don't know. That's a very good question, Lee. A very damned good question."

CHAPTER 26

After dinner Pete and I headed out into the cold—still no flurries—in Aunt Ibby's Buick. Two Christmas trees, even if one of them was small, wouldn't fit in or on the Corvette. Even if they would, there's no way I would risk that gorgeous paint job, and we knew that Chief Whaley would take a dim view of trees tied to the roof of a detective's unmarked car. Anyway, my aunt had insisted that we use hers and Pete figured he could stash the table tree for the kid's room in the trunk of the Crown Vic later.

"The tree lot with the really good selection is just past the Nathaniel Hawthorne statue," he said. "Close to downtown and well lighted. Opens early and closes late. The place is so popular they get tree shipments every other day."

"I'm excited about it," I said. "Will you help me get the tree stand and stuff out of the attic tonight?"

He squeezed my hand. "Of course I will. I know that place still spooks you."

I returned the squeeze. "Thank you," I whispered. "I'm sure O'Ryan would go up there with me, but he doesn't like it either."

"Is the white cat still hanging around?"

"I haven't seen her lately. We've figured out that she's feral you know, and it's really a wonder she trusts us as much as she apparently does."

We heard the Christmas music before we reached the tree lot. "I saw Mommy Kissing Santa Claus" rang out from hidden speakers around the large fenced area where varicolored lights twinkled among hundreds of trees of all sizes and shapes.

"So that's where the music comes from," I said. "I could hear it plainly way over by the museum."

"I know. We've had a couple of complaints about it from neighbors. They say he starts it as soon as he opens the lot in the morning and sometimes it plays until almost midnight."

"Only a couple?"

Pete smiled. "I was surprised too. But, it's pleasant music, and the weather is cold enough so that people have their windows closed." He shrugged. "This neighborhood is mostly stores and offices anyway and it's probably good for business."

"And dancing traffic cops," I said.

"Yep. Traffic cops too." Pete parked the Buick close to the temporary chicken wire fence. "Ready to pick out your tree?"

"Oh, yes." He opened the passenger side door and I stepped out into winter fresh air where snow flurries had begun to fall ever so softly. The scent of spruce and evergreen surrounded us. It was a magical moment.

It didn't take long for us to make our selections. A seven-foot Scotch pine for my house and a diminutive Fraser fir for Marie and Donnie's boys. (Yes, Pete's sister and brother-in-law are named Donnie and Marie.) Pete secured both trees to the roof of the Buick with bungee cords. "The Little Drummer Boy" provided background music as we started for home.

"That was really fun, Pete, really special. Thank you for thinking of it."

"I love sharing special times with you," he said. "I hope we can share lots more of them together."

"I do too," I said, meaning it. "Lots more."

Pete parked the Buick in the driveway behind the house and together we managed to maneuver the small tree into the trunk of his car. Then, with me on one side and Pete on the other, and with considerable muffled laughter, we wrestled the bushy-branched, seven-foot tall tree off the roof.

"Now we have to get it up two flights of stairs," I said. "How're we going to do that?"

"I guess we should use the front door instead of this one." He pointed to the back door. "That staircase is too narrow and twisty." We both dissolved into laughter again because neither of us had figured that out in advance. Pete returned the Buick to the garage, then with him carrying the trunk end and with me hanging onto the top, we trudged through the yard, around the house, and out onto the Winter Street brick sidewalk.

I pulled the keys from my purse and sneaked a look at the side window while I unlocked the front door. O'Ryan looked back at me. The right cat at the right door as usual.

Aunt Ibby greeted us as we entered the foyer. "My, that tree is a beauty," she said. "Good thing we have high ceilings in this old house."

"Did we disturb you?" I asked, concerned that our laughter and bumping around in the yard might have been too noisy.

"Not at all. I was watching TV with O'Ryan when he

ran to the back door, then changed his mind and fairly flew through the house to this one. So I followed him to see what was going on."

"No wonder he was confused. We changed our minds too," I explained. "Now to get this beauty upstairs."

"Good luck. Come on, O'Ryan."

We bumped and struggled our way up the (thankfully) broad staircase, through my kitchen and hall, moved my beautiful carousel horse to one side, and leaned the tree against the bay window.

Pete brushed his hands together. "Okay. So far, so good. You sure there's a tree stand up there?" He pointed to the ceiling. "And plenty of decorations? It's a big tree."

"Yeah. I noticed that. Let's go up there and get it over with."

Once out in the maroon-carpeted hall, with Pete at my side, I stopped short in front of the door to the attic. "Pete," I said, "I've been having visions about doors. About this one, and others. I'm really afraid to open it right now."

He put a protective arm around my shoulders and guided me back into the kitchen. "Here. Sit down and tell me about it. You don't have to open that door if you don't want to. I'll go up and get the decorations." He pulled out a chair for me, then sat in another one close beside mine. "You turned pale back there. You're really frightened. Talk to me."

So I did. I talked about the doors. Not just the vision doors, the ones about the attic and the front door of the house, but about the Chestnut Street doors and the Historical Charities door and all the other doors I'd been thinking about lately. Maybe obsessing about.

Pete listened quietly, never interrupting, just holding my hands, his eyes on mine, listening. When I'd finished, he remained silent for a long moment. "Oh, babe." He spoke softly. “I wish I could help you make sense out of all this. I wish we could figure out together what the doors mean, if they mean anything. Doors can mean good things, can’t they? New opportunities? Entering new fields? New beginnings? I don’t know. Good things. Happy things.”

“You’re right,” I said. “I feel better just telling you about them. I’m sure I’ll learn what they mean before long. I always do.”

“Yes. You do. Now I want you to just relax. I’ll make us some decaf, then I’ll go up and get the Christmas things.” He opened the coffee canister.” Do you think you’d like to decorate the tree tonight?”

“I think so,” I said, “and Pete . . .”

“Yes?”

“Nothing. I love you.”

I sat in my pretty kitchen and sipped on the coffee Pete had poured for me, feeling a little bit ashamed of myself for getting so emotional over some doors. Not even real ones. Visualized doors. Imaginary doors. Dream doors. Pete had gone up into the attic without me and I was truly glad that I didn’t have to go up there tonight. I’d been in that long, clean room, smelling of pine wood and cedar closets, numerous times since it had been rebuilt. Never liked it, but never felt the fright I’d felt standing in front of that door less than an hour ago.

Pete had left the kitchen door open, so I heard his footsteps as he descended the attic stairs. In a moment he appeared, smiling, on the threshold, both arms piled high with boxes, the green metal tree stand precariously balanced on top of the pile. “I think I got everything,” he said. “They were all right where you said they’d be. That has to be the most organized attic space I’ve ever seen.”

“I know it is. Aunt Ibby designed it that way. ‘A place

for everything and everything in its place.'" I reached up for the tree stand carried it into the living room. Pete followed with the boxes containing my collection of lights and tinsel and colorful balls and crocheted angels and crystal snowflakes and assorted Santas I'd accumulated through the years. We arranged the boxes along the length of the couch and on the coffee table.

"I was worried that you might not have enough decorations for such a tall tree," Pete said. "But you sure do. Anyway, I brought you another one." He handed me a small oblong box. "Go ahead. Open it."

I love presents. Always have. And I already knew that Pete was a really good present picker. I carefully lifted the lid from the box, and pushed aside blue tissue paper. It was a golden-colored blown glass cat and it was absolutely exquisite. "Oh, Pete," I said. "It's wonderful. I love it." I picked up the delicate ornament and turned it in my hands. Its painted collar was set with tiny jewels and the eyes were totally catlike.

"The man in the shop said it comes from Poland. Mouth blown, hand-painted glass. I was sure you'd like it." I knew he was as pleased because I loved the gift as I was to receive it. I reached up to kiss him. That kiss almost completely derailed our decorating plans, but after a while we opened the boxes on the couch and table, strung lights, placed ornaments and tinsel just so, and made sure that the new cat had a place of honor at the front of the tree.

It was close to eleven when we stood back, admiring our work, and leaving the Christmas lights glowing because we couldn't bear to turn them off, headed for the bedroom.

The dream, when it came, seemed familiar. It was very much like the vision I'd had in the museum store. I approached the front door of the Winter Street house. This time there were no cats, either white or yellow striped, peering from the side window. I pushed the unlocked door open. The foyer was empty. No hall tree. No paintings on the wall. I looked through the arched doorway into Aunt Ibby's living room. There was nothing there either. I walked across a bare floor to the dining room. Empty, as was the kitchen. I didn't look any further. I knew there would be nothing anywhere in the whole house.

CHAPTER 27

In the morning I told Pete about the nightmare, if that's what it was. I was surprised, as we lingered over morning coffee and toaster waffles with real Vermont maple syrup, how unemotional I felt as I relayed what I'd seen in the dream.

"So you opened the door and there was nothing behind it," he said. "That sounds like some kind of symbolism, doesn't it? Maybe our friend River would have some ideas about it."

"That's a good idea," I said. "I'll call her today."

I planned to do exactly that. River stays up so late because of the show, that I never call her before late afternoon. Francine and I were kept pretty busy during the day—I suggested a trip to the tree lot which turned out well. The proprietor of the place was a funny guy who told us some cute stories about customers. We got some nice shots of the dancing traffic cop too, though he couldn't leave his post to talk with us. He clearly didn't mind being on TV though and made some extra-fancy moves for Francine's camera. Later in the day we covered a craft fair at an assisted living community where residents had turned out an amazing variety of gift items. We got a feel-good segment for the viewers and I crossed off a couple more names from my list with the purchase of a pair of hand-knit mittens and a pig-shaped cutting board.

Just before I left the station at five I called River and asked her what she knew about door dreams. "Are they doors in your own house?" she asked right away.

"Yes." That surprised me, even though she's a witch and I'm getting used to her surprises. "How did you know that?"

She laughed. "I didn't know it, you big silly. I'm not a psychic for heaven's sake. I asked because that's usually a good sign. It can mean opportunity or fulfilment. It's like clearing the decks for something new coming into your life. Did it feel like that?"

I thought about the dream. "No. It wasn't a particularly good feeling. I felt, well, kind of detached about it, even though it was my house."

"Interesting," she said. "I think it could mean opening another door, a figural one, and learning that something you were sure was there, really isn't." Little sigh. "Sorry. That's not much help is it? I'll come over this weekend and read your cards if you want."

I thanked her, told her I'd let her know about the offered reading. The Tarot can be just as confusing as the visions and I was confused enough as it was.

Something I'm sure exists really doesn't.

I thanked her again. "The more I think about it, River, the more I think that second explanation might be the right one."

"You do? Good. You'll let me know when you figure it out, won't you?"

I promised I would and said good-bye. I stayed around

for Wanda's weather forecast. Cloudy and cold for the rest of the week. More snow coming later.

I drove home slowly and carefully and thought some more about what River had told me.

Something I'm sure exists really doesn't. It was a thought both comforting and frightening. I shook it away and concentrated on the road.

I could see my lighted bay window from Oliver Street even before I'd reached the house. Pete had fixed up an automatic timer so that the lights turned on at sunset. Beautiful! I parked, locked the garage, and still admiring my tree in the window, picked my way along the path which by then had a light coating of snow. O'Ryan had ventured outside, via the cat door, and waited for me on the back steps. I received the usual welcoming purrs and meows and once again, picked him up and carried him inside. "Your bottom must be cold, cat," I told him. "Thanks for coming outside for me in the snow." I put him down as I passed the laundry room. He ran ahead of me and started up the stairs.

"Is that you, Maralee?" my aunt called from inside her kitchen. "O'Ryan has been pacing the floor waiting for you. Is he out there with you?"

"He was," I answered. "He's already on his way up to my place."

She opened her door and peeked out. "He seems anxious about something."

"He does? Seemed like his old sweet self to me. I'll keep an eye on him."

"Good. He's been going up and down the front stairs, in your kitchen cat door, out the back one, and back in through mine."

"Sounds to me like some kind of new kitty game he's thought up. I'll keep an eye on him," I promised again, and started up the narrow, twisty staircase to home, cat, and Christmas tree.

As soon as I stepped into the living room, I realized that something was amiss. Colorful bulbs still shone, the golden cat still gleamed in their reflected glow. But beneath the tree, where I hoped to see presents piled soon, were several scattered ornaments. I looked around the room for the only suspect.

O'Ryan sat in the zebra print chair, calmly grooming his luxurious whiskers like some kind of feline Hercule Poirot. I pointed to the evidence. "Did you do this?"

He gave me his round-eyed "who, me?" look and proceeded to lick his right paw and begin his ear-washing ablutions.

"You're a naughty boy," I muttered, tossing my jacket, purse, and the bag containing mittens and pig onto the couch and bending to pick up the cast-off trinkets. "Look at this!" I scolded. "I got this plastic Santa Claus from my third-grade teacher, Miss White, for getting an A in drawing."

(Cat switches paws and washes other ear. Ignores annoyed woman.)

I held another ornament aloft, this one enhanced with red glitter. "Oh, you are in big trouble, cat. I bought this on my first trip to New York, to see the Macy's parade." I had to scooch down and reach under the lowest branches of the tree to reach the Santa Claus in a convertible sports car. "Johnny gave me this. You are a terrible cat." I sat on the floor and fought back tears. "This one was special. I'm really angry with you now." I hurriedly scooped up the remaining three baubles on the floor and began hanging all of them back onto the tree. I looked back at the offending animal, who by then sat upright in the chair, regarding me with an unrepentant stare.

I looked at the tree, then at the ornament in my hand—a Santa riding on a pink flamingo—a souvenir from Sunken Gardens in St. Petersburg—then back at O'Ryan.

"Wait a minute. They're all Santa Clauses."

Still holding the flamingo Santa, I sat on the couch and faced the cat. "You weren't just being naughty, were you? You're trying to tell me—us—something."

He crouched then, not breaking eye contact, and said what sounded surprisingly like "Duh."

"Yeah. I know. I should have figured that out right away. But what? What about Santa Claus?"

Apparently through with the conversation, he stretched, jumped lightly down from his chair, and with an impudent flick of his tail, left the room via the cat door.

I replaced flamingo Santa on the tree, gathered up my belongings from the couch, and walked slowly down the hall to the kitchen. I hung up my jacket, put the presents on the bureau, then sat at the table in the chair next to the window and looked out into the darkness.

Santa Clauses, empty rooms, doors, more doors, Scrooge, Agatha Christie. Something I'm sure exists really doesn't.

"Which all adds up to a big fat nothing," I told myself. "So get up and do something useful." I did. Two rolls of gift wrapping paper, one with Santa Clauses, one with snowmen, red and green crinkle ribbon, cellophane tape, gift tags, and boxes. I began wrapping presents to put under my tree.

CHAPTER 28

Isn't it always the case? It starts around Halloween and increases in volume and frequency until by December it's a pounding, constant din. Radio, television, newspapers, flashing neon signs, then 12 shopping days until Christmas! 11 . . . 10 . . . 9. It was getting awfully close.

Mr. Pennington's play—*Hercule Poirot's Christmas*—was scheduled for Saturday night. This was Friday and it was already sold out. Mr. Pennington gave me much more credit than I deserved for that. He thought the interview had worked PR magic. I knew better. The public has a short memory. Most playgoers wouldn't connect the play with current events anyway, however similar in nature they might be. Murder onstage is a lot different than murder for real. I was positive about that from personal experience. However, Mr. Pennington had gifted me with two tickets which I gratefully accepted, deserved or not. Aunt Ibby had a freebie too.

At the station, Francine and I had been kept pretty busy with a steady stream of feel-good holiday presentations. I fed carrots to reindeer at a petting zoo and informed viewers that reindeer, also known as caribou, are the only members of the deer family in which both boy and girl reindeer have antlers. (News to me!) I interviewed a glass blower and I, along with the WICH-TV audience, learned how blown glass Christmas ornaments are made and I gained a new appreciation for my golden cat. We did an outdoor stand-up at the annual Santa Claus parade while children and adults alike cheered his arrival by fire truck. Then we did an indoor stand-up at the children's ward at Salem Hospital where the same Santa delivered dolls and action figures to sick kids. There wasn't a flag on his red hat, so I assumed he was a professional Santa, not one of the many volunteer veterans.

It appeared that the much anticipated lighted boat parade would take place as planned on Sunday night, weather permitting. Aunt Ibby wasn't due to leave for London for a week yet, but her bags were already packed. I still had cards to address and packages to mail. That had to be top priority if they were going to get to their destinations by Christmas. Pete's nephews had a hockey game in Beverly, so my Friday night would be free. I made myself a solemn promise to spend it taking care of all of the addressing, and to get to the post office first thing Saturday morning for mailing.

I set myself up a neat workstation on the Lucite table, making sure I had several good pens, a black Sharpie, a pile of "If It Fits It Ships" boxes, my address book, and plenty of holiday stamps. Packages first. That was the easy part. Then on to the cards. I'd bought fifty, hoping that would be plenty. I signed the first one, tucked it into an envelope, and wrote the address as neatly as I could. I thought about the stacks of cards Lilly Jeffry had addressed in that perfect cursive and tried even harder for neatness—if not beauty—on the second one. And the third. And all the way up to forty-nine. (It's a good thing they include an extra envelope in those boxes. I messed up a couple of them toward the end.)

By ten-thirty I'd finished the chore, vowing to start in November next year, cleaned up the kitchen table, and stacked cards and packages on the living room coffee table, ready to take to the post office in the morning. I brought along the lone extra card too, and one of the pens in case I thought of somebody I'd missed.

Congratulating myself on a job well done, I put on my Lanz nightie, poured myself a glass of wine, told Alexa to shuffle Christmas carols, sat down with O'Ryan in the zebra chair, and admired my tree.

I don't usually fall asleep sitting up, but that Friday night I did, and I had a dream about Christmas cards. I saw myself putting a stack of cards into a wire basket marked "outgoing." I knew where I was in the dream. I saw the grandfather's clock and the closed door to Albert E.'s office. I looked down at the envelope on top of the pile. What lovely handwriting.

I woke suddenly. Had the cat moved? Had there been a sound from outside? I don't know. But on waking, I still had a clear picture of that envelope in my mind. All of it. I even saw the stamp with a red candle on it. I saw the complete address and the name of the company it was addressed to. Acme Plumbing. I know how fast dreams can disappear, so I grabbed the pen and scribbled the address onto that last envelope. Then I set my alarm for seven and O'Ryan and I went to bed.

In the morning I fixed my breakfast of orange juice, a Raspberry Toaster Strudel, and a cup of reheated coffee. I'll grab a fresh cup at Dunkin Donuts on my way to the post office. In the living room I picked up the pile of red, white, and blue mailing packages, put the addressed envelopes into a canvas Wolf Hill Nurseries bag, and with car keys and wallet in jacket pockets started for the door. I noticed the unstamped envelope on the coffee table with its messy scrawled address.

What's this?

A fuzzy version of the dream came back, not with detail, not with clarity, but enough so I remembered what I'd written and why I'd written it. The Acme Plumbing Company must be one of the companies Mr. Eldridge used. It was also the name on the white cargo van. The van bore no address or phone number. I'd found that odd at the time.

Maybe after I mail this stuff, I'll just buzz on past there.

I thought about what Pete would say, but it was broad daylight on a Saturday morning. What could go wrong?

I stuffed the envelope into my pocket, held the door open for O'Ryan, and followed him down the stairs. He ducked into his own entrance to Aunt Ibby's kitchen, and I went outdoors into a cold, sort of damp, New England winter morning. As I drove down Oliver Street with the heater cranked up I told myself once again how impractical my car is for winter in Salem—but then remembered how much fun it is all the rest of the year and decided not to worry about it. There was a line at the post office. (I'm not the only person around here who leaves card and package mailing until the last minute.) Everyone in the line was good natured about the wait and there were choruses of "Merry Christmas" and "Happy Holidays." It was with a self-satisfied feeling that I handed over my missives, paid extra to get the packages to their destinations by Christmas, climbed back into my impractical but gorgeous vehicle, and drove to the nearest Dunkin Donuts drive-through.

I pulled the crumpled envelope with its all but indecipherable handwriting from my pocket. The address wasn't far away, though it was in a neighborhood I wasn't particularly familiar with. Salem is a big enough city so that even people who have lived here for many years occasionally find themselves in places they've never seen before. That's what happened to me. It was a winding little side street. I drove slowly, watching for numbers on the buildings. There were several single homes and a couple of taller building which may have been apartment houses. Was this a wild goose chase? After all, I was basing this venture on a dream.

I finally spotted a mailbox with a number on it in front of one of the houses. It was an odd number, as was the number I'd written on the envelope. That meant I was at least looking on the correct side of the street. I slowed down some more and arrived at what appeared to be my destination. The small brown-shingled house with two large bay windows in the front was next to a vacant lot. The street number was posted over the door in tarnished metal numerals. It looked like a private home which had at some point been used as a small neighborhood store. There were even faint traces of letters that had once spelled out Salada Tea on one of the windows. I parked and looked up and down the street. Didn't see any people around, though there were vehicles parked on both sides. Still, I thought twice about getting out of the car. Then, once again, I told myself, It's broad daylight on Saturday morning. What can go wrong? I got out, locked the doors and approached the house. There was a lone dusty black valise in the Salada Tea window with various sizes and curvatures of white PVC pipe sticking out at odd angles along with a rusty pail containing assorted worn-looking wrenches and screwdrivers. A cardboard sign in the other window proclaimed ACME PLUMBING. I stepped into the covered entranceway between the bay windows and turned the knob. It didn't budge so, shading my eyes with one hand, I peered through the multipaned window in the top half of the door.

There was a desk in there. And a chair. I didn't see anything else. *How very odd.* I backed up for a moment, then looked in again. There was something on the floor just inside the door. Envelopes. Quite a few of them. Somebody in the Acme Plumbing Company hadn't picked up their mail recently. Was it my imagination, or did one of those envelopes have a stamp with a red candle on it? Was what I could see of the address written in perfect cursive?

I didn't have time to take a closer look. Maybe I'd been concentrating so hard that I wasn't paying enough attention to my surroundings. The voice came from directly behind me. The man stood at the edge of the sidewalk, blocking my way out of the space between the windows.

"Can I help you, young lady?"

I turned and faced Richard McNally. He wasn't smiling.

CHAPTER 29

"Are you looking for anyone in particular?" The man took a step closer.

It's broad daylight on Saturday morning and I'm scared to death.

Think fast, I told myself. "Um, my name is Lee Barrett. I'm a reporter for WICH-TV."

"Yes. I recognized you. How can I help you?" Still not smiling. Still blocking my exit.

"I, um, I wanted to apologize to a man who works for this company. I was working on a story and I guess I trespassed on his property. Well, I guess he's not here." I attempted a brave little smile of my own. "I'll try to catch him later." *I wonder if I can squeeze past this guy without actually touching him.*

"Oh. I get it now." He nodded his head, still not moving away from me.

"You do?"

"The butterflies."

Thank you, Scott Palmer. "Right," I said. "The butterflies. Will you tell that man that I'm sorry if I startled him?"

He stepped aside then. "That was quite a story."

"Yes. Well, you have a nice day." I moved toward my car, reaching into my pocket for the keys.

"Wait a minute." He touched my arm, ever so gently.

I froze. "What?" My voice sounded strange, even to me.

"What happened?"

"What happened?" I echoed.

"To the butterflies."

Has Scott's silly alibi become some kind of an urban legend already? This man is definitely not going to buy the Santa Claus ending.

Think fast. What becomes of wayward butterflies? A fifth-grade science class trip to Boston came to mind.

"I never did catch up with them," I said. "I heard that someone from the Museum of Science rescued them. Took them to their butterfly garden. Well, good-bye now. Merry Christmas." I sprinted toward the car, hit the unlock button, and slid into my seat. I dared a look back. McNally stood just where I'd left him, still watching me, still not smiling. I restrained myself from burning rubber all the way down that strange little street.

I'd intended to do a little more shopping, but after my encounter with the real estate owner, all I wanted to do was go home. I passed the Salem Common, paying particular attention to the bandstand where the community Christmas tree glowed with color, even in the daylight, and where I couldn't help picturing clusters of butterflies nestled among the branches. The squirrel lady was on her usual bench and dogs chased Frisbees, moms pushed strollers, several kite flyers took advantage of the brisk wind, and there was even one drone flyer there. All nice and normal.

I turned onto Winter Street, parked in front of the house, and hurried up the steps. I could already see O'Ryan peeking from the side window. I turned my key in the lock, welcoming the warm air and the scent from a basket of cinnamon-fragranced pinecones on the Sheraton table in the foyer. The cat greeted me with soft "merrous" and numerous trips in and out between my booted feet.

As I closed the door behind me O'Ryan darted through the archway into my aunt's living room, then sat, just over the threshold and looked at me, head tilted. It was his "well, what are you waiting for" look.

"You want me to follow you, right?" I asked. He scooted across the room, past the Christmas tree, which had many more presents beneath it than mine did, and into the dining room. "Aunt Ibby? It's me," I called as we neared the kitchen. "O'Ryan invited me in."

She stood beside the wide counter, wielding a pastry tube and swirling rich red frosting berries onto one of what looked like about a hundred cookies which already bore bright green holy leaves on white icing. "Come in, Maralee. I'm decorating Christmas cookies."

"I see that. Lots of them."

"I got to thinking about that women's shelter you visited. I thought they might enjoy some cookies over there, so I called. They said they'd love to have some." She gestured with the tube toward a stack of white boxes. "You can help me pack them up when I'm finished. I thought we'd tie each box with a red ribbon and put one of those big Santa Claus stickers on the top."

"Glad to," I said. "What a good idea. But watch O'Ryan around those stickers. He's developed some kind of attraction for Santas." I told her about the ornaments he'd knocked from my tree. "All Santas," I said, and lowered my voice. "Do you think it means something?"

She looked at the cat who was busily ignoring us, focusing his golden eyes on those invisible creatures cats sometimes seem to see dancing just above their heads. "It probably does, Maralee," she said, applying the last of the holly berries. "If it was just random items, that's one thing, but all Santas? That's specific."

I began arranging rows of cookies in the first box. "I know. But in a city crawling with dozens of them, how specific can it be?"

"Do you know any of them personally? That might be important."

"I've interviewed three of them," I said. "But I don't actually know any of them. Two of them go by Nick and Harry. The Santa who gave out gifts to the kids in the hospital didn't use any name except Santa Claus. Didn't want to confuse the kids I suppose."

"We can ask Rupert for his name when we go to the performance tonight," she said, "if you think it might be important. He told me that the city had hired one of the acting class students, a cast member as a matter of fact, to play Santa this year. Seemed quite proud about it."

"Probably isn't important, but since O'Ryan is interested in Santa, let's ask anyway." I tied a red bow on the box, put the sticker on top, and began the next one.

"Have you had an opportunity to talk with Sergeant Rouse yet? Ever since you spoke with the young man's mother I've wondered what will become of him."

"Joyce and I have been playing phone tag. I'll call her again right now." I tapped in the number. She answered right away. "Joyce," I said, "Got time for a quick question?"

"Hi, Lee. I guess you want to know about Joseph Marshall."

"I do. What's going to happen to him? Do you know?" Aunt Ibby leaned closer to me, straining to hear. "Mind if I put you on speaker? My Aunt Ibby is interested too."

"That's okay. Hi, Ms. Russell."

"Hello, Joyce. I hope you don't think we're just being nosey."

"Of course not. I'll tell you what I can. He's still under psychiatric observation. We're looking into the several complaints about his work. Turns out he's not licensed at all and we're trying to figure out if he's been able to obtain forged ones. That's where we stand right now."

"I see." I decided to push for a little more. "Have you learned anything interesting about the company he works for? I think it's called R. M. Real Estate?"

She paused. "There are things going on that I can't share. I'm sure you understand that, Lee."

"Sure do. Thanks Joyce. Merry Christmas if I don't see you before then."

We said our good-byes and went back to our cookie packing. "So now I wonder more than ever what's going on there, don't you?" my aunt asked. "What is it she can't tell us?"

"It's about the real estate company I think. I'd ask Pete," I said, "but I'm pretty sure he won't tell us either."

"Hmmmm," my aunt said.

"What hmmmm?" I asked. "What devious thing are you thinking?"

"Nothing. I wonder if that poor lad would like to have some nice Christmas cookies, that's all. Why don't we call his mother and ask her?"

"Well, she did say I could call her anytime," I said slowly, realizing that I've surely inherited the family devious gene. "I'll bet she's seen him, or at least spoken with him, since all this happened. Why not? I'll call her. About the cookies, I mean."

"About the cookies. Of course."

While my aunt finished the packaging, tying, and sticking, I dialed Mrs. Prescott. She was so pleased to see my name on her caller ID and she was so thrilled that I was calling her again, and all her girlfriends were so impressed that she knew a real TV star like me, and was it true that I used to be Crystal Moon?

With only the tiniest tinge of guilt, I insisted modestly that I'm not a TV star and admitted to being Crystal Moon. "My aunt and I were just decorating some homemade Christmas cookies, and it occurred to me that Joseph—um, Anthony—might like to have some, what with him being in the hospital and all."

"Oh, hon. If you aren't just the sweetest girl in the world! What a lovely idea. Thanks so much for thinking of my poor boy." She sniffled a little bit. "Brings tears to my eyes. Really. Say, you aren't married or anything, are you? Anthony is single, you know. Maybe, after all his trouble gets over with you two could get together!"

"I've got a steady guy," I said, trying hard to sound apologetic about it, "but you say Anthony is in trouble?"

"Sweetheart, you just don't know the half of it. Besides all those shrinks talking to him day and night, now some lady cop is over there yammering at him too." My listening aunt's head was on my shoulder by this time. I turned the phone as much as I could so she could hear everything. "It's bad enough," the distraught mother whispered, "that the poor kid was so scared that he was almost ready to jump off a building,"

"He was scared? Of what?"

Still whispering, "Somebody—he wouldn't tell me who, but it must be somebody important—told him that what he'd done could ruin everything and that they were going to make him pay."

"What's the 'everything'? Who's 'they' and what had he done?"

"See? That's what I don't know. Except for the business

cards and how bad could that be? But I'll bet he's going to keep acting crazy so they'll keep him safe in that hospital."

I felt sorry for her. "Do they let you see him?"

"I see him twice a week. I'll see him tomorrow. Through glass, you know, and there's a guard behind him." Her voice brightened. "But I'm sure they'll let him have cookies. They'll probably X-ray them though. Does that hurt them?"

"I'm sure it doesn't. If you'll give me your address I can drop the cookies off later today."

"Wonderful. Mind if I invite my girlfriend over? So she can see that I really know you?"

"Sure. That'll be fine. Around two o'clock?"

She recited an address not far from the women's shelter. That made our delivery schedule easy. We'd drop off half a dozen boxes at the shelter, then take the last two to Mrs. Prescott—one for herself and the other for Anthony.

After the conversation was finished and drop-offs decided on, my aunt made a pot of tea and two sandwiches—egg salad on toasted homemade sourdough bread—while I arranged a few left-over cookies on a plate. (Some of the cookies had turned out to be less than perfect, so we felt justified in consuming the evidence.) "She seems really concerned about those business cards." Aunt Ibby spoke thoughtfully.

"The cards say he's licensed and bonded. That would be false advertising at the very least," I offered. "I'm afraid he's got more problems than that. If Sergeant Rouse finds out that he's using forged license and insurance documents, I suppose the whole Prestigious Electrical Company is in trouble along with him."

My aunt agreed. "I'm guessing that's where the dead cousin Joey from Portland's identity comes in."

“He told his mom he was using the name for business reasons. I guess he was.”

“Monkey business.” She sniffed. “Sounds to me like he deserves whatever he’s got coming.” She looked down at the gaily wrapped red and white boxes. “But even criminals deserve a few cookies at Christmas, I guess. Shall we take my car?”

“Yes, please. Can’t fit much of anything in mine.”

CHAPTER 30

By one-thirty, lunch dishes washed and cookie boxes piled into the backseat of the Buick and with my aunt driving, we started for the women's shelter. "Wait till you see the kids," I told her. They're all so beautiful."

"I'm glad they have a safe, loving place to be for the holidays," she said. "Even though I'm sure it's stressful for them to be away from home."

"I know. Makes me even more grateful that I've always had you in my life."

"And you in mine. Listen. 'Away in a Manger.' Your friend the tree merchant certainly keeps the Christmas spirit going around here with his music. I enjoyed your interview with him."

"He plays it day and night, Pete says. But not too many people have complained about it so far."

"It just seems to suit the holiday mood," she said. "Snow flurries and Christmas trees and 'Silent Night' and 'Jingle Bells.' They all fit together perfectly."

Unlike my collection of index cards and visions and dreams and scattered tree ornaments and random doors and Agatha Christi and mythical butterflies. None of it fits together.

"And cookies," I added.

"And cookies," she agreed. We rode the rest of the way to the women's shelter with little conversation. "Where should we park?" she asked as we approached the shelter.

"Around back. There's a bell. Someone will let us in."

I balanced the six boxes while she pressed the doorbell. The general manager, Ms. Ahern, who'd greeted Francine and me, answered. "Come right on it, Ms. Barrett. We've been expecting you. We told the kids they're going to have a cookie party for snack time. They're so excited!"

I introduced my aunt and the three of us rode the elevator up to where the excited kids and smiling moms waited. A full-sized Christmas tree had replaced the small artificial one, and there were presents arranged beneath it. I realized that the kids had helped with decorations. Brightly colored construction paper garlands and strings of popcorn and cranberries were draped amid lights and ornaments. An angel in white satin with gauzy wings topped the tree, and muted Christmas music issued from a scuffed speaker box in the corner. Our guide took our coats and introduced us to the group, mentioning that Aunt Ibby was the one who'd baked the cookies. That brought a cheer. The moms and kids were invited to sit at a long table where a red plastic tablecloth and a centerpiece of candy canes and greenery added to the festive look of the room. Mismatched plates and drinking glasses were set at each place.

"Since Ms. Russell baked the cookies, perhaps she'll open the boxes," Ms. Ahern said. "Each of you may put two cookies onto your plate. Moms, will you take care of pouring the milk?" Aunt Ibby, looking pleased, distributed the cookies, pausing to speak softly to each child in turn.

I stood beside the GM, enjoying the scene. "Aren't they cute?" she asked. "They're so excited about Christmas. I had to limit them to two cookies each though. Too much sugar and I'll be pulling them down from the ceiling."

"Everything looks so nice here," I told her. "How are the finances coming along? Any improvement there?"

She sighed. "The contributions are up some, mostly due to your broadcast I'm sure, but we had an unexpected plumbing problem that set us back a bit. Our regular plumber did something wrong and nearly flooded the basement. Broken pipes. What a mess. So we had to call in another plumber to fix it. It's all working fine now, but it was expensive."

"I think my boss might let me do another piece from here," I said. "Maybe we can bring in some more contributions."

"What a blessing that would be," she said. "Every bit helps."

"Would you mind telling me the name of the plumber? The one who messed up?"

"Oh, I don't want to get anyone in trouble," she said. "He's a nice enough fellow. Just in over his head." She laughed. "With all that water in the basement, he nearly was."

"It'll be off the record," I promised. "I don't want to get anybody into trouble either."

"I could give you his business card," she said. "How's that?"

"Works for me."

"Hang on a sec. I'll run out to my desk and get it."

I joined my aunt at the end of the table, offering to help with the cookie dispensing. "Can't let you have all the fun," I whispered, untying the red ribbon from one of the boxes.

"Only two apiece," she warned. "Too much sugar isn't good for children."

"I know. You never let me have more than two when I was little either."

"And see how well you turned out!" She glanced at the clock on the wall. "How are we doing for time? Mrs. Prescott will be expecting us."

"You're right. I told her to expect us at around two."

Doris Ahern reappeared and handed me a card. I slipped it into my jeans pocket. "Thanks," I said. "We have to be leaving soon. More cookies to deliver. I'll speak to my boss about doing another piece about the shelter."

"Thank you both so much for coming," she said, then clapped her hands for attention. "Children? Say thank you to Ms. Russell and Ms. Barrett. I'll put the other boxes of cookies away for you to enjoy later."

That brought a low groan of protest about the cookie cut-off, then a rhythmic chanted "thank you Ms. Russell thank you Ms. Barrett." We retrieved our coats, wished the kids and moms happy holidays, and left that warm and welcoming room.

Aunt Ibby backed the Buick out of the narrow driveway and out onto the street. "Do you know how to get to the Prescott place?"

"I'm pretty sure I do. Not far from here. Couple of blocks down this street, then take a left." We found it right away. It was a trim two-story house with a small side yard surrounded by a chain-link fence. Like many Salem houses, the front door opened directly onto the sidewalk. An artificial Christmas wreath with a red plastic bow surrounded a brass pineapple-shaped doorknocker. I knocked and my aunt stood behind me carrying the two ribbon decked boxes of cookies.

We heard some high-pitched barking from inside, and

a "Hush, Snowball." Mrs. Prescott held a small, white Maltese in her arms, still barking but in a more subdued tone. "Come in, come in out of the cold. Gert! They're here." She waved her free hand toward a room on our right. "Hope you don't mind, I invited my girlfriend to meet you too. You must be Lee's Aunt Ibby Russell. Hi. I'm Clara Prescott. Come on in. I made coffee. You like coffee? I can make tea if you'd rather." We followed her through a tidy living room, past a white tree decorated with red and blue ornaments and blue lights, to the equally tidy kitchen. The mildly reprimanded Snowball, freed from his mistress's arms, scooted under the table, where a plump woman sat. Her white hair was streaked with spray-on color, red on one side, green on the other. She jumped to her feet on seeing us.

"Oh my God it's really you. I used to watch you all the time when you were on *Nightshades*. I loved that show. Clara says you're on the news all the time now."

"That's Gert," Clara Prescott said. "This lady with Lee is Ms. Russell, Lee's aunt."

"I think I know you from somewhere too," Gert said, squinting in my aunt's direction. "I know. The library. Right?"

"That's right," my aunt agreed, holding the cookie boxes in front of her. "Mrs. Prescott, I've brought a box of cookies for Anthony and one for you too."

"Oh, thanks so much." She accepted the boxes and put them on a nearby cabinet. "Thank you, Ibby. May I call you Ibby?"

"Of course, Clara. Pleased to meet you, Gert."

So that quickly, we were all on a first name basis.

"Please sit down, you two," Clara said. "Let's open one of these beautiful boxes and have them with our coffee. Would that be okay?"

"Of course it is," Aunt Ibby said, taking the chair next to the woman. "I do hope your son will enjoy his. You say you'll get to see him tomorrow?"

I sat beside Gert, who wanted to know if I knew River North and if she was as nice as she seemed to be. I assured her that River is one of my closest friends and one of the nicest people I'd ever met, which is true. At the same time, I didn't want to miss any of Aunt Ibby's conversation with Anthony/Joseph's mother. I leaned closer. Mrs. Prescott had lowered her voice but I caught the words "worried" and "shirts." My aunt nodded, her wise-old-owl expression in place, nibbled on a cookie, and sipped her coffee. "I see," she said. "I can see why you'd be concerned about that. What do you think, Maralee?"

"I'm sorry," I said, pleased that my wise-old-owl aunt was drawing me into the conversation. "I'm afraid I wasn't listening." Not true. I was listening intently. Just couldn't hear much of it. "You say you're concerned about Anthony?"

"It's the shirts. The work shirts. He said it's cold in that place, so he asked me to bring him a sweater. His Auntie Mae—she lives up in Maine—has knit him some beautiful ones. Sends him one every Christmas" She paused, looked at the floor. "I hope they'll let my boy come home for Christmas." She looked up, smiled, and continued. "Anyway, I went into his closet to get one"—she gestured with a cookie—"and I happened to look at his work shirts that were hanging there. Well, I like things neat, you know, and they were all like crooked on the hangers, so I went to straighten them out."

"Tell them what you found, Clara," Gert interrupted. "I think it's just weird. Really weird."

"Some of them had Prestigious Plumbing embroidered on the back."

Yeah. In red letters. Where is this going?

"But," Clara paused, perhaps for dramatic effect, "all the rest of them said another company. A company he never worked for."

"Perhaps he picked up another worker's dry cleaning by mistake," my aunt said.

"Uh-uh. Not with the name 'Joseph' embroidered on all the front pockets."

I knew the answer to my next question even before I asked it. "What's the name of the company?"

"Acme. Acme Plumbing."

I could almost feel that business card in my pocket burning a hole in my jeans.

CHAPTER 31

"Maybe Anthony is moonlighting. Maybe he got a second job," Gert offered with a broad wink in her friend's direction. "You know, Clara, to get out of his—um—bills."

"Oh, you might as well just say it out loud, Gert. You think my boy's gambling again."

"Well, why else would he need a second job? Hmmm?"

Anthony's mother frowned. "It's a couple of shirts, for God's sake. Nobody said anything about a second job!"

My aunt and I looked back and forth between the two—as though we were watching a Ping-Pong match.

"Excuse me," I interrupted. "But if Anthony had money problems do you think they were serious enough to make him want to—you know."

Clara dunked the edge of her third cookie into her coffee and nibbled on it thoughtfully. "Maybe. Maybe he's been betting on things again. But he hasn't been borrowing money from me for over a year." Another dunk of the cookie. "He's even been paying me board. No. I don't believe it's gambling. It's something else."

"I sure hope it's not the gambling," Gert pronounced.

"That was a rough time around here. Damn kid stole everything in sight. Sold his mother's engagement ring."

"He's going to buy me a new one someday." Clara's nod was positive. "Anyway, for my birthday he handed me his whole pay envelope. Handed it right over, he did. 'Buy yourself something nice, mum,' he told me."

Aunt Ibby spoke up then. "Clara, do you remember the name of the company he worked for? The name that was printed on the check?"

"No check. Anthony always gets paid in cash. In an envelope." She darted a look at Gert. "Yes, it was still sealed. He gave me the whole thing."

Somebody was paying Anthony under the table.

"Was there anything printed on the envelope?" I asked.

"Anthony wrote me a note on it. It said, 'With all my love. Buy yourself something nice, Mum.' He even drew a little heart on it. So, call me a silly old mom. I saved it. Want to see?"

Gert gave a dismissive flap of her hand. "One pay envelope! Big deal. He's never going to buy her that ring though. Mark my words."

Clara ignored her friend and stood. "Wait a minute. It's in my Bible." She walked back into the living room and returned quickly, unzipped a black leather case, carefully removing the worn black book. She handed me an envelope. "See? I told you."

She'd quoted the note, scrawled in black marker, word for word. The only other marking was a printed logo. It was an eight-sided geometric shape with a letter O in the center. Eight sides. An Octagon?

Octagon. Where have I heard that word lately?

Clara answered my unspoken question. "You're looking at that round thing with the square sides, aren't you? Anthony says that's his company's trademark. It's an octagon."

"That's the name of the building where Anthony worked, isn't it?" I asked. "I believe Mr. McNally owns that building, right?"

Clara shrugged. "Never met the gent. McNally sounds about right though. I recall it was an Irish name. Whoever it was didn't pay very well. Andrew gets the same pay every week, no matter how hard he works."

I downed the last swallow of my coffee. "This has been really pleasant, Clara, but we have to get along home. We have a play to go to this evening and I need to do something with my hair." I paused. "By the way, do you happen to have one of Anthony's business cards? The ones you told me about with the yellow lightbulb on them."

"Right here in the junk drawer," Clara said, reaching for the cabinet behind her and pulling the top drawer open. "Here you go." I slipped the card into my pocket next to the other one.

"You're going to a play?" Gert ran a hand through her own hair. "A play with real actors on a stage?"

"Yes. It's at the student theater on Essex Street, in the old Trumbull's Department Store building," I told her. "The actors are studying at the school there. They're really very good."

"I've heard about it," Clara said. "What's the name of the play?"

"*Hercule Poirot's Christmas,*" my aunt answered. "It's by Agatha Christie."

"I remember now. I saw him in a movie. Hercule Poirot is a detective." Gert leaned back in her chair. "With a mustache."

"I don't like mustaches on men," Clara announced. "I was glad when Anthony got rid of his. Shaved it off when he came home from Georgia."

"Chased some girl up there," Gert put in. "Glad he got rid of her too, aren't you?"

Clara silently glared at her friend.

It was clear that the conversation was rapidly deteriorating. Aunt Ibby gave a slight tilt of her head toward the door. I took the hint. "Well, it was good to see you again, Mrs.—Clara. Happy to meet you, Gert. I hope Anthony will enjoy the cookies." My aunt and I both stood, backing slowly toward the living room exit.

"I know he will. Come back and visit anytime." Our hostess picked up the now silent Snow Ball and escorted us to the door. She stood on her front step, waving Snow Ball's little paw in a good-bye motion until we'd pulled away.

"I can't imagine a cat putting up with that waving bye-bye nonsense, can you?" Aunt Ibby asked. "At least, ours wouldn't. What did you think about that shirt business?"

"I'll tell you in a minute." I didn't comment on the cat-waving thing, since I'd been guilty of doing it to O'Ryan. I was pretty sure she'd done it before too. I pulled both cards from my pocket. Each was printed on shiny white stock. The one Clara had just given me had a picture of a yellow lightbulb on it. The one Doris Ahern had given me featured a picture of a blue faucet. That card read ACME PLUMBING. JOSEPH MARSHALL MASTER PLUMBER LICENSED AND BONDED.

Wow. Getting confident on this one. Master plumber, no less, in addition to being licensed and bonded. All lies, no doubt.

"I think it's something more than moonlighting. Both cards have the same phone number."

"My goodness," my aunt said. "I wonder if Anthony has any other careers going?"

"I wouldn't be surprised. You know how Bruce Doan

likes all of us at WICH-TV to wear many hats? I think Anthony's employer likes his to wear many shirts."

"And his employer is?"

"R. M. Real Estate. Octagon Real Estate. Richard McNally."

"The same Richard McNally who serves on the board of the Historical Charities? His name is on their annual report."

"Unless there are two of them," I said, "and that's too much of a coincidence even for Charlie's Angels."

When we reached home I headed straight for my bathroom and shampooed my hair. I hadn't just been making up an excuse to leave when I'd mentioned that I needed to do something about the unruly mess of red curls on my head before curtain time at the Tabby's Student Theater. Between the use of the dryer and my electric straightening brush, I achieved a pretty good effect with plenty of time left before I'd need to dress. I picked up the paperback copy of *Hickory Dickory Dock* I'd left on the kitchen table and carried it into the living room.

I'd been reading the book in bits and pieces ever since I'd brought it upstairs. I was just past the midpoint of the story and Poirot had begun linking his clues together. "Here at last some vague pattern seemed to be taking shape," Christie wrote on page 126, describing the great inspector's thoughts about a possibly forged passport. I put the open book down on my lap and stared at the tree.

If Hercule Poirot thinks a complicated document like a passport can be forged, what about a plumber's license? Even a master plumber's license? How hard can that be?

Was a vague pattern beginning to take shape?

Maybe. I replaced the Creative Salem bookmark, put the book on the coffee table, and resumed staring at the Christmas tree.

Mr. Pennington had arranged for a limo to drive Aunt Ibby and a few other special guests to the performance while Pete and I planned to go in his car. I dressed carefully in a new soft wool blue dress. Pete's favorite color. I checked out my boot collection—yes, I know—I've become a boot hoarder—and debated between the high- and low heeled ones. I decided on silver glittered Doraty Mur low heels. Safer, if less glamorous on slippery sidewalks. My doorbell chimed "Bless This House" at exactly six o'clock. We'd decided to have a late bite to eat after the performance and to take advantage of the theater's locally famous cocktail and hors d'oeuvres intermission break. Suited me. I'd already had enough cookie calories.

Pete looked even more handsome than usual in his steel gray Armani. We admired each other at arm's length, and we laughed together when we realized that he was trying to avoid messing up my hair and I was being careful to avoid getting makeup on his white shirt. We arrived at the theater, found a space in the lot, and were fortunate enough to be in front of the lighted marquee when the limo bearing my aunt and the other VIPs pulled up to the curb. I recognized the photographer from the *Salem News* along with the society editor. My ex-student, videographer Therese Della Monica was there too, so I expected I'd see my aunt, glamorous in turquoise cashmere, on the WICH-TV eleven o'clock news.

I hadn't, however, expected to see Richard McNally step out of that limo directly behind her. He saw me too. We made eye contact, despite the camera lights, and he nodded in my direction, still unsmiling. I clutched Pete's arm. "Did you see that?"

"Your aunt? Sure did, babe. Think you'll still be that good looking when you're her age?"

"No. I mean, I don't know. Did you see Richard McNally right behind her?"

"Sure. He's a big shot around Salem too, isn't he?"

"I guess so," I admitted. "There's just something creepy about him. Did you notice that he was looking right at me?"

He put his hand over mine. "Babe, every man here is, was, or will be looking at you. I don't think you have any idea how beautiful you are tonight."

I wanted to bury my face on his shoulder, but I whispered, "thank you," and we proceeded past the "big shots" and my good looking aunt toward the theater entrance. The house lights were on, so we had no trouble finding our excellent orchestra seats.

"Looks like Mr. Pennington didn't need to worry about filling the place even if this is a Christmas play about a murder of a rich old guy. Art imitating life and all that."

"Have you seen it before?"

"Nope. Read the program notes." He waved the folded leaflet. "Sounds like a good mystery story." He pointed to the cast of characters page. "Think any of these people will ever become famous?"

"It can happen," I said. "Remember Daphne Trent?"

"Sure do."

"I'll be paying special attention to the men in the cast tonight though," I told him. "One of them played the Santa Claus I interviewed after the parade, and later at the kid's ward at the Salem Hospital, but I don't know which one."

"No kidding? Think you can spot him?"

"Shouldn't be too hard. Voice, general build, height, weight, you know. The usual description." I was pretty confident that I could do it.

"Weight won't count in this case, will it? Santa Claus is usually well padded, isn't he?"

I agreed, confidence fading just a tad.

"I watched your interviews with him," Pete said. "Maybe I can help figure out which actor it is."

"Your professional expertise is appreciated," I told him. "Uh-oh. There go the house lights. Show time. This part is always so exciting." We settled back in our seats and watched as the curtains parted and the magic of live theater began. The Tabby's student productions have gained a reputation for professionalism which regularly earn them excellent reviews from well beyond Salem's city limits. It was apparent from the start that *Hercule Poirot's Christmas* would be no exception.

I did pay special attention to the males in the cast. (There was no way the jolly old elf I'd spent part of a day with was a girl.) I immediately discounted Poirot as Santa because he couldn't have disguised that magnificent mustache. The actor playing Simeon Lee was too old and too short. The man playing Trassillian was too young looking. Superintendent Sugden's voice was all wrong and Chief Inspector Japp from Scotland Yard didn't look right at all for the Santa part.

By intermission time I still had no idea who played Santa and a peek at the program told me that no new characters would be introduced in the last act. I also checked to see if there'd been a substitution for any of the actors. There wasn't. Pete and I joined the well dressed crowd. I sipped champagne and ate diminutive crabmeat-stuffed mushrooms and dainty spanakopita.

"Figured it out yet, Nancy Drew?" Pete teased.

"Nope. Not yet. You?"

His nod was confident. "I'm pretty sure I've got it. I'll

tell you my guess after the final curtain and you can tell me yours. Okay?"

"Sure," I said, knowing I didn't have even a clue. "Look over there. Aunt Ibby is chatting with the mayor and I think that's the *Boston Globe* theater critic interviewing Mr. Pennington. And there's that McNally person again. See him? I don't like him. I hope he doesn't come over here."

"Hear that? The five-minute bell. Shall we head back inside?" Pete took my arm and guided me back down the aisle to our seats. The house lights dimmed and the curtain rose on the final act where Poirot figured out what was missing from the old man's safe, how poor Simeon Lee's dying screams had echoed so loudly through the house, and, of course, who had committed the murder.

After three well-deserved curtain calls, the cast of *Hercule Poirot's Christmas* took their final bows to a standing O, and Pete and I joined the departing crowd. I saw my aunt and Mr. Pennington hurrying toward us. "Quick, Pete, tell me who do you think Santa Claus is before Mr. P. gets here and tells me the answer."

Pete smiled. "Easy. It's Superintendent Sugden. Who'd you pick?"

"I didn't pick any of them," I admitted, and hurried forward to embrace my aunt and shake the beaming director's hand. "A wonderful performance," I said. "Enjoyed every minute of it. You must be so proud of everyone involved."

"I am indeed, my dear," Rupert Pennington agreed. "And did you identify your Santa Claus? Your lovely aunt tells me you've been wondering which of my talented actors had that honor."

"I'm afraid I still don't know which one it is. Please solve that mystery for me."

"Certainly. Your Saint Nicholas is my Superintendent Sugden."

I gave Pete a playful punch in the arm. "You were right. How did you do that?"

"Tell you later," he whispered, then thanked Mr. Pennington for our tickets, wished my aunt a good night, and propelled me toward the exit. We hurried across the street to the parking lot—the weather had turned much colder since we'd first arrived at the theater. Pete turned the heater on and we backed out onto Essex street. "It's still early," he said. "Want to stop by Greene's Tavern for a while?"

Greene's is one of our favorite places—kind of like TV's *Cheers*, where everybody knows your name. "Good idea," I agreed. "Then you can tell me all about how the heck you figured out that my Santa was the Superintendent. You didn't even meet him in person like I did."

"Didn't need to. Watched you interviewing him on television."

"That's all you needed?'

"I saw him when he was riding on the fire truck in the parade too."

We pulled into the tavern's backyard, where oddly, their front door is located, and hurried into the warm friendly room. The big stone fireplace blazed, the jukebox played Taylor Swift's "You Belong with Me," and familiar voices called out greetings. Sometimes we sit at the bar, but if we want to have a one-on-one conversation, which is what I had in mind for this night, we choose a wide comfortable booth. That's what we did. I ordered Irish coffee, Pete had regular because he was driving and you can't be too careful, especially during the holidays, and we shared an order of wings.

"Okay, shoot," I said, poking a straw through the

whipped cream topping on my drink. "Tell me how you figured it out."

"'Tell' is the operative word," he said. "I recognized a 'tell.'"

"Like in poker? The thing a player does unconsciously that gives a clue about what's in his hand? That kind of 'tell'?"

"Right. We use it in police work too. An unconscious habit sometimes helps us identify a suspect."

"And Santa Claus and Superintendent Sugden had one?"

"Yep. Your Santa had a habit of occasionally stroking his right eyebrow. The Superintendent made the same move three or four times during the play."

"You're right," I said, surprised. "Now that you mention it, I remember that. Wow. That's a very good thing to know. Thank you, Pete."

"You're very welcome," he said. "Enough shop talk. What do you want for Christmas?"

Since I hadn't given that question any thought at all, and I prefer surprises anyway, I turned the conversation back to "shop talk." Couldn't help it. I told Pete about the visit Aunt Ibby and I'd had with Mrs. Prescott. "I am still an occasional investigative reporter," I said, "and I'm still interested in why a not exactly honest electrician would be frightened enough to think seriously about jumping from a rooftop. I couldn't pry anything much from Detective Sergeant Rouse, so I went closer to the source. His mom."

Pete stirred his coffee silently for a moment. "What makes you think he was afraid of something? Not unhappy or depressed or any of the other reasons people do such things—why did you say frightened?"

"That's what he told his mother. He told her he was scared of somebody. Somebody who'd told him he might have ruined everything and that he was going to pay for it."

"Did she say who it was?"

"No. She didn't know and he didn't tell her. He didn't tell her what he'd done that was so bad either. All she could think of was the business cards. He'd had some made that claimed he was 'bonded and insured.' Of course you know he wasn't either."

"Uh-huh. We know that."

"He isn't a licensed plumber either," I said, watching Pete's eyes.

"So, Nancy Drew. You've been doing your homework. How'd you figure that one out?'

"He messed up the plumbing at the women's shelter. Those cards said he was a master plumber. Quite an exaggeration." I wanted Pete to know I was serious about my investigation. "Also he has shirts for at least two businesses. Prestigious Electrical and Acme Plumbing. They both have the same phone number. If you call it you get a recorded message saying to call back later."

"We know. You've done a good job," he said, then his expression turned serious. "But let's not forget, there's still a murderer on the loose. I guess interviewing old ladies won't put you in danger, but please Lee, be careful out there."

"I am careful, Pete," I promised. "All my investigating is done in broad daylight and I always have someone else with me."

He laughed at that." Little Francine and your sixty-something aunt. Not a lot of protection there. Just be careful, all right?"

CHAPTER 32

Pete walked with me to the front door, and patted O'Ryan who'd greeted us as usual. We shared a reasonably decorous front-door-with-the-outside-light-on good night kiss, and made a date for another early breakfast.

The copy of *Hickory Dickory Dock* was still on the table where I'd left it earlier. I remembered that I hadn't asked Pete about the relative ease of obtaining forged tradesmen's licenses. I'd ask him at breakfast. I kicked off my boots and hung up the coat and the blue dress. It would feel good to get into pjs and slippers.

I turned on the eleven o'clock news, hoping to catch Therese's coverage of the crowd at the theater. I was pleased to see that she'd caught the arrival of the stretch limo bearing my aunt and the other VIPs. Pete was right. Aunt Ibby is an extremely good looking woman. She stepped out of the elegant ride and, nodding to acquaintances in the crowd, made her way to the marquee area. She was followed by McNally, the mayor, the director of the museum, Lilly Jeffry, Conrad Gillette, and a couple of distinguished looking gentlemen I didn't recognize.

"I wonder who decided on the guest list for the limo,"

I commented to O'Ryan who sat on the windowsill, facing outward and studiously ignoring me. "I know Mr. Pennington made sure Aunt Ibby was included. Do you think he selected all the others too?" I began to tissue off my makeup.

There was no cat comment, and O'Ryan made a sudden dash to the cat door and out into the front hall, signaling that my aunt had arrived home. I tiptoed out into the hall and looked down from the third-floor railing to the foyer below. As the door swung open, I stepped back, not wanting her to think I was being nosey.

How would I feel if I caught her and Mr. Pennington kissing? How awkward.

I heard the door close as quickly as it had opened and my aunt's voice as she greeted O'Ryan. "Good boy. I'm home. You can relax now."

"That you, Aunt Ibby?" I called, leaning over the railing.

"Yes dear, it's me. Want to come down and talk about the play? I'm wide awake, but dying to get these heels off."

"Already took mine off," I said. "I'll be down in a jif."

"Hot chocolate?" she asked.

"Sounds good."

After a quick stop in the bathroom to finish the makeup removing, cleansing cream routine, I headed down the front stairs. O'Ryan had remained next to the front door, looking out the side window.

"What's so interesting out there, boy?" I looked through the top panes of the same window. Most of the houses on Winter Street had lighted decorations on display. It was a pretty sight. Multicolored bulbs reflected on scattered patches of snow and icy leafless branches of ancient oak and chestnut trees glistened in the street lamps' glare. I saw nothing out of place. No cars drove past. I thought for a moment I could hear strains of distant Christmas music from the tree lot.

The cat didn't join me as I crossed the living room, paused briefly to admire the enduring magic of bubble lights, then followed the alluring scent of chocolate into the kitchen. My aunt had replaced glamor with comfort just as I had. Makeup free, she wore a quilted bathrobe and pink bunny slippers as she poured the sweet-smelling drink into an antique chocolate pot. We sat facing one another at the round oak table sipping hot chocolate from delicate chintz-patterned cups and nibbling on homemade gingerbread.

"I am so lucky," I said. "And thankful."

A questioning look from my aunt. "Indeed?"

"Christmas." I waved my hand. "Here, with you, in this wonderful old house. Good things to eat. A job I love. Pete. Everything. I'm so lucky."

"I understand." She nodded solemnly. "You're thinking about the women and kids at the shelter and Clara and her mixed-up son and poor dead Albert. We are blessed." Her expression brightened. "Did you see me on television tonight? I didn't even notice the camera. It was such an exciting event for Salem—and for Rupert. He was delighted with the packed audience. Gives you a lot of the credit for that because of your interview, you know."

"The credit goes to Agatha Christie. As Shakespeare says, "The play's the thing!"

"It's a good mystery, no doubt. The audience loved it."

"I know. All the way to the end, I couldn't figure out who was guilty. It reminded me of what Pete said about Albert Eldridge's murder. He said, 'No one is a suspect because everyone is a suspect.'"

"Even so, Pete was able to identify your Santa Claus among the actors. Did he tell you how he did it?"

I explained what Pete had told me. "I'll watch for those things now. I'd never given it any thought before."

"Interesting. Maybe everyone has little habits, motions, expressions that count as 'tells' to an observant person."

"I wonder if that McNally guy has one," I said. "I don't like him."

"You don't?" She raised an eyebrow. Is that a tell? "I'd never spoken with him before tonight. He sat beside me in the limo. I found him rather charming. He spoke quite highly of you."

"Of me?" I would have raised an eyebrow at that, if I'd ever learned how to do it. "He doesn't even know me. I've only spoken to the man once in my life."

"He must have been quite impressed with you then. What did you talk about?"

That brought a laugh. "Butterflies," I said. "We talked about butterflies."

"Hmmm. No, he didn't mention anything about butterflies at all. He spoke about your beautiful automobile, and he's apparently a fan. Asked if you were planning to do some more of your investigative reports." She put her cup down suddenly. "Wait a minute. You don't mean Scott Palmer's butterflies, do you?"

"Afraid so." I told her about my trip to the Acme Plumbing Company office, and the dream that had sent me there. "My car is pretty noticeable. And I pretended I'd come there to apologize to that man who'd yelled at me. Scott's butterfly story was the only alibi that came to mind. I embellished it a little. Sent the butterflies to the Science Museum instead of Mexico."

"What did he say about that?"

I thought about it for a moment. "'Quite a story,' he said. 'That's quite a story.'"

"It is that," she agreed. "Now just what is it about Mr. McNally you don't like? Anything specific?"

"Nonspecific creepiness," I said. "River would call it psychic intuition or something like that."

"Maybe. Of course I find thorough research more dependable than instinct," she said. "Perhaps I'll see what I can dig up about him."

"Would you? I'd appreciate it."

The conversation turned then to more pleasant things, like her upcoming trip to London. "I'm looking forward to it," Aunt Ibby said. "I've been to London before many times, but never at Christmastime. It's going to be a treat, I'm sure. But Maralee, I still feel a bit guilty about not being here with you. Not cooking the big Christmas feast."

"Please don't worry about me. I'll miss you naturally, but I'll be fine," I assured her. "I'll be at Marie and Donnie's with Pete for Christmas dinner and there's a party at the station Christmas Eve. Pete and I have a standing date for New Year's Eve. You and I are both going to have wonderful holidays!"

"I'm sure you're right." She smiled. "Your Christmas tree looks beautiful from the yard. Just looking up at that sparkling window makes me glad. I love all the lights, don't you?"

"I do. Speaking of lights, it looks as though the boat parade is going to go off as scheduled. I expect I'll be covering it for the evening news. Are you and Mr. Pennington going down to Pickering Wharf to watch it?"

"I wouldn't be surprised," she said. "There are still quite a few things going on in Salem before I fly off to merry old London. The boat parade will be exciting, and then there's our Christmas Belles concert the night before we leave."

"The rehearsal I saw sounded really good. You girls are good at everything musical."

"The bells are pretty easy to master. Not much different from those colored numbered ones you played in second grade. We use musical designations—A, B, C instead of numerals. That's all. You could pick it up in a day."

"You give me credit for far too many talents, my loving auntie! I'm not musical. Remember my disastrous piano lessons?" I covered my ears with both hands. "That poor piano teacher must have suffered agony!"

"It was not that bad," she lied. "Anyway, you played your scales very nicely."

"Thank you, darling aunt. I love you too. But it's getting late and I have a breakfast date with a handsome detective." I rinsed out my cup and saucer, kissed my aunt good night, and walked through the living room to the foyer where O'Ryan still peered out the window toward Winter Street. "It's bedtime, cat," I told him. "Coming upstairs with me?"

He turned his head toward me, then back to the window, as though weighing his options. I started up the stairs and after a few seconds he followed. "Are you expecting company, big boy?" I asked, "or do you just like watching snowflakes?"

"Mrrupp," he said, making a dash for the cat door so that he could beat me into the kitchen. He likes to do that. I went straight to bed, but O'Ryan took up his position on the windowsill, quietly watching snow—or waiting. For what?

CHAPTER 33

I slept like the proverbial rock. No dreams, no visions, just lovely deep, restful sleep. O'Ryan must have given up his vigil sometime during the night. When I woke up at five-thirty he was curled up at the foot of the bed, snoring soft little cat-snores. Trying not to wake him, I gathered up my clothing for the day, tiptoed out of the room, turned on Mr. Coffee, and headed for the bathroom.

Yawning a wide pink-tongued yawn, O'Ryan emerged from the bedroom a few minutes before six, just in time to greet Pete at the back door. "You look gorgeous as usual," he said as he joined me for pre-breakfast coffee, "but this old cat looks like something some other cat dragged in. Is he okay?"

O'Ryan, ignoring the insult, stalked back into the bedroom, hopped up onto the bed, lay down, and squeezed his eyes shut. "I think he's fine. Just stayed up most all night staring out the window. Seems like he's expecting somebody—or something."

"Maybe he's expecting his lady friend. Frankie." Pete said. "Has she been around?"

"I'll bet you're right!" I said. "I should have thought of

that. No, I haven't seen her lately but if she gets too cold or hungry, I'm sure she knows by now that she's always welcome here."

"Ready to go? I'm really hungry. Those little hors d'oeuvres things at the theater and a couple of wings just don't do the job."

I decided not to mention my late night hot chocolate and gingerbread snack. "Okay. Let's try to beat the early morning rush." We took his car, and as we traveled toward the boulevard, the sweet strains of Barbra Streisand's "I'll Be Home for Christmas" sounded from the direction of the tree lot. "Really? This early?" I looked at the dashboard clock. "Does he always start this early? It's not even seven yet."

"Not usually. Just once in a while," Pete said, cranking down his window so we could hear better. "Listen. This is one of my favorites."

"Mine too, "I said. "The song was special to me during the years I lived in Florida. I'm so happy to be home again."

"I'm twice as happy about that," he said. "Please don't go away again."

"No plans for that," I promised.

I was right about the early morning rush at our favorite breakfast restaurant. Even though the only identifying marking on the building is a vertical neon "OPEN" sign in the window, it's a popular spot with Salem's early risers. Not many visitors have discovered it yet, which is fine with us.

We had to wait a couple of minutes for our favorite booth, but two mugs of steaming hot coffee were already on the table when we got there. "It's nice to be a 'regular,' isn't it?" Pete asked. "I like it that they know how we like our coffee and which table is our favorite."

"I like that too," I said. "But know what I don't like? I

don't like it when somebody I barely know, don't even want to know, has too much information about me."

Immediate transition to cop voice. "Who are you talking about?"

"Richard McNally," I told him. "Aunt Ibby sat beside him in the limo last night, and apparently he knows quite a bit about me."

"Specifically?" Cop face too.

I repeated what Aunt Ibby had told me, and filled him in on the brief conversation we'd had at in front of the Acme Plumbing store front. I explained the dream that had sent me there too.

"You didn't go inside the place with him, did you?"

"Of course not. There's nothing in there anyway."

"What do you mean, 'nothing'?"

"A desk and a chair and a pile of mail on the floor. Pretty much an empty room."

"Like that other dream you had? About the empty rooms?"

I'm sure I gasped. "I never thought of that! Yes. A door with an empty room behind it."

We were both quiet for a moment. Then I said, "Aunt Ibby is going to do a little research on R. M. Real Estate and on Richard McNally."

"I will too, babe," he promised. "I don't like it when somebody makes you uncomfortable."

"It's probably nothing," I said, feeling a little embarrassed. After all, McNally hadn't actually done anything. He admired my car. *Big deal. Everybody does.* He watches me on TV. *That's a good thing, isn't it?* "Hey, nonspecific creepiness isn't a crime, is it?" I smiled when I said it, hoping to lighten the mood.

"Nope. Sure isn't." He returned the smile, poured syrup onto his French toast. "But I'm going to check on him anyway. Now, is there anything else creepy going on you want to tell me about?"

"Well, there is one little thing. Not creepy. Just a question."

"Shoot."

"How hard is it to get fake documents made? Like licenses?"

"I don't think you could do it, but a person with the right connections, the right money, can get most anything," he said. "Why?"

"I'm wondering if Joseph Marshall has some fake papers that say he's licensed and bonded and all, even though he isn't."

"He does. Anything else bothering you?"

"Nope. No problems." *If you don't count visions popping up in unexpected places and a cat who leaves cryptic messages around the house for me to figure out.* I smeared extra strawberry jam onto an English muffin. "I'm going to be reporting on the lighted boat parade tomorrow night. Looks like the weather is going to cooperate."

"Hope so," he said. "I promised to take the nephews to see it. Where will you be?"

"Francine thinks the wall right behind the station will be one of the best spots to film from."

"I think she's right. The boys like to go to Pickering Wharf though, so that's where we'll be. All the shops, you know? Uncle Pete can be very easily talked into buying souvenirs, food, whatever they want."

"I get it," I said. "Everybody should have an Uncle Pete! I'll be doing a standup starting at dusk, live for the early news, then they'll rerun it for the eleven o'clock. The parade ends officially at nine, so I'll be heading for home after that."

"I'll call you. Maybe I could come by the house?" he

suggested. "Depends on what the kids want to do. School tomorrow you know. They can't stay up too late."

"Sure. Come over if you can. I hope O'Ryan won't stay up all night again. He needs his beauty sleep."

"Maybe Frankie has shown up by now."

"Maybe," I said. "If that's who he's waiting for."

Breakfast finished, Pete dropped me off at the front door, watching from his car until I was safely inside. O'Ryan waited at the window to greet me. I waved goodbye to Pete and picked the cat up and hugged him, noticing that he'd managed to wiggle his way out of the red ribbon and bell again. "I think Aunt Ibby may as well give up on decorating you, O'Ryan. You just don't like being belled, do you?" He answered with a quick lick on my chin.

Once again, I carried the cat up the stairs. "Don't get used to this kind of service," I told him. He purred loudly, clearly enjoying being lugged around as though he was a kitten instead of a big, old, slightly overweight boy cat.

CHAPTER 34

I knew I'd be doing some outdoor shots so I changed into flannel-lined jeans, a warm, cuddly, pink cashmere turtleneck, and thigh-high boots and topped it off with a white quilted jacket and pink and white knit hat. I packed my index cards, notebook. and the copy of *Hickory Dickory Dock* as well as the program from the play along with keys, wallet, and phone into my big handbag. There'd undoubtedly be time between assignments to do some note taking and maybe even some deep thinking—some hooking things together so that they make sense.

I stopped off at Aunt Ibby's kitchen on my way out. O'Ryan had already beat me to it and was busy emptying his red bowl—and wearing a new red ribbon with bell attached. "Leaving for work," I said. "I'm covering the boat parade so I'll be home late."

"Maybe you'll see me motoring by," she said. "I'll be on one of the decorated boats. Rupert arranged it. Isn't he sweet? A limo for the play and now a ride on a yacht! He's being very attentive lately."

Maybe Francine is right. Rupert is jealous of Nigel! That's so cute.

"You're worth it," I assured her. "He's very fond of you. Do you know the name of the yacht you'll be on? I'll be sure Francine gets a good shot of it."

"I don't," she said. "Sorry."

"It's okay. We'll be filming from the seawall behind the station. Wave to me when you go by!"

"I will. You look lovely in pink."

"Thanks. I don't know why they say redheads shouldn't wear it. See you later, by land or by sea." O'Ryan escorted me to the doorway and sat on the back steps watching as I backed out of the garage. I waved to him as I moved onto Oliver Street, but by then he'd turned his attention to the Winter Street side of the yard.

Is he still watching—waiting—for what?

I'd just parked and started walking across the WICH-TV lot when the mobile unit with Francine at the wheel pulled up in front of the building. She rolled down her window as I approached. "Just warming up the van," she said. "Rhonda already has a couple of assignments for us. You pick 'em up from her. I'll wait right here." I gave her a quick salute and hurried up the steps to the lower lobby, crossed the black and white tile floor, and pushed the Up button for the elevator.

I was pleased that Rhonda had something for us to do. Maybe it would be something newsworthy. Decorations and puppies and chocolates and dancing cops are fine, I told myself as the aged elevator clanked its way upward, but I'd always thought field reporters got to cover more hard news.

I'd covered a murder and a near suicide along with the candy dipping and the Santa parade! How much excitement did I expect in this job anyway?

I heard Aunt Ibby's voice in my head as I stepped off

the elevator onto turquoise carpet. " Be careful what you wish for," she often said. "You might get it."

Rhonda greeted me with the usual neatly typed assignment sheet. "Got a couple of places for you guys to hit this morning, and you already have the info on the boat parade tonight, right?"

"I think so." I studied the sheet. "What's up at the hotel? "

"The manager there has released some new videos that he says were taken the morning that Mr. E. died. The detective in charge is going to share the tapes and then walk the press through the exact path that they think the suspect took. They're going to announce a reward for information too."

"Sounds encouraging. Maybe they'll get an ID from someone this time." I flipped over to the second sheet. "Back to the Community Center? What's up with that?"

"Mrs. Jeffry asked for you especially. Sounds like a run-of-the-mill promo for the Christmas Belles."

"That'll be fun. I'm sure she has everything perfectly organized for the concert. She's wicked efficient—and nice at the same time."

"Mr. E.'s secretary, wasn't she?"

"Yeah. She was pretty broken up when we found that he was dead," I said, remembering how she'd felt for his pulse. "Poor woman thought he'd been working on his books ever since she'd arrived for work that day. And he'd been dead the whole time."

"Bummer," Rhonda said. "She's a strong woman though. Already been on the horn with Doan trying to get him to do a big Christmas telethon fund-raiser to get money for the Historical Charities—especially the woman's shelter, toys for kids, and all that."

"Good causes," I said. "I wonder if he'll do it."

"I'll be surprised if he does," she said. "Doan doesn't like to give away free air time. Well, back to the scene of the crime for you and Francine. They plan to show the videos at ten and I guess the stroll down the perp's path will be right after. Shoot the material right back to us. Therese will edit and we'll try for the eleven o'clock breaking news spot. Better get going."

"You've got us down for the boat parade for sure, right?"

"Sure do. The Doans got invited to go on some big yacht, but Buffy gets seasick so they turned it down."

"My aunt was invited to be aboard a yacht too. She's excited. We'll get this stuff right back to you, then we'll go straight on down to the Community Center."

"Have fun." Rhonda gave a little pinky wave and turned her attention to the TV monitor above her desk. (It was tuned to a rival station which meant that Mr. Doan was not on the premises.)

I hurried down the stairs because that way is actually faster than the elevator, then out the front door to the waiting van. I waved to Nick who stood with his camo kettle a little way down the street. He saw me and waved back. Fastening my seat belt, I read aloud to Francine from the assignment sheet. "Go to the hotel and wait there for Detective Sergeant Rouse. She'll give a brief statement, then we'll run some new time stamped videos from private surveillance cameras that Salem PD has already sent over. You will then follow Rouse's directions and proceed to record details of the path the person in the new video took. We are hoping this will encourage anyone who may have seen the person in that vicinity to come forward."

"New videos, huh? Sound to you like they're getting close to making an arrest?"

"Not really," I admitted "But maybe they're at least getting closer to finding out who the video guy is."

"Hope they figure it out soon. Having a murderer on the loose is bad for the whole city." She parked the van on the hotel's overflow lot and we carried the equipment we'd need to the lobby of the hotel where we were directed to one of the private conference rooms. Joyce Rouse was already there standing beside a TV monitor. I recognized one reporter from the *Salem News*, and the newswoman from WESX-Radio.

"Looks like this one is for local media only," I whispered.

"Sure," Francine answered. "Can't have every Tom, Dick, and Harry tramping all over everything."

"Thanks for coming, everybody." Joyce didn't use a mic. "This is kind of informal, I know. Please don't begin filming until we go outside. We've already sent the new video to your respective media. We've sent stills to the paper as well. I'm going to run the new video for you. These clips came from several home security devices. Quality varies, but some are quite good. We still don't have a good shot at facial features. His hat is pulled low and a scarf covers the lower half of his face. I can slow it down or pause it if you want." She turned on the set. "I'll answer your questions when we walk along the path that these new videos seem to indicate our person of interest took that morning." She pressed a remote control and the screen came to life.

The man approached a row of store fronts from the far left of the screen. I recognized an antique shop on the opposite side of the hotel. "We're parked close to there," Francine whispered.

I moved closer to the screen. "Now this is creepy," and it was. The figure grew more distinct as it approached the center. The large suitcase was plainly visible in his left hand, and in this sequence, unlike the earlier ones we'd seen, the hand motion Vinnie had described was obvious. The man extended his right arm, and lifted his hand, palm up, moving it toward himself as though he was signaling someone else to join him.

"Maybe we're looking for more than one person," the *News* reporter said to no one in particular.

The screen went black for a few seconds, then we viewed the man walking more slowly along the sidewalk across from the tree lot. His hand motions appeared more urgent. "Oh yeah," the WESX reporter said. "For sure he has a partner."

"If he even has anything to do with the murder," Francine chimed in. "What if he's just some innocent guy looking for his car?"

No one replied.

There was one more segment showing the man from the back, walking briskly along the boulevard. It was daylight. He no longer carried the suitcase and he seemed to be retracing his steps back toward the hotel parking lot. His clothing was different. He wore light-colored pants and a dark raincoat that looked too big for him. He still wore the same baseball cap pulled low and his collar was turned up so we still couldn't make out his face.

CHAPTER 35

"Well, that was interesting," the *News* reporter said, "but maybe Francine is right. What if he's just some guy trying to get his girlfriend to catch up with him?"

"She's probably carrying the rest of the luggage," the WESX woman suggested. "The heavy stuff."

"Right," Francine agreed. "Isn't that just like a man! Maybe the police are wasting time on this jerk while the real killer is long gone."

At this point I thought Joyce was probably wondering why she'd even planned this effort to identify the one actual person of interest they had. "It might be useful though to figure out who he is before we worry about his imaginary girlfriend struggling along with a steamer trunk on her back," I said, laughing. "Even if he isn't a killer, we know he was somewhere in the vicinity of a killing. I'll bet he knows something the police can use."

"You're probably right," Francine agreed. "I like my version better, but still—you're probably right."

"All right then," Joyce said. "We'll start from the point where he was first recorded, in the hotel's overflow lot. Then we'll cross Essex Street onto the boulevard and pick him up just north of the antique store. Pass the statue of Hawthorne and pick him up again across from the Christmas tree lot. We see him once more heading in the direction of Derby Street. Then we see him retracing his steps—without his suitcase—and lose him again just before he gets to the hotel. Notice that we pick him up once more on his way back toward the hotel than we did in the first videos." She opened the door and motioned for us to follow. "Please take photos, stills, and video. Make notes. Stay alert to every possibility. At the same time, try not to draw attention to yourselves. This is a little unorthodox I know. It's kind of a brainstorming session. We'll appreciate every bit of help we can get. Sometimes a pair of fresh eyes, especially reporters' and photographers' eyes, may pick up something we've missed."

So, off we went on a brainstorming adventure. Certainly unorthodox, as Joyce had pointed out, but maybe by using reporters' and photographers' eyes, so accustomed to looking for detail, something useful might develop.

We followed the detective and found ourselves walking along behind her single file like kids on a field trip—or, as Francine pointed out—like ducklings. We were last in line. The newswoman from the radio station videoed the walk and recorded her spoken observations. The representative from the newspaper photographed virtually every step. It looked to me as though he'd focused on everything from cracks in the sidewalk to the facade of each building we passed.

Francine used her shoulder-mounted camera and I used a handheld mic, and we transmitted directly to Marty at the station for editing later.

"This is Lee Barrett reporting from the eastern end of downtown Salem. You've seen the latest videos showing a person of interest in the murder of Albert Eldridge. This footage was obtained from several surveillance cameras positioned along the route this person walked during the minutes following the time of Mr. Eldridge's death. The newer footage from later the same day shows what appears to be the same person returning to the vicinity of the hotel." I paused while Francine panned the camera in a full 360 so that the viewers would know exactly where we were. "Salem police are hoping that someone will recognize the person in the pictures you've seen. We'll be showing them frequently here on WICH-TV. This person is not considered a suspect at this time, but a person of interest—someone who may have knowledge of what happened at the Historical Charities of Salem on the morning of December first."

I'd become so accustomed to the music coming from the tree lot, that I barely noticed it until we approached the source. "We Three Kings of Orient Are" blared from speakers across the boulevard from where we maintained our slow pace. "You can hear Christmas carols in the background, ladies and gentlemen," I said. "Such peaceful music, accompanying the search for a cold-blooded killer during this holy season seems so incongruous, doesn't it?"

I noticed that Francine had turned her camera toward a low brick wall surrounding a house with a tree-filled yard, set well back from the street. She signaled for me to mute the mic. "Look at this," she whispered. "This isn't far from the spot where they lost him. This yard cuts through all the way to Union Street. I know because I lived in this neighborhood when I was a kid. We used to cut through here all the time. Shortcut." She smiled. "The trees weren't here then and the people who lived there finally put up a 'no trespassing sign.' It's gone now. Maybe the jerk—I mean the suspect—hopped this fence and came out on the next street."

"I get it," I said. "Maybe they haven't checked for cameras over there." We hurried to catch up with the group, who'd already reached the corner of Derby Street.

At the head of the line, the detective held up her hand. "If we turn around here and head back the way we came, we'll be taking the approximate route of the person's daylight return in the direction of the hotel, this time without his suitcase. He was observed by one new camera along the way but not at all in the parking lot where we first saw him. Viewing that footage, you'll note that he's not wearing a scarf, still wearing a baseball cap, pulled low over his eyes. His collar is turned up, still effectively masking most of his face."

Again, we followed single file, not quite so slowly this time. I didn't include Francine's observation about the shortcut in my narration. I wanted to run the idea by Detective Rouse though, for sure.

The five of us gathered once again in the hotel's conference room. No recorders, no cameras. Joyce faced us from the front of the room. "I'm going to ask each of you to write down your impressions during this—should I call it an 'experiment?'—before you share anything but the bare facts with your readers and viewers. If you noticed anything, however small, you feel might be useful to the investigation, I'd appreciate it if you'd share it with me privately, in person, or by e-mail or phone. Thank you all for coming."

I poked Francine's arm. "You've got to tell her about that house with the trees in the yard."

"It's probably nothing," she said. "I mean the property might not even go clear through to the next street anymore."

"If you don't I'll have to," I insisted. "And it's your catch. You should get the credit for it."

"I don't know."

"There's a reward, remember? For information leading to the arrest?" I gave her a push in Joyce's direction.

"All right, all right. I'm going. Come with me?"

I followed close behind as she approached the detective. "This might not be important," Francine began. "I mean it was a long time ago, when I was a kid."

She had Joyce's attention. "You recognize the man from somewhere, Francine?"

"Oh, no. Not the man. The yard. The trees weren't there though"

Joyce threw me a helpless look. "Trees?"

"I think Francine noticed something on the man's route." I explained. "There's a house we passed about a block after where we lost sight of him."

Joyce nodded. "We checked every house and business on that side of the street for surveillance cameras."

"It's a house set back from the street. Lots of trees."

"Oh yes. I remember it. They don't have any cameras at all."

"You probably can't tell because of the trees, but that property goes all the way through to Union Street," Francine said. "At least it used to. What if the guy ducked through there and out the other side?"

Joyce pulled a phone from her utility belt. "Thank you, Francine. That might be helpful. If you think of anything else, anything at all, please contact me right away." She lowered her voice and turning away from us, spoke into her phone.

We gathered up our gear and headed for the mobile van. "You think my tip about cutting through that old yard could be important?" Francine asked.

"If I was a detective, I'd sure be in a hurry to check it

out," I told her. "Looked to me as though she phoned it right in."

"I hope it helps them find that creep. I can't forget about how Mr. E. looked when—you know." She unlocked the van. "Well, on to the next place on the sheet. The Community Center."

"Right. Rhonda said it's something about promoting the Christmas Belles concert."

"That's worth promoting." Francine wheeled the van through the entrance of the center's gated parking lot. "Everybody loves the Belles."

"That's for sure," I agreed. "Hey! Look at that." I pointed to a sleek black Lexus moving toward the exit gate.

"Yeah," she said. "Nice car."

"No, I mean I know who that is. Richard McNally. What's he doing here?"

CHAPTER 36

Lillian Jeffry waved to us from the glass cubicle where I'd met with her earlier, then stepped out into the corridor to meet us. "Lee, Francine! You girls are right on time. You know I like to do things in a timely manner."

So did Mr. Eldridge. I remember that about him.

"I have a few ideas about the Christmas Belles concert I'd like to run by you." She waved us into the office, directing us to two folding chairs. "Bruce Doan has kindly offered to give us a few ten-second spots every day until the concert."

I wondered if she knew how lucky she was. Mr. Doan doesn't often give air time away. "We can fit quite a lot of information into ten seconds," I said. "With some good graphics, the spots can be very impressive."

"I'm sure of that, Lee dear." She picked up a folder and handed it across the desk. "These are photos of previous concerts. Perhaps your people can prepare a montage. Another idea I have is for you to tape a few minutes of a rehearsal of our hand bell chorus, so that people who've never heard the bells can get an idea of how lovely they sound."

"We can do that," I said. "My aunt says you all have been rehearsing several times a week. When would be a convenient time for us to film?"

"Better be soon," Francine suggested. "We only have about a week before the concert."

"How about tomorrow night?" Lilly's smile was bright. "Six o'clock? Here?"

"I can arrange it," I said. "You, Francine?"

"Love to. I haven't heard the hand bells before."

"You're in for a treat then," Lilly said. "We're getting very good at all of the carols."

"You sounded good to me at the first rehearsal," I said. "By concert time the sound will be perfect."

"We hope so. We're still using the rehearsal bells, of course. Wait until you hear the professional set. Magnificent sound!"

"I expect those are still in Mr. E.'s safe," I said. "Has it been opened yet?"

"Why, no. I was mistaken about that. The bells we'll be using are here, safely locked away in this very building. The remainder of the set is still in Albert's safe. I'd quite forgotten that hc had the precious instruments delivered here, shortly before his demise." Again the bright smile. "Would you like to see them? I can arrange it. You can photograph them if you like. They're really quite beautiful."

"Great," Francine said, standing. "That's the best idea so far. A real attention grabber"

I agreed with Francine. "Can you work up a little history about them for my voiceover, Lilly? And maybe some recorded hand bell music?"

"Glad to. Come on. I'll show them to you." We followed her down the corridor to a room marked "Storage."

Really? From a secure safe in a private home to a storage locker in a public building?

The room appeared to be securely locked though, and Lilly unlocked yet another door to a much smaller space where white sheets covered two long tables revealing an outline not unlike a graduated row of miniature pointed mountain tops.

Lilly lifted a corner of one sheet and, with a magician-like flourish, removed it. "Voila," she said. "There are the twenty-five bells here we'll be using. There are nearly a hundred bells in the complete set, but we're not that good yet. We use mostly two octaves, with a few extra bells thrown in for special effects. For instance, in "The Carol of the Bells," our closing piece, Conrad has written a fabulous crescendo using bells all the way down to C-3. Ibby is kind of the star in that one."

Francine aimed her camera at the table where the bells gleamed golden in graduated sizes from the smallest to the largest. "They're really pretty. I'll bet you all will look great playing with the stage lights on. Will you all be dressed alike for the rehearsal tomorrow? That makes a better picture."

"We'll all wear black choir robes. Of course, the rehearsal bells aren't quite as beautiful as these, but the sound is comparable. Your audience will get the effect just fine. These beauties"—she gestured toward the bell display—"will have to wait until the night of the concert."

"If you'll give me just a minute to get this shot." Francine walked around the table, pausing once or twice, trying different angles. I took the opportunity to ask Lilly about the occupant of the black Lexus. "I saw Mr. McNally in the parking lot when we drove in. I know he's on the board of the Historical Charities. Is he associated with the community center as well?"

"Richard? Oh my, yes. He's very civic minded. He stopped by to be sure we have enough Christmas toys for the kiddies." She tilted her head to one side and fixed me in a laserlike violet-eyed gaze. "Why do you ask?"

"No particular reason. I've just run into him around town several times lately." I looked away. *That was a lame answer. Wish I hadn't mentioned it.*

"Uh-huh. Very civic minded. I'll tell him you were asking for him. He'll be flattered."

Now I really wish I hadn't mentioned it.

"You about ready, Francine?" I asked, a little too loudly for the small room. "I'd like to get back to the station to see what Marty's done with this morning's material."

"Finished here," she said. "Want to cover them up again, Ms. Jeffry?'

Lilly rearranged the sheet over the bells, folding it as carefully around the edges as though she was tucking in a child. "We try to keep them dust free, and always wear gloves when we touch them."

"Thank you very much for showing them to us," I said as we exited the room. "Looking forward to hearing the Belles at rehearsal tomorrow."

Lilly turned the key in the lock and slipped it into a jacket pocket. "I'll walk back to my cubicle with you and get back to work on some more promotion ideas for this place. Later I'll be back in my more luxurious office trying to catch things up at the Historical Charities building. Thanks so much for coming my dears. See you tomorrow evening."

"You surely do stay busy, Lilly," I said. "You remind me of my aunt. I'm trying hard to be more efficient, to get things done the way you two do."

"It comes with practice, dear child. Ibby and I have had many more years to practice." She gave a little wave and entered her glass-walled office. "See you later."

"She's a wonder." Francine clicked the key fob and

unlocked the van. "Working as hard as she does after going through such a rough time—and smiling through it all."

"A real Miss Lemon," I said, almost to myself.

"Who's Miss Lemon? Sounds like a schoolteacher."

"She's just a character in a book I've been reading. A perfect secretary who hardly ever, ever makes a mistake."

"Yep. That's Ms. Jeffry all right. Perfect." She headed to the exit gate and drove the short distance down Derby Street to the station. "I'll bet Marty has our stuff from this morning all organized. She's a Miss Lemon too, isn't she?"

"We're surrounded by efficiency, Francine."

"Maybe some of it is rubbing off on us," she said. "I mean, we've been getting everything done on time and most of it is damn good, don't you think so?"

"I just wish I could come up with something special for my little investigative reporter slot," I said, "but I think the field reporter job looks fine."

Francine parked the van and offered a high five. "We're a good team."

We used the side door entrance to the first-floor studio, knowing that's where we'd probably find Marty—who arguably wears more hats than anyone else at WICH-TV. We were right. She waved to us from a lighted set about halfway down the long black-walled room. "Hi kids," she called. "Just putting a few holiday touches on the sports set. Come on down." Francine and I joined her in the three-sided area where behind the sports desk a replica of the Stanley cup was flanked by a blown-up photo of Boston's Bobby Orr statue on the right and an artificial Christmas tree on the left. Marty was busy hanging decorations shaped like baseballs, footballs, hockey pucks, and other sports related paraphernalia onto the tree. "Cute, huh?" She stood back to admire her work.

"Guess you two want to see how your morning walk turned out, huh? Didn't have to do much to it. Cut some of the boring stuff. Got it down to a minute and a half. Wanna see?"

She pushed a few buttons on the sports desk monitor and once again we followed the route the person of interest had taken after the murder. The light was good, the camera angles tight. My narration sounded smooth. "When the viewers compare this with the original videos, they'll be able to follow his progress down the street," Francine said.

"Can we do a split screen and match them up, Marty?"

"I thought you might like that, Moon. It's already done."

Another button push, and there was the split screen, just as I'd pictured it. "You're a wonder, Marty," I said. "It's perfect."

"A regular Miss Lemon, huh, Lee?" Francine winked.

Marty smiled. "Agatha Christie, right? Thanks, but I'm better looking than Miss Lemon. Anyway, Moon, Doan approved both versions. We used the first one on the eleven o'clock this morning, but I say we run with the split screen tonight. You agree?"

"Absolutely. Both the five o'clock news and the eleven too?"

"No problem."

We left Marty to her tree decorating and climbed the metal staircase to the second floor. We told Rhonda about the Belles' rehearsal on the following night and picked up our assignment sheet for the lighted boat parade. "Mr. Doan said to tell you that since you have to come back for the boat parade, you guys can have the afternoon off," Rhonda said. "But keep your phones handy in case anything newsy turns up. Okay?"

An afternoon off was surely okay with both of us. "See you around six?" I asked Rhonda.

"Sure thing. I'm bringing a lawn chair. Going to watch from behind the building with you two."

"See you there," I said and joined Francine on the elevator. We exited onto Derby Street, where garlands and window candles enhanced the old Custom House where Nathaniel Hawthorne had once worked, and a lighted Christmas tree shone from a corner window in the Henry Derby house. "It's so pretty here at holiday time," I said, looking up and down the street. "I missed this in Florida."

Francine turned up the collar of her coat and jammed her hands into the pockets. "Bet you didn't miss this cold weather. Bundle up tonight. When the sun goes down it'll be wicked cold here. Damp too. You'll wish you were back on a nice sandy beach."

I laughed. She was right.

I started across the lot to my car and Francine hopped into her truck. I looked over to the spot where Nick the camo Santa usually rang his bell. Harry—he of the highly reflective brass kettle was there. I waved, but kept a safe distance away from that source of unwelcome visions and focused instead on the harbor and Pickering Wharf where decorated boats had already begun to congregate.

Once in the car, I turned on the heater, and checked my phone for messages. Pete had called twice but hadn't left a message. The dashboard clock showed a little before two. If he hadn't had lunch yet, maybe we could meet somewhere. I returned the call.

"Hi, babe," he said. "Want to grab some lunch?"

"You read my mind. Shall I meet you somewhere?"

"Got time for a roast beef sandwich at Bill and Bob's?"

"I have the whole afternoon off," I said, "and a hot roast beef sandwich and fries sounds wonderful."

"Great. Meet you there. I'm heading that way now. I've done a little checking on a couple of things." Uh-oh. Cop voice.

"What about?"

"McNally. See you in about ten minutes." That was the end of the conversation. I drove toward Beverly Bridge, roast beef, and maybe some answers.

CHAPTER 37

Pete was already at the restaurant when I got there. I parked next to the Crown Vic and hurried to the entrance. Bill and Bob's is small and warm and smells of good things. Pete had saved us a booth at the back of the room overlooking the gray expanse of cold salt water beyond the bridge. He stood when he saw me walking toward him. "What'll it be? The usual? Hot roast beef sandwich, fries, and a Pepsi?"

"Perfect," I said, accepting a side-hug and a kiss on the cheek. He went to the counter to order and I slid into the booth, wondering what he'd learned about McNally that he wanted to share with me. He returned with our lunches in a few minutes and sat facing me. "Well," I said, "am I right to distrust him? Is he as creepy as I think he is?"

Pete wore the cop face when he answered. "I don't know. Creepy doesn't count for much in my business. But I told you I'd do a little checking and I did. I haven't found anything exactly illegal on him, but a few things have turned up that I'd call highly unusual."

"Like what?" I picked up a hot fry with my fingers and dunked it into a little paper cup full of ketchup. "Where did he come from anyway? He seems like such a big deal around town but I don't remember him even being here before I left for Florida almost twelve years ago."

"That's right. He wasn't. He's been in Salem only about five years. Showed up here with a big bankroll apparently, bought a lot of real estate. Claimed he came from Atlanta."

"Atlanta?"

"Yes. Ring a bell?"

"Aunt Ibby says Lilly Jeffry came from Atlanta."

"We believe that's a fact. But she's been here quite a bit longer than McNally has. She's worked for Eldridge for over ten years. Apparently the perfect secretary."

Miss Lemon.

I thought about how well Lilly had adapted to her current situation. She'd been able to almost seamlessly transition from the profound grief I'd witnessed when she'd tried to revive the lifeless man on his office floor back into a superefficient Wonder Woman. It had happened literally within hours.

"Atlanta's a big city, Pete," I said. "Millions of people come from Atlanta. Is there a connection between Lilly and McNally? Other than the Historical Charities, I mean?"

"Rouse is working on that." Pete finished the last bite of his sandwich. "It's not my case after all. I just looked into it because you asked me to. I don't like it when somebody creeps you out." He smiled at that, but his tone was serious.

"But you don't think it's a coincidence, do you?" I pushed for more information. I know that Pete doesn't believe in coincidences. Neither does River.

"It's not my case," he repeated. "But you are. I'll keep an eye on things. You have good instincts about people, Lee. I don't believe in coincidences, but even cops believe in instincts." He reached across the table and squeezed my hand. "Don't take any chances, babe, but you keep an eye on things too. And for God's sake call me right away if anything creeps you out. Anything at all. Promise?"

I promised.

The visions are creepy. Does he want me to call when they happen? I knew the answer to that. Call him.

"I'll call you. I will. And will you tell me what you and Joyce find out about McNally? My instincts might come in handy."

"I'll tell you what I can. There's one more thing you might find interesting." He picked up our paper plate and plastic utensils and deposited them in a nearby receptacle, then returned to the table. "Want a coffee?"

"Yes, please." I watched as he went to the counter and ordered the coffee. One more thing? I liked it that he was sharing information with me. I liked it a lot. This was something new.

"Here you go." He handed me the paper cup and smiled across the table. "Now, where was I?"

"One more thing," I prompted.

"Right. Vinnie's mother bailed him out, but before he left we showed him the new footage we have of the suspect—I mean the 'person of interest'—in the Eldridge case."

"Did he come up with anything new?"

"Not exactly. But he made an interesting comment."

"What did he say?"

Pete leaned on one elbow, his fist under his chin. "He said that the way the guy moved reminded him of that dancing cop on the boulevard."

Pete had to go back to work so we took our coffees with us and went back out into the cold. I sat in the parking lot for a moment after Pete drove away while the heater warmed up, sipping my coffee, thinking of what we'd talked about.

Had Lillian Jeffry and Richard McNally known one another when they'd lived in Atlanta? No way, I told myself. As I'd reminded Pete, it's a big city. But they certainly had made a connection here in Salem. What was the common link between them? That was an easy one. The Historical Charities. Then what was Richard McNally's interest in me? Or was that all my imagination?

Pete said I have good instincts about people. My feelings about McNally are real, not imaginary. I'm going with my instincts on this one.

I backed out onto Bridge Street and started toward home. I turned left at Winter Street and was about to park in front of our house, then changed my mind and proceeded toward the Common. I wanted to take another look at that dancing cop. I wondered if I'd see what Vinnie Drake had seen.

I was in luck. The cop was there and he was in good dancing form. It occurred to me that as the temperature had dropped, the dancing had accelerated. By the time I reached the boulevard, the music rang out clearly while the officer rocked out to Eartha Kitt's "Santa Baby." The cat burglar was right. The hand motions were very similar to what Francine had called "some guy trying to get his girlfriend to catch up with him."

As long as I was on the boulevard, I decided that I may as well continue along the route we'd walked so recently—the route the suspect had taken, both after leaving the vicinity of the Eldridge house and, reversing his direction, on the way back. I did the same thing on wheels that he'd done on foot. I made a U-turn at the corner and drove slowly back along that pretty roadway, past the

Catholic Church, past the statue of Hawthorne, past the tree lot, past the hotel's overflow lot.

Where did he go?

With the question still rattling around in my brain, along with all the other questions I'd asked lately, I turned down Oliver Street and pulled into the garage. The Buick was there so I was pretty sure Aunt Ibby was at home. I wanted to tell her what Pete had told me about Richard McNally.

O'Ryan was already outside when I walked along the path beside the garden. He sat, looking patient and placid on the top step. That step is made of concrete and it occurred to me that it must be very cold on his bottom. (I had a fleeting image of O'Ryan wearing a pair of warm flannel pants, but since he couldn't even tolerate a satin ribbon for very long that image faded quickly.)

The cat and I entered the back hall and I tapped on my aunt's door. "Hi. It's me," I called as O'Ryan pushed open his cat door and gave me an over the shoulder I-got-in-first look.

"Come on in. It's not locked." Aunt Ibby looked up from the round kitchen table where several boxes of Christmas cards, sheets of name and address stickers, a small stack of holiday postage stamps, and an address book lay. With pen poised in midair, she said, "Got yours done yet?"

"Cards? Nope. Haven't started. But I bought some nice ones at the museum shop. Got a minute? Pete's done some checking on Mr. McNally."

She laid the pen down. "What did he find out?"

"Well first, Richard McNally is from Atlanta." I waited for her reaction.

It was the same as mine. "Lilly Jeffry is from Atlanta too."

"That's what I said. But you know them better than I

do. Do you think this is an association that goes back to before they came to Salem?"

She frowned. "I'd never given it a moment's thought. I don't really know Mr. McNally at all, but I consider Lilly a friend. I don't recall her ever even mentioning any man except for poor Albert and Conrad Gillette, of course. Those names were always in a business context." She stared out the window. "Hmmm. Atlanta."

"What do you think?"

The green eyes took on that special sparkle. "I think I'll do a little investigating. Anything else Pete had to say about him?"

"Said he hadn't turned up anything illegal on McNally. Some things, he said, were 'highly unusual.'"

"Okay. I can work with that." She stood. "I'll address the cards later. I know just where to look." She started to leave the room.

"Wait a minute. Where are you going?"

She turned in the doorway. "Oh Maralee, dear. I'm going to my office. You just go on about your day. I'll let you know what I find out." With that, she scurried away, O'Ryan trotting along behind her.

"I'll look for you at the boat parade," I called after her. "Bundle up. It's going to be cold."

"Yes, dear." I heard the office door open and close.

I sat at the table for a moment. No aunt. No cat. I shrugged, stood up, and returned to the back hall, facing the laundry room. "Might as well do a load of laundry while I'm here and have a couple of hours to kill." The wicker basket under the laundry chute was about three-quarters full. I dumped it into the machine, added non-allergenic, clear, fragrance-free laundry detergent, and pushed the proper buttons. Then I climbed the stairs to my place for a couple of hours of rest and a rethinking of my clothes. A cashmere sweater and sleeveless quilted vest would not be suitable for waterfront viewing of the boat parade, however cute.

Aunt Ibby's display of Christmas cards had reminded me that I should at least make a start on mine. I set up my kitchen table in a smaller approximation of hers, with my House of the Seven Gables snow scene cards, my stamps, one pen, and a copy paper printout of addresses instead of a book. Then I made a careful check of my closet for warmer outerwear. After a decade in Florida, my winter-wear was still minimal, but I had a powder blue ski outfit I'd used on a trip to Vail once, and a set of silk long under-wear along with plenty of hats and gloves. That should work out fine.

Between laundry, card prep, and wardrobe check I'd used up the better part of an hour. The sun had already set over Salem and the sky was reasonably clear with the tiniest sliver of a new moon. I changed clothes, reapplied makeup, and remembering Rhonda's idea of bringing a folding chair, stopped once again in the laundry room, tossed wet clothes into the dryer, picked up a blue canvas director's chair and headed for the garage, hoping I'd be able to wedge the folding chair into the passenger side of the car.

The Buick was already gone and there was a note under my windshield wiper. "Found something interesting," it read. "Talk to you tonight after the boat parade."

When I reached the TV station, chair safely stashed beside me, I was glad that my parking spot had my name on it. Most of the lot was filled and there were even a few hardy souls sitting on the granite sea wall. Cold bottoms there for sure and once again I thought about my stair-sitting cat. *I wonder if Frankie will come inside if it gets too cold. I hope so*. Carrying the director's chair, I hurried across the lot. The harbor was fairly aglow with the brightly lighted and lavishly decorated boats.

The Doans were in the reception area with Rhonda, Marty, and Francine when I arrived. There was a tray with mugs, a pot of hot chocolate, and a plate full of assorted Dunkin Donuts. Buffy Doan was resplendent in purple velvet with bunny fur trim. "Here's our field reporter," Mr. Doan said with a big smile, lifting his chocolate mug in salute. "Looks like this is going to make for good TV, don't you think so Ms. Barrett?"

"The boats are beautiful, sir," I said, "and the crowd is building."

"We'll be using two cameras tonight," Doan continued. "Marty will handle the live shots for the seven o'clock news. Palmer will be at the anchor desk. At the same time, Francine will be doing crowd scenes, cute kids, close-ups of the best boats. Then for the eleven o'clock Marty will combine the two for a five-minute segment. No voiceover, just musical background. Covington at the desk. Barrett, Rhonda has your script for the parade with the names of the boats and the owners. Got it?"

"Got it," Marty, Francine, and I chorused.

"Good. Mrs. Doan and I will watch from my office window—where it's nice and warm."

"We were invited to go on one of the yachts," Buffy Doan told us. "But I have a queasy tummy, so the office window view will have to do." She picked up her mug and a couple of jelly doughnuts and, giggling, followed her husband into the office marked MANAGER. The lock clicked behind them.

"Shall we brave the cold and the crowd?" Rhonda asked. "I already put my chair in back of the building. Marty rigged up a kind of barrier with sawhorses and a big sign that says WICH-TV staff only. No admittance. That should keep everybody out, including Lee's fans."

"My fans?" I lugged the director's chair back out to the elevator. "What fans?"

"Just kidding. But some guy came in asking about you this afternoon right after I gave you the kids afternoon off. Wanted to know if you'd be on the news tonight. I told him to watch seven and eleven o'clock both."

"Did he leave his name?"

"No. I didn't ask and he didn't offer. It was just a schedule question. Why? Do you think he's somebody you know?" She zipped up a navy parka, pulled on a matching watch cap, and handed me several sheets of paper, neatly typed.

"No. Not at all," I lied. "I was just curious."

Is the creep stalking me now?

CHAPTER 38

It wasn't uncomfortable behind the WICH-TV building after all. The building itself served as a windbreak and we congratulated ourselves on having the best seats in town for the boat parade. Old Eddie, the station's night watchman, security guard, and occasional mobile unit driver, helped Marty maneuver her rolling camera into position on the uneven ground, hooked up the lights, and installed a small monitor screen where we could all see it.

"Okay, Moon," Marty ordered. "Looks like the yachts are in position to start the parade around the harbor. If I've figured my angles right, they should begin passing in front of my camera in exactly eleven minutes. Scotty will signal me after the first commercial and we'll start shooting. That will be at seven-oh-eight. He'll introduce you. You do your standup then we'll show the boats and you read from the script Rhonda gave you. Got it?"

"Got it," I said.

"Good. Read it over. Francine, you can wander around and shoot what you think looks good. You know what Doan likes."

Francine adjusted the camera on her shoulder, "Got it. Not my first time at the rodeo."

She pushed one of the sawhorses aside and stepped out into the growing crowd. I've worked in front of the camera, one way or another, for most of my adult life, but I'd be lying if I didn't admit to having butterflies every time. (Monarchs?) Carefully, I stood on the seawall. It's only about a yard wide and a wrong backward step would have extremely unpleasant results. I watched the monitor behind Marty. Sound was off but I watched opening credits, then saw Scott at the anchor desk. There was a steady hum of engines as the boats began to move. First commercial came on—a national ad for chocolate-covered strawberries in a holiday box. Old Eddie focused the spotlight on me while Marty began a backward count. I smiled, held my hand mic in position.

"Six—five—four—three—two—one." Camera light glowed. Scott's voice came from the monitor.

"Lee Barrett is on scene at Salem's spectacular lighted boat parade, and it's certainly a beautiful night for it! Lee?"

"Thanks, Scott. You're right. The weather is perfect. We're here at the edge of Salem Harbor right behind the WICH-TV waterfront studios, just west of Pickering Wharf. A big, happy holiday crowd has gathered on the wharf, along the sea walls and in waterfront restaurants, homes, and condos all along the parade route, and as you'll see, they've gone all out with lights, costumed characters, music, and special effects." I turned sideways, cautiously, as the lead vessel moved through the water toward us.

"Here comes the *Rachel Marie*, a thirty-foot Grady White. Captain Rick Naves has gone with a *Frozen* theme, depicting an ice palace with his two daughters Allison and Debbie as the princesses Elsa and Anna. The music is

'Let It Go' from the movie. I'm going to step out of the picture now, Scott, so the folks can get a good view of these gorgeous boats as they pass by our camera."

I stepped down from the wall and out of camera range while I continued my narration, reading from Rhonda's notes and adding comments of my own here and there. It really was a spectacular sight and cheers from the crowd as each vessel passed showed their appreciation for all the effort and expense the owners had gone to. I wished Aunt Ibby had told me the name of the boat she was on so I could wave to her. We wouldn't get to show the television audience all of the yachts, sailboats, and even fishing boats circling the harbor, but Marty managed to capture more than a dozen of them in the time we'd been allotted for the feature.

At Marty's signal I stepped back up to my spot on the seawall, faced the light and camera, said thanks and good night to Scott Palmer, and wished the audience happy holidays.

I set my director's chair beside Rhonda's and prepared to enjoy the rest of the parade as a spectator. Francine turned her shoulder mounted camera over to Marty for video editing and joined us, still jumping up every few minutes to photograph parade and parade watchers with her own camera. I had my script on my lap, so I was able to name boats, captains, and themes as each one passed our vantage point. Marty and Eddie went back inside to secure the station's equipment.

"That's a pretty one," Rhonda said pointing to the passing parade of boats. "I love all the glitter, don't you?" The boat approaching our self-proclaimed reviewing stand was a big one—probably fifty feet or so and was one of the most extravagantly decorated ones we'd seen so far. "Too bad this one didn't make it to the news." Rhonda stood and moved closer to the seawall. Francine, camera poised, joined her. Since they were effectively blocking my view, I stood, put my script on the seat of my chair, and joined them. The boat featured several white Christmas trees in the stern, each one almost completely covered in silver glitter. The cabin had somehow been altered to resemble a sleigh, the entire thing sparkling with blue glitter. Revolving lights washed over the whole display, including a red-glitter-nosed reindeer extending from the bow looking for all the world as though he was flying, pulling the glistening, shimmering yacht.

"Whose is it?" Francine wanted to know. "What's the name of it?" I reached behind me for the script, holding it so that the lights from the boat illuminated the page.

"It's the *Octagon*," I said dully. "The owner is Octagon Real Estate."

And the owner of Octagon Real Estate is Richard McNally.

"Cool," Rhonda said. "Hey, Lee. Isn't that your aunt waving from the cabin?"

Of course it was. Rhonda, Francine, and I stood on the sea wall, waving madly to my aunt. Sitting beside her was Lilly Jeffry and at the wheel was a white-bearded Santa Claus which looked to me like my old friend Nick. He waved to us too.

I texted Pete who, I guessed, was still watching the parade over on Pickering Wharf. "Boat named *Octagon* heading your way. McNally owns it. Aunt Ibby and Lilly Jeffry in the cabin."

We watched the parade until nearly nine o'clock, when the stern lights of the last vessel disappeared around the end of the wharf, then folded our chairs and, using the side door to the first-floor studio, went back into the welcoming warmth of the television station. Marty, not surprisingly, was at work preparing the boat parade footage for Buck Covington's eleven o'clock news. Within moments Francine and Marty had their heads together figuring out how to jam Francine's footage of the *Octagon* into the five-minute presentation.

By nine-thirty I was ready to go. Pete's nephews wouldn't be ready to leave Uncle Pete for a while yet and my aunt was probably still aboard the *Octagon*. I put the folding chair back into my car, carefully backed out of the lot, and drove along Derby Street toward the boulevard and home.

Music drifted from the tree lot which still seemed to have plenty of customers milling around among trees of all heights and several varieties. I found myself tapping my fingers on the wheel and bobbing my head to the beat of "Run, Run Rudolph." Easy to see why the dancing cop danced on this corner.

The garage door rolled up. No Buick yet, but Aunt Ibby should be along soon unless she had plans with Mr. Pennington. I'd just hit Genie to close it up again when a short beep from outside told me that she'd arrived in—as her friend Lilly liked to say—a timely fashion. She parked the Buick, slid out the driver's side, and slammed the door. Hard. "Oh, Maralee, what a difficult evening this was!"

"Difficult? What happened?"

She hurried around the two cars, took my arm, and propelled me out the side entrance and into the yard. "I'll tell you when we get in the house. Oh, dear."

O'Ryan peeked from his cat door and ventured onto the top step, He greeted us with a loud "mmmrrow." My aunt picked him up and hugged him while I used my key and let us in. "Anything to do with the note you left on my windshield?" I asked as we all trooped into her kitchen. "You said you found something interesting."

"It has everything to do with it. Take off your coat. I'll make us some tea. Who knew I'd be alone on that boat with Lilly? And with that ridiculous Santa Claus person who didn't say anything except 'Ho-ho-ho' and 'Merry Christmas' throughout the entire boat ride." She tossed her own coat onto a chair and turned on the electric tea kettle. "What a difficult evening."

"You said that."

She sat down. "I know. And it was a lovely parade, dear. That part was fine. I saw all of you girls waving to me. That was nice."

"You were on the prettiest boat."

"Yes. Beautiful. Must have cost a fortune to do all that glitter." The tea kettle whistled. She put teabags into two cups and poured. "Want a cookie or anything?" She brushed a hand through her hair. "I'll be picking glitter out of my hair and off of my clothes for a week."

"No cookie," I said. "I want to know what you found and why you're upset."

"All right. Since we knew that both Mr. McNally and Lilly came to Salem from Atlanta, I wanted to see if there was any connection between them." She paused and took a sip of tea. "Oh, that tastes good."

"Aunt Ibby! Was there? Is there a connection?"

"Oh my, yes. There is. Sometimes, if you go back a generation or two, you can find surprising things on old newspaper microfiche. I searched for Atlanta McNally obituaries. Then I put in Richard McNally's name"

"But he's not dead."

"No. But his parents are. I found his father, John McNally's obit. He was survived by his loving wife Brenda, his son Richard, and his stepdaughter, Lillian Jeffry."

"He's her brother!" I gasped. "But why do they keep it a secret?"

"I have no idea. Furthermore, I didn't know Lilly would be on the boat with me tonight. I thought Rupert would be with me but he was on the big fishing trawler."

I got it. "So the difficult part must have been acting normal when you'd just found out her secret. They have the same mama, different daddy."

"So it seems."

We were both quiet for a minute. "I think Mr. McNally was at the station asking about me today. And I think I need to call Pete."

CHAPTER 39

Pete answered on the first ring. "Hi Babe. I was about to call you. I just dropped the boys off—full of junk food, with bags full of early Christmas presents from Uncle Pete. Great boat parade wasn't it? You home yet?"

"I am. Want to come over and watch me on the eleven o'clock? And want to hear what Aunt Ibby found out about creepy guy?"

"Sure do. I'm about fifteen minutes away. Want me to pick up anything?"

"I don't think we need anything. We're in my aunt's kitchen."

"No worries about food then. I'll be right along. Love you. 'Bye."

"Pete's on his way," I said. "I'll start the coffee."

"I think maybe I'll heat up that left-over stew in case he's hungry." She opened the refrigerator while I measured out the coffee.

"He might not be," I said. "He said they ate junk food on the wharf." She didn't bother to answer, just gave me the raised eyebrow look. Silly me. Aunt Ibby's Beef Burgundy? Of course he's hungry.

O'Ryan scooted into the back hall to greet Pete just as the oven timer dinged. Aunt Ibby grabbed the oven mitts while I opened the kitchen door. Pete gave me a big hug and a really nice kiss then turned his attention to my aunt who held the white ironstone tureen aloft.

"Hello, Pete," she said. "Have a bite to eat while we talk?"

"Thanks, I will." He took off his jacket and hung it on the back of his chair. "Now what's all this about the creepy guy?"

My aunt put napkin, silverware, and a full plate in front of Pete, then sat down. "I happened to be doing a little research on Richard McNally," she began, "and I've found a few things about him that you may not know."

"I trust your research, Ms. Russell, almost as much as I trust your cooking." He held up a fork. "This is fabulous, as always. What did you learn about McNally?"

Pete put his fork down the minute my aunt began to relate the story of McNally's father's obituary and the revelation that Lilly is McNally's half-sister. "Nice going, Ms. Russell," he said. "We knew there was a business relationship between them in Atlanta, but we hadn't caught onto the family ties at all. Nice going."

"There's more," I said. "Guess who she had to ride with in the boat parade."

Questioning look. "I don't know. Who?"

"Lilly Jeffry," my aunt said. "That's who. The whole evening with no one else to talk to." She frowned. "I mean except that goofy Santa Claus they had driving the boat."

"You didn't tell her what you'd learned, did you?"

"Of course she didn't," I interrupted. "She's on the case." That brought raised eyebrows from both of them.

"Anyway," my aunt continued, "I'm quite sure I managed to carry on a normal conversation without letting on that

I knew about her brother. But what does that mean, Pete? Why don't they acknowledge the relationship? I wonder if Albert knew. I wonder if that's how McNally got on the board so quickly."

"What about Conrad Gillette?" I asked. "He must have been a recent appointment too. He's not from Atlanta, is he?"

"No," Pete said. "He's local. His family's in real estate."

"Real estate. Like Octagon Real Estate?" I wondered.

"No. Gillette's family is much more high end," he said. "Octagon deals more in distressed property. Handyman specials, that stuff. They did the same in Georgia. Not quite slum lords, but almost."

"That would account for Octagon paying Joseph Marshall under the table," I said. "Wouldn't it? Inferior materials? Unqualified tradesmen?"

"Not my case," Pete reminded me. "But yes. It would."

"I wonder if Joseph got my cookies yet," Aunt Ibby said.

"You sent him cookies?" Pete asked.

"No. Of course not. I gave them to Clara to deliver to him."

"Who's Clara?" Pete asked.

"Mrs. Prescott. Anthony's mother," she said.

"I told you we went to see her. Remember?" I said. "She told us that her son was afraid of somebody."

He nodded, finishing the last rich drop of stew. "I remember. I just didn't know her first name. I passed that information on to Sergeant Rouse."

"Do you think he could be afraid of Richard McNally?" I asked.

"Not my case," he said again. "I can't discuss it. Do I smell coffee?"

I poured coffee for the three of us while Pete put his

plate and silverware into the sink. "Pete," I said. "I'm serious. If he was so afraid of somebody that he was about to jump off a roof, and if that same somebody is stalking me, I need to know about it."

"What do you mean, he's stalking you?" Pete put his cup down so fast it splashed coffee into the saucer. "McNally?"

"Well, maybe not exactly stalking," I admitted. "But he seems to show up where I am too often to be coincidental. I think he was at the station today asking Rhonda about me."

"Why didn't you tell me that? Okay. Now it's my case too. Rouse went to the hospital and talked to Marshall. He doesn't know for sure exactly where the threat came from, but he's afraid it was McNally."

"Do you know what Joseph—Anthony—did to make anybody angry enough to threaten him?"

"Nothing serious enough to commit suicide over, as far as I can see. Seems he was using company materials and company time to work some outside jobs. Trying to make a few extra bucks, I suppose."

"Maybe it's not McNally then," I said. "Wouldn't McNally just fire somebody that did that?"

"People are funny," my aunt put in. "You never can tell what somebody else might do. After all, stealing building materials is a lot different than taking ball point pens and paper clips from an office." Long sigh. "I know what rebuilding the top two floors of this old place cost. A pretty penny, I'll tell you."

Pete poured himself another cup of coffee and topped off mine. Aunt Ibby declined, pleading that it might keep her awake. "You're right, Ms. Russell," he said. "If what Marshall stole was worth a lot of money, someone might get very angry. Angry enough to make a serious threat."

"That doesn't mean the person would ever carry out the threat. People say things they don't mean when they're angry," I reasoned.

"You're right too," Pete said. "How about this? I'll get with Rouse in the morning and we'll compare notes. She'll understand that I'm concerned about you."

"It's almost eleven." Aunt Ibby tapped the face of her watch. "Let's watch the news on the big TV in the living room. I'm anxious to watch the boat parade from the camera's point of view."

"I just want to see the gorgeous field reporter," Pete said.

We followed my aunt to the living room where she sat in her regular chair, manning the remote control, while Pete and I sat together on the couch.

Buck Covington's handsome face loomed on the screen, while a parade of lighted boats moved past his head in the background. "Goodness. It looks as though he's really there," Aunt Ibby exclaimed. "But he wasn't."

The magic of television," I said. "Marty is a genius."

Buck ran through a few perfectly enunciated national news items, introduced a couple of commercials, then got to the scheduled parade spot. Buck used almost the same intro Scott had used earlier. "Our own Lee Barrett was on scene at Salem's spectacular lighted boat parade. We certainly had a beautiful night for it. Lee?"

I'm always critical of my performance every time I watch myself on television. The blue ski suit looked okay. My hair was too curly as usual but didn't look as bad as I thought it might.

The boat with the cute princesses and the *Frozen* theme came into view. Marty had zoomed in on the little girls who were totally adorable. Yacht after sailboat after fishing vessel, all aglow with lights, crossed in front of the camera, and WICH-TV's top camerawoman displayed each one to its best advantage.

"I wonder if Marty was able to include the footage Francine got of your boat, Aunt Ibby," I said, just as that very scene seamlessly appeared. Francine's lens had played, almost lovingly, over the entire length of the *Octagon*—from Rudolph's red glitter nose to the silver-sparkled trees in the stern. Aunt Ibby's and Lilly's smiling faces were shown in a neat close-up. Even the Santa Claus at the helm was shown in such detail that I was sure it was Nick.

I'll tell him next time I see him that I was impressed with his boat handling ability.

The segment wound up with the *Octagon* shot, and Buck returned with the new footage of the "person of interest" making his way down Hawthorne Boulevard and back. "If you recognize this man," Buck said, "call the number at the bottom of your screen."

"The man changed his clothes between the time he left the hotel parking lot and the time he returned there," Aunt Ibby observed.

"Yes, he did," Pete said. "We're hoping that if we keep showing these pictures, somebody, somewhere will recognize the clothes, if nothing else."

"According to Nielsen WICH-TV has a pretty big audience. We cover all of the North Shore and then some," I said. "Surely somebody out there knows who this is. Have you been getting tips at all?"

"Oh, sure. But so far none of them has panned out."

"That's assuming the person in the video is, in fact, the killer," Aunt Ibby, wearing her wise old owl face, pointed out.

"Even if he isn't," Pete said, "he was in the right place

at the right time. There's a good chance that even if he didn't do anything, he saw something."

On screen, Buck Covington was winding down the nightly news. "Stay tuned for Scott Palmer and The Salem Scoreboard with all the latest school hockey and basketball scores, followed by our own lovely Wanda the Weather Girl, with some not-too-lovely weather to tell you about."

Pete leaned forward. "Gotta see how the Salem-Beverly hockey game went. Both teams are playing really well this season."

"I'm interested in what Wanda has to say," Aunt Ibby declared firmly. "I heard there's a storm headed our way and I'm just hoping it won't interfere with my plane schedule. I'm flying off to merry England in a few days, you know."

"I guess you're probably all packed and rarin' to go," Pete said. "Do you need a ride to the airport?"

"Thank you, Pete. Rupert has offered to drive me there. Oh, look. There's Scott Palmer with your hockey scores."

The room grew quiet as Scott rattled off scores, statistics, and stars of the games, accompanied by highlight videos. We joined Pete in a happy shout as Salem scored a last-second goal to defeat rival Beverly 3-2. Wanda was next, wearing a spectacular gold lamé number with some quite astonishing cut-out effects in the upper body area. She did indeed have some dire storm warnings for travelers of an impending northeast storm that some meteorologists had already begun comparing to the great blizzard of 1978.

"I'll surely be keeping an eye on that storm," my aunt said. "It doesn't sound good at all, does it?"

"It might just blow out to sea," Pete offered. "We all know weather forecasting isn't an exact science, especially in New England."

"True enough," she said. "Let's hope for the best."

Buck Covington came back with closing words, reminding viewers to stay tuned for Tarot Time with River North. The scary movie tonight is a holiday special," he said. "You won't want to miss *Jack Frost*."

"I'm willing to miss that," Pete said. "How about you, babe?"

"I'll pass on *Jack Frost* but maybe I'll watch a few minutes of River's readings."

"I'll pass on both movie and readings." Aunt Ibby yawned. "And I'll say good night to you both." She clicked the TV off, a clear signal for us to go upstairs and watch our own TV.

We took the hint, said good night, and climbed the curvy front staircase, which was festooned with greenery, ribbons, and tiny bells.

O'Ryan had beat us upstairs via the back stairway and was already sitting on the windowsill, gazing out into the yard when we entered the kitchen.

"Do you suppose he's looking for Frankie?" Pete asked.

"I wouldn't be surprised." *And if Wanda's forecast is right, that smart little girl cat will be around soon, asking to be let inside.*

CHAPTER 40

"We left our coats downstairs," I said. "Shall I run down and get them?"

"I don't think either one of us is planning to go out again tonight," Pete said, "but if you think they might be in your aunt's way, maybe you should."

"I'll be right back," I promised. "Leave the door open for me. I'll have my arms full." I hurried down the broad staircase and through my aunt's living room, dark now except for the single electric candles in each window. The coats were as we'd left them on the chair backs. I gathered them up and climbed the two flights again, thinking about how some of my friends paid good money for stair-step machines. Not me!

Pete laughed when I returned to the kitchen. "I could hear you all the way up the stairs," he said. "You wouldn't be able to sneak in after curfew with all those little bells in the garlands ringing and dinging with every step."

"I kind of like the sound. Especially since I don't ever have to sneak in after curfew anymore."

"It's midnight right now, Cinderella. Want to see what

your friend River is up to tonight?" He turned on the kitchen TV and opened the freezer. "How about some vanilla ice cream?"

"Sounds good." I opened one of the cabinets above the counter. "I think I have some chocolate jimmies to put on it."

So there I sat with the man I love, at a vintage Lucite table with a disinterested cat on a nearby windowsill, eating premium vanilla ice cream with chocolate jimmies while watching my best friend's show on a wall-mounted flat screen TV.

It doesn't get much better than that.

River looks gorgeous for every show, but for this one she was celebrating the upcoming Winter Solstice in an all-white strapless sheath, accented with about a million sparkling crystals. She'd woven a crown of baby's breath into her long black hair and finished off the look with a fabulous 1950s rhinestone necklace. (I know because I was with her when she bought it.) When her theme music, "Danse Macabre" faded, River faced the camera. "I have something to share with you, my dear friend of the night, before I do my first reading." She walked across the set and stood beside a small tree in a bright red ceramic pot. It was decorated with twinkling lights and tiny silver bells. "I like to celebrate Winter Solstice at my house. It's on December twenty-first and this is my Winter Solstice tree. It's a live lemon tree. I keep it on my patio where it's warmed by the sun year round." She lifted a silver goblet and drank from it. "On the day of the Winter Solstice, the shortest day of the year, in the olden days in England farmers used to offer a toast in cider to the health of their trees and give thanks to them for producing fruit, encouraging them to continue producing abundantly. My Winter

Solstice wish for you, dear friends is that you too be blessed with vibrant health in the year to come, and may you produce wonderful things that bring you joy."

I liked what River had said. "That was interesting—about the farmers. You know, people like to learn something even when they're being entertained. I'm going to try to do more of that with my reports."

"I guess it's not too hard when you're talking about trees, but how about when you're trying to catch a killer?"

I thought about it. "I think people like to know the how and the why. How was he killed? Why was he killed? We still don't know either of those things about Mr. Eldridge, do we? A blunt instrument doesn't tell us much. And without the how we can't know the why."

"Never thought about it quite that way," he said. "But generally speaking, I suppose you're right."

I returned my attention to the TV. "Hello caller, your first name please?" River said, picking up the deck of Tarot cards.

Maybe if the person in the videos had a name, we could learn the "how" of Alfred Eldridge's murder. That should lead to the "why."

By the time River finished her first reading Pete and I were both yawning. O'Ryan had hopped down from the windowsill and was already curled up at the bottom of the bed. "Ready to call it a day, babe?" Pete looked toward the bedroom. "I can't stay awake even for *Jack Frost*."

"I can't either. If you'll hang up our coats, I'll take care of these dishes and we can call it the end of a very long day."

So with coats hung, dishes washed, makeup removed, Pete's gun safely stashed in the bureau, and the cat relegated to a soft cushion on a chair, I fell asleep in the strong arms of a loving man, untroubled by dreams or visions or nagging questions.

I awoke to the fine smell of coffee brewing. I could see Pete's reflection in the oval mirror as he set our New Hampshire Speedway mugs on the table. He was fully dressed for work. "You're up early," I called, swinging my legs over the side of the bed.

"Got a call. Have to go in early to meet somebody. Coffee's on."

"Smells good. I'll join you." After a quick face wash and tooth brushing, I picked up my full mug and joined him at the table. I looked up at Kit-Kat clock. "Chief Whaley called you really early. Must be an important meeting, huh?" I said in a not-too-subtle hint for information.

"Not the chief," he said. "You got any more of those Pop-Tarts?"

I opened the cabinet. "Raspberry or strawberry? Who called then?"

"Strawberry please." He smiled. "I know what you're doing."

I put two tarts into the toaster and tried to sound innocent. "What?"

"You're prying. Snooping. Interrogating." Another smile. "And you're getting better at it."

"I am? So you're going to tell me?"

"Yes. The call is from Mrs. Drake, Vinnie's mother. She says Vinnie remembers now where he'd seen the man who hired him to steal Ms. Jeffry's computer. She's going to stop by the station on her way to work to tell me about it."

"That should be helpful," I said.

"Maybe." He lifted the two tarts from the toaster. "Vinnie's kind of a flake though. I'll listen to what she's got. If it's anything I'll bring him in for some more questions. And Lee, I'm only telling you this much because I don't want you digging around looking for answers yourself. I can just picture you and your aunt now, going over to Mrs. Drake's house, laden with cookies, pumping the poor woman for information."

I put two more tarts into the toaster. Raspberry ones. "Okay. You've got me. No cookies. I promise." I pushed my luck some more. "Will you tell me what she says?"

"Maybe. Gotta go. See you tonight?"

"I'm going with Aunt Ibby to a Belles' rehearsal tonight," I said. "I could call you when it's over if you want."

"Yes. Call me." He kissed me. "We'll do something."

O'Ryan followed him to the back door. I poured myself another cup of coffee, put my raspberry Pop-Tarts on a plate, and turned on the morning news. Phil Archer was in the anchor chair advising viewers about the morning traffic which was somewhat messed up as usual. City councilors were warring among themselves, and citizens were warned that there were some Christmas Grinches stealing packages from front porches. So far, it didn't appear to be an exciting news day.

I had some extra time before I had to go to work, so I spent most of it taking a long hot shower, fussing with my hair more than usual, and doing an extra careful makeup job. I picked out lined blue jeans, a creamy Irish knit sweater Aunt Ibby had brought to me from Ireland, and my leather NASCAR jacket. I laid them all out in a neat row on the bed. O'Ryan leapt up, and with precise steps walked around and sniffed each piece.

"What do you think, cat? Do you approve?"

"Meh," he said and jumped down to the floor.

"What do you mean, 'meh'? I think it's a great combination. What do you know? You don't even wear pants," I told him as I dressed for work.

Phil Archer was right about the traffic. Christmas shopping was in full swing and Dancing Cop had his white gloved hands full keeping things moving. "Grandma Got Run Over by a Reindeer" provided background music for the intricate ballet of street-crossing pedestrians and slow-moving vehicles.

Things were moving along in an orderly fashion at WICH-TV too. Rhonda had my typed schedule all set and Francine had the mobile van gassed up and ready to roll. "You don't have any appointments set until your eleven o'clock at the Peabody-Essex Institute to see the doll houses," Rhonda said, "so Mr. Doan suggests that you take a ride around the neighborhood and see if you can find something worth a live shot that Phil can use before he goes off the air at ten. Phone Mr. Doan for his okay first."

"I've got an idea," Francine said as we headed for the elevator. "I saw a guy over on the common this morning. He was flying one of those little drones that take pictures. Do you think Phil could use a short interview with him?"

"I've seen him over there too," I said. "I've always wondered how those things work. I'll bet a lot of other people do too."

"I hope he's still there," she said. "My roommate and I used to have one of those remote-controlled model helicopters. I'm pretty sure it works something like that." She parked on the south side of Washington Square, next to the hotel. "Look, there he is."

Francine unloaded the camera and hand mic from the van while I called Mr. Doan. "Good idea, Barrett," he said. "I've often wondered how those things work."

"Me too," I said. I thought about my recent realization

that people like to learn something when they're being entertained. This was that kind of topic. As Francine and I drew closer to the drone flyer I was surprised to see gray hair. I'd expected a young techie type, not a man who might be around my aunt's age. He'd just landed his drone when we approached, so we had a good look at it. My first impression was of plastic and propellers with a small camera attached.

Would he mind being filmed live for WICH-TV? He'd love it. Francine signaled Marty to patch us in to Phil's show and we waited for her signal to proceed. Francine began a countdown. Three—two—one—

We, and our audience, became acquainted with Charlie on camera. He answered my questions succinctly and with good humor. He'd bought the drone on sale on Black Friday for his grandson's Christmas gift. He'd decided to try it out and had been "trying it out" every day since.

"Do you always fly it from here on the Common?" I asked.

"Most mornings at around sunup," he said. "I've been sending her different directions every day. Salem is beautiful from up there. I like that time of morning. Quiet and pretty. Well, usually quiet except for the danged music from over there lately." He pointed toward the boulevard. "I only get about twelve minutes flight time from one battery though. Bought an extra battery this morning," he said. "Couldn't wait until tomorrow to try her out. It looks like we've got some weather coming our way. Can't fly this baby in a snowstorm."

I asked the kind of questions I thought might both teach and entertain. I learned, along with my audience, that these tiny aerial acrobats have plenty of tech tucked into the lightweight frames. Unlike Francine's remote-controlled helicopter, the drone can fly, hover, or navigate without input from a pilot. "I give it a GPS position and it can self-stabilize," Charlie said. "The thing is amazing." He pulled a smartphone from his pocket. "I can use Wi-Fi and even communicate with her from this."

"Do you save all the videos you take?" I asked, hoping against hope the answer would be "yes," and that Charlie had been flying the little drone on the morning of December first.

"Sure do. I've been taking pictures since the day after Thanksgiving. Every morning. They're all archived on my website." He handed me his card. I read his name and website aloud, then slipped the card into my jeans' pocket.

I wound up the interview by asking what his grandson was going to get for Christmas, now that Grandpa had fallen in love with the drone. "That's easy," he said. "Another one of these."

As soon as I was back in the van I hit Pete's private number and left a voice mail message. "You might want to check with a man who flies a drone with a camera from the Common early every morning." I recited Charlie's name, phone, website, and e-mail from his card. "He was there on December first." I knew the idea that the drone had captured anything related to Eldridge's death was a long shot, but I was sure Pete would think it was worth a try.

I looked at the card again. Maybe I should show this to Aunt Ibby. Charlie was an interesting man and he wasn't wearing a wedding ring.

Silly me! She's already balancing two gentlemen friends. But his name would fit right in with her Charlie's Angels idea.

CHAPTER 41

At the Essex Institute we spotlighted a wonderful dollhouse built by a Salem cabinetmaker in 1876. The house has been electrified so we were able to peer with the camera into every elaborately furnished little room. It was decorated with Christmas trees, wreaths, garlands, and presents for every member of the resident doll family. Santa Claus and his reindeer stood poised in the rooftop.

"Kids are going to love this," Francine said. "Look at the tiny dishes on the table, the little lace curtains, the decorations on the tree."

"Not just kids," I said. "Moms and grandmas too. Every woman who ever had or wanted a doll house will love it. I hope they'll run this more than once."

Happy with our morning's work, we returned to the station shortly after noon. Phil Archer greeted us with fist bumps. "Good job girls. Nothing better to pick up morning ratings than live TV from the field." We checked with Marty about placement for the dollhouse story which was slated to be part of a children's Christmas special show. We'd just started walking down Derby Street to the Scratch Kitchen when my phone buzzed. Pete.

"Hi babe. Good catch," he said. "I got in touch with Charlie right after you called. We're going through his archives now. Chief says to tell you thanks too. There's a chance we may have something."

"Chief says thanks?" Tom Whaley and I got off on the proverbial wrong foot the very first time we met and things hadn't improved much since. "That's good to hear," I said. "And you think there may be something there? That the drone might have spotted something? Don't keep me in suspense. What did you find?"

"Not what we expected. I'll tell you what I can when we're sure. I just wanted you to know you were a big help. I'll see you tonight at the bell ringing thing."

"What'd he say?" Francine asked. "Charlie and his drone might be helping the cops?"

"Sounds that way. But he wouldn't say how." A cop boyfriend, however wonderful, can be a pain sometimes. "It's a cop thing," I told her. "Whatever it is, I never would have thought about Charlie if you hadn't mentioned him."

"That was just luck," she said, "but it looks like old Charlie may turn out to be even cooler than I thought."

"I have a feeling you might be right." We'd reached the restaurant and hurried inside, away from an increasingly cold wind. The giant television set over the bar was tuned to the weather report. The room was uncommonly quiet and all eyes were glued to the TV. Even the waitress who directed us to a table barely looked away from the screen. A voice from the bar broke the silence. "Looks like she's gonna be a howler."

"It must be the storm Wanda's been talking about all week," Francine said. "Everybody's been hoping it'd blow right past us and go out to sea."

"From the looks of that weather map it's heading right for us," I said. "It's grown bigger and closer since last night. It's a good thing the boat parade's over with. I hope everyone has their boats safely tied down."

"I'd better tell Eddie to get the van over to the garage for snow tires." She wrinkled her nose. "You know when this thing hits Mr. Doan will have us driving around town freezing our buns off so that the people all hunkered down nice and cozy can enjoy the storm on TV."

The normal hum of conversation in the room had picked up, and from what I could overhear, it was all about the coming storm. Francine's comment about snow tires made me think of my car. It would take more than new tires to make that sweet convertible storm-worthy. "I guess I'll lock the Corvette up in the garage and take a cab or walk when I need to get somewhere."

"Good idea. My truck has four-wheel drive so I'll be okay."

"I think my next vehicle will be a truck," I said. "More practical." We ordered our lunches and talked about me doing a standup on camera in a howling blizzard. It was an exciting, but terrifying thought.

By the time we got back to the station all talk there was about the weather. The weather and food. In New England, in the face of severe weather, we always assume that A.—we're going to lose power, and B.—we're probably going to be stuck in the house for days, and C.—we must hurry to the grocery store and stock up on water and bread and we must immediately cook everything that's in the freezer. Rhonda said that Wanda had brought three changes of clothes, figuring that she'd be updating the weather maps every couple of hours.

I called Aunt Ibby to find out what she wanted me to pick up at Shaw's market—besides bread and water. "Oh, Maralee," she said. "I was just about to call you. Two things. First, that interview with the man who flies the drone was wonderful. And the dollhouse segment was charming." She paused and took on a more serious tone. "Now for the second thing. Nigel phoned and he's concerned about the storm that's on the way. He's afraid my flight will get canceled. He wants me to leave tomorrow instead of Saturday."

"That's a pretty abrupt change of plans," I said. "Do you think you'll be able to get plane reservations on such short notice?"

"Nigel has taken care of that. We have a direct flight on British Airways from Boston to London tomorrow morning," she said, adding, "First class."

"Wow!" I was seriously impressed.

"Being an official at New Scotland Yard has its benefits," she said, "but Maralee, it presents another problem. A big one."

I knew what she was going to say. "The concert. You won't be here for the Belles concert. What are they going to do if you aren't there?"

"I've called Conrad Gillette and explained our situation," she said. "I told him I know of a competent substitute who can take my part"

"Oh, that's a lucky break. Who is it?"

"Why, it's you dear. I told him you had experience with the bells . . ."

"Aunt Ibby!" I sputtered. "That was in the second grade. They had pictures of ducks and bunnies on them!"

"Same principle. When we rehearse this evening, you'll stand beside me to get the idea of how we all work together. It's only three bells, for goodness' sake, and one of them is only used in the closing number." She sounded absolutely confident. "Mr. Gillette kindly offered to have the previous director—he retired when Conrad took over the Belles—work with you a couple of evenings if you think you might need to brush up a bit."

"Oh yes. I definitely would need to brush up on my hand bell ringing skills," I said, knowing my tone was sarcastic.

"Fine then. It's settled. See you when you get home." And she was gone. I still didn't know about the bread and water.

"Everything okay?" Rhonda asked. "You look a little confused."

"Hmmm. Yes, you might say that." I sat in one of the turquoise chairs. "But, no worries. I'll figure it out. Somehow."

"Good. Mr. Doan says we'll be using Wanda this afternoon and evening for every break so you and Francine can go early. Besides, he says Francine is going to film the bell ringers tonight for a couple of promos? That right?" Francine and I both nodded. "Anyway, the weather is the news today. That storm will likely be here by the weekend and it's getting bigger." Big smile. "Then you girls will see some real outdoor action!"

"Looking forward to it," I said. Big fake smile. "Guess I'll just head over to the grocery store then. Storm supplies you know."

Francine's truck was missing by the time I got to the parking lot. She'd probably beat me to the store. The mobile van was missing too. Gone to get snow tires I guessed. I looked up and down the street. Not a Santa in sight. I walked carefully across the lot to my beautiful car, bright Laguna blue against the backdrop of the dreary gray water of the harbor where waves were building, frothy white caps forming on their tops.

There was plenty of activity at the market. I pushed my cart up and down the aisles where the usual storm basics were fast being depleted. I grabbed the last case of Evian and selected three loaves of bread, one white and two whole wheat, and a large bag of O'Ryan's favorite kibble. A quart of milk and a package of Ring Dings found their way into my cart and remembering that I'd see Pete after the rehearsal I picked up a frozen pizza and a bag of salad mix.

After the rehearsal where I'd probably make a damned fool of myself.

When I arrived at home my superefficient aunt had already lined up her three suitcases in the front hall and arranged several oil-filled hurricane lamps, half a dozen flashlights, and a full box of candles along with a box of matches and a fresh package of batteries on the kitchen counter. "In case you lose power while I'm away," she explained. "There's wood for the fireplaces in the woodbin behind the garage, and the gas stove will keep the kitchen warm. Try to use up everything in the freezer, and . . ."

"Aunt Ibby, I'll be fine. Don't worry."

"I'm sure you will dear. But I wish now I'd installed a generator. And I wish I'd put a gas stove in your apartment instead of electric. And I wish . . ."

I laughed out loud. "Aunt Ibby, stop. I'm thirty-two. I've survived a couple of hurricanes in Florida. Just relax. Is Mr. Pennington going to drive you to the airport in the morning or do you want me to?"

"Rupert will be here at five tomorrow morning. My flight isn't until nine but there may be a crowd escaping the storm."

"Sounds like you've got everything handled. Frankly, I'm more worried about the hand bells than about the snowstorm."

"No need. You'll see. The main difference is the notes instead of numbers."

"And no ducks and bunnies," I muttered.

"I have every confidence in you, Maralee. I've called Lilly and she's arranged to meet us at the community center early so that you can look at the sheet music and handle the bells, get the feel of it all before the others get there."

"That's so nice of her and it'll help. I guess," I said. "I picked up water and bread at Shaw's. Do you need any of either one before I go upstairs and put them away?"

"No. I have everything I need. Let's leave for the center at a little before five. That'll give us an hour or so to get you acquainted with the bells."

"Okay. What should I wear?"

"It doesn't matter a bit," she said. "We all wear long black choir robes and white gloves, even for rehearsal."

O'Ryan and I went upstairs—he ran ahead of me and waited on a tall kitchen stool, watching as I unloaded the canvas bag. "Yes, I remembered to buy cat food. King-sized box. See?" I pulled the colorful package from the bag and tucked it into an overhead cabinet. "Plenty for you—and Frankie too, if she shows up." We both looked toward the window. No white cat. I patted O'Ryan's soft fuzzy head. "Don't worry. She knows she's welcome here."

I put the pizza into the freezer, checking at the same time for the vanilla ice cream supply. Half a gallon. *We'll have to eat it all before the power goes out. Pete won't mind that.*

With all of the supplies put away, I changed my heavy wool sweater for a long sleeved blue silk shirt, figuring the lighter weight would make bell ringing easier. I still had time to make some notes. First, I transcribed the information from Charlie's business card onto an index card. Next I wrote down everything he'd told us onto another—filling both front and back sides. What had Pete learned from Charlie's archived films? His message had been so cryptic. He'd seen something he didn't expect to see. What did that mean? I hoped that he'd share whatever it was—and soon.

We decided to go to the rehearsal in the Buick—probably safer and certainly warmer than mine. Aunt Ibby backed out onto Oliver Street and we were on our way with time to spare. The music still rang out from the tree lot as we passed. We both hummed along to "Hark, the Herald Angels Sing." I waved to the nondancing traffic cop who manned the corner after five o'clock and told my aunt that I'd saved Charlie the drone man's cards in case she was interested.

"I wonder if he flies that thing over our house," she said. "Does it peek in windows?"

"Never thought about that," I admitted. "I suppose it could. Pete's already looking at Charlie's archives. I'll ask him what he thinks."

We passed one of the smiling, bell ringing Santas in front of the building, and I recognized Lilly Jeffry's car when we pulled into the community center lot. The WICH-TV mobile was there too.

"Lilly is already here," Aunt Ibby said. "She's such a good friend. I just wonder why she's chosen to keep her relationship to Richard McNally a secret. Seems out of character somehow."

"Maybe there are hard feelings between them over something," I suggested. "I guess that happens even with brothers and sisters. I've never seen them together. Have you?"

"Yes. I have. They seem to have a cordial, businesslike association. Sometimes he even attends rehearsals. Maybe he'll be here tonight."

I took a furtive look around the darkened lot for the

Lexus and was relieved when I didn't see it. The WICH-TV mobile unit was already parked. Lilly welcomed us at the door, ushered us into the dressing room where we joined the rest of the Belles removing jackets and hats and donning black choir robes and white gloves. Then Lilly, in her typical take-charge manner, led us to the stage—and the bells.

The two tables were arranged end to end, center stage, each one sheet-covered. They looked just as the tables I'd seen in the storage locker had, with upright bell handles creating miniature mountain ranges. The stage lights were bright and I shaded my eyes with my hand, searching the audience for Francine. She was in the front row, camera aimed at the stage.

Lilly stood in front of the table and clapped her hands together for attention. "Before we begin, ladies, Mr. Gillette and I have a special surprise for you tonight." She moved toward where Aunt Ibby and I waited and extended her hand toward my aunt. "Ibby Russell, the surprise is really especially for you."

My aunt's eyes widened and she made a "who me?" gesture with both hands, as Lilly Jeffry continued. "Ibby will be on her way to England tomorrow, and will be unable to be with us for our annual Christmas Belles concert on Saturday." There was an immediate undercurrent of conversation among the Belles. "Don't worry, girls," Lilly said. "Ibby's niece Lee Barrett will take over her spot. Lee was playing the bells before any of us. She'll be fine."

I smothered a laugh at the preposterous statement.

"Ibby, will you assist me in removing the covering from the bells?" She led my aunt, who still appeared puzzled by all the attention, to the table. "You take that end and I'll take this one. We'll lift the sheets at the count of three. One-two-three!"

There was a collective gasp as the covers fell away, revealing not the expected rehearsal bells, but the glittering, gleaming unmistakable beauty of the bells Lilly had shown us in the storage locker.

"We wanted you to have the joy of playing these bells, Ibby, and besides, it gives the rest of us the opportunity to get used to them before the performance on Saturday. It's a win-win. Now, let's all get to work."

Aunt Ibby expressed her thanks as we and the other Belles took our places. Each table accommodated five ringers. One at either end and the other four facing the audience. There was much tentative gloved-finger touching of the shining bells.

"No need to be nervous," Lilly insisted. "They play the same way the rehearsal bells do, they just sound better. Richer. You'll see. But first, I have a presentation to attend to." She faced offstage. "Conrad? Would you come out here, please?"

There was a lull as Conrad Gillette entered the stage. Lilly moved toward him, holding an oblong, holiday wrapped package, provoking a chorus of giggles. "What's happening?" I whispered to my aunt. "What's so funny?"

"Joke present," she answered. "It's a really hideous Christmas tie. She told us about it last week."

"We couldn't resist buying this for you, Conrad," Lilly said. "With your impeccable taste in clothing, we knew this would be a worthy addition to your wardrobe and that you will enjoy wearing it for years to come." More giggles and shouts of "Open it!"

Conrad Gillette groaned, then smiled broadly. "Thank you all so very much. I know it will become one of my favorite things. Like the beautiful bright green sateen jacket with all four Teenage Ninja Turtles embroidered on the back which you gave to me last year." He tore the paper away and lifted the cover, and held the silk tie up for everyone to admire. It was totally hideous, extra wide, neon colored, with a mish-mash of snowmen, angels, Christmas trees, dogs and cats, and undecipherable doodles. All of the dogs, cats, snowmen, and angels had stick-on googly eyes. It was a masterpiece of bad taste. The Belles loved it. Gillette accepted it in good humor.

"I will save this for a very special occasion," he promised, then clapped his hands together. "All right, ladies, let's get to work."

Aunt Ibby took her spot at the end of a table and I stood close beside her. "These are my three bells," she said. "These are the only ones you'll have to worry about. Here's how we lift them. She grasped the smallest one by the handle. "Here's how we play them." She shook the bell from side to side. "See? Easy peasy. Now you do it." So I did. She was right. It was almost exactly like playing the second-grade bells, just a little heavier. I tried both bells and felt a lot better about my ability to pull this off without messing up. These bell ringers used sheet music on clipboards instead of numbered charts and unadorned shiny bells instead of primary colors and barnyard animals. We decided that Aunt Ibby would play the first song while I stood close by, watching her every move. Then I'd take over on the second while she watched me and we'd continue to alternate songs. It seemed like a good system for learning.

Conrad Gillette walked to the podium. I took my place beside Aunt Ibby. She opened the sheet music to "Jingle Bells," picked up the two smaller bells from the padded tabletop, and awaited the director's signal. He stood facing us, baton raised. The room was silent. There were a few spectators in the audience but Pete wasn't among them.

With a downward stroke of the baton, the bells began to chime. I watched my aunt's every move, looking away only long enough to glance at the music sheet. I studied her wrist motion, how high she lifted the bell, how carefully she returned each bell to the table. Remarkably, I remembered enough from my piano lesson days to follow the simple musical score.

Now if I can only coordinate the motion and the music, I'll be fine.

"Jingle Bells" came to a satisfying close. Gillette made a few gentle suggestions about meter. There was a faint rustling sound as the Belles searched their music sheets for "Good King Wenceslas," and I took my place in front of the two bells while my aunt stood beside me, watching, and once again the baton was raised. At that moment Pete arrived in the auditorium and took a seat in the back row. I picked up my two bells and focused on the baton.

The downstroke. I rang my smaller bell right on cue. I watched the baton in Gillette's right hand for the beat, the meter. So far so good. With his left hand, Gillette motioned to various positions on the long table. His cupped hand told the ringers when to chime in, his flat palm gave the signal to soften, to slow down. Like the dancing cop signaling to drivers and pedestrians.

No. Not the cop. These were the motions of the "person of interest." Possibly the motions of a killer. I had to tell Pete, but how? I struggled to maintain focus. Small bell, larger bell, both in unison. Small bell alone. One-two-three ring. One-two-three ring. I managed to make it through the song somehow without any significant errors. How was I going to get Pete's attention?

I'd turned off my phone, but it was in the pocket of my

jeans. Did I dare to pull it out and text Pete? Conrad Gillette made it easy. He pulled his own phone from inside his suitcoat and glanced at it. "Take a ten-minute break, ladies," he said. "Your next number is 'Joy to the World.'" He headed backstage and I reached into my back pocket.

Pete, I texted. Gillette is man in video. Hand motions.

CHAPTER 42

Pete stood and walked toward the stage, pausing at the exit leading to the dressing room. Aunt Ibby tugged on my sleeve. "Was that Pete?" she whispered. "Is anything wrong?"

"Yes. No. Maybe," I stammered. "I . . . I noticed something. I texted him. I guess he's checking it out."

"You noticed something? What is it?"

I looked around at the rest of the Belles. A hum of conversation buzzed around us and a few of the women flipped the pages of their music sheets. No one seemed to be noticing us. "Gillette is the man in the video," I whispered. "I'm sure of it."

"Conrad?"

"The tell," I said. "The music from the tree lot must have triggered the director's hand motions. What we thought was a beckoning gesture to another person was actually a signal to his imagined hand bell ringers. That was the tell."

"Of course it was!" She gasped. "Why didn't I see it? What will Pete do now?"

It didn't take long for us to find that out. From outside we heard the unmistakable wail of police sirens. Conversation halted. We all looked at each other. Lillian Jeffry, as usual, took charge. She stepped to the lectern on the vacated podium and held up her hands for silence. "Something's happening here, girls. I don't know what. Just relax, everybody. I'm going back stage and find out. Meanwhile, take a look at that crescendo at the end of 'Joy to the World.' It sounded a little ragged last time we played it."

Her words seemed to calm the group. Everyone stayed in place, although no one appeared to be studying the musical score as Lilly had suggested. I wasn't calm though, and neither was my aunt.

"Should we follow her?" Aunt Ibby asked. "Goodness knows what she's walking into back there if you're right."

The sound of the sirens had stopped. Other than the occasional tinkle of a bell, the silence was eerie. "Pete's there," I reasoned. "She'll be okay."

Two uniformed officers approached from the direction Lilly had taken. I recognized Officer Costa and Officer Marr. "Ladies, may I have your attention please?" Costa said. "There's been an—um—an accident in another part of the building. We're clearing the premises. Please gather your belongings and follow Officer Marr to the exit. Someone from your organization will contact you later. Thank you for your cooperation."

I stripped off the robe and gloves, picked up the clipboard with our music sheet on it, and headed for the dressing room, my aunt and the rest of the Belles close behind me. Any semblance of order disappeared quickly as the women grabbed coats and purses, hurrying to return to the auditorium where they'd be escorted to the front door. "Aunt Ibby"—I said, pulling my press pass from my purse—"you go along home. I'm going to find Pete and see what's going on."

"I don't want to leave without you," she said. "Come with me."

"I'll be fine," I assured her, at the same time motioning for Francine to join me. "There are police all over the place, so something is going down. We already have a camera here. This might be more important than Wanda's weather report."

"Call me as soon as you can then," she said. "And Maralee, be careful."

"I will," I promised, and with my press pass clipped to my shirt, and Francine close behind me, her pass on a lanyard around her neck, we headed for the long hall with its row of glass-walled offices. I could see a knot of uniforms outside of a lighted cubicle at the end of the corridor. I hurried toward them. Not unexpectedly, I was stopped. I turned to face an officer. "WICH-TV," I said, smiling and pointing to my ID. "Lee Barrett. Nightly News."

"Sorry, ladies," he said, smiling right back. "You can't go down there."

"It's all right, I know them." Pete's voice came from behind me. "Hello, Lee, Francine."

"Hello, Pete—Detective Mondello," I said. "What's going on?"

He took my arm, steering me away from the officer, back toward the auditorium, speaking softly. "I'm going to tell you what's happened, Lee, but you and Francine have to report from outside the building. This isn't anything in here you need to see. It isn't pretty. Francine, you'll have to go outside right now." He pointed toward the door. "Absolutely no cameras in here." Wordlessly, Francine obeyed.

"Is this about Conrad Gillette? Am I right?" I insisted. "Is he the one?"

"I didn't get to question him. Got here a little too late."

"He got away?"

"No. He's still here." Pete's jaw tightened. "But he's dead."

I didn't react to Pete's statement the way I felt that I should. Had I become somehow desensitized to death after I found Mr. Eldridge's body? Shouldn't I feel shock or at least surprise?

"What happened to him?" My question sounded flat. "It must have been sudden. He left the stage only about ten or fifteen minutes ago."

"An apparent suicide," Pete began. "He was . . ." Pete was interrupted by a woman's voice from the end of the hall.

"You have to let me in. It's my office and he was my associate." It was Lilly Jeffry's voice. "So, back off."

"Lilly?" I looked at Pete.

"'Fraid so. How did she get here so fast?"

"She left the stage right after you left the room. You didn't tell me how he died." I prodded. "Come on. I have to get out to my mobile unit."

"Apparently he hanged himself in a closet." Pete leaned closer to me, dropping his voice, "with a silk necktie. Stay here for a minute. I need to try to reason with Lilly."

I didn't have a minute to wait. Francine was outside waiting for the story. I had enough already for a breaking news spot. We'd tease with that, then hopefully I'd have some more for the middle of the seven o'clock news. I should have the whole story by the time Buck Covington's eleven o'clock show began.

I'd left my NASCAR jacket in the dressing room. No point in going back for it now. Besides, I had a warm Salem State sweatshirt in the back of the mobile, leftover from a spring break story last March. Trusting in my smile, my press ID, and the official look of a clipboard, I moved along the corridor toward the door and the lighted cubicle where Francine and I had met with Lilly and Gillette only a couple of weeks ago.

I heard Lilly's voice again, louder now, unlike her usual well-modulated tone. "How could Conrad have done this terrible thing? He was my friend. He was dear Albert's most trusted confidant, his strong right-hand man." Pete's back was toward me. I could tell that he was using his cop voice but I couldn't make out the words. I made it almost all the way to the exit before I was stopped again. The mobile unit was parked just outside the glass door, Francine standing beside it, shoulder mount camera ready. "Hello officer," I said. "Lee Barrett. Nightly News. Detective Mondello says we have to shoot from outdoors only."

That worked. He stood aside. "Okay Miss. If Mondello says so."

On my left was that lighted glass cubicle. I caught a brief glimpse past the uniforms, past Pete and Lilly Jeffry. I saw the top part of an open closet. It was impossible to miss the colorful scrap of silk tied to the closet pole. That had to be the ugliest Christmas necktie ever.

CHAPTER 43

Francine had already contacted Marty back at the station, made the necessary connections, and we'd be ready to roll at her signal. "Aren't you cold in that skinny little shirt, Lee?" Francine asked.

"I'll just grab my old sweatshirt. It's in the back of the van."

"Better hurry then. We can shoot a thirty-second teaser in five."

I climbed into the van and found the gray sweatshirt, no problem. Not the most appropriate look for a field reporter, but neither is pneumonia. I pulled it on, arranged the collar of the blue shirt over the V-neckline, took my place in front of the Community Center sign beside the glass door, picked up my mic, and waited for Francine's on-air signal. I looked around the parking lot. No Lexus. The bell-ringing Santa was still on the corner though, and that was somehow comforting.

Francine focused a spotlight on me and began a countdown. "Five-four-three-two-one." She pointed. I began. "This is Lee Barrett, speaking to you from outside the Community Center, here in Salem. The popular and well-known Christmas Belles gathered here this evening for a rehearsal of their hand bell Christmas concert. The evening has ended on a tragic note. A man has been found unresponsive on the premises, the victim of an apparent suicide. Stay tuned to WICH-TV for more details."

Francine gave me a thumbs-up. "Got some more details for midway through the news? Scott Palmer wants to know."

"Tell Scott don't worry. I've got more." I said, not giving details because other than the method of suicide I didn't have anything. If I couldn't dig up some more factual stuff before seven-thirty, I'd have to stretch my sparse knowledge of what had gone on in there tonight to fill five minutes. I texted Pete once more.

Got time to do a short interview?

I waited for what felt like an hour but was only minutes.

No can do babe. Maybe later.

Great. What was I going to do with five minutes of valuable air time and about two minutes of material? Lilly Jeffry, with what at first looked like her typical efficiency, came toward us. "Oh, Lee. You still here? Conrad's dead, did you hear?" She seemed to notice the lights, the van, and my mic for the first time. "Are we on television?" She covered her eyes with one hand and squinted in Francine's direction.

"No. Not right now. I hope to do a short report at seven-thirty though. Can you tell me a little about what's going on in there?"

She sighed. "Not a lot, I'm afraid. I tried to get into my office, but they wouldn't allow it. I understand of course, but I promised not to touch anything. Poor Conrad's body is still on the floor. It's decently covered, you know. They're waiting for the medical examiner to declare him dead." She covered her mouth and smothered a laugh. "How dead can you get, hanging in a closet with your Christmas necktie around your neck? Oh yes. Conrad's dead all right."

I realized that Lilly was obviously not herself. It would be cruel to question her further. I put an arm around her shoulders. "Do you have a ride home?" I received a blank look. Handing my mic to Francine, I steered Lilly back toward the officer who now stood in front of the glass door.

"Ms. Jeffry isn't feeling well," I said. "Can you find someone to assist her?" He gave Lilly a searching look.

"Right away. Ms. Barrett. Does she need a doctor?"

"Don't talk about me as though I'm not here, young man," she snapped. "I'm fine. No doctor. Just a little upset is all. How would you feel if your best friend wandered off and hanged himself for no reason? I'm just a little upset. Tell this boy that I'm fine, Lee. You tell him that. Now, where did I park my car?"

She clearly was not fine, and more than a little upset. What could I do? Francine tapped her watch as the minutes to seven-thirty ticked by. Lilly Jeffry's shoulders shook beneath my protective arm. The young policeman backed away from us. "I'll get somebody. Wait right here," he said.

My sense of relief was enormous when Pete appeared behind the officer. He pushed the glass door open, taking in the situation at a glance. "This has been difficult for you, Ms. Jeffry. I'll arrange for a cruiser to take you home. We'll secure your car." He turned toward me. "I can give you a brief statement, Lee. Will that help?"

I nodded, relinquishing my grip on Lilly's shoulder.

Pete spoke into his phone and a cruiser, lights blazing, moved from the parking lot toward us. Pete assisted Lilly, who seemed to have regained her composure, into the backseat of the cruiser. "Thank you, detective," she said. "Thank you too, Lee."

"Good night, Lilly," I said. "I'll call you tomorrow."

Pete moved closer to me. "How about you, babe? Holding up all right?"

"I am," I told him. "It's getting close to broadcast time. You said you could give me a statement?"

"A statement." He smiled his best smile. "No questions. Okay?"

"Okay. Can I ask questions when we get home though?"

"You can ask. Now where do you want me to stand?"

Francine took over the placement issue, positioning both of us in front of a community bulletin board where notices of upcoming events were displayed. The Christmas Belles concert poster was prominent among them. It was decided that we'd share one handheld mic and we stood facing one another.

Lights on. Countdown begun. "Five, Four. Three. Two. One." Francine pointed to me.

"Good evening, ladies and gentlemen. Lee Barrett here, outside of the Salem Community Center. What began as a joyous evening inside this building, when the popular ladies musical group, the Christmas Belles, gathered for rehearsal of their annual holiday concert, has ended in tragedy. Here with me is Salem Police Detective Pete Mondello. Detective, would you tell our audience what's happened here tonight?" I held the mic toward Pete.

"Thank you, Ms. Barrett." Sincere cop voice engaged. "I happened to be in the building this evening observing the Belles rehearsal. While there, I received a citizen's tip that a person of interest might be on the premises. I immediately called for backup, and on investigating, I discovered an apparent suicide victim in one of the many first-floor offices here."

My turn with the mic. I had to ignore the no questions ultimatum. "Detective, has the victim been identified? Can you disclose the name?"

He nodded, grim faced. "The man has been identified. We're not disclosing his name pending notification of family."

"I see." I pushed for more. "You mentioned that a person of interest had been seen on the premises. Any connection?"

"Not that we can determine at this time." Slightly annoyed look. He handed the mic back to me, and backed away. Interview plainly over.

"Thank you for your time, detective," I said, as he bowed slightly, politely toward the camera and walked away. "There you have it, ladies and gentlemen. An apparent suicide here at the community center. WICH-TV will continue to bring you the latest information on this unfortunate event."

Francine gave the "cut" signal and turned off the light. As I helped pack the equipment back into the van, a mobile unit from a rival station pulled in behind us. I couldn't help smiling. It's good to be first in this business.

Another set of headlights illuminated the bulletin board. The medical examiner had arrived. He exited the long black vehicle and strode toward the door, his black bag at his side. He paused briefly as he passed me. "We meet again, Ms. Barrett," he said, touching his fingers to the brim of his hat.

"Hi, doc." I returned his greeting, a little embarrassed by the circumstances. I'd been present for the discovery of two bodies in one month. How bizarre.

"Want to hang around and see if we can come up with anything new for the eleven o'clock news?" Francine asked.

"Maybe. First I need to see if they'll let me back inside to get my purse and jacket." I approached the officer at the door who must have been sufficiently impressed with press pass, clipboard, and acquaintance with the lead detective to believe I was worthy of admission. "You'll have to go around to the street door though," he said. "That's how the choir ladies all left. I'll call over there and tell them to let you in."

I followed his instructions and since Officer Marr, who I already knew, recognized me, I was indoors right away. I approached the auditorium and was surprised to see that the set of hand bells was still on the table. These were the super expensive bells. I knew that they were too valuable to be left out in plain sight. Once again, I called Pete.

"You still here, Lee? Do you need a ride home?" He didn't sound annoyed about the questions I'd asked. That was good. I'd almost forgotten that I didn't have my car.

"Maybe later. I just came back inside to get my jacket," I told him, "and I noticed that nobody has put the bells away. They're pretty valuable. I know where they're supposed to go. Maybe you can get somebody to unlock the storage room and stick them inside for now."

Patient cop voice. "Okay. I'll be right there."

I walked onto the stage, cut across to the dressing room, and found my belongings just where I'd left them. I pulled on my gloves and tossing the jacket over my shoulders, I waited for Pete by the long padded tables and the bright brass bells. I reached for the largest bell, the C-3 which would only be used in "The Carol of the Bells." I hadn't yet had a chance to use that one. I had gloves on. I guessed it would be all right to touch it. I hefted it in my right hand. Heavier than the others, I guessed it weighed eight or ten pounds. Not too heavy to swing back and forth though. I was confident I could handle it at the concert—if there'd be a concert, with the music director dead. The two sheets that had covered the bells were neatly folded on a nearby chair. I picked them up, holding them in front of me with both arms.

Pete appeared from the wings. "These are valuable, huh?" He pointed to the bells.

"Lilly says so. They belong in the storage locker at this end of the main corridor. The door is marked. You'll need the key I suppose."

"Somebody must have a set," he said. "The tables have wheels. I'll push them one at a time if you direct me to the locker." Pete unlocked the wheels and moved the first table easily, almost silently, not even disturbing the bells, still upright on the cushioned surface. I directed Pete to the storage locker. "So far, so good," I said. "Now to get it open."

Pete tried the door. It swung open at his touch. "Looks like nobody bothered to relock it after they got the bells out," he said. "Maybe the bells were the only valuable things in there."

He maneuvered the table inside. I tossed one of the sheets over the bells, carefully tucking it in around the edges, the same way Lilly had. We repeated the process with the second table.

"Probably we should lock it now," I said. "Lilly will know where the key is when—if we need the bells again." I took one more look around the narrow room, noticing a rack of Halloween costumes, a penguin-shaped piñata, and a sprinkling of blue glitter on the floor. Pete was right. The bells were the only things of value in the locker. He pressed the lock button, then escorted me back to the front door.

"I'll be working around here for a while yet," he said. "Are you going to do the late news broadcast from here?"

"I expect so. We have a couple of hours before then. Francine will drive me home first so I can get a warmer coat then she'll pick me up later. Any more information to share right now?"

"We've contacted Conrad Gillette's family," Pete said. "It's okay for you to release his name if you need to."

"Thanks," I said. "Call me later?"

"I will." There were too many people milling around for us to kiss, so we said a polite good night, and I went out the front door and walked around the building to where Francine waited in the van with the heater running full blast. It felt good.

CHAPTER 44

On the way to Winter Street I phoned the new information to Mr. Doan. "Come in and do it live on Covington's show," he said. "Let Francine go home and you lose the sorority girl sweatshirt for this one, okay?"

I'd have time to change into something appropriate for studio TV, and to catch Aunt Ibby up on what was happening. I called Pete yet again and told him what I was doing. "I don't want to drive my car with the weather so iffy, so I'll take a cab to work," I told him. "I should be through by eleven-fifteen if the offer of a ride home is still good."

"Works for me" he said. "It's been a really long day. Looks like that storm is stalled offshore. Maybe it'll miss us after all."

His "maybe" was doubtful. If the witches believed it was going to be a bad one, I was pretty confident that it would be. "Anyway," I said, "I hope it holds off long enough for Aunt Ibby and her girlfriend to get on that flight to London."

Francine dropped me off in front of the house. O'Ryan greeted me in the foyer and my aunt's cheerful voice called to me from her office. "Hello, Maralee. I'm just printing out my boarding pass. I'm so excited! My flight is on schedule. Rupert will pick me up here at five in the morning and Nigel will be at Heathrow to meet us. Everything is falling into place as it should." She appeared in the doorway. "It's dreadful about Conrad. I've spoken to Lilly. She's completely distraught and no wonder. Come in and sit down for a minute. Is it true that he hanged himself with that joke necktie? Do you think it's because he actually was the man the whole city's been looking for?"

"I'm afraid it is. It's up to the police to figure out why, I guess. Did he kill Mr. Eldridge or did he know who did?" I sat on the living room couch and she sat in her usual chair. "It's a mystery piled onto another mystery."

"What does Pete say about it?"

"Not much." I said. "You know Pete. Did you watch my little interview with him?"

She nodded. "Yes. He wasn't very forthcoming, was he?"

"Goes with the job." I stood. "Speaking of jobs, mine isn't over for the day yet. Mr. Doan wants me to do a few minutes with Buck Covington at eleven to talk about what happened. I'm going to change clothes and call a cab. Pete will bring me home."

"I'm glad you're not driving. Lilly said that she had to leave her car at the community center. A policeman drove her home."

"Yes. Pete arranged that. She wasn't quite herself."

"I should think not. Losing two friends in one month—what a shame." She made a "tsk-tsk" sound. "What do you suppose will happen with the concert? I know the music director we had before Conrad took over is still available, and they say he directs a hand bell chorus at a church in Marblehead. 'The show must go on' and all that."

"They'll have to make a decision quickly. Tomorrow the witches celebrate Winter Solstice, the concert is scheduled for Saturday and Sunday is Christmas Eve. Busy weekend ahead, and maybe a blizzard to boot." I started for the front stairway. "Why don't you try to get some sleep, Aunt Ibby? Your weekend begins early tomorrow morning."

The bells on the garlands and the one on the cat all jingled merrily as we climbed the stairs. "Pete's right about the bells," I told O'Ryan. "There'd be no sneaking in late around here when there's a ring-a-ding-ding with every step." I unlocked the kitchen door, clicked on the TV on my way to the bedroom, and opened my closet. I decided on a red wool midi with knee-high boots and was about to check my jewelry box for earrings when I heard Wanda's voice. I hurried back into the kitchen. "This storm, which formed off the coast of South Carolina, has the appearance of an extratropical cyclone," she said. "There's also an Arctic cold front bearing down in our direction." Wanda sounded anxious. Unusual for her. "If the cold air mass merges with the storm," she warned, "it can create a dangerous low-pressure system. Stay tuned for an update from the National Weather Service at eleven." She didn't give her usual trademark low bow at the end of her comments, even though the deep V-neckline of her hot pink satin mini was obviously designed for it.

"Wanda's worried," I spoke aloud. "That's not good."

"Mmm-mmm," O'Ryan said. That didn't sound good either.

I called the cab company and requested Jim Litka, my favorite cabbie. He's not only a good driver but also an amazing source of all kinds of information. I looked forward to the short ride, partly because I didn't want to drive, but mostly because I wanted to hear what Jim's "sources" had to say about Conrad Gillette's death.

O'Ryan and I waited in the downstairs foyer for the

green and white taxi to roll up to the curb. I opened the front door the moment I saw it, but Jim was already bounding up the front steps, taking my arm. "Careful, now, Ms. Barrett. Wouldn't want you to slip and tumble down these stairs." He bent to pat O'Ryan, who licked Jim's hand and purred a happy greeting. "Hi there. How're you doin', old boy?" Jim saved O'Ryan's life once, so it's no wonder the cat loves him.

Jim lets me ride up front with him, so he opened thc passenger door and handed me in as carefully as though I was an egg. "Okay," I said as soon as the cab started moving, "what do you think about it?"

"About which? About is the storm going to bury us in snow and knock out the power for a week or about who offed that Gillette guy?"

"Offed Gillette? You think Conrad Gillette was murdered?"

"I don't think anything about it one way or the other, but one of our dispatchers dates a guy whose brother's roommate is one of the cops who was at the community center when they cut down the man who was hanging in the closet. He says Gillette was strangled before somebody strung him up with a necktie."

"Whew. I don't know what to say." I was really shocked. "If that's true, somebody did it fast. I was there when Mr. Gillette told us to take a ten minute break. Whoever it was must have been waiting for him in that office."

It was Jim's turn to look surprised. "You were there?"

"I was," I said. "My aunt is one of the Belles and she has to be out of town on Sunday. I've been taking a crash course in hand bell ringing so I can take her place."

"Gotcha. 'Course, I don't know if any of that strangling stuff's true. I'm just sayin', but if it was murder, somebody was trying to shut Gillette up about something, right?"

"Looks that way, doesn't it?" This was a whole new puzzle to solve. If Gillette had become more than a person of interest—perhaps a suspect—in Albert Eldridge's killing—was that the reason for someone to kill him? We arrived at the station too soon for any discussion about the oncoming storm. Too bad because he undoubtedly had some special insight into that too. I paid my fare with a generous tip and promised to call Jim if I needed a ride home. "Doesn't matter how late it is, Ms. Barrett. You know that."

Rhonda was at her desk when I got upstairs, even at this late hour. "Do you ever sleep, Rhonda?" I asked—only halfway kidding. *Does she?*

"Mr. Doan is still here too," she said. "He's nervous about the storm and now the second person associated with Historical Charities is dead. It's all too interesting for either of us to leave. Afraid we might miss something." She lowered her voice. "Besides, I'm getting time and a half pay. It helps with the Christmas shopping." She handed me a sheaf of papers. "Here. I transcribed what you said in your earlier spots about the thing at the community center. Thought you might be able to reuse some of it."

I thanked her and headed for the news room hoping I'd have a chance to see River. Since she and Buck Covington had become an item, sometimes she arrived early and watched his show in studio. I was in luck. She was there, already in full late-night show glamor mode—a concoction of black velvet, black lace, and black feathers, provocatively arranged. I imagined it might be difficult for poor Buck to read his teleprompter with such a vision within sight.

"River," I said as I slipped into a chair beside hers in the audience area. "It's good to see you. I'm tempted to ask you to read my cards sometime soon! There's so much going on lately, it's getting hard for me to think straight."

"I'll do it whenever you like." She reached for my hands and held them both. "Take deep breaths. Meditate. Call me whenever you need me." I took her advice about the deep breaths.

Buck invited me to sit beside him at the anchor desk. (I liked the view from there. Maybe someday?) He led with a brief question, asking about what I'd observed while I was at the Community Center. Using Rhonda's transcript and my own impressions, I was able to fill five minutes easily. I revealed Gillette's name this time, mentioning that he and Mr. Eldridge were both associated with the Historical Charities of Salem, and asked once again for viewers to call the scrolled police station number on screen if they had information to share. "Stay tuned to WICH-TV for continuing coverage. We'll also keep you informed as to the status of the Christmas Belles concert." Buck thanked me. River waved and blew me a kiss. I hurried back to the reception area and texted Pete that I was ready to go home if he was.

He was, and the Crown Vic picked me up at exactly eleven-fifteen.

I leaned back in the seat, so glad to be going home. "Long, long day," I said. "I didn't even wait to hear what Wanda had to say about the storm."

"Radio says it's going to smack us by Christmas day."

"That's Monday."

"Yep. Looks like a white Christmas for sure."

Pete parked in his usual spot and we walked together toward the house, pausing to admire the lighted Christmas tree in my bay window. When we passed the garden gate I saw O'Ryan poke his head out though the cat door, then quickly withdraw it. "Too cold for you out here, cat?" I teased.

"Smart cat," Pete said. "He was just checking to be sure it was us, then went straight back to sleeping in the nice warm house."

"That's what I'm ready for too," I said. "I'm sure Aunt Ibby is tucked in all snug in her bed. "

"Visions of sugar plums?" Pete asked.

"I hope that's the only kind of vision around tonight, thank you."

"Been seeing things, babe? Want to talk about it?"

"Maybe later."

We started up the twisty back staircase, treading as lightly as we could, out of consideration for my sleeping aunt. "At least there aren't any noisy jingle bells on this one," Pete whispered. "Ooops. Spoke too soon." O'Ryan, wearing the dreaded bell on a ribbon around his neck, scooted past us to the third floor, jingling all the way.

We entered the living room, which smelled deliciously of fresh evergreen. Pete walked ahead of me, turning on lights as he went. "Want to turn on the TV? See what Wanda has to say?"

"Good idea," I said, "and I'll hang up our coats if you'll start a pot of decaf."

I opened the package of Ring Dings for a sugary weather-watching snack and joined Pete at the table. Wanda repeated the report she'd given earlier and added a warning about coastal flooding. She looked a little happier about it than she had earlier. She agreed with the radio reporter that we'd most likely get hit on Christmas. This time she remembered her trademark low bow.

Pete poured our coffees. "We've seen each other more than usual today, but barely had time to talk."

"I know."

"I was planning to question Gillette before I got your text."

"You were? What for?"

"Remember that I told you about Vinnie Drake and his mother coming in to see me this afternoon?" he asked, not waiting for an answer. "Seems the kid remembered where he'd seen the guy who'd hired him to steal Jeffry's computer."

"He did? Where?"

"Saw him on WICH-TV with a red-headed lady reporter talking about the Eldridge murder."

"That would have been me," I said. "And that would have been Gillette. So why would he need to steal Lilly's computer?"

"Something was on it he didn't want anyone else to see."

"But you checked her computer. You said it was all boring figures and some personal messages."

"There was one we need to take another look at from Gillette, dated the night before the old gent died. It said, 'E. knows.'"

I stirred cream into my coffee. "E. knows what? Did you ask her?"

"Sure we did. She said it had to do with Eldridge's Christmas present. They had the first house in the Heritage Village project all set to show him. A perfect vintage house bought and paid for, she said. They were starting to do the period paint and wallpaper and he found out about it. Spoiled the big reveal. That's all."

"You checked it? "

"Yep. It was all true. If that's what Gillette was talking about. Now we're not so sure."

"You think Mr. Eldridge discovered something wrong with the figures?" I thought about the ledger I'd seen on his desk. "And that Gillette had something to hide?"

"It gets worse," he said, "and I may as well tell you since you helped us out with the drone."

"You said you saw something in Charlie's film you didn't expect to see."

"It was at the very end of the twelve minutes he shot that morning. It showed Lilly Jeffry getting into Gillette's car in that overflow lot behind the hotel and driving it away."

"It was before we found the body?" I asked.

"Hours before that. Whatever this is, Lilly Jeffry is up to her efficient little nose in it."

CHAPTER 45

"As long as we're both awake, want to see what River has going on tonight?" I suggested, "while I try to process what you've just told me?"

"Sure." He reached for a Ring Ding. "I have a feeling it's going to get even more complicated before we figure it all out."

River's music, "Danse Macabre," issued from the TV accompanied by a photographic image of snow falling on Salem's Charter Street Cemetery—a pretty scene in a twisted sort of way. River appeared and announced that in keeping with the season, the night's scary movie would be *Gremlins*.

"Good movie choice," I said. "Everybody loves it and it's not one of her nightmare-inducing flicks."

River began the show by announcing that since it was a few minutes after midnight, the Winter Solstice had begun. "This marks the longest night of the year," she said. "The days will grow longer now, and the hours of darkness will decrease. Please know, dear friends of the night, that if something in your life is shaded in darkness right now, from today on, the darkness will decrease and the light of day will reveal the answers you seek. I wish you all a happy Winter Solstice. Now, let's begin with a reading for our first caller." She reached for her phone console. "Hello caller, your first name and birthdate, please."

"I hope she's right," I told Pete. "I hope the light of day will help to clear up a murder or two around here." I tried to concentrate on the pattern of cards River placed on her table.

"I have a feeling it will," he said, "but it will be because of good, solid police work, not the number of hours between sunrise and sunset." He looked toward the screen, then back at me. "What do you mean, a murder or two?"

Oh-oh. That's what I get for listening to cab company gossip.

"There's a rumor going around that maybe Conrad Gillette was already dead when somebody put him in that closet with a necktie around his neck to make it look like suicide." I watched his face. "Could that be true?"

He gave a grim-faced nod. "The ME is checking into that possibility."

Neither of us was watching the television. "Then it's possible that Gillette was murdered?"

"Possible? Yes."

"It's also possible that Gillette may have killed Mr. Eldridge then," I said.

"I can't comment on that, Lee," he said in his firm, no-nonsense, cop voice. "Want to turn the TV off and go to bed now? Or do you want to watch the movie?"

"Both maybe. I'll use the downstairs bathroom." I went into the bedroom and grabbed a pair of flannel pjs with lots of Donald Ducks on them, then headed out into the front hall. I thought O'Ryan might follow me, but he stayed on his windowsill.

I hadn't quite reached the second floor when I noticed

that the door to the study was ajar—just about enough to admit a cat. I walked slowly along the maroon carpet and pushed the door open, then reached around and pressed the light switch on the inside wall. At first glance, nothing seemed to be out of place. I walked into the room, looking up and down the shelves. "Ha! O'Ryan's been up to his library tricks again," I said as I bent to pick up a book from the floor. I recognized it immediately. Another one from my childhood. In fact, this particular copy of Lewis Carroll's *Alice's Adventures in Wonderland* had once belonged to some long ago great grandparent and I'd always found the John Tenniel illustrations frightening. Even as I replaced it on the shelf, the cover picture of little Alice and the huge Cheshire cat in a tree, grinning his horrible smile at the child, still gave me a chill. I pushed the book into its proper space, turned out the light, and closed the study door, being sure it was securely shut, and made my way to my childhood bedroom and bath.

When I returned to my own apartment, Pete was already in bed, the TV was on, *Gizmo* had been fed after midnight, a commercial for Whole Foods was running, and O'Ryan had curled up in a chair. Pete patted the space beside him inviting me to join him under the covers.

I snuggled up with him, comfortable but still not sleepy. "Pete," I said, "if Gillette was cooking the society's books and Eldridge found out about it and Gillette killed him and Lilly covered up for Gillette somehow, and then somebody killed Gillette, don't you have to question Lilly? And what about her half-brother? Is he involved too?" I sat up straight in bed. "What if they leave town? Shouldn't we do something?"

He pulled me close. "Relax, babe. You know it doesn't work that way. What you say is possibly what's happened, but we need proof every step along the way to make an arrest. For now, we're keeping a close eye on Lilly Jeffry. We've subpoenaed the society's books as well as the ledgers that Mr. Eldridge kept personally. That's a first step. We still have no murder weapon, remember? That's important. As to Richard McNally, his companies seem to do almost all of the carpentry, plumbing, electrical, and painting work on the society's properties as well as the various charity's buildings too. That's unusual, but not illegal. Relax," he said again. I thought again about River's advice. *Take a deep breath. Meditate.*

I didn't get to the meditation part. A few deep breaths were all it took to put me to sleep. It had so far been, after all, a very busy, crazy, confusing shortest day of the year.

I'd set my alarm for four-thirty. I wanted to be awake when Aunt Ibby left for the airport. I got out of bed, trying not to disturb Pete, pulled a bathrobe from the closet, and tiptoed into the kitchen. O'Ryan jumped down from his windowsill and looked up at the cabinet where his breakfast kibble was stored. I took the hint, fed the cat, started the coffee, wondering if the weather would affect my aunt's flight plans. I turned on the early morning news show on WBZ-TV in Boston. Their weather report was mostly concerned with the oncoming storm, but so far there were no canceled flights from Logan Airport. If luck held, Aunt Ibby's direct nine o'clock flight to London would take off and land without incident—meteorological or otherwise.

Leaving cat and boyfriend in my apartment, and with a full coffee mug, I went downstairs to wish my aunt bon voyage. She was already up, dressed, and sitting on the hall-tree bench beside her suitcases. I'd already given her the scarf I'd bought at the museum gift shop and I was pleased to see it peeking out from the collar of her coat.

"Oh, Maralee, you didn't have to get up early just for me," she scolded. "You need your rest."

"You sound just the way you did when I was a teenager." I gave her a big hug. "And if I was flying away for Christmas, you'd get up early for me."

"You're right, of course. But someone else showed up early this morning too. Frankie came strolling through my kitchen cat door less than an hour ago! I've fed her, and I gave her a bell like O'Ryan's, but hers has a green ribbon. She seemed pleased with it."

I glanced around. "Where is she? I'm so glad she came home."

"Oh, she's around somewhere. You know how she is. Likes to stay out of sight." She stood up and looked at the mirror in the hall tree, patted her hair. "Lilly Jeffry is an early riser too, you know, and she e-mailed me this morning that the concert will go on as planned. Isn't that good news? Our old director, Claude Balfe, will take over. You'll all be in good hands." A slight frown crossed her face. "That is if the police get through with their business in the building. It's terrible, what happened there, but suicide isn't against the law."

I wasn't about to pass on cab-company-originated rumors of murder, even though Pete had almost corroborated the story. "Whew," I said. "I hope it's good news about the concert. I'm flying blind here, with no rehearsal to speak of and a new director and those million-dollar bells."

She waved that dismissive hand. "This is the Christmas Belles dear, not the Mormon Tabernacle Choir or the New York Philharmonic. Remember the Irish step dancers? The all-girl cast for *A Christmas Carol* where I played Scrooge? We're not known for perfection." She laughed. "I'm pretty sure the audience would be disappointed if one or more of us didn't hit a clunker!"

A sudden jingling announced that O'Ryan was coming down the stairs. Aunt Ibby stood up and the cat streaked by on his way to the front door. "That will be Rupert," she said as O'Ryan assumed his position at the side window and the doorbell chimed "The Impossible Dream." She opened the door, admitting Rupert Pennington, who immediately picked up the three suitcases, one under his arm and one in each hand. "Good morning, Ms. Barrett, good morning, Ibby. Best we hurry. Airport's a busy place this time of year."

Aunt Ibby hugged me once more, reminded me to open the dampers if I had to use the fireplaces, and to please use the Buick if I had to drive in bad weather. "I'll call you," she said, and whoosh! They were gone.

O'Ryan and I climbed the stairs back up to my apartment. Pete was awake, shaved, showered, dressed for the day, coffee mug in hand. "Has your aunt left already?" he asked, looking up at Kit-Kat clock which read just five. "I meant to say good-bye to her."

"Oh, you know Mr. Pennington," I said. "He's in a rush to get her there in plenty of time to get through security and see her safely onto her plane. And guess what? Frankie is back. Aunt Ibby fed her and tied a bell around her neck this morning."

"That's good news, babe. I know you've been worried about her. Maybe she heard about the bad weather we're expecting. Smart cat. The other guy, Nigel, was wise to have your aunt leave early," he said. "I'm betting there won't be any flights leaving Boston by tomorrow night. The thing is stalled off the coast of the Carolinas now. They're calling it an 'extratropical cyclone.'"

"I know. Maybe the Christmas Belles' concert will be

canceled," I said, almost hopefully. "Even though Lilly has already e-mailed Aunt Ibby that it'll go on as planned."

"She's probably right," Pete said. "Salem is pretty traditional about the way Christmas is celebrated here. People like the Santa parade and the tree lighting on the Common and the Holiday Walk—things that happen year after year, you know? Familiar things. And the Christmas Belles concert is one of those things. Besides, it's a major fundraiser for the Historical Charities."

"What if the rumors about Mr. Gillette being murdered are true? The whole place will be festooned with yellow tape. Closed up tight." I refilled my coffee cup. "Can't do anything about that."

"They'd probably just move the whole shebang over to the high school or the Senior Center," he said. "Stop worrying. From what little I heard at the rehearsal, you play the bells just fine. And I'm pretty sure we'll be out of the way sometime today."

"You going to work early again?" I asked. "You're all dressed and ready for the day and I'm still wandering around in robe and slippers."

"I'm taking an early shift so I can get off tonight and watch your debut as a bell ringer." Big grin. "Wouldn't miss it for the world!"

I covered my face with both hands. "God, I hope I won't embarrass you. Aunt Ibby says the Belles' audience always expects somebody to hit a clunker and this time I'm afraid it'll be me."

"So what if you do? He took my hands in his. "You're taking this too seriously. Just have fun with it—like you did in second grade."

He'd nailed it. I felt better immediately. "You are absolutely right. I'm just going to look at those expensive fancy bells and picture bunnies and chickens and ducks on each one."

"There you go," he said. "Got any more of those Pop Tarts?"

"Aunt Ibby said to use up the stuff in the freezer. How about waffles?"

So we began the shortest day of the year. Pete left right after breakfast. I dawdled around for a while, cleaning up the kitchen, making the bed, folding laundry. I looked but didn't see the elusive white cat anywhere. I put a blue bowl full of kibble next to O'Ryan's red bowl, then followed my aunt's advice and drove to work in her Buick. For all the whoop-de-do about the weather, the day seemed quiet enough, with little wind and no snow. "The calm before the storm," Rhonda said.

Marty had put together half a dozen ten-second clips of the bell ringers from the previous night's rehearsal as Lilly had requested. We previewed them on Rhonda's monitor. The Belles sounded darned good, including the little bit of "Good King Wenceslas" that featured me! Marty added graphics encouraging people to buy the few seats that were left.

Once again, Wanda was designated star of the day, with scheduled weather updates on the half hour—necessitating a significant wardrobe budget increase to maintain her fashion image. Francine was assigned to accompany Scott Palmer to a Polar Bear Club event at Deveraux Beach, where hardy citizens donned bathing suits and took the annual plunge into the frigid Atlantic. This left Old Eddie and me to stand by at the station in case something worthy of live reporting turned up. It also freed me to do some free-lance snooping into the Gillette-Eldridge-Jeffry connection.

I was sure there was a connection there, other than the obvious work-related one.

I got a key to the dataport from Rhonda and armed with phone, pen, index cards, and a street map of Salem, got to work. First, I called my old friend Detective Sergeant Joyce Rouse. "Hi, Joyce," I said, "I'm trying to dig up some background information on the Eldridge death for an investigative piece I'm putting together. What I need is some pretty basic stuff—nothing confidential."

Her "Well, Lee, you know it's an ongoing case" was hesitant.

"I understand. By the way, Francine was wondering if her tip about that backyard running all the way through to Union Street turned out to be useful at all."

"We're taking another look at it now that there are indications that the person in the video may possibly have been Conrad Gillette. I'm sure you've heard about that. As I told you earlier there were no cameras around so we can't be sure. It's nowhere close to his apartment though." She paused. "But do tell Francine I appreciate her trying to help even if it turns out to be nothing. If more people who see something would say something . . . you know how that goes."

"I do, Joyce," I said. "I'm sure you've checked with people on the Union Street side of that property. Anybody over there see anything? Say anything?"

"It was barely light out so the few tips we've had from that area are pretty sketchy and not that reliable. Sorry."

"That's okay. I'm just digging around, trying to make sense of all the loose ends."

"So are we, Lee. So are we. I've got to go now. Good to hear from you. Merry Christmas."

"Merry Christmas, Joyce," I said. I'd already spread the map out on the scarred desktop. Using one of my index cards as an improvised ruler, I drew a straight pencil line from the lot with all the trees on it across Union Street and the next two parallel streets after that. I put down the pencil and leaned back in the chair. If my hunch was right, and I was pretty sure it was, all Conrad Gillette had to do that morning was cut through a few yards at the proper angle and he'd wind up at the back door of the Acme Electrical Company.

The dots were beginning to connect themselves—forming a chain of murder from Albert Eldridge to Conrad Gillette to Lilly Jeffry and straight to Richard McNally's back door.

CHAPTER 46

I filled in quite a few index cards that day in the privacy of the dataport. True, some of my scribbled card comments still ended with question marks, but some of my earlier questions had found answers.

Unfortunately, my connect-the-dots theory had created a new question. A big one. Of the four people in my imaginary chain, two were already dead. Murdered. If Richard McNally was at the head of the chain, as I suspected he was—that's where the thing called instinct comes in—did that mean that Lilly was in danger? If McNally didn't want any weak links in his chain, would he harm his own sister?

Another question mark had popped up on several cards. What was McNally so desperate to hide anyway? It must have something to do with his various businesses, I was sure of that.

The mysterious e-mail on Lilly's computer said "E knows." I knew from Pete's comments about it that he didn't believe the story about Mr. Eldridge discovering his Christmas surprise. I didn't believe it either. But Mr. Eldridge had clearly discovered something—and that something was big enough and important enough to get him killed.

I shuffled those cards around on the desk for the better part of an hour but there were too many questions and not enough answers. I was concerned about Lilly though. She'd begun to show signs of weakness. When we'd discovered Eldridge's body, I'd seen it in her grief. I'd seen it again the previous night at the community center. The smooth veneer of the perfect secretary, the completely in control woman, Hercule Poirot's Miss Lemon—had begun to crack. That weakness could have serious consequences. For Lilly.

Joyce had said, "If you see something, say something." But had I really seen anything? Outside of a string of so far undecipherable visions, I hadn't. Discouraged, I snapped an elastic band around the cards and returned them to my purse. Besides all that, I still had to face the hand bell concert. But by tonight that particular concern would be over with. The rest would still be with me.

I wish Aunt Ibby was here to help me make sense of all this.

I checked the round clock on the dataport wall. Twelve-thirty. Aunt Ibby and Mrs. Abney Babcock were about halfway to London. I was sure she'd probably call me once she got settled in her hotel. Maybe I could bounce a few questions across the ocean. I locked up the dataport and dropped off the key with Rhonda.

Once upstairs I looked around for someone to come to lunch with me. No luck. Francine wasn't back from the beach yet and Rhonda had brought microwavable Lean Cuisine. I thought about going home, but there I'd have no one for company except O'Ryan and he prefers to eat on the floor. I opted for a drive-through and headed the Buick to the nearest Golden Arches.

With a large coffee in the cup holder and a quarter pounder with cheese and extra pickles on the seat beside me, I drove back to the station. I pulled into one of the visitor spaces closest to the building, overlooking the harbor. No lighted boats in sight. The sky was growing dark and the harbor water looked angry, with choppy waves tossing soapy looking foam up and over the seawall. I turned on the radio and unwrapped my sandwich. The weather was the main topic on the all-talk radio station. A National Weather Service forecaster declared that an eye-like formation had been noted in the center of the storm.

That didn't sound good. I turned off the radio, shut off the engine, rewrapped the sandwich, and carried it along with the coffee to the first-floor studio door. The scenery inside had to be more pleasant than the gloomy vista viewed from the WICH-TV parking lot.

I stopped short before opening the door. Was that a black Lexus across the street? The black car passed by quickly. Was I getting paranoid? There had to be hundreds of them in a city of this size. I took a deep breath as River had advised and felt better right away.

Kind of better.

Marty was in the studio directing work on the set being built for the big Christmas Eve day show. "Hey, Moon," she called. "What do you think of the giant blocks this guy is building for the fund-raiser? Cute, huh?" A man in a carpenter's apron looked up from the box-shaped item, frowned slightly, then went back to sanding the edges of the cube. "They're supposed to look like kid's building blocks," Marty explained. "It's a toy land set, and there'll be kids here in the studio. We're going to be featuring your dollhouse piece too. It was short notice for an all-day pitch for donations to the Historical Charities, but after seeing your Women's Shelter piece, and the Veteran Santa Clauses and all, and after Ms. Jeffry's pleading for help for all the worthwhile things the Histy does, he weakened and donated the air time."

"He gave away air time? And he's paying for all this?" I waved at the blocks, the giant nutcrackers, the Rudolph with a glitter red nose.

She snorted. "Paying? Don't be silly. The Historical Charities pays the carpenter, Jeffry got the mall to lend us the nutcracker, and Rudolph came off a boat parade boat." She patted the Rudolph on the antlers. "That woman's a dynamo. Gets 'er done. There'll even be a Santa Claus guest appearance."

"I hope the storm holds off," I said. "Christmas Eve could be kind of wild around here if it doesn't."

The carpenter put down his sandpaper and stared in my direction. "I know you," he said. "You're the one who took pictures of my truck."

Uh-oh.

"I am? I mean, I did?"

"Yeah. It's okay. My boss explained about the lost butterflies. Glad they got rescued."

He turned and picked up his sandpaper. The red embroidery on the back of his khaki shirt spelled out Perfection Carpentry. The name on his pocket said he was Kenny, but I'd be willing to bet he wasn't.

So. The Historical Charities of Salem—the Histy—is picking up the tab?

"Do you happen to have a business card?" I asked. "I'm thinking of adding some cabinets to my kitchen."

"Um—can you pay cash?" He winked. "I can give you a good price."

I winked back. "No problem."

"Sure." He reached into his shirt pocket. "Here you go."

The shiny white card had an illustration of a red hammer with little lines coming from it and the copy declared that the carpenter was licensed, bonded, and insured. I was willing to bet that he was none of them.

Marty looked at him, then looked at me. "Butterflies?" she said.

"Long story," I said. "Tell you all about it later. My lunch is getting cold." I hurried for the metal door that led to the stairs.

I sat in one of the turquoise chairs in the second-floor corridor, took a bite from my rapidly cooling sandwich, and pulled an index card from my purse. I wrote "Perfection Carpentry, Acme Plumbing, Prestigious Electric. How much did Historic Charities of Salem pay to these companies in a year?" Then I texted the same words to Pete.

It didn't take long to get a reply. Checking same thing. STAY OUT OF THIS.

Okay, I texted back. You don't have to yell.

CHAPTER 47

Wanda continued to dominate every break so once again Francine and I were dismissed early. Francine headed for the mall and more shopping, and I went home to Winter Street and cat who greeted me with great enthusiasm. I knew he must be lonely without my aunt's vibrant presence, and gave him extra cuddling and patting and the expensive cat food that comes in tiny silver cans.

The Community Center location for the Belles' concert had been okayed, and there had been no official announcement yet that Conrad Gillette's death had been anything other than a suicide. The corridor with the glass cubicles was closed off from the rest of the building with saw horses and DO NOT ENTER signs, but no yellow tape. Concertgoers would enter from the front of the building just as they always had.

Had my taxi driver informant been wrong? I asked Pete the question when he phoned to see if I needed a ride to the concert.

"The ME hasn't made a final determination yet," he said, "but meanwhile we'll keep the involved part of the building closed to the public."

Next question. "What about the companies I asked you about? And yes, I'd love a ride. You're going to hear my debut, aren't you?"

"I wouldn't miss your debut for the world. Pick you up at six. We'll talk about those companies later. Meanwhile, stay out of it. Promise?"

I promised, then fussed with hair and makeup for about an hour. I figured the black choir robe and gloves would cover everything else.

Pete picked me up at exactly six. The concert wouldn't begin until seven, so the Belles had a little extra time to prepare for the much anticipated event. He dropped me off at the front door, as arranged earlier and went to park the Crown Vic in the back lot. All of the women seemed a little nervous, even those who'd worked with the retired director before. There was some random tentative shaking of bells here and there, and whispered conversation.

Claude Balfe presented a much more formal appearance than had Conrad. He wore a tuxedo, black tie, and all. His white hair was longish in a classical sort of way. The concert wasn't due to start for half an hour yet, but we were all in our positions and Maestro Balfe (he preferred that term) already stood erect at the podium facing the two long tables with the brass bells uncovered. He rapped his baton on the lectern. "May I have your attention, ladies? Thank you." He pointed the baton toward the table. "I noticed that these bells, these precious instruments, have been stored in a common locker along with coloring books and craft supplies, covered only by common bed sheets." Long, effective pause. "This is unacceptable." He raised his voice. "WHERE IS THE BELL CASE?"

Exactly. Where is the bell case? What if that wasn't a suitcase Gillette had carried away from the scene of Mr. Eldridge's murder? Maybe it was a special case for twenty-five bells, ranging from teeny tiny to extra large. I'd noticed Pete ducking into the last row of seats at the rear of the room after he'd parked the car. I shaded my eyes with one hand and peered into the darkness. He was still there. I saw him stand at the director's shouted question and start for the exit.

"Pete! Wait!" I called, and with choir robe flapping, ran down the steps to the auditorium floor. "Wait!"

Pete waited. The director rapped his baton. "This is highly irregular. Come back here, young woman."

I ran down the aisle. "Pete! The case is at the Acme Plumbing company. The empty room. It's right in the window all full of pipes and tools!"

"Thanks, babe." At a dead run, phone in his hand, he was out the door. He was going to miss my debut for sure.

I returned to the stage using my most ladylike slow walk. I apologized to the maestro who simply glared at me, and with my heart still racing, took my place at the long padded table. By then the audience had begun to file in. Even with the warnings of bad weather on the way, it looked as though we'd be playing to a full house. I saw Therese come in with her shoulder-mounted camera, moving toward the front row, ready to begin filming the event for WICH-TV. I was glad she hadn't been there to record any of the previous action, though I was sure she'd hear all about it soon enough.

The program began with the simple one-octave selections. I tried my very best to concentrate on the music score before me—to watch the maestro's hand signals which were much more subtle, yet easier to follow, than all of Conrad's enthusiastic waving and beckoning had been. By the time we'd reached the fourth selection, "Joy to the World," I'd begun to feel quite comfortable with both score and instruments. I even remembered to smile as I jingled each bell.

There was a brief intermission midway through the program. Lilly Jeffry stepped to the lectern and, facing the audience, announced that Bruce and Buffy Doan had graciously offered to host a Christmas Eve day telethon for the Historical Charities of Salem on WICH-TV.

"The main beneficiaries of the Doans' generous gift of valuable TV time will be the Women's Shelter and the Veteran's Christmas Toys for Kids project," she announced. "Will Bruce and Buffy please stand up?"

The Doans stood, to loud applause from the audience, the maestro, the onstage Belles, and me.

"Be sure to watch WICH-TV for this incredibly important event," Lilly implored. "Make your most generous pledges. Checks can be sent to The Historical Charities of Salem." She gave the address. Twice. Then she returned to her spot behind the bell table.

I felt grudging admiration for the woman. Even though, as Pete had said, Lilly was involved in whatever was going on "up to her tiny little nose," she'd managed to shake loose the always "thrifty"—some say "cheap"—Bruce Doan from thousands of dollars' worth of salable TV time.

The hand bell program continued with "Bring a Torch, Jeanette, Isabella" followed by "The Little Drummer Boy." By this time I was really getting into the spirit of the music. The tunes were getting progressively more complex and difficult, and I was getting progressively pretty damned good at this bell ringing gig.

Just before our big final number, "The Carol of the Bells," Maestro Balfe rapped for attention once again and faced the audience. "Ladies and gentlemen," he began, "our next offering is a special arrangement of a timeless classic Christmas song—'The Carol of the Bells.' This beautiful arrangement is the work of our dearly departed friend and dedicated patron of the arts, Conrad Gillette. It is with a sense of great humility that I am honored to conduct the Christmas Belles playing this magnificent piece for your enjoyment." He turned and faced us once again, both arms upraised. "Ladies?"

I was ready. I'd studied the score and this was going to be a piece of cake. These bells might just as well have chickens and bunnies on them. I really wished Pete had been able to stay. The music began with most of the action happening at the opposite end of the table with the gentle tinkling of the smaller bells, like distant church chimes. The music swelled as the song progressed. The audience was silent, spellbound, I thought. I wished Aunt Ibby was here to enjoy this.

The melody soared toward the ending crescendo. I eyed the shining C-3 bell, then watched the maestro's hand, waiting for him to point the baton at me. I looked back and forth. The bell. The baton. The bell. The baton moved in my direction. I reached for the bell. The swirling colors began.

No not now! Not a vision now!

I lifted the bell, willing myself not to look at the picture beginning to form on its gleaming surface. The maestro pointed the baton at me. I moved the C-3 exactly as my aunt had instructed. "It works just like the little bells," she'd told me. "It's just a bit taller."

I rang that bell with all my might, and throughout that big auditorium there sounded, and resounded, a mighty clunker.

The audience grew silent. The maestro glared. My fellow Belles glared. A smattering of applause began, and grew louder until the usual ovation expected at a Christmas

Belles' presentation erupted. Smiles returned to the Belles' faces as we all moved from behind the tables in orderly lines, just as we'd rehearsed, and took our position in front of them. We joined hands and took a bow. Then another. And another. Maestro Balfe joined us and took a couple of bows himself.

I guessed that the standing O meant I was forgiven for the off-tune bell ringing. Aunt Ibby had said the audience would accept a few clunkers. The Belles began to leave the stage, one by one. The audience began to thin and I was about to leave too, when I noticed that Claude Balfe, instead of exiting the stage, had approached the tables and picked up the C-3 bell, holding it carefully by two gloved fingers. He looked back at where I stood, not speaking. After a long moment I joined him beside the table. The building had grown silent. He stood there, holding the bell and looking at me in a most accusing manner.

"I'm sorry, sir," I said. "I don't know what I did wrong. I'm really sorry."

"Hadn't you ever rung this bell before? At rehearsal?" he asked.

"No sir. I never had. Neither had my aunt. And last night, after what happened, we never finished the rehearsal."

"I see. Well, let's try a little experiment, shall we?" He lifted the bell, and without hesitation, rang it. Another clunker. "Thought so," he said. "If the bells were kept in their proper cases, this sort of thing wouldn't happen."

"What sort of thing?" I asked. "What's wrong with it?"

"Why, somebody's dropped it or mistreated it somehow." He held the bell up close to his eyes. "I can't see the dent, but I know it's here somewhere; You sure you didn't accidently drop it, young lady?" Again the distrustful glare.

I shook my head. Vehemently. "No sir. I never even tried to ring it before tonight."

"It's no wonder," he grumbled. "Imagine it! Keeping hand bells in a closet with crayons and glue and playthings. I wouldn't be surprised if they've allowed the children to play with them." He clutched the bell to his chest. "Barbarians."

I didn't comment further. I thought of the brief glimpse of a vision I'd seen in that same bell. It was a blur of red. A blood red Santa hat.

"Excuse me, sir," I said. "I think we need to call the police."

CHAPTER 48

I knew Pete was probably trying to get access to the Acme Plumbing office by then, but I called him first anyway. There was no response after a couple of rings and I was about to hang up when he answered. "Yep. What?" Brusque cop voice.

"It's the big bell. The C-3," I told him. "It's dented. I think the bell is what killed Mr. Eldridge."

"Have you got it there? The bell?"

"Maestro Balfe is holding it right now. Carefully."

"With gloves?"

"Of course."

"I'll be right there. Chief's getting a warrant for the Acme place. You were right. The suitcase is in plain sight in the window. We're looking for McNally now to let us in. Is Lilly Jeffry still there?"

"I don't know." I looked around the empty stage, and out into the empty auditorium. "She went with the others."

"Okay. I'm in my car now. Sending help your way. Just stay where you are. I'm coming." He hung up.

I was wrong about Lilly. She hadn't gone with the others.

Enter Lilly Jeffry. Stage left. A tiny woman in a choir robe with a large gun.

"I believe I heard one of dear Albert's bells ringing out here." She made a sideways motion with the gun. "Put the bell on the table, Claude," she said. "I'll take care of it."

Balfe held the bell tighter and moved away from the table. "No." he said. "It needs to be repaired. It's a wonderful bell. It can be fixed as good as new. I'll see to it."

"I'll take care of it," she snapped. "That stupid damned Conrad must have dented it swinging it at the old fool's head."

"Do as she says, Maestro," I spoke softly. "Please put it on the table."

Pete had said he was sending help. I looked toward the back of the auditorium. Listened for sirens. Nothing. Claude Balfe hesitated, then placed the bell back onto the table in its proper position. Lilly grinned. "Good boy, Claude. Now back away. That's a good boy."

I don't know why Lilly even thought for a minute that she'd get away with stealing that bell. She barely made it out the door to the hall. Then, handcuffed, she was led away without a word. Pete arrived a few minutes later, put the bell into a large evidence bag, and turned it over to a man in a CSI jumpsuit.

"I'll send you home in a cruiser, Lee," Pete said. "I've got a lot of loose ends to tie up here. You okay? You were a real help tonight. Chief says thanks."

"I'm fine," I said. "Did you get the bell case from the plumbing store?"

"We did."

Balfe spoke up then. "You found the case? That's good

news. Could I have it please? I'd like to put these bells away properly."

"Sorry," Pete said. "It needs to be cleaned up. They've been using it for tools and junk for nearly a month. Besides that, there are traces of blood in it. We expect it's Albert Eldridge's blood."

"Is Lilly going to jail?" I asked.

"She's under arrest. Asked for a lawyer already."

"You know I have to call all this in to the station," I said. "It's my job."

"I know. Call you later." He paused. "By the way, your photographer is still outside. I wouldn't be surprised if she got a picture of Lilly Jeffry in handcuffs in time for the eleven o'clock news."

"Hmm." The maestro spoke quite firmly. "Awkward."

I frowned. "Awkward?"

"Why yes. I believe your photographer recorded Ms. Jeffry speaking glowingly of the owners of your television station." He pursed his lips and made a tent of his hands. "Now she has quite likely photographed Ms. Jeffry being led away in handcuffs. It'll be awkward to reconcile the two events, won't it?"

He was right, darn it. I ditched the choir robe and gloves, grabbed my coat, and went outdoors in search of my former student, now professional videographer, Therese Della Monica. I didn't have to look far. She was waiting for me just outside the front door. The wind had picked up and it had begun to snow.

"Some excitement here again tonight, huh?" She smiled. "How come the nice lady who said all that good stuff about the Doans got arrested?"

"You got your car, Therese?" I asked.

"Sure. Mr. Doan didn't think this event justified using the gas hog mobile unit. He just wanted a few little clips for the news." Another smile. "I guess he didn't know she was going to introduce him and Buffy. What's going on?"

I sighed. "It's a long, long, story. Let's get the video back to the station and figure it out."

"My car?"

"Yes please. I was supposed to get a ride home in a cruiser, but it looks like we'll be working late." I told the officer who'd been volunteered to provide taxi service for me that I'd found a ride with a friend. Therese and I left the Community Center and drove back to the TV station. We huddled in the downstairs studio with Marty who, as usual, had all the answers. We'd use some short clips of the music, which was the original plan. We'd omit Lilly's flowery speech about the Doans' generosity. It was too late to stop the telethon after they'd blocked out time, advertised it all week, and built a special set for it. Anyway it was still a good cause. The shelter needed the money and who didn't want little kids to have toys? We'd run a still shot of Lilly getting into the backseat of the police car and have the newscaster report that Ms. Jeffry had been detained by police and that she'd retained counsel. Period. Awkward moment neatly averted. It had taken less than an hour. We'd made it in time for the eleven o'clock news with ten minutes to spare.

Scott Palmer stopped on his way through the studio to the newsroom. "Hey, you folks looked out the window lately?"

"There aren't any windows down here," Therese reminded him. "Why?."

"Looks like our long-awaited blizzard has started," he said. "Snowing pretty hard out there already."

"No kidding? I haven't seen a really good snowstorm since I got back from Florida." I hurried to the side door and looked outside. It was quite beautiful. The snow made halos around the street lamps and it was already sticking to the branches of trees, turning the brown twigs and brushwood into graceful sugary shapes.

"Close the door," Scott said. "It's cold out there. Wanda says it's making its way up the coast and it's going to dump a lot of snow on us. Power outages. Limited visibility. Strong winds. The whole shootin' match. White Christmas in spades. You got copy ready for Covington to go with the video about the bell thing? I'll take it upstairs. How'd it go anyway?"

"Went off like clockwork." Marty handed him the copy for the music clips and a separate sheet for the brief squib about Lilly. "There you go, Scotty."

"Thanks. See you girls later."

"I'm going to stay here tonight," Therese announced. "I don't like driving in the snow. I'll just curl up on the couch in the break room. Want me to call you a cab, Lee?"

"No thanks. Call me crazy, but I only live on the other side of the Common. I'm going to hoof it across. It's not really blowing hard yet and it's so pretty."

"It's cold though. You think you'll be warm enough?"

I pushed up the sleeve of my parka. "See? Silk long johns. Used to wear them skiing in Vail. Warm as toast under ski pants and sweaters."

"You sure about this?" Marty frowned. "You could stay here too. There's a couch on River's Tarot Time set and another one on the Home and Garden display."

"Gotta go," I said. "My cat worries about me. See you guys at the Christmas party." I pulled my hat down covering my ears, pushed open the side door again, and stepped out into that beautiful snowstorm.

I was excited. I remembered playing on the Common during storms when I was a kid. It was true that I hadn't seen a good old-fashioned winter nor'easter in many years, Too many years. This was going to be fun.

I stayed close to the side of the building and emerged onto Derby Street. The Christmas lights looked even prettier viewed through the whirling snow. I looked both ways before crossing, but I didn't need to. Not a vehicle in sight. I hummed the chorus of "Joy to the World," then realizing that no one was around to hear me, sang the words out loud. What fun!

I hurried along Hawthorne Boulevard, smiled up at the statue of Nathaniel Hawthorne sitting there, oblivious to the snow making a pointy hat on his distinguished literary head. There was no activity in the tree lot. No music either. That was a disappointment. The dancing cop crossing guard wasn't there. No need. The stores were closed.

I suddenly felt all alone in my city.

The hotel was just ahead and I focused my attention on the lighted windows. I knew there were people behind those windows, warm, happy people. I felt better. It occurred to me that I could check into that hotel right now and join the warm, happy people. But, no. I was halfway to Winter Street already. Soon I'd be home with two cats and my Christmas tree and a lovely cup of hot chocolate.

The Common is just past the hotel and around the corner from the Historical Charities of Salem building—Albert Eldridge's home. No Christmas lights there. Odd. They'd been on earlier in the evening. I remembered seeing them. The community Christmas tree in the bandstand glowed brightly even through the snow, which was accumulating really rapidly on the ground around me. Visibility was fast decreasing too. I entered through the arched gate, and using the bandstand as a beacon, headed straight across the Common for home.

I hadn't gone very far when a sound puzzled me. I stopped to listen. The sound stopped too.

Imagination.

I walked a little faster. There was a distant popping sound and the street lamps surrounding the Common went out. Boom. Just like that. I stopped and looked back at the hotel. Those friendly oblongs of yellow light were gone too.

Well, that's what Wanda said was going to happen, Dummy. Widespread power outages.

I was happy to see that my beacon, the Christmas tree, was still on.

Must be run on batteries or maybe it has its own little generator.

I began to walk again, glad for the tall boots, not so happy about the heels. I heard that sound again. It came from somewhere in the darkness behind me. I walked faster. Stopped. Listened.

It's getting closer.

I started, stopped, listened. Started, stopped, listened. Time seemed to have slowed down. How long had I been trying to cross the Common? And how long had I known that I wasn't alone there? At last I reached the iron gate that exits onto the street. I was being followed. I needed help.

Pulling off one glove, I fumbled for the phone in my jeans. No signal. No light. Blank screen. How can that be? Can a storm knock out a cell phone? I shook the phone. Tapped it against the gatepost. Nothing. I slipped it into the parka's big front pocket and walked faster. Listening.

CHAPTER 49

There hadn't been a snow plow through the neighborhood yet, and the snow in the middle of the street was just as deep and wet as it was in the middle of the Common. I wanted to run but my feet felt as though they had iron weights on them, pulling me down. Was the sound growing closer? My breath was coming in deep, painful, burning gulps.

Take deep breaths. Relax. Breathe. Breathe. Good. Now run.

I ran then. Somehow my feet pumped up and down. I was across the street. I felt, rather than saw, the massive boulder that formed the Civil War monument on the corner and moved to the left of it toward the brick sidewalk that led to my front door. To home. To safety.

The thing, the person, the animal, Jack Frost, Gizmo, Jack Skellington—whatever whoever was behind me was getting closer. I was sure of it. I could hear it breathing.

No. That's me. Breathe. Breathe. Relax. Run.

Right foot up. Right foot down. Left foot up. Left foot down.

There were intermittent flashes of light. Lightning?

Exploding transformers? I saw the house. The front steps. The front door.

Keys. Keys? Where the hell are my keys?

I tore off the gloves and dropped them onto the snow. Reaching into the deep front pocket of the parka, closing icy fingers on the keyring, crying tears of relief—I'd made it home. I climbed to the landing, felt for the keyhole with my left hand, struggled to force the key into the lock with my right.

Too late. The footsteps were directly behind me on my own front steps. Whoever it was—whatever it was had caught up with me.

"You okay, little lady?"

I whirled, slipped, fell. Strong arms grasped my waist, steadying me. I faced my pursuer.

Santa Claus?

"You okay?" he asked again, voice gruff.

"Nick? Is that you?"

"Sure is. I've been trying to catch up with you all the way across the Common. What are you thinking, woman? Out all alone on a night like this! You crazy? Here. Give me that key."

Wordlessly, I handed it to him. After a couple of tries, the door opened. There were no welcoming cats in the front hall. Odd. Pulling off the wet boots I kicked them aside. I remembered the candles and matches Aunt Ibby had placed on the Sheraton table and, in stocking feet, felt my way toward it. I heard the door close behind me. "Wait a sec. I'll get us some light," I said, striking a match, glad of its radiance. There were half a dozen red candles in holders of varying heights on the table. I lit all of them. A pretty Christmas arrangement. A welcome source of light in the inky darkness. *River uses red candles for lots of spells. Mostly* good ones.

I picked up the candle in the tallest candle holder, turned toward where Nick stood in front of the door. He looked big, very big—and his shadow, wavering in the candlelight, looked even bigger. He took a step toward me, the light reflecting in his eyes, making them glow red. A few specks of blue glitter sparkled in the beard. He smiled then, not the friendly Santa Claus smile I'd grown accustomed to, but a grin—the wide, mouth stretching grin of the Cheshire cat.

That awful smile had frightened me when I was a child. It frightened me now. I backed away from the man, feeling the newel post of the staircase against my back. The bells in the festive garlands gave a merry little jingle at my touch.

He took another step in my direction. The nice warm Santa smile was back. "Figured it out, have you, sweetheart?" Then the nice warm Santa smile was gone. The warm ho-ho-ho Santa voice was gone too. He was right. I'd figured it out. Too late, but I'd finally figured it out.

The smile. The smiling cat. That's what O'Ryan had tried to tell me with the Alice book. Look at the smile. I'd seen it on more than one person. I'd even commented on it. Lilly Jeffry had that smile and used it to advantage. Lilly's stepbrother, Richard McNally, had it but rarely used it. Behind the fake beard, the brush-on ruddy complexion, Nick had it.

"McNally," I said. It wasn't a question.

"Right. I knew when I saw you snooping around at the plumbing store that you'd have to be dealt with eventually." The cat-grin was back when he took another step in my direction. I moved backward onto the first step, facing him eye-to-eye.

Dealt with?

I reached for the railing. The little bells tinkled again *Relax. Breathe. Breathe. Think.*

I thought. In the big dark house I had the advantage. I knew my way around in it. I knew where every room, every doorway, just about every stick of furniture was. In my environment Richard McNally was comparatively blind. I backed up one more step. I slipped my hand into the pocket, feeling for my phone. Would it work now that I was inside? I didn't dare to try it.

House phone! There are still a few house phones here.

"Did you know your sister was arrested tonight? She might need your help."

"Figured that out too, did you? Pretty good. We got away with scamming the old man for years on that. But she screwed up. He found out about the money. That what they got her on?"

I took another step in my backward climb upstairs. He smiled the nice smile and moved one big Santa-booted foot onto the first step.

"She had a gun," I said. "It wasn't about money."

"Everything is about money, sweetheart," he said, putting the other foot on the first stair. The little bells jingled. "We had a good thing going until the old man put on his Santa hat and decided to visit all his contractors." He laughed an unfunny laugh. "He found the same thing you did. Empty store fronts. Buildings full of crap materials. Unlicensed phony tradesmen."

"So Mr. Eldridge had to die."

"Of course. But Gillette wasn't supposed to do it. That was supposed to be Lilly's job." He climbed another step. So did I. It was almost totally dark where I stood. "Who was she going to shoot anyway? Old Lil hasn't been right in the head since the old guy got whacked with the bell."

"She was trying to get the bell back," I said. "The police know it was the murder weapon."

"That was stupid Gillette's fault. I took care of him

though. Had to. He was ready to crack. I hid in the storage locker and texted him to come right away and meet me in the office. I couldn't let him confess the whole thing. Made it look like a suicide. How'd you like that necktie trick?"

I didn't—couldn't answer that. "Lilly moved his car to another lot that morning after he took the bell case to the Acme store," I said. "He changed clothes in the store and picked up his car as though nothing had happened."

"See? I said you were smart. Couldn't risk him getting Eldridge's blood in the car. We burned the clothes, cleaned and polished the bejesus out of the bells, and dropped them off at the Community Center. One of the workers threw a bunch of junk into the case. Looked normal that way. Perfect." He sighed. "It was a sweet deal while it lasted. I sent the padded bills on the right billheads, Lilly made out the checks, and the old man signed them. I cashed them. Four-way split. Me, Lilly, Gillette, and whatever was left over for the charities. Sweet."

He made a sudden move forward then. I turned and ran up the stairs, jingling all the way. He was right behind me. We were both in total darkness, but I was in stocking feet and knew where I was. I knew how many stairs there were in each flight. He didn't know his way around my house and besides, he was big and the costume made him clumsy.

Advantage: Lee.

"Doesn't matter where you go, little lady," he growled. "These bells tell me right where you are."

Advantage: McNally.

I had two steps to go before I'd be on the second-floor landing. There was a house phone in my old bedroom. But when the bells stopped ringing, he'd know where I'd stopped. I paused on the landing. *Think. Think.*

Ahead of me, on the stairway to the third floor, the bells continued to ring. How could that be?

The cats! I stepped off the landing and onto the soft, plush carpet of the second floor and tried not to breathe, hoping McNally couldn't hear the pounding of my heart as he thundered past me following the bells to the third floor. I heard the cat door swing open. Good. O'Ryan and Frankie could rattle some things around in the kitchen. I knew they would.

I tiptoed to my bedroom. I knew how to open my door soundlessly. (Just about every high school kid who's occasionally sneaked in after curfew can do it.) Once inside, I turned the knob that locked it. It was a pretty flimsy deterrent, but it would slow an intruder down for a minute or two. Good thing my kitchen door upstairs had a proper lock on it. That would take a while to breach.

I moved in tiny baby steps. Even in this familiar space I couldn't afford to knock anything over, make any noise. I felt for my bedside table, for the reproduction pink Princess phone. A house phone. Holding my breath, I listened for a dial tone. Got it. I punched in 911, whispered my name and address. "Hurry," I said and hung up. I knew there was a flashlight in the little table's single drawer, but could I risk a light showing under the door?

The bathroom would provide at least one more lock. I could use a light in there too. I picked up the flashlight, padded my cautious way to the bathroom just as I heard my kitchen door shattering.

"Got you now, bitch," he shouted. "Thanks for leaving the flashlight on the table." I could hear him stamping around overhead. Heard the occasional sound of glass breaking. How long would it be before he discovered that I wasn't there? Now he had a light. He could search from room to room. Did I dare to dash out into the hall, run downstairs, and back outdoors? Was I fast enough?

Too late. He was on his way back down the stairs. Stamping. Jingling. I closed the bathroom door behind me. Turned on my flashlight. Was there anything I could use as a weapon in this tiny, windowless room? I heard the guestroom door swing open. Aunt Ibby's room would be next. Then, this one.

I pulled open drawers, the medicine cabinet, even the laundry chute. I heard my bedroom door begin to splinter as he pounded on it. "I know you're in here, bitch! I'm going to break your pretty neck and throw you down these stairs." A satisfied grunt as the door gave. "Are you under the bed, girlie? They'd think you just fell down stairs in the dark. Come on. You can't get away."

The laundry chute!

It was my only way out. I stuck my head into the opening. Flashed the light down into the darkness. The chute was lined with aluminum. I remembered that. Aunt Ibby had been specific about it. Absolutely smooth walls with no rough edges that might snag or tear fabrics on their way down to the wicker basket in the laundry room—the laundry room just a few steps away from the back door and freedom!

I'd crawled into that chute once before on a dare from a girlfriend. But I'd been a skinny twelve-year-old at the time and it had been a terrifying experience. But it hadn't killed me, and staying where I was just might. I stripped off the jacket, the jeans, the sweater, and pushed them through the top-hinged door. At least there'd be something soft to land on when I hit bottom. I tossed the flashlight in too. When I was down to the silk long johns and socks, I lifted the top-hinged door as high as it would go, and holding onto a towel rack I put one leg in, then prayed that the towel rack would hold my weight for the few seconds it would take to put the other leg into the oblong hole in the wall. It held, but just barely, the anchoring screws shifting in the old plaster wall. I braced myself against the aluminum walls with both feet while I lowered the door, darned hard to do with socks on, but thankfully, still thin enough to do it. Then I used both hands and feet to ease myself along, and unlike the twelve-year old's straight shot down the approximately fifteen-foot drop, I managed to do a Spiderman type of vertical crawl on my way down to the basket.

The pounding, splintering began again, and the bathroom door gave way sooner than I'd thought it would. Before long he'd find the chute and figure out where I'd gone.

It took him only seconds. The flashlight beam was blinding and his voice bounced and echoed from aluminum walls. "Gotcha!" The laugh that followed was chilling. I knew he couldn't fit into the chute, so he'd have to come down the stairs and then figure out where the dirty clothes wound up. That might slow him down.

I dropped the rest of the way onto my parka and jeans in the basket. I still had a flashlight too, and no reason not to use it. I turned it on, pulled on the jeans, flung the parka across my shoulders, and dashed for the exit.

He was on his way down the twisty back staircase, not bothering to be quiet. I knew I'd locked the door to the stairs, but it wouldn't take him long to kick that down. How had he figured out the location of the laundry so fast?

He's a contractor, dope. He just had to follow the plumbing—bathroom to bathroom to laundry.

I wrenched the back door open, shining the light into the yard. I could run for the garage, I could get into my very fast car and drive away. I felt in the parka pocket for my keys.

Keys. I'd handed the whole keyring to MvcNally.

A jingling sound issued from the back stairs. Bells? The footsteps slowed. "You behind me? How'd you do that? You must be smarter than you look." I heard him take two more steps, thundering on the old wooden stairs in those big black boots. Then, more bells; these seemed close to the bottom of the stairway. "Damn it! I can't see you. How're you doing that? You in front of me or behind me?"

I wasn't doing anything at all except trying to get away. I knew who was doing the bell ringing though, A couple of Christmas ribbon decorated cats.

I'd given the Winter Street address to the 911 operator, so I thought I'd better run to the front of the house. I still hadn't heard any sirens yet. Maybe the storm had slowed them down.

Hurry! He'll be outside in seconds.

I dared a look back at the open back door just in time to see him on the top step, his flashlight sweeping big arcs of golden light across the rapidly accumulating snow. My sock-clad feet were wet and near freezing, and I knew there was a good chance he'd see my footprints in the deepening snow. I'd already doused my light and ducked behind a row of tall arbor vitae, peeking between feathery branches heavy with snow, not daring to move, to give away my hiding place. I gauged how long it might take him to catch up with me if he figured out the direction I'd taken. He still had boots, but he was probably going to be weighed down some by the padded red suit. What if the 911 operator hadn't heard my whispered message? If I ran to the nearest neighbor, wouldn't they be in danger from the crazed Santa chasing me? Would they even answer the door?

Do I hear sirens? Or is it the wind?

He turned toward his right. Good. He was facing the wrong direction, giving the tell-tale footprints time to fill with snow. Suddenly, he fell forward, tumbling down the granite steps, the flashlight lurching erratically. He spun around, whirling faster than a man of his size should be able to. The light flashed intermittently on the reason—the reasons—for this strange behavior.

There was a cat firmly attached to each thigh. One yellow cat—one white one.

I saw my chance and took it. I ran—through the yard, past the front gate, and out into the middle of Winter Street, just in time to see the beautiful flashing red, white, and blue lights of several police cars.

EPILOGUE

When the police arrived, just like the U.S. Cavalry in some of the old movies Aunt Ibby and Mr. Pennington like to watch, I directed them to the backyard where Richard McNally was arrested while in an awkward and undignified position. (Think runny makeup, saggy red suit, clinging to a fence post with two yowling, belled, and beribboned cats claw-deep into his legs.)

My 911 call had indeed been difficult for the operator to understand, but they were able to track my little old pink Princess phone. What had seemed like hours to me, from the time I'd made that phone call, slid down the laundry chute, and run out the back door until those welcome sirens screamed their way down Winter Street was less than fifteen minutes—not bad considering they'd had to figure out where I was, then had to plow through darn near a foot of wet snow to get to me.

Pete had been in the first patrol car to reach me in the middle of the street that night. He'd picked me up, put me in the front seat, cranked the heater up, kissed me, and said, "Take off those wet socks. I'll be right back."

McNally's wild rampage through the house had caused

some damage—mostly in the form of demolished doors. (I thought about my door vision. I remembered the scattered Santa Clauses under my tree too. How big a hint was that?)

Richard McNally lawyered up immediately and refused to admit any wrongdoing ever, anywhere, anyhow. His stepsister Lilly Jeffry, however, decided that cooperation with the law was her best option, and she knew where all the Historical Charities skeletons were buried!

It had all been Richard's idea, she insisted. She'd really liked her job. Liked the old gent too. Besides, he'd often told her she'd be mentioned in his will. Ha! She'd sneaked a look at the will about five years ago. He'd mentioned her all right. Barely. After all her hard work and dedication, the senile old Scrooge had left her a measly ten thousand dollars. She'd called her stepbrother to complain about it.

Things had gone bad in Atlanta so Richard showed up in Salem with his big idea.

It didn't take him long to put it into motion. The Historical Charities of Salem was the only client they'd need. Millions passed through their books every year, and Lilly kept the books! The old buildings needed constant repair and maintenance. Unskilled labor with phony IDs and substandard materials can trim expenses significantly. The charities themselves were grateful for whatever they got and didn't complain.

But leaking pipes, failing electricity, and shoddy carpentry caught up with them when Anthony and some of the other workers began moonlighting and customers complained. That started the license investigations and things went rapidly downhill. Lilly Jeffry seemed especially repentant about the money the veteran Santas had collected. The three had stolen all of it . . . and Richard

McNally wasn't even a veteran. Lilly, the perfect secretary, began to make mistakes.

McNally, after a trip to the hospital to treat his cat-inflicted wounds, was charged with kidnapping (me), and willful destruction of property (the doors). The serious charges, like murder, fraud, impersonating a veteran, and a long string of others came later. He will be in prison for a very long time. Lilly Jeffrey will do time too. Accessory after the fact in the murder of Mr. Eldridge, grand theft, defrauding the government, and much more. Besides, they are both in trouble with the IRS. A surprising amount of the stolen money was found in bank accounts and safety deposit boxes belonging to the three. It will take a while and working through red tape to access it, but along with the generous donations of a grateful community, the Historical Charities of Salem with new leadership will continue its good works.

Anthony, alias Joseph, along with his fellow handymen were all found guilty of a variety of charges involving their licensing deception. Power was restored just in time for the WICH-TV Christmas party which turned out to be fun despite the snow. My investigative report on The Case of the Holiday Homicide (with apologies to Nancy Drew) was picked up by a national network, which may result in a promotion for me. Maybe. Fingers crossed.

I had a mild case of frostbite on both feet, but with plenty of TLC from Pete, and some unlovely, no-name sensible shoes, I recovered quickly. Our Christmas dinner with Donnie and Marie and the boys was wonderful. Made me think about someday having a family. But not yet. I gave Pete two tickets to the Daytona 500 NASCAR race next February for Christmas. A Florida vacation will feel good about then. He gave me a gorgeous Georg

Jensen stainless teardrop shape serving bowl I'd been admiring for over a year in my friend Jennie's antique shop.

Aunt Ibby and her friend are still in London looking forward to the big New Year's Eve celebration there. They'll be watching fireworks at the London Eye. Exciting. Pete and I plan to have a quiet New Year's Eve. We might even watch the fireworks from the fire escape outside my kitchen window, with the cats. Yes, Frankie is still here. With any luck, all of our doors, including cat entrances, will be replaced by the time my aunt arrives home. (No, I didn't hire Kenny from Precision Carpentry.)

I won that bet about the two swords that thief on the Tarot card left behind. I'd bet Pete that the killer had left two clues behind when he was confronted in Eldridge's office. He had—the ledger with the phony figures in it that Lilly had provided, and the Santa hat Mr. Eldridge had worn when he'd discovered that his high-priced contractors were empty storefront maildrops and a four-story building full of scrap lumber, used parts, and secondhand tools. We'll be having dinner, on Pete, at Gulu Gulu soon.

About those Monarch butterflies. I told Scott about Aunt Ibby's suggestion that he write a children's book about them. He says he's already wearing too many hats. The story's been told around Salem so much, lots of people already think it happened. We even had a call at the station from the Museum of Science about it. Maybe somebody, somewhere, some day will write that little story.

ACKNOWLEDGMENTS

Many thanks to the usual suspects for unfailing support, advice, and encouragement. Special recognition to fellow writers from Bay Area Professional Writers Guild, Wordsmiths, Sisters in Crime, Mystery Writers of America, and Pinellas Writers (with a special salute to author David Wood for inspiring Lee's "empty room" dream). Much appreciation to my publisher Kensington, especially editor Esi Sogah and publicist Karen Auerbach. A big hug to Barnes & Noble, both locally and nationally, for their consistent tasteful promotion of cozy mysteries. But most of all, I need to acknowledge my husband Dan—who's turned out to be a darned good mystery plotter!

Aunt Ibby's Never-Fail Meringue

This meringue cuts beautifully and never gets sticky.

1 tablespoon cornstarch
2 tablespoons cold water
½ cup boiling water
3 egg whites
6 tablespoons sugar
Dash of salt
1 teaspoon vanilla extract

Blend cornstarch and cold water in saucepan. Add boiling water and cook, stirring until clear and thickened. Let stand until completely cold. With electric mixer at high speed, beat egg whites until foamy; gradually add sugar and beat until stiff, but not dry. Turn mixer to low speed, add salt and vanilla. Gradually beat in cold cornstarch mixture. Turn mixer again to high speed and beat well. Spread on filled pie shell. Bake in moderate oven (350 degrees) about 10 minutes.

(Aunt Ibby says to make sure the beaters are absolutely clean for this, or any meringue recipe.)

Don't miss the next in the
Witch City Mystery series

FINAL EXAM

Coming soon from
Carol J. Perry
and
Kensington Books